# DOROTHY GARLOCK

# Larkspur

**WARNER BOOKS**

A Time Warner Company

WARNER BOOKS EDITION

Copyright © 1997 by Dorothy Garlock
All rights reserved.

Cover design by Diane Luger
Cover illustration by Michael Racz
Hand lettering by Carl Dellacroce
Book design by Elizabeth Sanborn

Warner Books, Inc.
1271 Avenue of the Americas
New York, NY 10020

Visit our Web site at
http://pathfinder.com/twep

W A Time Warner Company

Printed in the United States of America

First Printing: February, 1997

10 9 8 7 6 5 4 3 2 1

TD

ie

**"Please, Kristin. Please stay here at Larkspur with me."**

His words echoed to the core of her being. *What did he
mean?* She summoned all her determination to ask. Her
voice came out thin and weak. "As housekeeper?"

Without conscious effort he was drawing her closer
to him. Finally his hands slid behind her back and she was
leaning against him, her head pressed against his shoulder. Buck turned his face into her hair.

Lord help him say the right words. Happiness such as
he never dreamed of having was right here in this sweet
woman. Somehow he had to make her see him as a man
who needed love and who had love to give . . .

ie

Books by Dorothy Garlock

*Annie Lash*
*Dream River*
*Forever Victoria*
*A Gentle Giving*
*Glorious Dawn*
*Homeplace*
*Lonesome River*
*Love and Cherish*
*Midnight Blue*
*Nightrose*
*Restless Wind*
*Ribbon in the Sky*
*River of Tomorrow*
*Sins of Summer*
*Tenderness*
*The Listening Sky*
*This Loving Land*
*Wayward Wind*
*Wild Sweet Wilderness*
*Wind of Promise*
*Yesteryear*

Published by WARNER BOOKS

This book is dedicated to
MARCIA VOLK
a friend for all seasons

# LARKSPUR

Larkspur, larkspur, growing free
Purple, pink or pearly white,
What will your petals bring to me
As I contemplate the empty night?

Is that poison in your bloom
More deadly than the life I lead
In my brother's house: my lonely room,
My servile state, my soul in need?

You bear a claw beneath your flower
It warns of danger lurking there.
A challenge! Shall I cringe or cower?
No—this time I need to dare.

Larkspur, larkspur, magic weed,
You haunt me, taunt me, call me west
To where the earth supports your seed,
To where, at last, my heart can rest.

I'll journey to that far-off place
Where one whose face I do not know
Has willed to me his stake, his space,
His "Larkspur" land.  Oh, yes, I'll go!

—F.S.I.

# Chapter One

1883

## River Falls, Wisconsin

"You will not go! I forbid it!"

Ferd Anderson went to the fireplace and leaned his arm against the thick oak mantel. His narrowed, angry gaze fastened on his sister's face.

"I'm not a child, Ferd." Kristin spoke calmly despite her nervousness. "I'm twenty-three years old and—"

"—A twenty-three-year-old *spinster*—" he interrupted rudely, "who has enjoyed the hospitality of my home for the past ten years and who has never been more than thirty miles from the place where she was born."

Kristin refused to allow her brother to see the hurt inflicted by his remark.

"—And you expect me to allow you to travel alone to some godforsaken, uncivilized place called Big Timber in Montana Territory."

"Mr. Hanson at the *Sentinel* wrote that Montana will become the forty-first state soon."

"I don't give a damn if it'll be the *first* state! And what does that crackpot Hanson know about anything? You're *not* going there. That's my final word."

"Women have more freedom now. This is the 1880s, not the Dark Ages. I'm no longer a child. Technically you have no say in the matter."

"Don't I? Don't I?" he repeated, pushing himself away from the mantel. Outrage reddened his face, sparkled in his eyes and compressed his lips. "Who in thunder has been taking care of you all these years? Who put food in your mouth, clothes on your back and coal in the furnace to keep you warm? Huh?"

"You did, brother, and I've worked here in your home for my keep."

"—And as soon as the opportunity comes for you to pay me back, you get it into your head to leave my protection, grab an inheritance from a ne'er-do-well uncle and squander it."

"He couldn't have been too much of a ne'er-do-well. He acquired property."

"I remember my ma saying he was too lazy to spit."

"*My* mother liked him. Uncle Hansel told Gustaf that Uncle Yarby was a good-hearted man with an adventurous spirit who wanted to see some of the world before he settled down."

"Uncle Hansel!" Ferd snorted in disgust. "He left his sons nothing but a half dozen cows, a span of oxen, and a farm with a mortgage. He also left them a houseful of womenfolk to feed and a do-nothing dawdler like Gustaf who refuses to stay home and help ease Lars's burden."

Kristin was quiet for a moment. It would do no good to argue that Gustaf was *not* a do-nothing dawdler. Ferd had always resented him for his good looks and charming ways.

"I didn't realize that you considered me a burden, Ferd," Kristin said, in an effort to move the subject from Gustaf. She moved around the chair and straightened the white crocheted doily that lay on the back. "When my mother died, you insisted that I come here. And when you sold the farm, it was my understanding that my part of the money would go to pay for my keep."

"How long do you think that lasted? It was used up long ago."

"I've been an unpaid housekeeper, Ferd. A nursemaid to your children, a seamstress—"

"Oh . . . oh—" The trembling words came from Ferd's wife, Andora. "That's not true and it's mean of you to say so. You . . . came here and just took over. We gave you a roof over your head and—"

"Be quiet!" Ferd snapped; and when Andora began to cry, he shouted, "Stop that!"

Andora gave a tiny scream, fell back on the couch and assumed her best pouting position.

Ferd turned back to the mantel again, breathing heavily. He was a big man; hardworking, prosperous, ambitious. His lumber business was growing along with the population increase in Wisconsin. He had planned to open a branch in a neighboring town. The money from the inheritance would have made it possible.

Fourteen years older than his half sister, he had paid scant attention to her other than to be aware that she was there, looking after the girls, tending the house for him and his wife, who was beautiful and as irresponsible as a child and would always be.

Andora suited Ferd admirably. He could dress her up, show her off to his business friends and be certain she would reveal nothing of consequence because she knew nothing. She had been trained to compliment the right people and to gush at the right moment. The fact that she was a failure in bed meant nothing. There were others far more capable and willing to satisfy his sexual needs.

"I don't understand. I just don't understand." Ferd's jowls quivered with agitation. "Why *you*, for God's sake? Yarby had three brothers beside Pa. All of them are dead now, but he had ten nephews. If he didn't want me to have it, he could have left the land to Sven, Lars, Karl, James—"

"—And four nieces," Kristin amended. "And I don't know why he left it to me."

"If Yarby Anderson had the brains God gave the rest of the family, he'd have known that women are not supposed to clutter up their minds with business matters and decisions," Ferd continued his tirade as if Kristin had not spoken.

"I can't believe you'd just up and leave us," Andora whimpered. "As soon as you get your hands on a little money you go away so none of us will know what you do with it, and after all we've done for you."

"I've done just as much for you, Andora," Kristin said, trying not to show her frustration. "Ever since you married Ferd, you've had a maid who worked for room and board. You've never had to cook the meals, wash or iron, or get up with the children in the middle of the night."

"I've . . . cooked—"

"Something fancy you wanted to show off."

"Ferd paid you to cook!"

"A dollar a month." Kristin's patience was strained, and her voice rose angrily.

"You'd not have had a roof over your head if not for Ferd. If you had an ounce of gratitude, you'd give the money to him. You're . . . selfish and mean and you've turned the girls against me!"

"You're spoiling them rotten, Andora. They'll grow up to be just like you."

"What's wrong with that? They'll not be old maids like you!" Andora retorted nastily.

Kristin looked down at her sister-in-law, who had sunk back down on the couch and was dabbing at her eyes with a lace-trimmed handkerchief—one that Kristin had made.

"I didn't realize this before, but maybe I have been selfish, Andora. I loved doing for the girls, but I hate seeing them grow up to be so self-centered and unlovable. I liked keeping the house and took pride in it. In doing so, I may have fostered your irresponsibility and contributed to your uselessness."

"Hold your tongue! You have no right to chastise Andora," Ferd shouted, and gave his thigh a terrific slap with the palm of his hand.

"I have as much right as she has to chastise me."

"Oh! I'm not . . . useless. Ferd loves me the way I am! You've ruined everything. Who'll take the girls to their music lessons and . . . how'll I get my dress finished before the Fourth? All the seamstresses worth their salt have been engaged by now." Andora burst into tears and ran from the room.

Kristin sighed. "You might try doing it yourself, Andora."

"Stop this bickering!" Ferd shouted, then turned on his sister with a brutality he seldom showed. "Papa pampered you from the day you were born. His big mistake was having you educated. Mine was continuing on with it after he died."

"Only for part of a year," Kristin reminded him. "After you married Andora, you soon learned that though she was pretty, she wasn't capable of running the house."

"If you'd been walking behind a plow these past ten years and milking cows like your cousins, you'd not have your head crammed full of fancy notions."

"Ferd, I don't want to leave with hard feelings."

"You'll not leave."

"Ferd—"

"—I've had my say and you'll not defy me. Besides, I've already sent a letter off to that lawyer fellow who has someone who wants the land. I told him to get an offer. Not that I'll take the first one he makes, but it'll give me an idea of what the land is worth."

"You had no right to do that without consulting me."

"As head of this family, I made it my right. Now I'll hear no more about it."

"And you won't." Anger straightened Kristin's back and put a fighting spark in her eyes.

"I thought you'd be sensible about it."

"Ferd, it isn't that I don't appreciate what you've done for me. It's just that this is something for me, not you, to decide. I'm leaving for Montana Territory in the morning."

Ferd looked stunned. His raised brows wrinkled a forehead made high by his receding hairline. He was taller than his sister, but his rounded shoulders and paunch made him seem shorter. He set himself solidly, legs well apart, and pushed out his chin.

"And where did you get the money for a train ticket?" he asked in a voice that was deceptively calm.

"Cousin Gustaf lent it to me. He's taking me to Eau Claire to catch the train."

Ferd said nothing for a long while. Then, noting a ripple of movement that revealed a tightening of every muscle in his body, Kristin put her hand to her throat and stared at him.

Never before had she seen such pure rage in her brother. His fists were tightly clenched, his mouth clamped shut. His face was red, and violence roiled in his eyes. For a moment she feared that he would strike her.

"Gustaf," he spat. "I'm not surprised that that hornswoggler stuck his bill in. If he wasn't going to get Yarby's money, he intended to make sure that I didn't."

"It isn't cash money," Kristin said patiently. "It's . . . land called Larkspur. It may be worthless."

"You would take that light-foot's advice over mine, and, like a common slut, travel alone to some godforsaken place where you will more than likely end up in a whorehouse! You've not got the brains to take care of yourself." By the time Ferd finished speaking, his face was crimson and he was shouting.

"You don't have much confidence in me, do you?"

"You will embarrass me before this whole town. Everyone will think I've lost my mind, allowing you to go willy-nilly out to this wild unsettled place." Ferd was so angry that he never heard a word she said. "If you go, after all Andora and I have done for you, never darken my door again."

"I'm sorry you said that, Ferd."

"And never show your face in this town either. It will be hard enough for us to live down the shame of your betrayal."

"You're my closest kin. I don't want to leave with this between us."

He turned to the door.

"Ferd."

He didn't answer.

"Ferd?"

Without a look or a word he went quickly up the stairs.

Kristin stood for a long moment with her head bowed.

*Betrayal* could mean only one thing: Ferd had bragged to his friends about the land *he* had inherited in Montana, and now everyone would know it had been left not to him but to his sister. Pride stiffened Kristin's back. She refused to take blame for taking charge of her own future. If Ferd suffered a loss of esteem, it was of his own doing.

Moving slowly, knowing it would be for the last time, she closed up the house for the night, as she had done for the past ten years, and went to her room adjoining the kitchen. As the family had increased, it had become necessary to convert the large pantry into a bedroom, and Kristin had willingly left the children's room for the privacy of this small space.

The gray dress she planned to wear for the trip hung over the back of a chair, her good black shoes sat under it. On the seat were her undergarments, her hat and a dark shawl she thought wise to wear because Cousin Gustaf had said the train would be smoky and dirty. Her clothes were in the trunk along with family photographs Ferd did not care for, personal items, sheets and towels. On top of all were her sewing equipment and writing materials. Everything she owned was in the trunk, the box, and a tapestry bag containing toilet articles and a pistol Gustaf had given to her and insisted she carry. He had taken her out to the woods and shown her how to load and shoot the gun. He cautioned her to keep it with her at all times.

"If you need it, it'll be there," he had said. "And don't be afraid to use it. If a man comes at you and refuses to back off, he's going to hurt you. It'll be you or him."

"I don't know if I could shoot anyone, Gus."

"You could if you had to. Keep the gun loaded. Unloaded, it's no use at all. Hold it straight out and pull the trigger slowly."

They had practiced until Gustaf was satisfied she at least knew how to handle the gun. Now Kristin felt safer knowing that she had the weapon. And Gustaf was right; she would use it if she was forced to do so to protect herself.

Kristin had planned to have a tub bath, but after the unsettling set-to with Ferd and Andora, she decided to carry warm water from the kitchen and wash in her room. Afterward she put on her nightdress and, standing before the small mirror above her washstand, looked at herself. She didn't think she was pretty, but neither was she ugly. Kristin took the pins from the braids that wrapped around her head. She had washed her hair that morning in fresh rainwater, not knowing when she would have the chance again. Silvery blond hair was not unusual in this Swedish community, but it was her most startling feature. Her eyes ran a close second. They were large and blue-gray, deep-set, under well-defined brows only a shade darker than her hair.

She leaned closer to the mirror. Faint lines of worry had appeared lately between her brows and at the corners of her eyes and mouth. Her face had a pensive look. The shadows beneath her eyes told of sleepless nights. Her wide mouth, its lower lip fuller and softer than the upper one, was turned down at the corners, reflecting her less than happy mood.

Ferd had called her a spinster. She guessed she was, but she had not thought much about it. She had been courted by several men when she was younger. None suited her brother, which had not mattered because none had suited her either. Now word was out that a man had to go first through Ferd to reach his sister, and lately not one had thought the effort worthwhile except for a couple of widowers who had been left with young children and little else. The thought of bedding with either of them made Kristin's stomach heave.

She had not settled as happily and as gratefully into the life of sister-servant as Andora and Ferd had believed. The girls, ages six and eight, were resentful of her authority. Andora indulged them in whatever they wanted to do, and of late they had begun to follow their mother's example and treat their aunt as a servant in the house.

Many times, when resentment bubbled up in Kristin, she longed to have something of her own and to see some of life other than the small confines of her brother's house here in River Falls, Wisconsin. Cousin Gustaf had helped to feed that ambition. He had told her of life beyond this small town and had even urged her to consider taking a position as governess or housekeeper in Eau Claire or St. Paul. Until now she had not had the courage to make the break.

Her life had taken a sudden change when the letter had come from Yarby Anderson's solicitor, a Mr. Mark Lee, telling her that after his being missing for a year, Yarby's remains had been found and identified. In a will dated twenty years earlier, when Kristin was four years old, he had left her all of his worldly possessions, which now consisted of ranchland called Larkspur.

To Kristin, who had never had more than five dollars of her own to do with as she pleased, it was a miracle. She had been elated until Gustaf had explained that several thousand acres of land in Montana might not equal forty acres of good farmland in Wisconsin.

Nevertheless it was something.

Kristin sat down in her mother's rocker. She would have liked to grieve for this uncle who had remembered her in his will, but she was not very successful. She had never seen him and all she knew of him was from what Gustaf remembered about him and that he had written her mother two letters after her father had died. She had searched the trunk for them, but they seemed to have disappeared. It gave Kristin a warm feeling to know that somewhere there had been a man who had cared enough about her to bequeath her some property.

She'd had no idea the furor that would result when she showed the letter to Ferd. He railed against Uncle Yarby for being so stupid as to leave an estate to a woman, railed at the time it would take to get the estate settled and the money in the bank.

After a week of hearing about the wrong done in her favor to the rest of the family, Kristin began to get not only stubborn but angry. She decided that if it was the last thing she did on earth, she was going to see this land that was hers now and stand at the grave of the man who had left it to her. She had every legal right to go there, and she was backed by her cousin, who insisted that he finance the trip. She accepted after promising to return the money as soon as the estate was settled.

Kristin and Gustaf had been born on the same day on adjoining farms. They had played together as children and had gone to school together. At sixteen Gustaf had left the farm to work on the boats carrying freight up and down the Mississippi River. Since then he had come home, at times, to help his brothers put in the crops or to harvest them, considering it his duty to help provide for his mother and unmarried sister.

Ferd considered Gustaf a man without substance, but her cousin had always been dear to Kristin, and she looked forward to his visits home. Without Gustaf's urging, Kristin doubted that she would have had the courage to defy Ferd and set out on this long and uncertain journey.

*Heavens!* The farthest she had been from home was Eau

Claire, and that was only one time when Ferd wanted her to tend the children while he and Andora mixed with the social set.

The lamplight threw Kristin's shadow on the wall. She watched it as she rocked. It was very strange to be sitting here, ready to leave this place where she had spent the past ten years. It didn't seem that any of this had really happened. She wished with all her heart that she wasn't leaving with an irreparable rift between herself and her brother.

*What in the world would she do if this turned out to be a hoax and there was no inheritance?* She would do as she had always done, she told herself sternly. She was not helpless. She could cook and sew and . . . milk cows.

*I'm sure they have dairy farms in Montana.*

# Chapter Two

$D$awn came.

Kristin had slept only fitfully all night. For the last hour she had been awake and listening for the birds to chirp in the trees above the house and for the roosters on the next street to announce the new day. At the first sound she got out of bed, went to the window and looked out. The sky was clear. This was the first day of her new life. She would be starting it in fine weather.

After lighting the lamp, Kristin used the chamber pot. She usually waited until she was dressed and then went to the outhouse, but this morning she felt defiant. She smiled knowing that her bit of revenge was childish.

*How long would it be before Andora thought to empty the pot?*

Last night anger and hurt had vied with one another in her heart, but this morning she felt as brave as an angry lioness. During the night the fear of the long journey and what she would find at the end of it had left her. Come what might, she would at least see another part of the world. She washed her face and hands in cold water from the pitcher, not bothering to fetch warm from the cookstove reservoir. She dressed, braided her hair and fastened the coils around her head with the large ivory hairpins Gustaf had brought her from some faraway place. Her stomach growled as she put the small-brimmed straw hat on her head and secured it with a hatpin. She had been so nervous last night that she had scarcely eaten anything at all.

She had been careful with what she packed to take with her. Besides her clothes and a few mementos, she took only what she had brought with the dollar a month Ferd had given her for her special use after she had nagged him for weeks because she wanted to buy a *real* toothbrush.

The house was quiet as she carried her baggage out to the front yard. She struggled with the small trunk, returned for the box and then for the bag and shawl she would carry on the train. Gustaf was coming to take her to Eau Claire to catch the train. *Train.* Never had she imagined that she would be going to a distant land on a train. With her baggage piled just inside the yard gate, she returned to the house one last time to pause in the front hall and listen. No footsteps sounded from the upper rooms. All was still.

*Ferd was not coming down to say good-bye.*

By the time she returned to the front gate, Gustaf had arrived. Dear Gustaf. What would she do without him? He hopped down from the buggy and tied the horse to the hitching post. The cousins could have passed for twins though Gustaf was a half head taller than Kristin and his blond hair was a shade darker. It matched the rakish mustache on his upper lip. He wore a smile on his handsome face. His eyes went past Kristin to the darkened house.

"Ole Ferd still got a kink in his tail?" Gustaf picked up the trunk and carried it to the boot of the buggy.

"He's terribly angry."

"He'll get over it." Gustaf settled her box beside the trunk, then with his hand beneath her elbow, he helped her up into the buggy.

"No. He told me never to come back."

"He said that?"

"And more." Kristin flipped the shawl around her shoulders to ward off the morning chill.

"The man's a fool," Gustaf growled as they drove away.

Kristin, her heart aching, looked back at the house to see if Ferd or Andora had relented and had stepped out onto the porch to wave good-bye.

The door was closed. The porch was empty.

The streets of River Falls lay empty except for a few merchants sweeping the walks and porches as they prepared for a new business day. They turned to stare at the buggy and to wonder what Ferd Anderson's sister and her vagabond cousin were doing out so early. Gustaf chuckled at their curiosity and saluted gaily as the buggy passed. The only sound was the clip-clop of the horse's hooves on the brick-paved street.

Kristin gloried in a mounting sense of freedom. Was this how a small bird felt when it left the nest and flew for the first time?

"Hungry?" They had left the town and were on the open road to Eau Claire.

"You heard my stomach growl," Kristin accused.

"Naw. I figured ya'd have a big ruckus with Ferd and be too upset to eat. Ma fixed a basket. It's there under the seat."

"Bless Aunt Ingrid." Kristin lifted the basket up onto the seat between them.

"The fritters are on top. The rest is for ya to take with ya. It should last all day and part of tomorrow. By then you'll be in

Fargo, where you change trains. Ya can refill it there with food enough to last until ya get to Big Timber."

"Won't buying food at the station cost a lot of money?" Kristin took a bite of the fritter.

"Ya got to eat. Ferd didn't give ya a dime, did he?"

"No." Kristin would have been embarrassed to admit this to anyone but her cousin. "Gustaf, I'll pay back every cent—"

"Hush about payback. Ya've got crumbs on your mouth."

"Ferd will tell your brothers that you gave me the money. They'll be angry knowing you had it and didn't put it toward your mother and sister's keep."

"I give them money each time I come home, and I take nothin' from the farm. Lars and Kevin will tell Ferd to mind his own business. I'd go with ya, Kris, but I promised to stay until Lars gets on his feet."

"How is he?"

"He's gettin' around on a crutch. He should be all right in a few weeks."

"I wish you were coming now."

"Ya'll be all right. Get a room in the hotel in Big Timber and look up that solicitor. What's his name?"

"Mark Lee."

"If ya need me, send a wire in care of Tommy Bragg." He gave her an impish grin. She grinned back.

"You're setting me up good and proper. Ferd Anderson's spinster sister leaves town and wires the notorious town rascal."

"Don't sign it. I'll know who it's from."

"So will the rest of the town if it comes from Big Timber."

"Do ya care?"

"I thought I would, but I don't. Oh, Gus, what if it's all a hoax? What if the inheritance doesn't amount to a hill of beans?"

"Then ya've had a grand adventure out of it."

"But . . . I can't come back."

"I'll come to wherever ya are and snag ya a rich husband."

"Oh, Gus. Be serious. I haven't heard a word from that Mr. Lenning who has been managing the property."

"He's probably an old goat like Yarby and can't write. I betcha Ferd's heard plenty from Lee."

"No! You think he'd do that and not tell me?"

"Hell, yes! When we get to Eau Claire, I'm going to send a wire to Mark Lee and tell him to be expecting ya. I'll also tell him that if he don't treat ya right, I'll come out there and bust his head."

"You can't say that in a wire."

"No, but he'll get the message."

Kristin put the basket back down on the floor of the buggy. Aunt Ingrid had packed slices of bread and butter, cheese, hard-boiled eggs, apples and fritters.

"What time does the train go?"

"Eleven o'clock. We've plenty of time. Nervous?"

"A little."

"Ya'll be fine. Just remember what I said about not making eye contact with a man that's giving you the once-over. Be alert and act as if you owned the world. A stuck-up woman will turn a fellow off quicker than anything if he's got any brains. If he has none, use your hatpin. If that doesn't work, use the pistol to discourage him."

Kristin laughed. "I doubt that I'll be bothered all that much."

"You'll be noticed, you can bet your boots on that. You're pretty, Kris. I've been telling you that for years."

"Oh, pooh! You say that because you like me."

"I'd say it if I didn't like you. I've been up and down the river a dozen times and seen all kinds. You're a handsome woman and you got brains, which is more than that worthless piece of fluff Ferd married has."

Kristin laughed. "You talk as though men will be following me as if I were the Pied Piper."

"Who's he?" Gustaf screwed his bill cap down tighter on his blond head.

"Way back in the thirteenth century the town of Hamelin in Germany was plagued with rats. A mysterious stranger came and offered to rid the town of the pests. He played his pipe, and the rats came swarming out of the buildings and followed him to the river, where they drowned."

Kristin knew how Gustaf loved a story so she continued.

"When the town leaders refused to pay the piper, he returned and once more played his pipe. This time all the children in town followed him. He led them to the mountains and they were never heard from again."

"Yo're pulling my leg. It ain't true . . . is it?"

"It's a legend. Robert Browning told the story in his poem, *The Pied Piper of Hamelin.*"

"Don't that beat all?"

"Oh, Gustaf!" Kristin looked at her cousin with tears in her eyes. "You're my dearest friend. I'm going to miss you."

"Well, I should hope so. Not every young lady has such a handsome cousin."

"Nor such a . . . boastful one." Kristin sniffed back the tears.

"I'll come out to Big Timber as soon as I can cut loose from the farm."

"Gustaf! Will you? When did you decide that?"

" 'Bout two minutes ago." He grinned. "I always wanted to see what was over the mountain."

"How will you come? Will you have the money?"

"A man needs no more than two hands and a strong back to get to where he wants to go."

As they approached the outskirts of Eau Claire they heard a train whistle. Gustaf pulled his watch from his pocket.

"That one's not yours. We've got an hour."

Five minutes later Gustaf was unloading her trunk and box on the depot platform. Kristin stepped down from the buggy and walked with him into the station. Her heart was beating so fast that she could hardly breathe. The agent spoke to Gustaf.

"Hello, Gus. This the young lady going out to Big Timber? Ain't never sold a ticket to that place before. Guess it's a wide spot in the road from what I hear. Got baggage?"

"A box and a trunk out on the platform."

"I'll tag 'em. Here's your ticket, young lady. When you get to St. Paul, the train will sit there for half an hour. Stay put while another engine hooks on. You'll ride that car to Fargo, where you'll change cars, maybe even trains. Your baggage will follow you and be unloaded at Big Timber."

"Will it be night when I get to Fargo?"

The agent consulted a schedule. "Midnight. Westbound leaves at 5:00 A.M. Don't worry though, ma'am. The station agent will be there. Show him your ticket, and he'll see that you get on the train. You'll have another layover at Miles City and reach Big Timber Wednesday evening about six o'clock."

Back out on the platform Kristin stood beside Gustaf and looked down the tracks. The heavy hand of loneliness gripped her, wrapping its icy fingers around her heart. She reached for Gustaf's arm.

"Am I doing the right thing, Gus?"

"To my way of thinking ya had two choices." Gustaf's eyes settled on her anxious face. "A person's got to go forward or stand still. Ya could have stood still and been a servant in your brother's house for the rest of yore life. Yo're too much of a woman for that. Uncle Yarby gave ya a chance to get out. You'd a been a fool not to take it."

"You're right, of course."

"If I had thought ya couldn't take care of yourself, I'd not have let ya go. You've got money to live for a few weeks and still enough to come back."

"I can't come back."

"Yes, ya can. Ya can come to the farm."

"There's so many there that—"

"—Just till ya get settled. But ya won't have to do that. I'll come out to Big Timber in a few weeks. Maybe ya'll give your poor relation a job."

"Oh, Gus!" She leaned over and kissed his cheek. "You've always seen the bright side of things."

"Of course," he said jauntily. "I'm a fine fellow."

From a distance came the sound of the train whistle. A drummer came out of the station and set a large bag on the edge of the platform. On the side of the bag was printed: AMERICAN THREAD COMPANY.

A richly dressed young couple with eyes only for each other stood with hands clasped—a new hatbox and carpetbag at their feet. In comparison, Gustaf looked shabby in his baggy pants and soft-billed cap. But to Kristin he was a rock, her anchor in a sea of sudden confusion.

"Remember now what I told ya about men," Gustaf said hurriedly. "I'll wire that Lee fellow and tell him to meet ya, but if he isn't there, go to a hotel—the best one in town. Ya can afford it for one night. When ya get yore bearings, ya can get a room in a roomin' house to save money. Don't sign any papers until you have someone besides Lee look them over—"

"Oh, Gus—Two nights on the train."

"Ya'll be all right," he said firmly. "Ya've got a level head and ya'll use it."

His words were almost drowned out by the scream of the train whistle, then the screeching of iron wheels on the iron tracks. Sparks flew as brakes were applied, and the train came to a jerking halt. The conductor in a fine black suit stepped down from the platform at the end of the coach and placed a stool beside the step. He went into the station.

Passengers in the car looked out the windows.

Baggage was being loaded in the car ahead.

Kristin held tightly to Gustaf's arm.

"I've never even been this close to a train. It's scary."

"There's nothin' to it. Keep this over your arm at all times. Even when ya sleep." He reached out and touched the straps on her pouch bag.

"I wish I knew more about Uncle Yarby."

"Ya know all that you need to know." Gustaf put the basket in her hand. "Ma tucked a cup in here. There's usually a watercooler on the car."

The conductor came out of the station and stood beside the steps at the end of the coach.

"A . . . ll . . . a . . . bo . . . ard!" His rolling voice sent a shiver of excitement down Kristin's spine.

The drummer stood aside and waited for Kristin to board. Gustaf held her arm and motioned for the young couple to go on ahead. Then he kissed Kristin on the cheek.

"Fly away, little bird," he whispered.

"Have I told you that I wish you were my brother?" She almost choked on the words.

"Many times. Now get aboard."

Kristin moved up the steps on wooden legs. At the top she turned back.

" 'Bye, Gus. I'll write."

The drummer was swinging up the steps behind her, and she had to move on. The coach was only half-full, and in the middle of it Kristin found a seat next to the window. She slid into it and looked at Gustaf's grinning face. He stood with his hands in his pockets and his cap at a jaunty angle. Tears filled Kristin's eyes. She was leaving her dearest friend. The only person in the world that she felt cared for her. Really cared.

The train jerked and began to move slowly. Kristin waved. Gustaf walked along the platform, keeping pace with the train for as long as he could. She turned in the seat and continued to wave until he was out of sight before she turned back.

She was on her way. It was too late to back out now.

When the train left the station in Eau Claire, Kristin held tightly to the edge of the seat and watched the trees and the wire poles fly by. Gradually she became accustomed to the speed at which she was traveling and relaxed a little. When the train stopped briefly at a small town, she waved to some children standing beside the track. Later, when the train crossed a trestle, she experienced a moment of panic as she looked out the window, and down. Seeing only water, she closed her eyes tightly and prayed. She had the illusion that there was nothing beneath her. Finally, when she heard the rails singing a different tune, she opened her eyes, relieved to see piles of coal along the tracks and buildings in the distance.

The whistle blasted continuously as the train pulled into the station in St. Paul. The conductor came down the aisle.

"Thirty-minute stop here if you want to get off and stretch your legs."

Everyone left the car except Kristin and a man who was sleeping with his head propped against the window and his hat over his face. Kristin took her cup to the watercooler. She drank a full cup before she thought about what she would do when she had to empty her bladder.

The coach was still half-full when they left St. Paul but was filled after the stop in Minneapolis. Kristin was glad she had a window seat. A pleasant-faced woman sat down beside her. After chatting a few minutes about the crowded coach, the woman said she was going to St. Cloud to visit her daughter and that she made the trip twice a year.

"I've never been on a train before," Kristin confided. "I'm wondering what a person does who must use the . . . water closet."

"Water closet? Oh, you mean the lavatory. It's at the front of the car. The conductor locks the door while the train is in the station."

"You can't . . . use it while the train is stopped?"

"No. You see the ah . . . waste falls out the bottom of the train and is strung out along the tracks."

"Oh, my goodness! I couldn't go up there while people are in here watching me. They'd know exactly what I'm going to do."

"That's the drawback. I used to take my little girl and pretend it was *she* who needed to go when it was usually both of us. If you can wait, there's a lavatory in almost every station."

"Oh, dear. I don't get off until I get to Fargo."

"You needn't wait that long, my dear. The train will stop at

St. Cloud for fifteen minutes. Get off the train when I do. I'll show you where to go."

"The train may leave without me."

"We'll tell the conductor. He'll make sure you're on before he gives the signal to move out."

By early evening, Kristin was used to the rolling, rocking rhythmic movement of the train and began to enjoy the trip. She had eaten bread, cheese and a fritter and was saving one of her four apples to eat later. She was one of the lucky ones who had a seat to herself after the stop at St. Cloud.

As twilight approached, she daydreamed about what she would find at the end of her journey. Would she be welcomed by Mr. Lenning, Uncle Yarby's manager? Would he have a pleasant wife who would understand that she had no desire to interfere with the running of the farm . . . ranch? And that she just wanted to see her land?

Walk on it.

Feel it.

Laws! It was hard to believe that she *owned* land.

# Chapter Three

## Montana Territory

Someone was watching him.

Buck Lenning rose to his feet slowly, careful to make no sudden moves. He had been on his knees drinking from the clear cold stream when he saw pebbles from a spot on the bank fall with tiny splashes into the water. He had no idea who or what was there in the willows ahead and to the right, but the pebbles had not fallen without a cause.

His senses had been honed to sharpness by a lifetime of constant vigil. Something was not right. Trouble had a breath all its own, and he could feel it trembling on the back of his neck. Bending low to make himself as small a target as possible, he moved up the bank to his horse.

Was an Indian or a Mexican skulking just out of sight? Unlikely. Mexican bandits were scarce in this part of the country, and an Indian warrior would not have been so careless. Whoever it was, if ambush was his reason for being there, he had missed his chance.

Lenning had left the grasslands of the Larkspur and cantered along the Sweet Grass Creek bottom for a couple of miles. When it turned back up toward Crazy Mountain, where tall pines were scattered here and there among birch and aspen, he followed its course. Willows skirted the banks of the creek where he had paused to drink and to water his horse.

While looking over the back of his saddle, he pretended to adjust the cinch. Suddenly a brown thrasher flew out of the willows and swept past his head like a darting arrow. He continued to scan the bank along the creek. Then his sharp eyes saw color where none should be. A tiny bit of red had caught his eye.

Fixing the position in his mind, he led his horse a short distance before he mounted and headed him in the opposite direction. A hundred yards down the trail he turned up toward the mountains and came back to approach the willows from the hillside.

Buck Lenning had not planned to be away from the ranch for long. He hated to spend the extra time investigating, but logically he must assume that whoever was hiding along the creek bank was an enemy and needed to be flushed out. Moving slowly, he walked his horse back to a place above where he had seen the pebbles fall into the water.

When he noticed that something or someone had been dragged along the soft green grass, he swung down out of the saddle. Moving with catlike grace he followed the sign toward the creek and the dense growth of willows. He heard no sound, and the only movement was a cool breeze stirring the tops of the pines.

He might not have seen the slender, young Indian girl at all had he not spotted the red cloth tied to the ends of her long braids. Her dress of soft brown linsey blended with the patches of grass beneath the willows. She was frightened but defiant as she watched him with large dark eyes. Considering what happened sometimes to young Indian girls when come

upon by some white men, he did not blame her for being
afraid.

The reason she had been dragging herself over the grass
was obvious to Buck. Her leg was broken below the knee.

"I am friend."

She only stared at him. If he had any brains, he told himself
sternly, he'd get the hell away from her. The Sioux were
plenty mean, and especially where their women were concerned. But, christamighty, he couldn't just ride off and leave
her here with that broken leg. Yet if he laid a hand on her, she
might yell loudly enough to raise the dead. If there was a band
of Sioux nearby, his life wouldn't be worth a pile of horse-
hockey.

He took a step nearer and smiled down at her. She bran-
dished a small knife, motioning for him to stay away.

"I am friend. I help you."

"Go!"

He motioned to her leg. "It's busted. You die without help."
He spoke in what he thought was passable Sioux and gestured
with his hands toward the mountain. "Wildcat, cougar in these
parts. White men who are bad."

"Go."

"I'll cut splints and bind your leg."

He went to where he had left his horse. After tying it
nearby, he took a small hatchet from his saddlebag. Without
speaking to her again, he cut two lengths of straight, stout willow sticks, trimmed and smoothed them as best he could with
the hatchet. While he was doing this, he unobtrusively
watched the girl and saw her cut a strip from the bottom of her
dress with her knife. He was relieved that she was accepting
his help.

Kneeling down he touched the break with gentle fingers.

"This'll hurt like hell," he muttered in English.

"It is so."

He looked up. "Ah . . . you understand me?"

"Little."

"What your name?" He made conversation to take her mind off what he was doing.

"Little Owl."

"I'm Lenning."

"Lenning."

Working carefully, he pulled on her leg. There was no sound from the girl as he fitted the bone in place. But when he looked at her, he saw small white teeth sunk into her lower lip, and her eyes were tightly closed. He placed the splints on either side of her slender calf and wrapped the strip of cloth tightly around it.

"You're a nervy little gal. Where's your camp?"

"Back there." She pointed toward Crazy Mountain.

"How far?" When he saw her brows come together in question, he repeated the words in Sioux.

"Sundown . . . on horse."

Good Lord! If he took her there it would be midnight before he got back to Larkspur. He had to get back within an hour, two at the most. He could give her his horse and walk. The roan would come back to the ranch if turned loose. But Indian's didn't consider taking a horse as stealing. And he was a mighty fine horse.

"Buck Lenning," he muttered to himself, "you can get yourself into some mighty poor situations."

While he was mulling these thoughts over in his mind, he saw that the girl had cocked her head in a listening position. She leaned back and placed her ear to the ground. A look of panic came over her face. She fluttered her hands in a shoo-ing motion.

"Go! Go! Bad men come."

Now Buck could hear the sound of horses approaching.

"Indians?"

The girl shook her head. "Bad! Bad!"

"White men? Are they after you?"

She nodded. "Bad!"

Buck looked around. This wasn't exactly the place he would have chosen for a hostile encounter, but it would have to do. He would be on his feet and they would be mounted.

"Sit still. We'll see what they have to say."

Buck stood behind his horse and watched two men come down the trail. One was leading a spotted pony. The tough-looking men reined in sharply when they saw Buck. They stared at him hard before resting their eyes on the Indian girl.

"I see ya caught our squaw." The one who spoke was not much more than a kid. He had a thin beard, narrow, deep-set, mean eyes, and wore a sleeveless vest decorated with tufts of hair.

"She be a looker, ain't she." The older man was heavyset—fat. His gun belt rode beneath his belly. He urged his horse forward. "Glad ya found her. We thanky for the trouble. We been lookin' for her for a couple a hours."

"We'll jist take 'er off yore hands." The kid squeezed the fire from the end of his cigarette with his thumb and forefinger and dropped it in his breast pocket.

"It was no trouble. I'll take her back to her village." Buck spoke matter-of-factly.

"Now why'd ya think we'd stand still for that?" The young one, to Buck's way of thinking, had an attitude that would get him killed before he was twenty.

"Can't you see that she's got a broken leg?"

"Her own fault fer jumpin' off that pony. Me an' Lantz here cut that squaw out for ourselves. Ya want one, get 'er like we got ours." With his eyes on Buck he spoke to Lantz. "Get her."

"Stay away from her." Buck's voice cut through the quiet sharply. "You blasted fools will get yourselves killed. Her tribe will be all over you like a swarm of ants."

The fat man cackled. The other man threw his leg over his saddlehorn.

"He's got some mouth on him, ain't he?"

"Ain't a Sioux in five mile. Get her, Lantz."

Buck stepped back from his horse. "It appears to me you boys are looking for trouble."

"Trouble? From you? I ain't seein' no backup." The young one grinned, showing a missing front tooth.

"Ain't you that Lenning feller from out at Larkspur? 'Pears to me ya've got trouble enough without takin' on more."

"You're no trouble." Buck uttered the words softly. "Where I come from you'd not stand knee-high to a short frog. The way I see it you're not very smart or you'd not be sitting there bunched up for shootin' with *one* gun. I'm plannin' to use *two*." His words fell like stones in the silence. "Drop the rope on that pony."

"The hell I will!" The kid's lips drew back in a snarl. "Ya can't take both of us."

"It'd be like shootin' fish in a barrel. If you're figgerin' on making a try for this girl, you'd better think about spending the next week or two here on the mountain. It'll take about that long for the scavengers to pick your bones clean. I'll not waste my time buryin' you."

The fat man shifted in his saddle. He was suddenly aware

that he had turned his horse so that he was sideways and would have to turn half-around to get off an effective shot.

It was obvious to Buck that the kid fancied himself a gun-hand. More than likely he had already killed his first man—some poor soul who knew more about a plow than a gun. He wore his gun slung low with the holster tied down. He was the one to watch. Buck decided not to wait for him to make the first move. His hand flashed down and came up with his gun.

"Unbuckle your gun belts . . . now! Drop them or I'll open up and you'll be buzzard bait."

Lantz cursed. "Air ya knowin' who yo're goin' against?"

"Yeah. A couple a two-bit turd-heads that aren't men enough to get a woman without grabbing a helpless little girl."

"Helpless? She's 'bout as helpless as a nest a rattlers!"

"I hope she bit you good. Now drop your belts. I've said it the last time."

"Yo're gettin' yore way this time, but I'll be seein' ya again." Lantz unbuckled his gun belt and dropped it in the dirt. "Colonel Forsythe's got plans for ya."

"Forsythe's got scrambled brains if he thinks he's going to get the Larkspur. Now you, fat man," Buck snarled. The man unbuckled his gun belt and let it drop to the ground. "Turn and walk your horses back down the trail. Not too fast. I'll be right behind you."

Buck mounted his horse, jerked the pony's lead rope from Lantz's hand and flung it to the girl who sat on the ground. He made a motion with his hand for her to stay. He walked his horse behind the two men for a quarter of a mile to the place where the trail ran alongside a steep bank of the creek.

"Stop here," he commanded. "And get down."

"What for? Ya goin' to shoot us over a squaw?"

"Take off your boots."

"Godamighty!"

"I ain't a doin' no such." The fat man hauled himself down out of the saddle.

"Suit yourself." Buck drew his gun. "I'll fill 'em full of holes with you in 'em."

Lantz sat down on the ground and pulled off his boots. The fat man leaned against a tree and toed his off.

"Sit down." Buck stepped from his horse. He stood for a moment staring down at the two. They both had big holes in their socks. The fat man's big toe stuck through the end of his. Buck picked up the boots. "Phew! Don't ya ever wash yore feet?"

"What'er ya doin'?" Lantz demanded.

Buck walked to the edge of the bank and sailed first one boot and then the other far out into the rocky stream.

"I'll get ya. I swear to God—"

Buck ignored the outburst. "By the time you find your boots, you're feet will be cleaner than they've been in years." He took off his hat and hit each of their horses hard on the rump. "H'yaw! H'yaw!" he yelled. The startled horses bolted and took off down the trail.

"It's goin' to be a pleasure a-burnin' ya out."

Buck turned on Lantz. "What did you say?"

"The Colonel ain't lettin' ya have that land."

"You speaking for him now?"

"I . . . hear talk—" Lantz turned his eyes away from Buck's direct stare.

"Ya ain't got no claim now the old man's dead."

"Keep talkin'."

"Well—"

"Shut up, Lantz. Don't tell him nothin'."

"He ain't goin' to be so smart when—"

"Shut up, gawddammit!"

Buck mounted his horse. "You're welcome to start lookin' for your boots soon as I'm outta sight." He turned his horse up the trail, then turned back. "If I was you, I'd hightail it out of the country. That little Indian gal is Red Cloud's sister."

Buck allowed himself one of his rare grins as he rode toward where he had left the girl. He didn't know if she was kin to Red Cloud, but saying it turned the fat man's face two shades whiter than a snake's belly.

The girl was where he had left her. She had managed to stand. She stood on one foot, holding on to a sapling. Buck picked up the gun belts he had forced the pair to drop and slung them over his saddlehorn.

"Can you ride?"

"Pony take me to my people."

He picked her up carefully and set her astride the pony. She grimaced with pain, but made no sound.

"I'll ride with you a ways. Then I must go back."

He mounted his horse and took the lead rope from the girl. Watching to make sure that she was able to keep her balance, he led the pony up the craggy mountainside and down to the flat plain before he stopped and dismounted.

"Can you make it from here?"

She nodded.

He took the smaller of the two gun belts from his saddlehorn, removed the pistol and checked to see if it was loaded. It was.

"Can you shoot?"

She nodded again.

He shoved the gun back down into the holster and swung the belt around her small waist. With his knife he poked a hole in the leather and slid it through the buckle. The girl sat in total silence.

"If you need it, hold it in both hands and pull the trigger. If you should fall off and can't get back on the pony, shoot the gun every once in a while. Some of your people may hear and come help you."

The girl reached out and touched his shoulder.

"You *good* white man. Red Cloud, my uncle, will thank the man from Larkspur."

"Your *uncle?*" Buck chuckled. "What'a ya know. I didn't miss it by much." When the girl looked at him with a puzzled frown, he explained. "I told those two saddle bums that Red Cloud was your brother."

"Red Cloud old man. Black Elk my brother. Crazy Horse was cousin."

"You got powerful kinfolk, little lady." He mounted his horse. "I got to be gettin' back." He tipped his hat. "Good-bye, Little Owl."

"Good-bye, man from Larkspur."

Buck watched her ride away. She sat with back straight, head up. The thought of the fat man and the kid violating her made his skin crawl.

He turned his horse back down the trail, cut across the hills and headed back to Larkspur. The sun was directly overhead. He'd been gone for a good three hours, and it would be another hour or two before he got back to the house.

These were uneasy days. He rode down through the pines to where he could look across a magnificent sweep of country. Larkspur land lay at the foot of a two-mile-long ridge. Aside from the sweet grass meadows the place was pretty well covered with gambel oak and ponderosa pine. Aspen followed the folds of the ridge and trailed down to the meadows.

"No wonder Forsythe wants it so bad." He had spoken aloud, the habit of a man who spent long hours alone. "Well, he'll pay hell getting it."

Pushing the horse, he came out on the high meadow and followed the stream down to the good bottomland. There was a fair stand of grazing under the scattered trees that stretched back to the mountains from the edge of the meadow. Below, another meadow was bordered with grooves of aspen. The range had everything a man needed; logs for the buildings and corrals, stone for the fireplaces. Larkspur was closed-in land where few range hands were needed and where hay could be cut to lay up against the cold of winter.

There were places in the Crazy Mountains where small valleys or ravines opened out into the meadows which allowed him to control the grazing in the small valleys that cut deep into the mountains. He had found such a place and built upon it so that there was no access except right through his ranch. Moreover, he had built each of the outbuildings like a fort, and it was easy to move from one to the other without exposing himself to rifle fire from the outside.

The buildings were bunched amid the pines. He knew every stick and stone of the place. Seeing what he had built with his own two hands and with the sweat of his brow never failed to give him a deep sense of pride.

*This was home;* the only real home he'd ever had. He had sunk his roots here, and here he would stay till the end of his days, be it tomorrow or forty years from now.

Hurrying the roan on down the lane, he scanned the area he had brushed with a branch before he left and was relieved to see no new tracks. He rode past the house and around to where a room had been built on the end of the bunkhouse.

"Howdy, Sam," he said to the shaggy black-and-brown dog

who sat beside the door with his tongue hanging out the side of his mouth. "Anyone been around?"

Buck stepped down from his horse, took a key from his pocket and opened a padlock on the door. Always fearful of what he would find when he returned after being away for several hours, he flung open the door.

An old man with a white beard sat on the bunk attached to the far wall. His elbows were on his knees and his face in his hands. Buck went to him and knelt down.

"You all right, Moss?"

"My name ain't that."

"Sure it is."

The old man's face was lined by a lifetime of struggle against the elements. The sunken blue eyes that looked up at Buck were filled with tears.

"Who'er you?"

"You know who I am," Buck said gently.

"I can't find my pa."

"He'll be along soon. Are you hungry?"

"It snowed this mornin'."

"Let's go to the house, and I'll fix you something to eat."

"Cousin Walter burned his house down."

"I hated to leave you here, old-timer, but I was afraid you'd wander off while I was gone, and I wouldn't be able to find you."

"Ollie Swenson froze to death."

"I know—"

"It takes four pecks to make a bushel."

"It sure does."

"I don't like it when you go."

Buck peered into the old man's wrinkled face. Was this one of his infrequent lucid moments?

"I rode over to Sweet Grass Creek to see if they'd dammed it up."

"Had they?"

"Nothing's been there. Not even a beaver."

The old man got shakily to his feet and looked up at Buck. Years had worn away the muscles of his youth. The flesh on the arms he wrapped around Buck's waist were loose and sagging. His frail body trembled. He clung to Buck as a child would cling to its mother.

"You takin' me home?" he asked beseechingly.

"Yeah, sure. I'm takin' you home."

# Chapter Four

## Big Timber, Montana Territory

$\mathcal{M}$ark Lee crossed the street to the bank and climbed the wooden stairs attached to the side of the building. FORSYTHE LAND DEVELOPMENT was painted in gold script on the glass pane of the door. The young lawyer walked into the office with a feeling of dread. The news he had for Colonel Forsythe was sure to anger him.

Lee knew that Forsythe was shrewd, cunning and a conniver of the first degree. He also knew that he would use any method to get what he wanted, keeping himself in the background of anything smacking of crime or wrongdoing. Mark wanted a piece of the good life Forsythe enjoyed: prestige, good food, a soft bed and Havana cigars. To get it, he would play along.

When Lee opened the door, Forsythe was putting on his hat, preparing to leave the office for the day.

"Hello, Colonel. I'm glad I caught you."

"I was just leaving. What's on your mind?"

"I . . . just got a wire. That woman is on her way out here. She'll be here Wednesday night."

"What woman?"

"The Anderson woman."

"Jesus Christ! Didn't you send the letter to her brother?"

"Yes, but he hasn't had time to get it."

"What does the wire say?"

"Kristin Anderson will arrive Wednesday 6 P.M. Meet her. Take care of her. G. Anderson." Mark read the message and handed over the paper given to him by the agent. "I thought her brother's name was Ferd. Maybe it was Gerd."

To Mark's surprise Forsythe smiled after reading the message.

"Good. Meet her at the train. Get her a room at the hotel and treat her to dinner in the dining room. Give her a little taste of what money can do. Thursday morning bring her here to the office. I'll show her a map marking the tract of land, and she'll see how far it is from town. I'll tell her about the Sioux raiding parties, and the low beef prices. Then I'll produce a stack of greenbacks. It'll be more money than she ever dreamed of having. She'll sign the deed and you can put her back on the train in the afternoon."

Mark sighed with relief. When he had found the twenty-year-old will in the files of the old lawyer whose office he now occupied, Forsythe had been delighted. It would be less bother to have it probated than to go through the process of trying to find the next of kin to get a clear title to Larkspur. Mark had written immediately to Kristin Anderson informing her of her inheritance and in less than two weeks had received word from her brother that they wished to sell. Anderson had taken great pains to explain that he was too busy with his lumber business to manage the land properly.

On the way back to his own office Mark Lee wondered why the woman was coming here. According to her brother, she was a spinster who lived in his home and took care of his children. Mark always felt more confident, however, after speaking with the colonel. Forsythe would charm the Anderson woman into signing her land over to him and they would be rid of her.

Kyle Forsythe was such an imposing figure. Although some considered him pompous and overbearing, others realized he was a sharp businessman whose air of aristocracy served him well. The War Between the States had been over for eighteen years, but he still used Colonel before his name. He had obtained the lesser rank of Lieutenant Colonel through the influence of Judge Ronald Van Winkle, uncle of his late wife.

Getting title to the land beyond the Yellowstone River was his all-consuming interest. He was hurrying to get his claims locked in before the territory was made officially a part of the United States. When that time came, he fully intended to be one of the largest landowners in the state with a good chance of becoming its first governor. By then he would have a tight hold on the wool market. With a bridge across the Yellowstone River, Big Timber could become the largest wool shipping point in the West. Larkspur, however, had the potential of being more valuable than grass or steers or sheep. He was determined to have it, regardless of the cost, before these yokels woke up to its possibilities.

Taking possession was another matter. Lenning was wild and unreasonable. He'd not give up without a fight. Although Mark had met him only one time, once had been enough. The man had picked him up and tossed him off his porch as if he were a stray cat. His dignity and his backside had suffered a mighty blow.

Forsythe had said not to worry about Lenning, and Mark Lee was perfectly willing to let Forsythe handle him. From what he had heard and knew about the man, he was one mean son of a bitch when pushed.

*     *     *

Dazed with fatigue, Kristin looked out the window at the lonely, empty land. She had not seen a farm since Fargo, at least not one like the farms in Wisconsin. The only milk cows she had glimpsed were in small pastures on the edge of the few towns or villages they had passed.

The first night of her trip she had not slept a wink, and had only dozed occasionally on the train the next day. At Miles City she had gone with the three other women passengers to a dormitory-type rooming house that sat alongside the railroad track. She had paid the exorbitant sum of a half a dollar for a cot in the room with the other women and had slept for just a few hours. But at last she had been able to wash the smoke and grit from her face, neck and arms.

Today, after they stopped at a small town named Billings and took on firewood and water, the conductor told her the next stop would be Big Timber. She both welcomed and dreaded the end of the trip.

As the train approached the town, it seemed to Kristin to be a mere blob on the vast landscape. But as they neared, she could discern a well-laid-out town sprawled alongside the tracks. Of course, it was a mere village compared to Eau Claire, but it was larger than several of the towns they had passed since leaving Miles City.

As Kristin set her straw hat firmly on her head and fastened it with her hatpins, she heard the engineer announce the train's arrival with several blasts of the train whistle. There was the now-familiar sound of scraping of iron against iron as the train slowed and jerked to a stop. She caught a glimpse of the sign on the end of the gray-painted building that served as the station. BIG TIMBER. She was here at last.

Kristin followed two men to the end of the car. She acknowledged their courtesy with a nod when they stepped aside so that the conductor could assist her down the steps. The platform was crowded with people and baggage. Holding tightly to her bag and her basket, Kristin moved over to stand next to the building. She looked about her in dismay at the roughly dressed men. Most were wearing guns. Two women were preparing to board the train. One consoled a small child who cringed and cried. At the car ahead the baggage man was unloading boxes and trunks onto a high-wheeled cart.

Kristin walked to the end of the station and looked up the road toward the town. It lay between two rows of buildings and held a stream of spring wagons, buckboards and saddle horses. She would walk if Mr. Lee didn't show up to meet her.

She felt strangely calm and confident.

Almost everyone had left the platform when a man came out of the station and looked around. He was dressed in a dark suit and wore a high-crowned hat with a wide white band. Finally his eyes fastened on Kristin. She tilted her chin and looked away. *Don't make eye contact with any strange man.* She remembered Gustaf telling her that. Kristin turned her back to him. He couldn't be Mr. Mark Lee. He was far too young and too handsome.

"Are you Miss Anderson?"

Kristin turned to face the man who had stared at her. Their eyes were on a level. He was short. His tall hat had made him seem taller at first glance. He had dark eyes and hair and a carefully groomed mustache. As far as she could see there was not a speck of dust on his dark suit.

"I'm Kristin Anderson."

"Mark Lee. I got your brother's wire saying you would be arriving today."

"My brother sent a wire?"

"It was signed G. Anderson."

"My cousin, Gustaf, sent the wire. He took me to the train."

"He said take care of you, and I will. I've reserved a room for you at the hotel. Pardon me for one moment while I make arrangements to have your baggage sent over, and then we will go there. I'm sure you're eager to refresh yourself."

Kristin waited while he spoke to the agent. Mr. Lee seemed nice enough, even though he wasn't what she expected. The only lawyers she knew were the two in River Falls, and they were gray-haired old men. She watched him return to her and realized that he was quite proud of himself. He walked with a kind of a swagger. Gustaf would say he was a *dandy*.

"Your trunk and box will be brought to the hotel presently. Shall we go?"

He took the basket from her and, with a hand beneath her elbow, escorted her around to the front of the building where a fancy buggy was hitched to a fine mare.

"How was your trip?" he asked after he had settled her in the soft leather seat and climbed in beside her.

"Long. Dirty. But interesting."

"Have you traveled by train before?" The mare trotted up the well-traveled road to the main part of town.

"No."

"Traveling in the East by train is much pleasanter than it is here in the West, where the cars are uncomfortable and the stops far between." He laughed. "I doubt that you will find this desolate country to your liking. I certainly don't. I'd rather be where things are happening than here in the midst of all this space filled with nothing more worthwhile than a few skinny steers."

"I think it's a fascinating land."

"It would be if there were something worthwhile on it. Out

here the land is parched, the Indians hostile, and the people worn-out from the struggle to keep body and soul together."

"Someone must like it or there wouldn't have been enough people to build a town."

"Business brings men West. Men can endure most anything as long as they're making money. Most of the women I've met can't wait to get away from here."

"And you? Are you eager to leave?"

For a moment her question surprised him, and he was silent. Then he turned a charming smile in her direction.

"I've no intention of spending my life here. I'll be going back to Chicago very soon. Perhaps tomorrow or the next day. We can travel back East together."

Kristin was silent. She wasn't in the habit of making quick judgments, but something about Mark Lee didn't ring true. It struck her that he didn't want her to like it here and was planning on her leaving right away. Why?

The hotel was on a corner, a long two-storied building with tall narrow windows. It was newer, but not so fine as the one Kristin had stayed in the time she and the children had gone with Ferd and Andora to Eau Claire. She didn't care. All she wanted was a room with a lock on the door and a bed to sleep in.

"Sign the register, please." The desk clerk, a dapper little man with hair parted in the middle and slicked-down, placed an open book before Kristin and handed her a pen he had dipped in the inkwell.

"Is there fresh water in the room?" Mr. Lee asked.

"Yes and also a pitcher of very warm water. I had it sent up when I heard the train come in."

"That was kind of you," Kristin murmured.

"I hope you enjoy your stay with us, ma'am."

"I'll walk you to your door." Mark Lee urged her toward the stairs. "You're in room 104, the second on the right." At the door he inserted the key, swung it open and handed the key to Kristin. "Your trunk will be here shortly. I'll be back in a couple of hours to take you to dinner. The hotel serves a fine menu prepared by a chef who formerly worked for the Savoy in Denver."

"Thank you for the kind offer, Mr. Lee. But I'd rather stay here. I may just sleep the clock around."

"I'm sorry you won't be joining me, but I understand. I'll leave word at the desk to send up some dinner." He went to a long cord with a tassel on the end. "When you're ready, give this a couple of tugs. A bell will sound in the kitchen and your meal will be brought up."

Kristin was uncomfortable. It was most improper for him to be in her room even with the door open. Mr. Lee didn't seem to think anything of it. He surveyed the room carefully before he went to the door.

"I hope you'll be comfortable here tonight. I'll be back in the morning to take you to the office where we can discuss your inheritance. Will eight o'clock be too early?"

"You needn't come get me, Mr. Lee. I'm perfectly capable of finding my way to your office if you tell me where it is."

"It will be my pleasure. And . . . don't concern yourself about the hotel bill. It is part of my fee for handling your legal matters."

*And how much will that be, Mr. Lee?* Kristin did not voice the question, but her mind, tired as it was, was working rapidly.

"Thank you for meeting me. I'll see you in the morning."

"Have a nice evening, Miss Anderson."

As soon as the door closed, Kristin went to it, inserted the key and locked it. Alone at last for the first time in three days and two nights, she removed her hat and hung it on the peg beside the door. She felt as if she were still moving, as if the floor beneath her feet was not standing still. A heavy knock sounded at the door and she opened it to two men carrying her trunk and box. They set them inside the door and hurried away.

How heavenly it was to wash herself from head to toe in the warm water. Since soap and towels had been provided, she left her own in the trunk. After putting on her nightdress, she brushed her hair vigorously and plaited it loosely into one long braid. Then she looked out the windows at the main street of Big Timber, and admitted to herself that she was disappointed. The town was so new, so raw.

Refusing to allow her mind to wonder about the events of tomorrow, she tucked the bag containing her money and the pistol under the spare pillow, climbed into bed and sank into a deep, dreamless sleep.

Mark Lee took the buggy to the livery back of the hotel, and then walked the two blocks to the Forsythe house. The two-storied white Victorian-style house with a wraparound porch and large carriage house was set in the middle of an acre of well-groomed yard, surrounded with a white picket fence.

Lee used the brass knocker on one of the double doors. A minute or two passed before it was opened by a woman with soft brown hair and an unlined face. Ruth DeVary was Colonel Forsythe's housekeeper and much more, Lee suspected. Always well groomed and well mannered, she also acted as hostess when the Colonel occasionally entertained a person from out of the district whom he wished to impress.

"Afternoon, Mrs. DeVary."

"Afternoon, Mr. Lee. Come in. I believe the colonel is expecting you."

"Thank you." Lee hung his hat on the hall tree and followed the woman down a short hall to the room the colonel called his study.

Forsythe was not alone. He appeared to be in deep conversation with Del Gomer and Mike Bruza. Lee did not like or trust either man.

The dark-haired man, Mike Bruza, was long-armed, short-legged and thickset and enjoyed using his big hairy fists. He was tough and liked to play on the winning side. Long ago he had decided that Forsythe was smart and obviously wanted to be a kingpin. That was all right with Mike. He'd just ride along and gather up information along the way that might someday help him to topple the *king*.

Mike's ambition was to be a lawman. He relished the power that went with the job. As lawman *he* would be in position to tell the high muckety-mucks how the cow ate the cabbage—even the *colonel*.

Del Gomer was unlike any man Mark Lee had previously met. Lee considered him as dangerous as a cornered snake. He was clean-shaven except for a waxed mustache, tall, broad of shoulder, hard-eyed and quiet—so quiet he was scary. In contrast to Mike Bruza, he was neat and clean about his person and his possessions.

When things did not go to his liking, Del said little at the time. He was inclined to sit back and wait. Sooner or later his pent-up anger would explode into sudden, ugly violence. He was cold-blooded and utterly without conscience. He would kill a man without hesitation and with about as much concern as if he were swatting a fly.

Del had one weakness. He was completely, hopelessly in

love with a woman who cared absolutely nothing for him and who ignored him as if he were a mere speck on the wall.

Forsythe looked up and saw Lee standing in the doorway.

"Come in. Help yourself to a drink." He motioned to a sideboard that held a decanter and glasses.

Lee downed the drink. He needed it. He was always uncomfortable with Gomer and Bruza. They were everything he wasn't: big, rough and physically capable of taking care of themselves in almost any situation. Forsythe was impressed that Mark was a nephew of Robert E. Lee, but it meant nothing to these two. He could feel their contempt whenever he was with them.

"Well," Forsythe prompted, "what do you think of our little pigeon?"

"She wasn't the middle-aged spinster I expected."

"Older or younger?"

"Younger. I'd guess she's in her early twenties."

"Hummm . . ." Forsythe poured himself another drink. "Ugly as sin, I hope. Ugly ones are easier to manage."

"She's no raving beauty, but not bad-looking. She's got kind of silvery blond hair. At first I thought it was gray. She had it skinned up and under a hat. She's medium height, slender, but not a weakling. I invited her to dinner. She turned down my invitation."

"Smart woman." Mike smirked at Lee.

Forsythe gave him an angry stare. Outwardly Mark Lee ignored the remark. Inwardly he seethed.

"She appears to be a strong-minded woman."

"We'll have to change that. Bring her to my office tomorrow. Do you have the papers ready?"

"One paper is all that's necessary. If she signs over her claim to Yarby Anderson's estate, that's all we need."

"What if she won't sign?" Mike hated to be left out of the conversation.

"She will," Forsythe said confidently.

" 'Course, she will." Mike's laughter was harsh and out of place in the refinement of the room. "A little scare might help change her mind . . . fast."

"No rough stuff . . . yet."

Mark Lee poured himself another drink without being invited. *Good Lord!* Forsythe wouldn't turn these two loose on a woman, would he? Lee had a feeling about Miss Kristin Anderson. She was not going to be as easy to manipulate as the colonel expected. As badly as he wanted this deal over and done with, he didn't want to see a woman hurt.

It was mighty still, so still Buck could hear one aspen leaf caressing another. Once in a while he could hear a horse shift his feet in the corral. A bird made a slight inquiring noise. Nothing else broke the silence but the occasional whispering of birds in the aspens that sounded like a bunch of schoolgirls getting settled for the night. The moon was wide and shining just above the dark, somber spruce massed together north of the house.

Buck Lenning sat on his porch and looked up at the stars—a million of them. He wondered if Little Owl had gotten back to her village and if Lantz and his fat friend had found their boots. They couldn't have walked far without them. Buck chuckled. The fat man probably rode his horse to the outhouse—the lazy bastard!

They'd hightail it to Forsythe the minute they got back to Big Timber and report his being away from the homestead. From now on he'd have to be more careful or they'd sneak in and take possession or burn his place down while he was away.

Buck marked off with bent fingers the five weeks that had passed since the patrol had stopped for the night and he'd given the letter to the sergeant to mail. It would take the patrol a week to get to Helena, that is if nothing unforseen happened. Cleve Stark *might* have received the message by now, but a Federal marshal was not free to cut loose and come to a friend's rescue on the spur of the moment.

Looking back, Buck wished he had sent for Cleve *before* the body had been found and identified as Yarby's.

And there was that damn will. Who in hell would have thought that twenty years ago Yarby Anderson would have written out a will and have had it notarized and recorded? Buck thought back over the ten years of sweat he had put into this place. Yarby had more than likely forgotten about the will by the time he had found Buck half-dead from gunshots in four places and had dragged him over the snow to his cabin. After he recovered, Buck had stayed on and the two had become more like father and son than friends.

Buck wondered about the woman in Wisconsin. Yarby hadn't been young even twenty years ago when he made out the will. Was she a lost love? By now the woman probably had grandchildren. It was unreasonable to assume that she'd make a trip all the way out here. Forsythe would have downplayed the inheritance—let her think the land was not worth much. Of course, he'd not put it past him and Lee to arrange for an imposter to claim the Yarby's estate, then sell it to them.

Buck stood and stretched.

*Cleve, you better hurry. All hell will break loose if they ride out here to take my home.*

# Chapter Five

$\mathcal{K}$ristin was up, washed and dressed, as daylight began to creep into the room. Feeling renewed and more confident in a dark gray skirt and white shirtwaist, she stood by the window and waited until there was activity on the street below before she put on her hat and fastened it firmly with her hatpins.

There were a number of things she wanted to find out before she met again with Mr. Mark Lee, and she couldn't do that unless she stirred herself out of the room.

With the bag that now held her room key as well as her money and pistol over her arm, Kristin went down the stairs to the lobby. Two men sat in the straight chairs. One was reading a newspaper, the other smoking a foul-smelling cigar that was as fat as a sausage. Kristin paused at the desk, but the clerk was nowhere in sight. She went out the door and onto the boardwalk fronting the hotel.

A man on horseback passed. He tipped his hat. Kristin nodded. Down the street a buckboard stood in front of a store, and across the street, the barber was sweeping the walk in front of his shop. A half dozen horses waited patiently at the hitching rails. She was toying with the idea of asking the barber about an eating place when a man whose long beard and hair were snowy white hobbled around the corner of the hotel leaning heavily on a cane. Without hesitation, she stepped out and greeted him.

"Good morning."

"Howdy, ma'am."

"Sir? Is there an eating place in town other than the one here in the hotel?"

"This'n suppose to be for the high-toned folks."

Kristin smiled. "That's exactly why I'd rather go somewhere else. I'm not high-toned folk."

"Me, neither. I ate there once. Flapjacks they give me wouldn't cover the top of a teacup." The old man snorted. "Bonnie, down in the next block, sets a decent table. It's where I'm goin'."

"Thank you. Do you mind if I walk along with you?" She moved beside the old man, fitting her steps to his.

"Pleased to have ya. Bringin' Bonnie a new customer might get me a extra biscuit."

"I don't know when I've been so hungry."

"Come on the train, didn't ya?"

"How did you know?" Kristin laughed and waited for him to step down off the walk to cross the street.

"News travels in Big Timber, missy. Bet there ain't nobody standing on two feet what don't know that yo're old Yarby's niece from Wisconsin come to claim the Larkspur."

"Well, for goodness sake! That takes the cake! And I thought there were busybodies in River Falls."

"Hee! Hee! Hee!" The old man clearly enjoyed her surprise. "Yup. Ain't no town out here big enough for a pretty woman to pass through without folks takin' a notice."

"Thank you for the *pretty* part of that."

"Yup," he said again. "We're all waitin' to see how long it's gonna take Forsythe to hornswoggle ya out of what Yarby left ya."

"Forsythe?"

"See that sign yonder?" He pointed to a sign over a stairway next to the bank. LAND BROKER. "Some folks call him Land *Grabber* or Get-Rich-Quick Forsythe. He knows more ways to part a man from his money than a duck's got feathers."

"I'll not be having anything to do with him. The lawyer that's handling Uncle Yarby's will is Mr. Mark Lee. Do you know him?"

"Pshaw! *Land lawyer!*" He snorted with disdain. "Watch the little shyster. He's square in Forsythe's pocket."

"Did you know Uncle Yarby?"

"Shore. Everybody 'round here knowed Yarby. Too bad. It was a shame; a pure-dee old shame what happened. Well, here we are." He stopped in front of an open door.

"Thank you," Kristin said softly before stepping inside.

"Keep yore wits about ya, girl." The old man's whisper came from behind her and was just as soft. Then he murmured, "Repeatin' what I said could cost me my life."

For a second Kristin thought the man had said something about "costing his life." It was preposterous, of course. Her mind swam in a sea of confusion and bewilderment. She went into the restaurant looking much more relaxed and confident than she felt. Half a dozen men were seated at the long oil-cloth-covered table. The other table was occupied by a lone diner.

"Mornin', Cletus. You're right on time for a fresh batch of biscuits." The woman who spoke had a pleasant, smiling face and was approximately Kristin's age. "You got a knack of timing it just right."

"Mornin', Bonnie."

"Your place is waiting for you, Cletus." She turned friendly brown eyes on Kristin. "Come in, ma'am, and have a seat."

The old man had taken the only vacant seat at the front table. Kristin moved to the near-vacant table and sat down at the end. The eruption of an unladylike growl that came from her stomach reminded her that she hadn't eaten in almost twenty-four hours.

Three chairs were empty between her and the only other person at the table: a rather handsome man with light, neatly combed hair and a freshly shaven face. His back was to the wall giving him a full view of the door, the kitchen and dining area. He looked at her briefly with light, steel gray eyes, then ignored her.

Kristin placed her bag on the floor at her feet and watched the woman set platters of biscuits on each end of the table where the old man sat and then bring a smaller plate of biscuits and one of fried meat and flapjacks to her table.

"Coffee or tea?"

"Coffee, please." Kristin turned up the cup that sat beside her plate.

Bonnie smiled. "Somehow I knew you'd say that. Be right back with a fresh stack of pancakes and bacon. Or would you rather have oatmeal?"

"Pancakes would be fine."

She returned immediately with a coffeepot and filled Kristin's cup. The gray-eyed man pushed his cup across the table, his eyes on Bonnie's face. She filled it without looking or speaking to him and went back to the serving counter.

Kristin ate heartily. The flapjacks were light, the butter fresh and sweet. She asked the man at the table to please pass the syrup pitcher. He did so without as much as a glance in her direction.

It was evident that Bonnie was popular with her customers. She took their teasing with a laugh and tossed their sallies back at them. Her reddish brown hair was thick, and curly wisps of it stuck to her damp forehead. Her sleeves were rolled up past her elbows, and an apron was tied about her small waist that emphasized her well-rounded breasts and hips. On one of her rounds of the tables she paused beside Kristin.

"Would you like some plum butter to go with your biscuits?"

"I would." The quiet man at the table answered before Kristin had a chance.

When Bonnie brought the jar, she set it on the table and went back to the cooking area without a word. Kristin saw her speaking to the man standing before the large black cookstove. He was angry. She was trying to calm him.

The diners left two and three at a time. Finally Kristin, the man at her table, and Cletus, were all that remained. The only sound in the room was the rattle of pans and the clink of dishes as the cook washed them and passed them to Bonnie to dry and place on the shelves behind the counter.

To Kristin the silence was deep and somehow . . . threatening. Instinctively she knew the tension between Bonnie and the cook had something to do with the man who sat at her table. Each time she glanced at him, his eyes were on Bonnie. Kristin wanted to go and yet she wanted to stay and talk more with Cletus and maybe get to know Bonnie.

Just when her excuses to linger were running out, the man stood and went to the peg on the wall where he had left his hat. He was tall, slender and neatly dressed. He placed a coin on the counter, and when Bonnie did not turn to face him, he went to the door where, with hat in hand, he looked back at her.

"Good-bye, Bonnie," he said just before he went out. He

stood in front of the restaurant for a moment, then carefully put his hat on his head and walked down the walk toward the hotel.

The man behind the counter spun around. Kristin heard a loud *thump, thump, thump* just before he broke into a spate of angry words.

"That cold-eyed son of a bitch! He never took his eyes off you all the time he was in here."

"So what?" Bonnie retorted. "Looks can't hurt me."

"He'll hurt you! He's not giving up. How long's it been? Six months? Eight?"

When the cook came from behind the counter, Kristin realized that the thumping sound she had heard was the end of a peg on the wooden floor. The knee of the man's left leg rested in the cradle of a peg held by straps wrapped about his thigh and the stump extended out behind. The thumps sounded again as he came around to pick up the money left by the cold-eyed man.

"Mother a Christ! A dollar for a fifteen-cent meal." He dropped the coin back on the counter. "I wonder who he killed to get it."

"Bernie, calm down." Bonnie brought the coffeepot and refilled Cletus's cup. "Would you like more coffee, miss?"

"No, thank you. I'm killing time. I hope you don't mind. By the way, do you know where I can hire a buckboard and a driver to take me out to Larkspur?"

A deathly quiet followed her words as the woman and two men looked at one another. The one-legged man finally answered.

"You'll just be asking for trouble if you try to go out there, ma'am. They'll not let you keep the Larkspur!" Bernie spun around easily on the peg and dropped the dollar in a tin under the counter.

Bonnie looked pained. "No use trying to be polite, Miss Anderson. Everybody in town knows who you are and why you're here. I'm Bonnie Gates and this hotheaded blabbermouth is my brother, my twin, Bernie Gates."

"I'm happy to meet you. And please don't apologize. I'm from a town not much larger than Big Timber. I'm used to everyone's knowing everyone else's business. Did you know my uncle?"

"We didn't. We haven't been here a year. Cletus knew him."

"Nice a man as ya'd want to meet," Cletus said. "I hadn't seen him for a couple a years when all this happened. Never believed a bit of it."

"Never believed . . . what?"

"Wal . . . that Yarby'd do anything . . . wrong."

"I don't remember ever seeing my uncle. But it was wonderfully kind of him to remember me in his will. I want to see Larkspur. I've never owned anything in my life and never dreamed that I would." Her eyes shone and her full mouth tilted at the corners. "I want to walk on my own land and to know that I have a place on this earth that's mine."

Bonnie came and sat down beside Kristin. Pain and disappointment were stamped on her face as she looked at her brother, then turned to Kristin.

"It must be a grand feeling to own your own place with nobody to tell you to get out. Bernie and I always wanted a little place. Almost had one . . . once."

"I hope Mr. and Mrs. Lenning won't mind me staying for a while."

"I ain't heard of Buck gettin' married. Might of. He ain't been to town for quite a spell." Cletus cleared his throat.

"Miss, I ain't got no business stickin' my bill in, but"——he lowered his voice and glanced toward the door—"they ain't goin' to want you goin' out there. They'll want ya to sign and get outta town . . . fast."

"Who'll want me to . . . get out of town?" Kristin had a puzzled look on her face.

"Forsythe and his bunch. Bet they was in a snit when you showed up."

"Will they try to stop me from going to the Larkspur?"

"I ain't swearin' they would. I ain't swearin' they wouldn't."

Bernie snorted in disgust. "Cletus, you know as well as I do that they'll . . . do whatever it takes to get Larkspur. Look what they've done so far. Why do you think that hired killer hangs around?"

Kristin looked from brother to sister. They both had reddish brown hair and soft brown eyes, but that was where the resemblance ended. Bernie was stocky, with broad shoulders and chest. Bonnie was soft and slim with hair curlier than her brother's.

"You'll scare her, Bernie," Bonnie chided gently. She stood and wrapped her hands in her apron.

"Somebody'd better scare her, Sis. If I was you, Miss Anderson, I'd either take the piddling amount Forsythe will pay for Larkspur and catch the next train out, or I'd hightail it out there and hole up with Buck Lenning."

"I'm not selling, and I'm not leaving. I've nothing to go back to."

"They'll see to it that you sign the papers. It's what they did when they got the Samuels' place. Took the woman out to near the Sioux camp. She thought it was where the ranch was. The Sioux run them off their hunting grounds just like they always do. Woman didn't know that. As soon as they got back to town, she signed the papers and caught the eastbound train. I'm not sure how they got Silas Midland's land, but when he left, he was walking with a cane."

"My cousin told me not to sign anything until at least two lawyers have looked at it."

"You'll sign if your arm is twisted up behind your back, or they got your finger in a vise."

"They'd . . . do that?"

"Or turn his hired thugs on you."

"I'm meeting with Mr. Lee this morning. I'll tell him straight out that I'm not selling—"

"Don't do that!" Cletus spoke quickly. "Oh, 'scuse me, miss. I ain't got no cause to be givin' advice."

"Oh, please. I'll appreciate any advice I can get."

"I'd stall 'em along. Tell 'em you'll think about it. Meantime me'n Bernie'll try to figure out a way to get ya out to Larkspur without them knowin'. I'm thinkin' you'd be better off with Buck."

"You'll help me? Oh, thank you. Thank you. I must go. I'm so glad I ran into you. I didn't quite trust that Mr. Lee. I felt he didn't want me to like it here."

"Yes, you'd better go. Here come the railroaders for their breakfast. Don't forget . . . not a word about what we've said." Bonnie glanced at her brother.

"Don't worry. We only passed the time of day."

"I've got me a idey," Cletus said. "Go to Mrs. Gaffney's and rent a room—anyone can tell you where she's at. Get your stuff out of the hotel this afternoon. If we can arrange anything, I'll get word to Mrs. Gaffney. Now you'd better get. They know I sit here for a spell after breakfast."

"I . . . don't know how to thank you. I'll do my best to see that they never find out what you've told me."

Kristin walked slowly back toward the hotel. She could not fully comprehend all she had learned the past hour. The good Lord must be watching over her and had brought her together with these folks who would help her at risk to themselves. They had taken a chance on her. She must not let them down.

*Oh, Gustaf, I wish you were here.*

"Sit down, my dear."

Mark Lee had introduced Kyle Forsythe to Kristin as his business partner, and the polite phrases had been uttered.

"I trust you had a pleasant breakfast."

"It was all right."

"I stopped by the hotel, thinking we could become acquainted before this meeting and was surprised that you were not there."

"I'm sorry. If I had known, I'd not have gone out walking while I waited for Mr. Lee. I saw people going into a place down the street and followed along, not knowing it was a place mostly for men." Kristin laughed nervously. "After I went in, it was too late to back out the door."

"You met Miss Gates. Lovely girl. I hear the food is good there. I've not tried it myself."

"We don't serve such large pancakes in Wisconsin, and the meat is not so greasy. I was surprised that potatoes are not served in some form for breakfast. Back home it's standard fare."

"Is that right? Come to think of it, they serve them in Tennessee, too."

"Potato pancakes?"

Forsythe laughed. "No pan-fried."

Kristin smiled. "We Swedes are also fond of potato dumplings." *He really was charming. She was so thankful she had been warned.* She turned to the young lawyer who had been sitting quietly. He was her lawyer, but it was Colonel Forsythe who was doing all the talking. "Mr. Lee, about my uncle's will—"

"Show it to her, Mark. The young lady is anxious to get her affairs settled."

Mr. Lee took a yellowed document from a leather case and placed it on the desk in front of her.

"It's a standard will of the time. Witnessed, notarized and recorded at the territorial capital."

> I, Yarby Anderson, being of sound mind,
> do bequeath to my niece, Kristin Anderson,
> River Falls, Wisconsin, all my earthly
> possessions at the time of my demise.
> Yarby Anderson September 5, 1863
> Witness: Judge James Williams
> Roy R. Smothers

Kristin read the document twice. When she looked up she had tears in her eyes.

"Bless his heart. I never knew him. It was dear of him to think of me."

"From what I hear he was a nice old man," Forsythe said kindly. "He must have thought the world of you."

"I hope he didn't suffer."

"He was found deep in the woods. I suspect his heart just gave out, and he sat down and died without fear or pain. A wonderful way to go."

"I guess so." Kristin dried her eyes.

"Now, young lady, I'm sure you want to get this business over with so you can get back home. I'm prepared to give you

the best possible price you could get for that land." He reached
into a drawer and brought out a stack of bills.

"But, sir, I've no idea what the land is worth."

"That's understandable. That's why I'm here. Land is my
business. I've been buying and selling it for many years."

"And my brother says there's probably a herd of cows."

"Cows? If he was referring to a herd of steer, my dear, I'm
sorry to disappoint you. Indians and rustlers made off with
your uncle's small herd long ago."

"Didn't Mr. Lenning try to stop them?"

"Mr. Lenning." He paused with a look of disgust on his
face. "The man is a saddle bum who wandered off the trail and
onto the Larkspur. Your uncle was kind enough to take him in.
He probably worked hand in glove with the rustlers for a cut
of the cash."

"There is so much I don't know—"

The Colonel thumbed through the stack of bills then placed
them on the desk in front of her.

"Here's two . . . THOUSAND . . . dollars. A fortune. I'm
willing to pay this for your inheritance sight unseen because
you're a young woman of refinement. Many here in the West
would take advantage of a young lady alone without family.
I'd be grateful if someone would be as considerate of my
daughter should she be put in your position."

Kristin allowed her eyes to linger on the bills he was sliding
through his fingers.

"It's a lot of . . . money—"

"Yes, it is. If managed right, it will keep you comfortably in
your *own* house for the rest of your life."

"I know." Kristin began to smile, and she called on all her
acting abilities to keep the look of loathing out of her expression.

"It's a simple process, my dear. All you have to do is sign the paper Mr. Lee has prepared, and you're a rich woman."

"Papa had certain rules about things." Kristin called up what she hoped was a dreamy expression. "One of them was—don't be impulsive. He used to say, 'Always sleep on a *big* decision.' My brother, Ferd, thinks I've no business sense at all, but when I go back with all that money, and tell him that I didn't do anything impulsive, that I slept on the deal like Papa always said was the smart thing to do, he'll sit up and take notice. I'll see you in the morning, Colonel Forsythe."

"If you feel that's what you must do, my dear."

Kristin stood. "I'd like to stay a few days after we get things settled. Do you know of a rooming house suitable for ladies?"

"As a matter of fact I do." Forsythe placed the money back in the drawer. "A friend of mine, Mrs. Bartlett, has rooms to let. I saw the sign this morning. She's on the first street west of here. Big house with gables and beautiful stained-glass windows. But, my dear Miss Anderson, you'll be able to afford the hotel—"

"No, sir. I'm going back to River Falls with my inheritance intact. You don't know how much satisfaction it will give me to wave it under my brother's nose." Kristin reached for the will to pull it from Lee's hand. He held on to it and put it back in an envelope along with another paper. "I just want to look at it, and look at it."

"Mr. Lee will have it when you're ready to sign." The colonel chuckled, moved close to her and instead of clasping her elbow to escort her to the door, his fingers surrounded her lower arm.

"Your hotel bill has been paid by Mr. Lee. Tell the clerk to see that your trunk is delivered to Mrs. Bartlett. We'll see you in the morning."

"You sure will, sir." Kristin offered her hand and he clasped it warmly.

As she went down the steps, the smile she had been holding slid off her face. The shysters! The bald-faced liars! She had been around Ferd's business friends enough to recognize a couple of connivers when she met them. Of course, she might not have caught on so fast had she not been warned by Bonnie, Bernie and Cletus.

The *charming* colonel thought he would get her under the watchful eye of his friend, Mrs. Bartlett! He really was a slick operator, but was he as dangerous as her new friends believed him to be?

Kristin turned into the mercantile, approached the man at the counter and asked for directions to Mrs. Gaffney's rooming house.

In the upstairs office Colonel Forsythe turned back into the room after seeing Kristin to the door.

"We've landed our pigeon. Not many women can resist that impressive stack of bills." He chuckled. "They were mostly fives with a few twenties on top."

"She wanted the will."

"Well, she didn't get it. She'll be back in the morning. We didn't even have to show her the map . . . or tell her about the Indians."

"It seemed to me that she folded awfully easy."

Forsythe slapped Mark Lee on the back and offered him a cigar.

"Trust me, my friend. You underestimate my power over women. Especially the love-starved ones. Even though she's young enough to be my daughter, I'll bet you a five-spot I'll be in her bed before she leaves town."

# Chapter Six

Mrs. Gaffney was short and plump with a twinkle in her eyes and a twist of thick gray hair fastened to the top of her head.

She was also very hard of hearing.

When the drayman brought Kristin's trunk and box to the back porch, she told him to put them in the hall. When he offered to carry them upstairs, she walked away as if she had not heard him. Rather than run after her and repeat, he had driven away.

Kristin liked Widow Gaffney immediately. Her home, on the edge of town, with a large meadow behind, was immaculate and her attitude about her disability amazing. At times she treated it as if it were an advantage. Kristin soon discovered that if she spoke with her lips close to the woman's ear, they could converse in normal tones.

Mrs. Gaffney had two roomers. Both men worked on the railroad and used the rooms only three days a week. At the present time they were away.

After supper Mrs. Gaffney put on her hat and shawl and announced to Kristin that she was going to Bible study at the church and that Kristin could sit on the porch or in the parlor while she was away.

"You'll be all right here," Mrs. Gaffney said in a heavy Irish brogue when she saw unease on Kristin's face. "I best go alone."

"You've helped others before?"

"One time." Her eyes hardened and her lips snapped shut. "I get even for what they done to Isaac."

"Your husband?"

"My friend. They took his land. 'Twas only a little place, but 'twas his. He loved it." She shook her head sorrowfully. "It broke his heart to pieces."

Kristin sat on the porch. She wondered what Gustaf would think of all that had occurred. If there was a way to send him a message without putting her new friends in further danger, she would. He had said he would come to Big Timber when Lars was better. Still she was afraid for Gustaf if he should come here and find out what Mark Lee and his cohorts were doing. They might hesitate to harm her; but if they were as dangerous as Bernie said, they'd not hesitate to kill him.

When it grew dark and Mrs. Gaffney hadn't returned, Kristin began to worry. Finally she went into the parlor and lit the lamp. A half hour passed slowly before she heard steps on the porch and the door opening. Kristin waited patiently while Mrs. Gaffney removed her hat and shawl. When she picked up the Bible and sat down on the settee, Kristin sat down beside her.

"I think a man is watching through the window," she said, as if she were reading a passage aloud. "Bonnie come to church to say that Bernie be here at two-thirty in the morning to take you to the freight camp." Her lips scarcely moved as she spoke. Kristin was surprised that a woman so hard of hearing could speak so softly.

Words on the page suddenly jumped out at Kristin. She moved her finger from line to line to point out words:

YE . . . be . . . in . . . trouble.

Mrs. Gaffney shook her head. "I hear nothing. I'm deaf, you know." She closed the Bible and bowed her head as if in prayer. "I think he be gone now. Stupid man."

They were sitting just inside the kitchen door when Kristin heard a faint sound outside. As she went out onto the porch, a topless buggy came silently around the side of the house and stopped. Bernie hopped down, spun around on his peg and hurried to the porch.

"Bernie, I'm afraid for you and Bonnie," Kristin whispered. "I wish you were coming with me."

"We ain't goin' to be able to stay here much longer. That hired gun of Forsythe's is got his eye on my sister. I'm no match for him face-to-face. But if he don't back off, I'll shoot him in the back and they'll hang me." He hoisted Kristin's trunk to his shoulder.

After her belongings were stashed on the boot of the buggy, Kristin put her arms around Mrs. Gaffney and kissed her cheek.

"Thank you, thank you," she said with her lips against her ear.

"Good-bye, darlin'. Tell Buck that Rose Gaffney's goin' to whip his hind end fer not slippin' in to see her."

Kristin looked at her in astonishment. "You didn't tell me you knew . . . him."

"Ya didn't ask, lovey. I'd not be lettin' ya go out there if I didn't think Buck could take care of ya. Get along with ya now. Bernie, I'll turn on the windmill and let my stock tank run over till the tracks are washed out."

Kristin climbed into the buggy and Bernie turned the horse toward the pasture behind the house. She was impressed with how careful he was and glad, now, that she had put on a dark dress and tied a three-cornered cloth, peasant style, over her silvery blond hair. The horse's hooves were covered with gunny-sacks and the well-greased buggy made hardly a sound.

Bernie didn't speak until they were well away from the house.

"Cletus is an old-timer here. He was one of the best wheel-wrights in the Territory in his day. He knows a good many freighters. A train of three wagons came in this morning. They'll be setting out at three o'clock. They go early and rest the stock in the middle of the day. It's easier on the teams. You'll ride on one of the freight wagons. They'll drop you off at Larkspur and go on."

"I told Colonel Forsythe I'd come back this morning and sign the papers. What'll they do when they find I've gone?"

"They'll be fit to be tied."

"Will they hurt Mrs. Gaffney?"

"They don't dare. She's rather a favorite in town due to her care of the sick."

"How about you and Bonnie?"

"Del Gomer won't let anything happen to Bonnie that he don't want to happen," Bernie said bitterly.

"Del Gomer. He's the one who watched her this morning."

"He's there for every meal if he's in town. He came to the restaurant when we first opened. He was nice and mannerly. Bonnie liked him. They talked for an hour at a time. He met her a couple of times after church and walked her home. She was halfway in love with him when we found out what he is—a hired killer. He works for whoever pays the highest price. There's been a half dozen random killings this past year that can be chalked up to Forsythe's gunman."

"If she left town, would he follow?"

"Depends on how tight he's hooked up with Forsythe."

After a silence, Kristin asked, "Is the house at Larkspur more than just a shack?"

"I don't know. I've never been out there."

"Do you think they'll follow and try to get me to sign the papers?"

"From what I hear, Lenning's no slouch when it comes to protecting what's his. He and Anderson had been together for a long time. Forsythe tried serving eviction papers and his men got a tail full of buckshot."

"As long as I own the Larkspur, you and Bonnie are welcome. I would be glad for the company. Cletus said he hadn't heard that old Mr. Lenning had married."

"I ain't heard that he's all that . . . old."

"Will you remember what I said? I've not known you and Bonnie even twenty-four hours, but that's not important. Friendships are forged in an instant. Please don't put yourself in danger by shooting that man. Remember that you have a place to come to."

"I'll remember."

Dirty white canvas covered the loads that rose up over the six-foot-high sideboards of the freight wagons that were parked on a grassy knoll. The camp was astir. Three teams of mules were being hitched to each wagon.

"You'll be all right with these men. Cletus knows them all and vouched for them," Bernie said.

A heavily bearded man came to the buggy as soon as it stopped.

"This the passenger Cletus wants us to drop off at the Larkspur?"

"She's the one."

"Come on, miss. We're 'bout to pull out."

He helped Kristin out of the buggy and led her to the last

high-wheeled wagon in the line. She turned to say good-bye to Bernie, but he had turned the buggy around and another man was unloading her trunk.

Looping the handle of her carrying bag over her shoulder, she climbed up the high wheel as if she had done it a hundred times before. It wasn't until she turned to sit down that she had a moment of fright because the seat was so high off the ground. She wanted desperately to tell Bernie good-bye and to thank him, but it was impossible to peer around the load that loomed up behind her.

*Kristin Anderson, what in the world are you doing here in the middle of the night with these strange men? Lordy! You'll never live another day like this one.*

The thought had no more than left her mind when the bearded man sprang up onto the seat beside her. He gathered the reins in his hand and then stood to sail a black-snake whip out over the backs of the mules. "Y'haw!" The mules strained, the big wheels moved and Kristin grabbed hold of the side of the seat.

The freighter asked surprisingly few questions.

"Where ya from, miss?"

"Wisconsin."

"Is that back near Ohio? Knew a man oncet from Ohio."

"No. It's just across the Mississippi River from Minnesota."

"Hummm— Ain't never been there. Been to Dakoty."

"I came through there on the train. The towns were miles and miles apart with a lot of flat land in between."

"This is the best country I ever knowed. It's got most a ever'thing a man would want. Rivers, lakes and mountains. Now take Crazy Mountains. They be the prettiest place ya ever did see. Ya can see 'em from the Larkspur."

"How did they get the name *Crazy* Mountains?"

The freighter chuckled. "One story be that the Indians killed a crazy woman what lived alone after her man died. Another be that the locoweed that grows on the foothills drove the horses crazy. Be that the case it may be why the Larkspur is call Larkspur. Larkspur be almost as poison to stock as locoweed."

"I didn't realize Larkspur was a poisonous weed. It has such a pretty flower."

"Yes'm. It's a sight to see a patch in bloom. Folks keep their stock away from it. Indians use it to kill body lice and itch mites."

It was almost daylight when the freighter told her they would be crossing the Yellowstone River.

"It ain't nothin' to get in a sweat over this time a year. River's low and there be a good rocky bottom where we cross."

Kristin looked at the wide river and refused to give in to the panic that swamped her. Determined to sit quietly and take what came, she gripped the side of the seat and kept her eyes on the wagon ahead.

*It'll be all right. They've crossed many times. Don't look down. The mules aren't afraid. They're going right into the water. Oh, my goodness! Did the wheels slip? Landsakes! We're in the middle of a river!*

The driver was giving all of his attention to the team. Even when the water reached the mules' bellies, they continued on in a steady gait. On reaching the bank on the other side, they dug in their hooves for purchase to climb the bank. Kristin had not realized she was holding her breath until it left her with a sigh of relief.

"Ya got grit, missy." The freighter grinned at her. "Scared spitless, warn't ya? But ya didn't let out a peep."

"It's the first time I've ever been on a freight wagon, much less crossing a river."

"Ya did good. I feared ya might go belly up on me."

"Faint? I've never fainted in my life."

"We get to that grove ahead we'll make a short stop to rest the mules a mite. Ya can stretch your legs. Boss man usually makes camp midmorning and cook breaks out the vittles, but Cletus wanted we get ya on up to the Larkspur. We'll just keep going and make Larkspur by noon. We'll call it a day 'bout midafternoon."

"Did Cletus think that someone would follow me?"

"I ain't knowing that, but the boss puts a heap of store in what Cletus says. Boss says, too, he's a damned old fool, and if'n he ain't careful, he'll end up like Yarby."

"Yarby Anderson? You knew my uncle?"

"Never set eyes on him, miss. Sorry to say. Here we are. Ya just sit tight till I get the mules settled and I'll help ya down."

Kristin noticed the men went into the trees on one side of the line of wagons. She hesitated a moment, then went into the bushes on the other side. It was embarrassing, but necessary. Her bladder was full almost to overflowing, and it was such a relief to empty it. Back at the wagon, her shoulders slumped with fatigue. Mrs. Gaffney had insisted that she sleep a little while she waited for Bernie. But she had been unable to do more than doze for a few minutes at a time.

Now five hours later, Kristin's back ached and her eyes burned from lack of sleep. Her lips felt gritty when she licked them. Hunger pangs reminded her of the jam-filled biscuits Mrs. Gaffney had wrapped in a cloth and placed in her bag. She shared them with the driver, who appeared to be enormously grateful.

The horizon ahead seemed to melt into the sky. Nothing moved except the long grass bending in silver ripples before the breeze. It was a vast, empty, still country with the mountains ahead. And it was quiet. Quiet beyond anything Kristin had ever imagined.

"This is beautiful country." Her mouth was so dry she could hardly talk. The wagon had bumped along for what seemed to Kristin an eternity. She hated to ask the driver for another drink of water from the fruit jar he kept at his feet. "Is the Larkspur like this?"

The teamster spat over the side of the wagon, then looked at her with a cocked eyebrow.

"We be *on* the Larkspur."

"Oh, my goodness!"

"It's big. Mighty big. It goes clear up to them mountains. We been making good time. Boss figures it pert nigh thirty mile 'tween Larkspur and Big Timber."

"Where's the house?"

"Over yonder in that grove that backs up to the mountain. There be a stream ahead. Boss'll want to stop and water and rest the stock. Then we'll be knowin' how he figures to get ya over there."

Kristin felt her heart leap, then settle into a pounding that left her almost breathless. *This is my land. Yonder is my home. I own a small piece of this earth. Mr. Lenning, please, please welcome me. Please help me to keep it.*

The mules were drenched with sweat when the train stopped beside the stream. A robust man with iron gray hair came to the wagon and extended a hand to help Kristin down.

"Miss, it's been a long hard pull for my stock. They're pert nigh wore out. It's about a mile over to the ranch. Do ya reckon ya can walk it if a couple of my men go along and carry your plunder?"

"Yes, of course." Kristin pulled the cloth from her head and wiped her face with a corner of it. The men gawked at her silvery blond hair. "I hope someday to be able to thank you properly for helping me."

"It didn't put us out none a'tall, miss. Cletus seemed to think them scallywags was 'bout to hornswoggle ya outta yore place here. That Forsythe's got a mean bunch a hangin' round him, for all his smooth ways."

"I never got to thank Cletus, or Mr. Gates. I was lucky to meet up with them."

"I'm thinkin' yo're right 'bout that. Folks are gettin' mighty fearful a losin' their land. It be hard to fight a bunch with the law and money behind 'em."

Two men came to the back of the freight wagon with a canvas stretched between two long poles. They fitted Kristin's trunk and her box in the sling, lifted the poles to their shoulders and started toward the grove at a fast clip.

"They don't mean to carry them? We could leave them here and Mr. Lenning could come with a wagon."

"It ain't no chore, miss. Them two could carry a buffalo."

"Good-bye." Kristin held out her hand. "When you get back to Big Timber, tell Cletus how much I appreciate what he's done for me."

"Luck to you, miss. Buck Lenning's a good man. He'll help ya all he can."

Kristin hurried after the men carrying her trunk. As tired as she was, she was glad to be on her feet and walking. Her hipbones and buttocks ached from the rough ride on the big wagon, and there was a constant ache between her shoulder blades. With her bag over her shoulder, she waved her scarf at the teamsters and headed across the grassland toward her new home.

She felt a surge of elation when the ranch buildings came in sight. The log house, squatting comfortably on a small knoll, blended perfectly with the background of the grass-covered, tree-dotted foothills of the mountain. The logs were thick and fitted snugly together. There was no chinking in this house, for the logs had been smoothed with a broadax and adze, and laid face-to-face. A cobblestone chimney rose above the roof on one end. The peaked roof slanted down to cover a porch. Kristin could see several other buildings and a series of split-rail corrals, but they were all a mere background for her lovely new home.

Kristin had expected her uncle, an old unmarried man, to have lived in a shack somewhat like the poorly constructed ones she'd seen from the train. This was a lovely homestead. Beyond it was an endless sea of grass and above it an endless span of sky.

"Are you sure this is it?" Kristin had to run a few steps to catch up with the men as they reached the porch and unloaded her trunk and box.

They looked at her strangely.

"Yes'm. This is Larkspur Ranch."

"Thank you. Could you not stay for a . . . drink of water?"

"No, ma'am. The boss'll be ready to move when we get back." The man rolled the canvas around the poles and hoisted them to his shoulder.

"Good-bye and . . . thank you."

They tipped their hats and hurried away. Kristin felt a moment of panic. It was so quiet. She stood just at the edge of the porch and waited for the door to open. It didn't. She stepped upon the porch and rapped on the door. After a moment, she hesitantly tried the door. It was locked.

*Please, let someone be here.* Although she realized it was futile, she rapped again. A short time later she stepped off the porch and went around to the back of the house. A dozen head of horses were in a large split-railed corral. She rapped on the back door. The silence was deafening. Her eyes clouded with worry. Had Mr. Lenning given up the fight with Forsythe and abandoned the property?

As she turned from the door, she saw a black-and-brown animal come streaking across the corral, leap the rail fence and head straight for her. Fright kept her immobile for a second or two. Then she turned and frantically clawed at the door. Miraculously it opened. She rushed inside and slammed it shut. A second later she heard the ferocious growls of the animal and then claws scratching the door.

For a long moment she was even too frightened to move. Of all the dangers she had expected to encounter, a wolf would have been on the bottom of the list. She could hear the animal growling outside the door. Making sure it was closed securely, she went to the one glass window and looked out. All she could see was the corral. But the scratching on the door told her the beast was still there.

*Thank heavens she had made it inside.*

Kristin set her bag on the table and went to the waterbucket that sat on the end of a long counter fastened to the back wall. She drank two full dippers of water before she hung it back on the nail above the pail. Then she surveyed the room. It extended across the back of the house. At one end was a fireplace, at the other a black cookstove, work counters and shelves. In the center was a heavy table, its plank top rubbed to a glowing finish. The cookstove was still warm, and a pan of soiled dishes soaked in the dishpan.

Two hide-covered chairs sat on each side of the fireplace and on the mantel a tall oak clock, its pendulum swinging back and forth. It was a friendly sight. Kristin had a fondness for clocks. A handsome slant-top desk sat against the inside wall.

Two rooms opened off the kitchen. One of them was large. A heavy door with a bar across it opened onto the porch. The room was furnished with a bed, a chest and several other pieces of furniture that appeared to be totally out of place with the others, as was the handsome desk in the other room. A fancy square table, covered with a fringed cloth, a green velvet chair and a banquet lamp with a painted round globe were more suitable for a parlor than a bedroom. Hugging the side of the inside wall was a very narrow stair leading to the attic room. A man's hat and coat hung on the rack on the wall.

The covers on the bed had been straightened. The room was not cluttered, but was not very clean. The plank floor needed to be swept, and cobwebs hung from the ceiling.

The room off the kitchen area was smaller. The only furniture was a bed, a chest and a trunk. Several shirts and a coat hung on pegs on the walls.

Mr. Lenning and another man had definitely taken over her uncle's house—her house now. It was to be expected, she reasoned. How long had Uncle Yarby been missing before his body was found? A year?

Kristin washed the trail dust from her face and hands and took down her hair. She massaged her scalp with her fingertips. When was the last time she had had a chance to brush it? Searching for her hairbrush, she emptied the contents of her carrying bag out on the table. She still had the money Gustaf had lent her and the pistol, so she was not completely helpless. At the hotel she had put a pair of clean drawers as well as stockings in the bag.

She stood beside the window looking out at the mountains behind the house and brushed her hair until her scalp tingled. She braided it in a loose rope and pinned it to the back of her head. It would not do for Mr. Lenning to return and find her looking like a trollop with her hair hanging down her back.

What to do now? She felt like an intruder; and if not for the beast outside the door, she would have gone out onto the porch. She peered out the kitchen window again but was unable to see if the animal was beside the door. She didn't dare open it to find out.

Kristin sat down in the cowhide-covered chair. Mr. Lenning was likely away doing roundups and branding and the sorts of things cowboys do. Ranches were supposed to have lots of cowboys. Dear Uncle Yarby. She wished she could thank him for leaving her this lovely house. What a joy it would be to tend to it.

One of the first things she would do would be to move the table farther from the cookstove, and wash away the soot and the cobwebs behind it. As soon as she could find enough rags she would make a rug to go in front of the fireplace.

The glass windowpanes needed to be washed. They would shine when she finished with them. Someday, when all this trouble was over, she would go to Big Timber and buy curtain material.

*My, this chair was comfortable.* She leaned her tired head against the back, telling herself that she would close her eyes for only a moment.

"Wake up! What the hell are you doin' here?"

Kristin came dazedly out of the wells of sleep when she heard a man's voice. With an effort she opened her eyes. They traveled up long legs to where a gun was strapped around narrow hips and on up to eyes that held such anger that for a second or two she froze with fear.

*Oh, dear Lord! They followed and found me!*

# Chapter Seven

Kristin shot up out of the chair and ran to the table where she had left her pistol. Grabbing it with both hands, she pointed it at the man.

"Stay away from me."

"Mother of Christ! Who the hell are you?"

"You know who I am, you . . . you bounder, shyster, crook!" she sputtered. "I'm not signing, no matter what you do. Break my fingers, twist my arm, do what you will! I'll not sign my land over to you and that's that!" By the time she finished speaking she was shouting.

"What the hell are you talking about?"

"You'd better get out. Mr. Lenning will be back soon. If he doesn't shoot you, I will." She steadied the hands holding the gun. Not for anything would she let him know how frightened she was.

Eyes the color of oak leaves beneath thick dark brows never moved from her face. The man stood there strangely quiet. He gazed at her for a long while before he spoke.

"I'm Buck Lenning."

"You're . . . not Mr. Lenning," she scoffed. "He's an old man like Uncle Yarby."

"Mother of Christ!" he said again. "You're . . ."

"Miss Kristin Anderson. And you . . . get out of my house!"

"*Your* house?"

He was a tremendously tall, sun-darkened, wild-looking man with green, amber-flecked eyes. Thick black hair curled and twisted around his head in complete disarray.

He stared. She stared back.

"Put the gun down before you shoot yourself."

"Not till you leave."

"I'm not going anywhere. What're you doing here?"

"Where else would I go? I couldn't stay there. That slick scallywag was going to force me to sign over my inheritance. They'd have . . . hurt me. They've done it before."

"Forsythe?"

"Oh . . . oh—"

There was no sound to alert her to the presence that filled the doorway behind her, but she knew it was there and whirled around to point the gun at the animal who watched her with fangs bared.

"Don't . . . shoot!" The man leaped. His big hand grabbed hers, forcing the gun point to tilt toward the floor. "Give me that thing." He wrested it from her hands. "Hell and damnation! If you'd a shot my dog, there'd a been hell to pay."

Kristin glared at him defiantly, not wanting him to know that she was so tired and unsteady on her feet and that she felt faintly giddy. Beads of sweat stood on her forehead and upper lip.

"Dog? That's not like any dog I've ever seen." She tried to put strength in her voice and failed miserably. "It's a wild, vicious . . . beast. It came running at me and would have killed me if I hadn't gotten in the house."

"How'd you get out here?"

Their eyes met in a duel across the table. His were instruments of power. His unwavering stare sent a series of tremors up and down her backbone.

"A friend arranged it."

"What's your game, sister?" He ejected the bullets from the gun and tossed them and the gun on the table. "Come here, Sam." The big dog came silently into the room and stood by the man. "How'd she get in here, boy?" He spoke to the dog, but his eyes remained on Kristin as if to pin her to the floor. Strong fingers reached down to scratch the woolly head. "Have you been out smelling around that wild female again?"

"That dog's dangerous. You can see the claw marks on the door."

When Lenning said nothing, Kristin raised her brows. Eyes, the color of a cloudy winter sky, looked down her nose at him even though he was a head taller. Confidence was etched in every line of her face, belying the fact her insides were quivering with fear. Pins had come loose from the hair at the nape of her neck and the long coil of silvery blond hair had slithered down her back. She was aware of the disarray but too proud to give it notice.

It came to her that perhaps she had acted in a harebrained fashion—that it had been stupid to come to Montana, stupider yet to come out here, alone, to Larkspur.

"I'll not take your word that you're who you say you are," she said stubbornly. "It was my impression that you had worked for my uncle for a very long time and would be a much older man." Her voice was hoarse and jerky and didn't at all sound like her own.

"I'm sorry to disappoint you. I thought I had aged mightily this last year. And . . . why should I take your word that you're who you say you are?"

"I can prove it. I have letters addressed to me in my trunk."

"That's no proof," he scoffed. "It would be like Forsythe and Lee to send you out here with a trumped-up identity to put me off my guard, then slip in here and burn me out. It's the land they want, not the house and the buildings."

Kristin's features took on a look of utter disbelief. She seethed with anger. His high-handed attitude grated on her nerves like chalk screeching against a slate.

"You think I'd have any part of swindling someone out of what's rightfully theirs? I have letters in my trunk addressed to Kristin Anderson, River Falls, Wisconsin."

"I never for a moment thought you'd come out here unprepared to prove that you're the heir to all this!" His voice dripped with sarcasm as he spread his arms wide. "But I've not got time now to look at them. Come on, Sam."

"Mr. Lenning, if you are Mr. Lenning. Keep in mind that my uncle left this ranch to me and that you work for me now."

"I'll not forget that, Miss Anderson, ma'am. That is if you are Miss Anderson. And there's something you'd better keep in mind too—watch your manners if you plan to spend the night in *my* house."

"You may have lived here with Uncle Yarby. But the house is mine now."

"You're wrong, Miss Know-it-all Anderson. This is *my* house—and every stick and stone of it is sitting on *my* land. Yarby's house is yonder through the grove and it may very well be sitting on my land, too. It's difficult to get an exact boundary line. You'd better get over there and clean out a place because that's where you'll spend the night."

Kristin froze in shocked silence. Her mind shut down for seconds, then cleared with amazing speed. A rosy redness rushed up her neck to flood her cheeks.

"Very well. I trust you'll control your . . . ah . . . dog."

"He'll not bother you now, unless I tell him to."

"That's kind of you," Kristin snarled. "I'll not bother you anymore today, but tomorrow we've a few things to straighten out." She put the pistol and the bullets in her bag, slung it over her arm, grabbed up her shawl and walked out the door and into the bright sunshine.

She had trespassed. Humiliation and fatigue set her lips trembling. Only pride enabled her to press them together to trap the sob that longed to escape and to straighten her back. She would not apologize for her mistake. To do so would give him a tactical advantage.

Buck watched her round the house to the front porch. Her back was stiff as a board. The blond braid that hung to her waist was a sight to see. In spite of his irritation at finding her in his house, the corners of his grim mouth relaxed, and a shadow of a grin crossed his face. He had no doubt that she was Miss Kristin Anderson, Yarby's kin. She even resembled the Yarby he had known long ago. Traces of blond still lingered in Yarby's gray hair at their first meeting. He also had been just as proud and as stiff-necked as his niece.

Buck had not even known about Yarby's will until Mark Lee came out to the ranch. The puffed-up jackass had taken great pleasure telling him about it. Then Buck had thrown the slimy, little piece of horse-dung off his porch, hauled him up out of the dirt, marched him to his buggy and told him to get the hell off his land.

It had come as a complete surprise to Buck that Yarby had left his share of the ranch to Kristin Anderson. He had wondered if she was a woman Yarby had once loved and perhaps lost to another member of the Anderson family. The sissified lawyer had not mentioned her being Yarby's niece. What in tarnation was he going to do about her? It was clear that the woman had more grit than brains. Didn't she realize the chance she had taken coming out here alone?

Getting her out of the way for a while had given him time to think. And seeing Yarby's shack would give *her* things to think about. She had blurted out something about twisted arms and broken fingers. Would Forsythe and his bullyboys sink so low as to harm a woman? The answer to his question flashed into his mind. *You can bet your boots they would!*

*Damn them!*

*Cleve, hurry and get here before I'm forced to kill someone.*

His thoughts plunged ahead. If she'd signed Yarby's land over to them, he'd have really been in a bind. And . . . who was the friend who had helped her? It was more than thirty miles to Big Timber. He had kept his eye on the road to town and nothing had come down it but Glazer's freight wagons.

Holy hell! If she came out with the freighter only one man could have arranged it. *Cletus Fuller.* That stubborn old fool was going to mess around and get himself killed. Only a couple of people in town knew what was going on out here, and Cletus was one of them. The wily old man must have had a pretty good reason for getting her away from Forsythe. But how was he going to take care of Moss and her, and hold on to the ranch until Cleve got here?

With Sam following him, Buck crossed the yard to the room at the end of bunkhouse, unlocked the door and swung it open. Moss was sitting at a table painstakingly plaiting thin strips of leather into a lariat. It was a skill he'd not lost. Buck kept him supplied with the narrow strips of rawhide because he was afraid to let him use a sharp knife.

"Hello, Moss."

"I'm obliged."

"You've done a lot this morning."

"The steers will go loco eatin' that larkspur."

"I remember you telling me that, old-timer."

Buck placed his hand on the Moss's shoulder. It had been hard to watch his old friend's mind deteriorate to the point where it was impossible to converse with him. Moss couldn't remember what he had done minutes before, but sometimes he'd get a glimmer of something that had happened years back and blurt out a name or a place or some bit of information like that about larkspur.

Buck watched Moss's nimble fingers working the strips of leather. He was content for the moment. Buck went back outside and looked in the direction of the shack Yarby had built when he first came to the territory and bought and paid for the land with money he had made in the gold fields. What would that woman do if Forsythe sent his hired guns out to burn him out? Would she fall to pieces?

*It was strange having a woman to worry about.*

Weeks back, Buck had thought it likely that Forsythe would send men to rustle his herd. As a precaution, he had sent Gilly Mullany and two Indian drovers to drive the herd onto Indian land in the mountains and had struck a deal with the Oglala: a hundred head of cattle for grazing rights. He had always played square with the Sioux, respecting their right to their land.

Gilly was a drifter who had wandered in a few years ago, a man who had had many disappointments in life and who feared being old and alone. He had proved to be a good hand who never undertook to make a decision on his own, but was content to follow orders. He would stick to the last ditch if it came to a fight, but would not seek one. Because of the way the ranch buildings were situated, Buck felt that he and one other gun could hold off an attack for a good long while. Had it not been for the grizzled old cowboy, the two Indian boys, and the Sioux squaw who came down from time to time, he'd not have been able to take care of Moss and tend to his stock this past year.

The woman's being here complicated matters.

Colonel Forsythe had moved in several years ago and had begun to take over the ranches in what was generally known as the sweet grass country. The Larkspur was the key. A year ago Forsythe had thought he had it, but Buck had managed to foil his plan. If Forsythe secured possession of the Larkspur, he'd control a large chunk of the best grassland in the territory and could shut off water rights to a number of small ranchers, all of whom were scared or unable to put up much of a fight against him.

Buck looked toward the grove. Miss Anderson would be all right for a short time. He was sure of that, or he'd not have let her go over there alone. The prissy town-woman had been so tired she could hardly stand, yet she had headed off toward the grove as if she were marching to Zion.

Amusement crinkled the corners of his eyes and lifted the ends of his wide mouth as he wondered what she thought, now, about the house she had inherited from her Uncle Yarby.

Kristin's arms felt as if they were being pulled from their sockets. Had the box been this heavy when she had carried it from her bedroom to the porch the morning she left River Falls? Of course, she'd not been so tired and she had not felt ready to sit down and cry as she did now. She stumbled over a chunk of dead wood hidden by a growth of grass. The rope slipped from her hand and the box fell on her foot.

"Darn! Darn—" The pain was not severe but her body was so tired and her mind so unsettled that tears sprang to her eyes. Certain that she could not be seen from the house, she lifted the hem of her skirt and wiped her face. She was not even curious about the other house. She just wanted to get there and sit down. How would she get that heavy trunk through the woods? She was sure of one thing—she'd not ask *him* to help her.

Leaving the box on the ground, Kristin walked on, parting the bushes as she went. If at one time there had been a path, it had long ago disappeared into the heavy growth of brush. She passed through a belt of high grass and stunted scrub pines, and suddenly there in front of her was the old homestead.

She understood immediately why Buck Lenning had looked so smug when he said, "Your house is yonder in the grove."

Before her was the most desolate, run-down place she had ever seen. It looked as if it had been deserted for years and years. The door hung on one leather hinge. The windows were glassless and without shutters. The roof sagged, and brush grew up to the door.

Kristin went toward it in a near stupor. When she looked inside, she could see that sticks and leaves had blown in the openings and formed a layer of litter that covered everything. Inside were built-in bunks, a table and a split-log bench. All were deep in dirt and flecked with animal droppings. A piece of an old blanket lay in the corner and looked as if it had been used as a nest by an animal. The only thing that appeared to be intact was a stone chimney.

Kristin was unaware of it, but her hand was clasped tightly over her mouth as she surveyed the dilapidated homestead. Her shaky legs carried her to the bench, and heedless of the filth on it, she sat down. With her arms wrapped about the bag she held close to her chest, she rocked back and forth.

*Her dream of starting an exciting new life had turned into
a nightmare.*

The dam crumbled. Misery came gushing out. She could no
longer contain the hurt and the disappointment within her. Her
face convulsed and huge racking sobs came from deep within
her, disrupting the silence in the gloomy, pitiful shack.

The troubles had begun with Ferd's rejection and anger
over her inheritance. Then had come the anxiety and discomfort of the long train trip. The encounter with Mr. Forsythe,
the sleepless night, the strain of having to steal away from Big
Timber in the middle of the night, and the long hard ride on
the freight wagon would have been bearable. But this, the
house she had so looked forward to, and the insufferable Mr.
Lenning, were too much.

She cried openly. Tears rolled down her cheeks. She made
no attempt to wipe them away. Had she thought about it, she
would have realized that she had not cried like this since her
mother died ten years ago.

When the figure filled the doorway and blocked out the
light, she was so deep in her grief that she wasn't even frightened of the lean-faced, shaggy-haired man in jeans and worn
boots.

Buck had heard her sobbing as he approached and was
shaken at the sight of her tears. He could not remember when
last he had seen a woman cry. It didn't matter to him that she
was a woman who had come here to lay claim to what he and
Yarby had worked for. She was alone and scared. Her wet
lashes and tear-streaked cheeks made her look as helpless as
a child. Buck had always been softhearted when it came to a
helpless creature's suffering.

"Miss Anderson." He waited for her to answer, and when
she didn't, he said, "Come on back to the house and . . . we'll

talk." She was a pretty woman, he realized when he looked at her through eyes unbiased by anger. Even with swollen eyes she was pretty. Spunky too. Maybe too spunky for her own good—like Yarby.

"You are inviting me to come back to *your* house, Mr. Lenning. I have to take your word that it is yours." As miserable as she was she was still defiant.

"It is my house," he said more gently than he had said it the first time. "This is Yarby's house and Yarby's land. He and I lived here for a couple of years. I wanted you to see it and get down off your high horse so that we could talk."

"I'm completely at your mercy. I've nowhere to go." Her eyes were full of tears, and she drew her lips between her teeth to keep them from trembling.

"I suppose that is true. I've no way of getting you back to town . . . at least for a few days."

"I couldn't go back there if you did. They'll be furious at me because I didn't stay to sign their papers. Cletus thought they might do things like twist my arm or break my fingers. After I had signed away my inheritance, they'd have gotten rid of me. It wouldn't do to let me hang around. People might find out that they had bought my land for two thousand dollars."

Buck whistled through his teeth.

"That much? Generous of him. It might be best for you to go home and let a lawyer handle your claim."

"I've nothing to go home to." It was an admission she regretted making the instant the words left her mouth. Lenning's knowing her circumstances made her more vulnerable.

"Forsythe is determined to get the Larkspur one way or the

other. You could find yourself in the middle of a war for possession."

"I'm aware of that. He's hired killers."

"You picked up a lot of information during the time you were in Big Timber."

"I was lucky."

"Well . . . luck is a fickle thing."

"What do you mean?" She hugged the bag tighter to her chest.

"Not what you're thinking. You've nothing to fear from me, Miss Anderson, ma'am." There was a tinge of sarcasm in his voice. "You'll not need the pistol. I'm not that desperate for a woman."

"Especially an . . . old maid." The words were out before she could stop them.

He laughed . . . before *he* could stop it. Kristin rushed into speech to hide her embarrassment.

"Colonel Forsythe said you were a saddle bum who had drifted in and rustled off Uncle Yarby's cattle. Cletus said you were an honorable man. So did Mrs. Gaffney. She thought I'd be safer here than in town. I really don't understand it all. Is there no law here in Montana?" Her throat choked with bitterness. She turned her eyes away from him, only to have them swing back of their own accord.

"You met Rose?" His face changed completely when he smiled. He looked years younger; not so wild and . . . dangerous.

"She's a dear lady. She helped me at great risk to herself." Kristin got to her feet.

"You met some of the most decent folks in Big Timber."

"I met Bonnie and Bernie Gates, too. Bernie has a peg leg.

Also at great risk to himself and his sister, he came at two in the morning and took me to the freight wagons."

"I'm surprised Glazer brought you out."

"He was very nice. All the men were."

At the urgent barking of the dog Buck became instantly alert. He stepped away from the doorway.

"Come on," he called over his shoulder.

He loped through the grove. Although Kristin tried, she could not keep up with him. When he reached the spot where she had dropped the box, he reached down and picked it up, hardly breaking his stride.

Sam continued to bark.

When Buck came out of the grove, he could see the dog fidgeting and looking toward the creek. He hurried across the yard, dropped the box near the back door as he passed it and broke into a run. He cursed himself for lingering to talk to the woman, forgetting to lock the door and allowing Moss to wander away. If Forsythe's spies were about, they would surely see him.

Moss was heading for the creek through the knee-high grass on the flat land. Knowing that he'd not answer if he was called and that he would reach the creek before he could be reached, Buck shouted for the dog.

"Sam! Go get him."

The dog bounded away and within a minute or two had grabbed on to the leg of the old man's britches. Moss hit at Sam, but the dog held on and finally pulled the frail old man down onto the ground. He was still sitting there pulling up tufts of grass when Buck reached him. He looked up at Buck and grinned as innocently as a child.

"Maw give me tater dumplin's for supper."

"Sure, old-timer. Come on." Panting from the run, Buck lifted Moss to his feet.

"A bunch of damn two-bit thieves shot Lars Jensen in the belly." Moss continued to talk as they made their way back to the homestead.

Kristin waited beside the door and watched as the men approached. Buck was leading the old man by the hand as if he were a child. The dog, Sam, who had frightened her earlier in the day trotted along behind them with his tongue hanging out. Kristin had heard Buck send the dog, and her heart dropped to her stomach when he pulled the old man to the ground. But then, the animal had stood there watching him until Buck arrived.

They were a strange threesome: the shaggy vicious dog, big, wild-looking Mr. Lenning, and the little gray-haired man, smiling and talking up to him. As they neared, the old man's bright blue eyes fastened on Kristin.

"And when he has a punkin pie, he shares it with the others." He dipped his head and spoke in a singsong voice.

Buck looked at Kristin for her reaction to the strange greeting. Their eyes locked for an instant before she smiled at Moss.

"That's from the song 'Yankee Doodle.'"

"This is Moss. My . . . pa."

"Hello." Kristin held out her hand. Moss grabbed it and held on tightly.

"Kitter's farm was on the side of a hill."

"I bet he had a hard time plowing." Kristin's eyes went to Buck and then back to the gentle little man.

"Moss was the smartest man I ever knew. Lately his mind has gone backward."

"I understand. One of our neighbors back home suffered

the same. She was past sixty but acted like a three- or four-year-old child."

"Moss is harmless."

"You don't need to explain."

Moss was still holding to Kristin with one hand. With the other he reached up and gently stroked her hair. Buck watched him closely.

"Are you my maw?" A fleeting look of longing crossed Moss's face, then it was gone. Buck was sure Kristin hadn't noticed, but he'd not be able to keep her in the dark for long.

"No. I'm your friend."

Moss's eyes rested on her face for a long time without movement, without any discernible emotion, then he grinned.

"Let's get inside." Buck looked down at the dog and patted his head. "You did good, Sam. Watch and let me know if you see anything."

Moss tugged on Kristin's hand, and she followed him into the kitchen. She tried to free it from his grasp so that she could put down her bag, but he held it tightly. Buck gently pried his fingers loose, and Moss turned to go back out the door. Buck hurried to shut it and drop a bar in place.

"As soon as I have time I'm going to make a door with a screen in it. One I can fasten at the top so that he can't reach it."

"What do you do with him when you have to be away?" Kristin hung her bag on the back of one of the big chairs.

"This past week, I've locked him in the room next to the bunkhouse."

"Locked him in! That's terrible."

"More terrible than letting him walk off and get lost in the mountains, or fall in the creek and drown?" he answered testily.

"You're right. I apologize. I can, at least, help you with your father while we're getting this mess straightened out."

Like a curious child, Moss was looking in her bag. Kristin remembered the pistol and hurried to pull the bag gently from his hands. She reached in and brought out her hairbrush. With a smile she drew the stiff bristles through the gray hair that came down over his ears. Then she put the brush in his hand.

"Can you brush your hair?"

"He ate blueberries till he got hives," Moss said.

"He'll follow simple orders like when you hand him his shirt, and tell him to put it on, or take him to the washpan to wash his hands," Buck said.

"Granny Dows did that, too." Kristin held out the gun. "Where can I put this?"

"Keep it locked in your trunk." Buck unbarred the front door and went out onto the porch. He carried the trunk to the small room off the kitchen, then went to the back step for the box. "It's not the Grand Hotel in Big Timber—"

"—Well . . . thank goodness for that. If you'll bring in some wood for the cookstove, I'll make supper. You do eat, don't you?"

"When I get the chance. Cooking is not one of the things I do best. Now, Moss could stir up a decent meal out of almost nothing."

"Why do you call your father Moss?"

"Habit," he said testily. "What did you call yours?"

"Papa." Kristin shook down the firebox on the stove and lifted the two round lids on the top.

Buck returned with an armful of cut wood and a pail of chips.

"Can you make biscuits?"

"Of course."

"There's been times when I'd have given a dollar for a decent biscuit." He started the fire in the cookstove and replaced the iron lids.

"If I had a penny for every biscuit I've made, I'd be rich. I don't know much about ranching and roundups and things like that, but I can cook and clean and milk cows."

"Things are not too clean—"

"Do you have dishes other than the ones in the dishpan?"

"Whole set under the curtain. They've been there a while. Moss and I usually use the two granite plates you see in the dishpan. Help yourself to whatever you need." Buck gave her a quizzical look and picked up the waterbucket. "If you'll keep your eye on Moss, I'll get a bucket of water, and some meat from the smokehouse."

Kristin glanced at Moss and nodded. He was sitting in one of the big chairs contentedly holding her hairbrush. He was surprisingly clean—both his clothes and his person, and she began to feel a grudging respect for Buck Lenning.

She washed her hands and opened the big tin containing the flour. Although she still smarted from the humiliation of mistaking *his* house for *hers*, the tension between them had eased . . . for the moment.

# Chapter Eight

Colonel Kyle Forsythe made no attempt to conceal his anger as he paced the length of his study. It had been a mighty blow to his self-esteem that the woman whom he had bragged about as being in the palm of his hand had failed to show up to sell him her land, and now he was told that she had skipped out in the night.

Mark Lee had been smart enough not to remind him that he had allowed her to walk away from the office without signing the power of attorney. But the young lawyer had been cool and aloof since the meeting began a half hour ago. He wanted this land deal completed, so that he could collect his money and leave this two-bit town.

Del Gomer, on the other hand, appeared not only to be unconcerned but uncaring that Forsythe's plans had gone awry. When he had arrived a half hour ago, neat as a pin as usual, he had greeted Mrs. DeVary politely, and then had gone into the study where he now sat holding his drink in his long slim fingers, his silver-colored eyes never settling long on any one person or thing.

*The bastard wouldn't bat an eye if his mother were being burned at the stake.* The thought passed through Lee's mind even as he spoke of other things.

"I had Cam Spencer watch Mrs. Gaffney's house last night

after the drayman told me she'd gone there." Lee wiped his brow with his handkerchief and returned it to his pocket. "She stayed at the house while the old lady went to church. When she returned, they went up to bed."

"Then I suppose Spencer left his post and went back to the saloon," Forsythe said sarcastically.

"Around midnight . . . he said."

Forsythe paced back and forth for a full five minutes. The only sound in the room was the clink made by Lee lifting the stopper on the whiskey decanter and the soft thud of the colonel's highly polished shoes on the thick carpet. Abruptly, he spun on his heel and went to the door.

"Ruth!" he bellowed.

Almost immediately Mrs. DeVary came into the room with her usual pleasant smile.

"Afternoon, gentlemen."

"You know Mrs. Gaffney, don't you?" Forsythe's voice was gruff, impatient.

"Not very well. She's very hard of hearing and it's difficult to visit with her."

"Get over there and see if you can find out where the girl went."

"What girl?"

"Kristin Anderson, old Yarby Anderson's kin. The one that came in on the train yesterday. Who did you think I was talking about—Lily from the Red Dog Saloon?"

A puzzled frown came over Mrs. DeVary's face. "I've never called on Mrs. Gaffney, Kyle. What excuse can I give?"

"How the hell should I know?" he shouted. "Take her some of those damn cookies you bake for the church bazaar or ask her advice on something. Earn your keep for a change!"

Ruth DeVary's face turned white and then red as she looked down at the floor.

"Very well," she said quietly, and left the room.

Mark Lee was embarrassed for the woman. He had discovered long ago that Forsythe had a mean streak, but he had not seen him use it against Mrs. DeVary.

"Somebody helped her, by damn! She didn't get on the train. Bruza checked. At least *he* can do something right." Forsythe paced back and forth across the room. He stopped in front of Mark. "She ate breakfast at that hole in the wall run by the cripple and his sister. If I find out they had anything to do with getting her out of town, I'll string him up by his balls and put her to work flat on her back out at Flo's."

"You'll do no such thing." The words fell calmly into the silence after Forsythe spoke.

"What did you say?" His mind fogged by a heavy cloud of rage, Forsythe spun around to face the cold-eyed man.

"You heard me. Leave Miss Gates alone." Del never raised his voice. His colorless, unblinking eyes fastened on the colonel.

"Who the hell is running things here?"

"Run things anyway you want but leave Bonnie Gates out of it. I won't tell you again."

"Are you horny for that woman?" Forsythe stood before Del with his hands on his waist, his feet spread in a cocksure stance meant to intimidate. It had no effect at all on Del.

"That is none of your business," he said quietly.

"Christ!" Forsythe threw up his hands. "If you're hot for the bitch, go screw her and get it out of your system."

Del stood and placed his empty glass on the sidebar. His movements were slow and relaxed. When he spoke, his voice was as calm as if he were talking about the weather.

"I suggest that you be more respectful of Miss Gates. Don't call her a *bitch* and never speak of *screwing* in connection with her."

A deathly quiet settled over the room. Mark felt a chill slither down his spine. He could almost smell sudden, violent death.

Colonel Forsythe suddenly realized he had made a dangerous mistake and that this man would kill him without a second thought. His fertile mind searched frantically for a way to put things right. He locked his hands behind his back and arranged his features to make himself appear more contrite.

"I'm sorry, Del. I got carried away. You're absolutely right. It was not a gentlemanly thing to say about a lady." When he swung around to speak to Lee, his voice was not quite steady. "I hear that Lenning has moved his herd up onto Indian land. That'll complicate matters a bit."

"His drovers are Oglala Sioux." Lee glanced at Del Gomer. Lee was thankful his eyes were on the colonel and not him. "A couple of fellows that I've hired off and on came in," Lee continued, anxious to defuse the tension. "They had a run-in with Lenning out on Sweet Grass Creek a few days ago. He had a Sioux woman with him."

"I hadn't heard he'd taken up with a squaw."

"The point is, he was about eight miles from the ranch."

"Well, now." Forsythe rubbed his hands in glee. "If his men are away, it might be a good time to strike."

"The place is like a fort. There'll be no sneaking up on him."

"I'm not thinking to attack the ranch. If Lenning is found eight or ten miles from his ranch, who can say what happened to him. Could be a Sioux wanting his horse, or a jealous husband wanting his squaw back. Without him and the woman we'd have no trouble getting that land."

"Are you talking about ambush?" Lee wished he'd had the nerve to say *murder.* This land-grabbing scheme was going into a phase that made the young lawyer uncomfortable.

"It happens all the time. This is a dangerous country. Who do you know that's good with a rifle?"

Buck slept only intermittently throughout the night, uncomfortably aware that Kristin Anderson was in the next room. Having a woman in the house was strange. More than strange, it was downright unnerving. Earlier he had walked Moss outside to relieve himself before he put him to bed, but as soon as Moss lay down he began to expel gas in such a loud explosive manner that the sound was sure to reach into every corner of the house. And, of course, Miss Anderson would not know it came from Moss.

He had at first planned that he and Moss would sleep in the bunkhouse, but that was before it had occurred to him that Forsythe's men might have followed Miss Anderson. He couldn't leave her in the house alone.

Sam would let him know if anyone came to within a hundred yards of the buildings, that is if his desire to mate hadn't drawn him away from his post as it had done earlier in the day. A bitch wolf-dog had been in the area lately, and her scent caused Sam, at times, to forget his duties.

Another reason for Buck's sleeplessness was that Moss occupied his bed and he lay on a bedroll on the floor. He was becoming soft, he told himself while shifting around to find a comfortable position. For years he had slept on the ground, or wherever he happened to be.

He had tied the long soft strip of cloth about the old man's waist and fastened the other end to the bedpost as he did when Moss slept in his own bed. He had fashioned this safety measure to keep Moss from wandering around the house in the night and possibly hurting himself or setting the place on fire.

Morning was just a suggestion of pale light when Buck got up, dressed and went out onto the porch in his stockinged feet. The stars were fading. A quail called questioningly and received a reply.

*Lord, how he loved this country, this place.*

Buck breathed deeply the fresh, cool mountain air and stretched his long frame. This morning he had to have a talk with Kristin. Sometime during the long sleepless night hours he had begun to think of her as Kristin rather than Miss Anderson or Yarby's niece. He had resigned himself to the fact that she was here . . . for a while. Even if he knew of a safe place to take her, he couldn't leave Moss, and he couldn't take him along.

Having met Kristin had brought back Buck's old yearning for a woman of his own, to bear him children, to be by his side during the day and in his bed at night. He was troubled by the desire that hardened his body and clouded his mind. He tried to shake off the feeling.

*Christamighty! He was as bad as Sam lusting after the bitch wolf!*

This past week had been difficult without Gill and the Sioux drovers to help him keep an eye on the old man. Buck ran his fingers through his shaggy hair. Good Lord, when this problem started a year ago, he'd had no idea it would get so complicated. How much should he tell Kristin and how would she stand up under the strain? If he told her all, would she even believe him?

\*     \*     \*

Early-morning light was sifting through the window when Kristin awoke from the drugged sleep of exhaustion and lay listening to the soft cooing of morning doves in the distance and the nearby scolding of a bluejay from an oak tree beside the house.

Lying in the strange but comfortable bed, she was overcome with a poignant wave of homesickness, and she longed with all her heart to be a little girl again back home in Wisconsin with her mother and father.

The clatter of a bucket in the room beyond her door brought her out of her dreamlike state. She lifted her head to listen. When she heard the faint sound of iron striking iron and recognized the sound as a lid being placed on or removed from the cookstove, she got out of bed, whipped her nightdress off over her head, dressed, brushed and braided her hair. She found her precious hairpins where she had placed them on the top of her trunk the night before, and fastened the coiled braid to the nape of her neck.

What would her brother Ferd make of her spending the night alone, miles and miles from town, with a strange, wild-looking man? He'd declare that his predictions were true— she had become a fallen woman. Kristin smiled at that. She'd felt as safe here as she had in the hotel room in Big Timber.

After tying an apron about her waist, she pulled open the door. Because she was an unwelcome guest in this house, she was determined not to abuse the man's hospitality.

He was at the cookstove with his back to her. If he had heard the door open, he did not let on. He was dressed except for the boots that sat beside one of the chairs. His shirt hung loose and his dark hair was wet and combed straight back from his forehead.

"Good morning." Kristin spoke before going farther into the room.

"Morning."

"I'm usually up before this. I slept like a log."

"I've not been up long myself."

"I'll . . . cook breakfast."

"I was counting on that. I added water and more coffee to the pot."

Kristin crossed the room to the open door and looked out into the still morning.

"Go on out. Sam would let me know if there was anyone about." Buck glanced at her over his shoulder. "He'll not bother you."

As she hurried down the path to the outhouse, she had a feeling that during the night Buck Lenning had made a decision about her, and she felt suddenly chilled and unsure of herself. He was not like any man she had met before. He was a man of contrasts. She thought of the events of the night before. Just as she had finished making up her bed with sheets from her trunk, Mr. Lenning had rapped on the door. She had opened it to find him standing there with a lit lantern in his hand.

"Come. I'll show you the outhouse." He had spoken as unconcernedly as if he were speaking of wheat or cattle prices. "Keep the light low. I never know who is watching the place."

Her face had been flushed with embarrassment as she followed him to a small building set at an angle between the house and the bunkhouse. He had handed her the lantern and walked quickly back to the house.

Reflecting on the action now, she realized it was a thoughtful gesture. At least she'd not had to ask him the location of the necessary building, and she had been grateful for the light.

Kristin thought of her choices now that the house Uncle Yarby had left her was not livable. She had land, but no idea how much, or if she could sell enough of it to build a house. She couldn't go back to Big Timber unless she was willing to sell out to Colonel Forsythe—take his two thousand dollars and leave town. But where would she go? She wished Gustaf were here to tell her what to do.

By the time she left the outhouse, she realized that she had no choice but to trust this unpredictable man who had at first seemed as dangerous as a rattlesnake, but was so gentle with his aged father that she felt completely safe in his house. The thought occurred to her that the man called Moss could be Uncle Yarby's trusted ranch manager and that when he could no longer carry out his duties, his son had come to take over. Cletus had known her uncle. She wished now that she'd had more time to talk with him about the man who had remembered her in his will.

She went to the washstand as soon as she returned to the kitchen, washed her face and hands and began preparing breakfast. She could hear Mr. Lenning in the other room talking in a low calm voice to his father. It surprised her that he bothered when the other man didn't understand what he was saying.

Kristin put a dab of grease in an iron pan and set it on top of the stove to melt. After stirring up a batch of biscuits, she pinched off small hunks of the dough and dipped them in the hot grease before arranging them in the pan. She had the pan in the oven and her hands washed when the door opened, and Buck came out with Moss. The old man was dressed in worn, but clean duck pants and a soft shirt.

He paused in the doorway and looked at her.

"Good morning," Kristin said and smiled.

Moss came to where she stood beside the table. As innocently as a child, he put his arms around her waist and placed his head on her shoulder. For a few seconds, she was unsure what to do. Then she put her arms around the frail body and hugged him.

"I like you too, Mr. Moss."

"He lived in the woods with the grizzly bears."

"Are you hungry this morning? I can make you some cornmeal mush."

"Buck won't give up without a fight."

Startled by the words, Kristin looked quickly at Buck over Moss's shoulder, her brows raised in question. His expression never changed. He took Moss's arm and gently tugged him away from Kristin.

"Come on, old-timer."

Kristin glanced out the window and watched the two men walk down the path to the outhouse. How in the world did Mr. Lenning get anything done? Taking care of his father was a full-time job. And . . . his patience with him was astounding.

Kristin felt a strange tenseness come over her as if she were standing on the edge of a cliff. Today, this morning, things would be decided that would affect her life for the weeks and months ahead and ultimately for the rest of her life. She was uneasy as she set the table. There was something hard and sure about the man who would be a part of the decision-making. She sensed that he was the kind of man that people trusted. Cletus had certainly trusted him. Rose Gaffney, too.

She also sensed that he was a man who wanted roots. He had built this house and filled it with this strange assortment of furniture. The fancy chair and table in the other room, the rolltop desk, didn't go with the homemade table and chairs and rope beds. And the set of china dishes—

Last night she had looked for dishes with which to set the table because there had been only two granite eating plates soaking in the dishpan. On a shelf behind a curtain, she had found a set of gold-rimmed china dishes complete with cups, saucers, platters and vegetable bowls. They were of such good quality she had not been sure if she should use them until Buck spoke from behind her.

"Use them if you want. But they've been sitting there a while and will need a wash."

"Are you sure? They're far too fine for everyday use."

"They are?" He frowned. "I've never used them."

Once again she admired the lovely china and wished she dared bring out a cloth from her trunk to spread over the table's bare wood.

Later, as Kristin sat at the table with the two men, she was surprised to realize that she felt comfortable passing the biscuits, putting sorghum in the mush she had made for Moss. He appeared tired and ate very little. Buck would remind him to eat every once in a while by reaching over and dipping his spoon in the bowl and watching while it made the perilous journey to his mouth.

"Wolves brought down a sheep this mornin'." Moss looked from Kristin to Buck and back again. "Nothin' smells as good as sawed wood."

When Moss made these offhand statements, Kristin could feel Buck's eyes on her face, judging her reaction. Buck said little even though he was polite and had been helpful pointing out where the supplies were in the kitchen. He ate large amounts of the food she had prepared and seemed to relish the meal.

"I don't know if I've ever eaten a better biscuit." The compliment came suddenly and unexpectedly after Kristin had cleared the table and was pouring water over the plates in the dishpan.

"Thank you. If I had butter, eggs and milk I could cook a much better meal." She was increasingly aware that he was in a different mood this morning. "Would your father have coffee if I watered it down so that he'd not burn himself?"

"He's about to fall asleep. He's been sleeping a lot lately." Buck gently pulled the old man to his feet, guided him to one of the big chairs and returned to the table. "Some days he'll sit there for hours."

"Is that when you get your outdoor chores done?" Kristin placed the heavy mug of coffee on the table in front of him. She could not bring herself to use the delicate china cups.

"Lately I've not been able to leave him here alone. That's why I fixed up the room at the end of the bunkhouse. It has nothing in it but a bed and a table."

"How long has he been like this?"

"About a year and a half. But not this bad."

"Then he was sick when Uncle Yarby disappeared?"

"Yes." Buck's eyes met hers and held.

"Where is my uncle buried? I'd like to pay my respects."

"In the Big Timber graveyard. I hear he's even got a grave marker."

"Ah . . . I wish I had known when I was there," Kristin said sorrowfully. "Did he have a decent burial?"

"I don't know. I wasn't there."

Her eyes widened with surprise and indignation.

"You'd been with him for many years and yet didn't attend his burial!"

"It was a good ploy to get me and my men away from Larkspur. If I'd gone, it's more than likely that I'd not have had anything left when I got back, if I'd gotten back."

"You have men working here?"

"Of course. They're taking the herd up to Indian land to keep them out of Forsythe's hands."

"Colonel Forsythe said there was no herd."

Kristin waited for Buck to say more and when he didn't she gave him an exasperated look.

"Mr. Lenning, I'm not prying into *your* affairs. I'm trying to evaluate my own situation and decide what I should do. I don't enjoy being an unwelcome guest in your home. Cletus said something about not believing what had happened to Uncle Yarby. You more than anyone should know what happened to him. I think I'm entitled to know."

Time ticked away as they looked at each other openly from across the table. Neither spoke. Finally he pulled his eyes away from her and swung them slowly around the room. When his eyes returned to hers they held a quiet serious look. Kristin was beginning to think that he had no intention of telling her anything when he began to speak.

"A little more than a year ago a hanging posse rode out here looking for Yarby. He was accused of raping and murdering a woman from a wagon train camped down on the Yellowstone."

When the meaning of his words sank in, Kristin gasped.

"Oh, my goodness! A *hanging* posse?" She was shocked by the story. She shuddered and turned her eyes away from him.

"A hanging posse," he repeated. "They would have hung him on the spot if he'd been here."

"Thank heavens he wasn't."

"Why do you say that? How do you know he didn't do what he was accused of?"

"Of course he didn't do it! He was my father's brother.

There isn't a mean streak in any of the Andersons. Well, maybe a little but never mind that now."

"There wasn't a mean bone in Yarby's body. I know that for a fact. The only thing he could do was disappear."

"The poor man was so frightened he ran away." She was silent for a long time. Then, in a strange tone of voice, she said, "Shouldn't he have stayed and tried to clear his name?"

"Forsythe had people ready to swear he was there and saw him leave shortly before the woman was found. He didn't stand a chance against paid accusers. If Yarby had hung, you would have been notified a year ago of your inheritance. As long as the will had been recorded they would have had to recognize it."

"They had found the will and thought they'd stand a better chance getting me to sell if they got rid of my uncle?"

"That's the size of it."

"Why . . . the . . . cussed creatures!"

"They cared not a whit if Yarby was guilty or not."

"My uncle had been gone a year when he was found dead in the woods?"

"By Forsythe's men. Then they produced the will making you heir to all Yarby's possessions. I doubt they ever thought you'd show up here."

"I almost didn't. My brother wanted to take Mr. Forsythe's offer." She clicked her tongue against the roof of her mouth. "Poor Uncle Yarby. He must have suffered terribly being falsely accused of such a terrible thing and not being able to defend himself."

Buck continued to study her. She was a tall, slim, capable woman. Gutsy, too, or she'd not have come out here alone. Her eyes were not quite blue and not quite gray. Loose tendrils of silvery blond hair framed delicate cheekbones flushed with uneasiness.

She was pretty.

She was about the prettiest woman he'd ever seen. She had called herself an old maid. He wanted to laugh at that. Men here in the West would kill for a woman like her. He admired her calm voice; it was low and soothing. In fact he liked quite a few things about her.

He wondered why she smiled with her mouth closed, when she had such good white teeth.

While Buck was building his house, he'd had in the back of his mind the plan to find a strong, calm woman to bear his children. He didn't want to live in this house alone, grow old alone. What good was it to work to build something without someone to share it with or leave it to?

He and Yarby were so busy during Yarby's good years that he'd not had time to go looking for a woman. He wondered if Kristin would be outraged by the suggestion that they team up, travel in double harness.

A tightness crept into his throat, and he thought how foolish he was to think that she'd even consider such a thing. She would be sure that he was an ignorant, ill-mannered, saddle tramp hoping to get her share of the Larkspur.

She was looking him over with the same degree of interest as he was looking at her. The straightforwardness of her stare convinced him that there was nothing pretentious about her and that her expression of compassion for Moss was real.

Kristin's fingers were stroking the smooth surface of the table.

"This is a lovely table. Did my uncle make it? Cousin Gustaf said he liked working with wood."

"I made it a couple winters ago." Buck looked critically at

the top wishing he'd done a better job rubbing down the surface and applying oil.

"It's a lovely piece. Did you build the workbench and the washstands in the other rooms?"

"Yarby helped some. He taught me all I know about carpentry." Buck smiled as if remembering pleasant times. The smile rearranged his features in a fascinating way. "He made the chest. Said it was like one—" He cut off his words. His eyes followed hers to the flattopped chest beneath the window.

"I wish I'd known him. He must have been a lot like my papa." The words came off not-quite-steady lips.

"He never talked about his family." The smile vanished as quickly as it came. He looked over his shoulder at Moss, who was sleeping in the chair.

"He never mentioned me?"

"Not one time."

# Chapter Nine

*He* was silent for so long that a queer little shock of something almost like panic went through her. *Had he been irritated by her questions?*

Resentment edged its way into her thoughts. Well, what if he had? She moved her hands to her lap and clasped them tightly together. It was her life, her future they were discussing.

"Mr. Lenning, I've gleaned a little information from you about my uncle, but I still know nothing about what I may, or may not, have received from him."

"It seems clear to me. You'll get Yarby's land and half a herd of about two thousand head of steers."

"Two . . . thousand?"

"More or less. By the time we get the herd to the buyer there will be considerably less. Rustlers know I'm shorthanded. If not for the Sioux they would already have them."

"Forsythe told me that Uncle Yarby's cattle had been stolen and that you were in with the thieves and would get part of the money."

"Steal my own cattle? I'm not surprised he'd say that. He's got a mouth that spouts what he thinks folks will swallow. He can make some believe black is white."

Hearing that made Kristin smile, and dimples appeared in

her cheeks. Buck felt a jolt of something warm and exciting deep in his belly.

"He's smooth as silk. If not for Cletus and the Gateses warning me, it would have taken me longer to catch on to his palavering. My brother has business friends with blathering tongues, but none of them can hold a candle to Colonel Forsythe."

"Were you not tempted to take his money and go back home?"

"Not for a single second." She looked away from him, hoping he would not see the hurt of Ferd's rejection.

"Why not?"

"Personal reasons."

"Do you have someone back there that . . . you care about?"

"Only my cousin Gustaf." Kristin took a deep shuddering breath. "My brother would be happy to know of the predicament I'm in. He said this was a wild-goose chase and I'd end up in a . . ." She caught herself before she revealed her bitterness toward her brother.

"He didn't want you to come out here?"

"He forbade it."

"Then why did you? Couldn't another member of your family take care of things for you? This Gustaf for instance?"

"Gustaf encouraged me to come. It was my chance to be independent, to have something of my own. You couldn't possibly understand unless you had lived on someone else's charity all your adult life."

His dark brows drew together in a frown. "I guess not."

"I'm sorry to bring my troubles down on you, Mr. Lenning. I just don't know what to do. But it's not your problem, is it?"

"It's a problem for both of us. You're here, and I've got to decide what to do with you."

"I'm truly sorry to be a bother to you. But, please understand that I'd planned to make my home here, walk on my own land, sit on the porch and look at the sunset, watch the moon come up, plant a garden, prepare food for winter knowing that I could stay here until I died. I could let my hair hang, go without shoes if I wanted"—she smiled at that and Buck couldn't take his eyes off her face—"I would have no one to tell me to leave or that I must do this or that for the sake of what folks would think."

"Life isn't that simple."

"It should be. If you put all your hopes, dreams and toil into a place, you should be able to enjoy the fruits of your labor. Of course, I've not put any toil into a home yet, but I'm willing. I need to find a place for myself."

"Yarby had toiled for this place. Someone was willing to kill him for it."

"You helped him, didn't you?"

"Everybody needs somebody."

"It's strange that you'd say that. You seem to be the most self-assured person I ever met. I can't imagine you *needing* anyone."

She waited and was rewarded. He smiled again.

"I've had a lot of practice looking after myself."

"Didn't your father look after you when you were young?"

"I guess so."

Buck had never sat over breakfast and visited with a pretty woman before. As pleasant as it was, he knew that they had to get a few things settled between them.

"I just don't know what to do," she said for the second time, giving him the opening to say what had been on his mind, what he'd mulled over for most of the night.

"You can stay here and . . . help me with Moss. It will give me time to deal with Forsythe. After that we can decide what to do about Larkspur."

He saw the narrowing of her eyes. She opened her mouth and closed it without saying anything. When she spoke it was with stiff lips.

"Stay here in the house . . . with you?"

"You can't stay in Yarby's house."

"Without another woman present it wouldn't be decent!"

"Who's to say what's decent and what isn't? You said you wanted to be someplace where you didn't have to worry about what folks think." His voice was set; his eyes on hers were unwavering. A look of angry frustration ran rampantly across his face. "Do you consider yourself a decent woman?"

"Of course!"

"If folk thought otherwise would it change that?"

"Of course not! I know what I am."

"Then why care what they think? If you're afraid I'm going to force myself on you, rest at ease. Getting you in bed is the last thing on my mind." Watching her to see if she believed the lie, Buck held his breath until his chest hurt, then breathed deeply to ease it.

His tone of voice as much as his words had brought a deep flush to Kristin's face.

"You needn't be crude." She voiced the rebuke because she could think of nothing else to say.

"It's just an offer. Gilly will be back in a few days. If you don't want to stay here on the Larkspur, he'll take you to wherever you want to go. I doubt that there'll be anyone along before he gets back." A strange unaccustomed loneliness possessed him at the thought of her leaving.

"I'm not ungrateful, Mr. Lenning. It's just that this . . . ah arrangement would be . . . scandalous back in River Falls. An unmarried woman would not live in a house with a man even if his aged father did live there."

"Do you think the ladies in Big Timber will look down on you for living out here with me and Moss?" Her lips tightened, and she refused to answer. "If you're here in the West long enough, you'll learn that out here folks are not so quick to jump to judgment. I've known whores who play the piano in church and sing in the choir. On Sunday you can't tell them from the virgins."

The thought came to Kristin that a man as roughly handsome as Buck Lenning would have known many whores. Horrified that he might be able to read her thoughts, she suddenly rose to her feet, went to the cookstove and stood with her back to him.

"If you stay, I'll sleep in the bunkhouse if it'll make you feel . . . safer. Moss and I would have slept there last night, but I wasn't sure if you'd been followed and didn't want to leave you in here alone." He spoke quietly, but his voice roared in her ears.

"You think the colonel will send men out here to . . . try to kill us?"

"What do you think? Without you and me, the Larkspur is his." He laughed without humor. "I'm hoping my Sioux drovers will bring back a few relatives who'll help stand guard. If so, we'll not be completely surprised when the colonel's men come. I've a place up in the hills behind the ranch where I can hide you and Moss."

She went back to the table and sat down.

"You've done it before?"

"Several times. I've had to tie Moss to a tree and gag him."

"How . . . awful."

"It saved his life," he said quietly, his eyes so narrowed she could hardly see the green glint between the thick lashes.

"I didn't mean to criticize. It's like a war, isn't it? You really shoot at each other."

"Yes. Someone will die before it's over. I intend to make sure that it isn't me, or Moss, or . . . you."

She looked at him quietly, trying to read his thoughts. The silence stretched between them like a taut thread. The moment came to an end when she drew in a ragged breath.

"You're right, Mr. Lenning. What people think about me shouldn't matter. It's what I think of myself that's important. I accept your offer and thank you for it." She reached across the table to extend her hand. "I'll look after your father and tend your house in exchange for your protection."

Buck grasped her slender hand tightly in his large rough one. When she smiled, her eyes moved over him like a touch. Watching her lips spread and her eyes light up, he was filled with a quiet peace. He suddenly felt the desire to hold this soft woman in his arms, kiss her lips and beg her to stay here in this house he had painstakingly built and tried to furnish, and to care for him in all the ways a woman cared for her man.

The thought was so real that before he could comprehend what was happening, his own body responded to his thoughts. He dropped her hand quickly and turned to Moss, who had risen from his chair.

It was dark by the time choir practice was over and Bonnie Gates came out of the church.

Del Gomer was waiting.

Bonnie recognized him immediately and put her hand in her pocket and grasped the little derringer Bernie insisted that she carry.

In the three days since Bernie had helped Kristin Anderson get out of town Del had eaten every meal at the restaurant.

Mike Bruza had been there several times. He was loud and a braggart, but he'd been polite to Bonnie. Del always waited until the man had gone before he left himself.

"Miss Bonnie—" The tall man stepped out of the shadows and came to walk beside her. "You shouldn't be out alone at night."

"My safety is no concern of yours."

"It is very much a concern to me."

"I have a derringer in my pocket and I won't hesitate to use it."

"You need a real gun. That little pistol wouldn't stop a man unless you hit his heart."

"It would stop him if I aimed it between his legs," Bonnie said staunchly, and continued walking.

"It would slow him up a bit, that's sure." His hand cupped her elbow, she shook it off, stopped and waited for him to walk on. He stayed beside her.

"I don't need your protection."

"Yes, you do, Bonnie. But don't worry. Anyone who bothers you will answer to me."

"How many times do I have to tell you that I don't want your attention. I don't even like you."

"Yes, you do," he said again. "You just won't admit it." He walked along beside her as she hurried down the road. "I've been watching to see that you're not bothered."

"Spying on me, you mean."

He chuckled. It was a strange sound coming from a killer, soft and musical.

"It wouldn't take much spying to know what you do. You work too hard. All you do is go to the mercantile, to church, to visit with Mrs. Gaffney. You didn't even go to the ball game on Sunday afternoon."

"If you hurt Rose Gaffney, I'll shoot you! I swear I will."

"She's in no danger from me."

"That's very kind of you."

He ignored the sneer in her voice.

"Would you like to go to Laramie or Denver, see a stage play and buy some nice clothes?"

"In exchange for what? Sleeping with you? No, thanks. My brother and I have a business to run. That takes up most of my time."

"Let me take care of you, Bonnie. Don't you get tired of waiting on men who take a bath once a year?"

"Look, it doesn't matter to me if they *never* bathe. I'm doing honest work. I don't kill people for *my* living."

"I'll be away for a few days."

"Lucky me! Is Forsythe sending you out to kill someone? How much is a life worth to you, Mr. Gomer?"

"Watch out for Mike Bruza. Don't get close to him. If he grabs you, shoot him."

"I'll shoot anyone who grabs me, and that includes you."

"Bonnie." He stepped in front of her so that she had to stop. "I'll never hurt you."

"How about my brother? If Forsythe told you to kill him, would you do it?"

"It depends."

"On how much money he'd pay you?"

"No. It'd depend on if I wanted to or not."

"You're a cold-blooded bastard." She spat the words with disgust and tried to step around him.

"You liked me once."

"I didn't know what you did for a living then." She moved again to go around him. "Get out of my way. My brother is expecting me home."

"Believe me. I'll never hurt you."

"And you believe me. I don't want anything to do with you."

"I accept that for now." He cupped her elbow with his long, slim hand. "Don't pull away," he said sharply. "I'll see you safely home."

Bonnie walked along beside him, hoping and praying that her brother would not be waiting for her at the foot of the steps leading up to their rooms over the restaurant.

She had liked Del when she first met him. He had come to town shortly after she and Bernie had arrived and opened the restaurant. He was quiet, well mannered, attentive, and appeared to be genuinely interested in her.

He lived in the hotel, came and went at odd times and never seemed to be short of money. That bothered her as did his evasiveness about his personal life. She began to suspect that he was married. Then later, he had killed a man in the alley behind the mercantile, and no explanation was ever given.

Jim Lyster was the law in Big Timber. He made a big show of it, walking up and down the street with a big tin star on his chest. He never arrested anyone except a drifter or a railroad bum. It was well-known that he was on Forsythe's payroll.

No one knew the man Del had killed or why he had killed him. He never mentioned the incident to Bonnie. Cletus had told her of Del's connection to Forsythe. At first her disappointment had been great. Then she began to chide herself for being so blinded by his good looks and polite manner.

Now she despised him.

Bonnie saw with relief that Bernie was not waiting for her. As soon as they reached the stairs going up the side of the building, she jerked her elbow loose from Del's hand and hurried up the steps.

"Good-bye, Bonnie. I'll be back at the end of the week."

She ignored him, but at the top of the landing she looked back. He was standing there, waiting for her to go inside. She rearranged her angry features so as to not alarm her brother, shoved open the door and stepped into the room. She looked toward Bernie's bed, where he usually lay reading this time of night, giving his knee and stump relief from the wooden peg.

The bed was empty. Her brother lay on the floor beside it, his face a bloody pulp. Her breath caught in her throat. She let out a little cry of anguish and rushed toward him.

Abruptly she was grabbed from behind. A wiry arm wrapped around her neck as another arm locked hers to her sides and pulled her tightly against a chest.

"Hold on, sister. I ain't through with that bastard on the floor yet. I ain't goin' hurt ya none if ya behave yoreself."

Fear knifed through Bonnie and with it came a shriek that was cut off by a hand over her mouth and nose. Her attacker was holding her head so far back that she couldn't see Bernie. She struggled and tried to kick backward. The hand tightened, cutting off air to her lungs. Then a voice penetrated the roar in her ears.

"Let go of her."

The arm around her dropped as did the hand over her mouth and nose. As she gasped for air, she heard a loud *bang*. Staggering to a chair, she grasped the back of it to steady herself. While she drew air into her lungs, she looked around. Through a daze she saw Del Gomer shoving his gun back into the holster that lay against his thigh. The man he had shot had been flung back against the wall and lay crumpled on the floor. Bonnie's frantic eyes sought her brother.

"Bernie? Please . . . no! Ber—" Her voice deserted her. She dropped to her knees beside him.

His face was almost unrecognizable. Blood poured from his

nose and seeped from the broken skin on his face. It oozed from a deep cut on his forehead. His crippled leg was folded beneath him as if his good leg had collapsed, letting him fall to the floor.

"I've got to get a doctor!" Bonnie jumped to her feet only to bump up against Del, who was holding a wet towel.

"Put this on his face and let's see how bad he's hurt."

Bonnie grabbed the towel. At this moment she would have accepted help from the devil himself. Del knelt down on the other side of Bernie and carefully lifted his hand and placed it on his chest. Bonnie gently mopped her brother's face.

"Please, Brother, don't be hurt bad," she whispered over and over.

Her sight was blurred by the tears that fell on her hands as she wiped the battered face. She wasn't aware that she was crying or that it was Del who placed a pan of water on the floor beside her. She rinsed the bloody cloth and dabbed at the wounds again while Del straightened Bernie's leg. She was aware, however, that it was Del who brought the lamp, set it on a chair, knelt down and looked closely at the wound on Bernie's forehead.

"He needs a doctor."

"Doctor's gone to Billings."

"Oh, Lord." Bonnie reached for Bernie's hand.

"Don't touch it, Bonnie." His fingers closed around her wrist. "His fingers are broken."

"Oh . . . oh merciful God! Why did he do this?" Her eyes flew up to meet his.

"I'll put him on the bed, then go get some things to patch him up. I think the bastard knocked him out and then stomped him. That cut on his head needs a couple of stitches."

"You can do that?"

"I can do it. First I've got to get rid of that trash in the corner."

Bonnie's legs were so weak when she stood that she stumbled to hold on to the end of the iron bedstead.

"Who is he?"

"Can I borrow this towel. I'll wash it in the horse tank and bring it back." Without waiting for permission, he wrapped the towel about the dead man's head, picked him up and slung him over his shoulder.

"Who is he?" Bonnie demanded again.

"A mouthy piece of horse dung named Miller."

"Why'd he come here to hurt Bernie?"

"Because he knew *you* wouldn't be here."

"He didn't even have a gun in his hand when you killed him," she said accusingly.

"He had *you* in his hands. He knew better."

Del looked out the door before he went out and down the stairs. He walked quickly between the two buildings and back toward the livery and the pole corrals. When he reached the fence, he dumped the body over the rails. The horses nickered and shied away. Del reached through the bars and snatched the towel he had wrapped about the bloody head to protect his clothes.

"Dirty bastard," he muttered. "You knew what you'd get if you put your hands on her."

It was an hour past midnight.

Kyle Forsythe lay in his bed with his hand cupped about the naked breast of his housekeeper, Ruth DeVary, and ignored the sniffles the woman was trying to conceal. He cared not a whit if she bawled all night. He teased her by rolling her nipple around between his thumb and forefinger, plucked at the pelt of hair between her legs and yawned sleepily.

In his younger years he had been able to achieve an erection each and every night that a woman was available. Tonight he had exhausted himself trying to gain satisfaction. Lately it had been taking longer and longer for him to reach his climax and he hated it. It must be the woman's fault. Finally, frustrated, he had slapped her hard across the face with his open hand. After that, either she had worked harder, or else his dominance over her had created a spark that had fired his blood. In a matter of minutes he had rushed to completion.

He would have to remember that.

His thoughts traveled back to all the women he'd had. Barmaids had been enamored of his good looks and his station in life. Society women, including his late wife Cindy Read Forsythe, had fallen in love with him. He'd charmed an Arkansas hill woman and had married her under the false name of Kirby Hyde. After he'd tired of her, he'd gone off to war, and let her believe he'd been killed. Later she'd had a child she *claimed* was his.

Good grief! Time had passed quickly.

The ringing of the bell on the door broke into his thoughts. *Hell! What now?*

"Ruth!" He elbowed the woman beside him. "Go see who's at the door. Tell them to come back tomorrow. Then get back here. I may want you again." In the back of Kyle's mind was the slap he'd given her. He wanted to try it again and see if that was what had aroused his limp flesh.

Ruth hurriedly left the bed. She donned a dressing gown before she lit the small lamp and carried it out into the hallway and down the stairs to the door. The night caller was persistent.

The bell continued to ring up to the time she opened the door and saw Del Gomer standing there.

"Mrs. DeVary." Always polite, Del tipped his hat. "I want a few minutes with Colonel Forsythe."

"He's in bed, Mr. Gomer."

"Then tell him to get up."

"He told me to tell whoever was here to come back in the morning."

Del pushed gently, but firmly, on the door and she backed away as he came into the foyer.

"I'll see him down here or upstairs."

"Please . . . don't, Mr. Gomer—"

The lamp she was holding cast a light on the swelling on the side of her face and on an eyelid that drooped. He lifted his hand and trailed his fingers across her cheek, then took the lamp from her hand.

"Where is he?"

"First door on the right. Please . . . don't say anything—"

His cold-eyed stare stayed on her face until she turned her head away.

Ruth followed him up the stairs, not knowing whom she feared the most, Del Gomer or the colonel.

Forsythe sat up in bed when Del entered the room.

"Del? Godamighty! What's happened?" As he spoke he swung his legs over the side of the bed.

"Mrs. DeVary tried to keep me out. But as you can see, I'm bigger than she is."

"Yes, yes, of course. If I'd known it was you— Ruth, get my pants."

"Don't bother, Mrs. DeVary. He needn't dress to hear what I've got to say. Did you send Cliff Miller over to the Gateses?"

"Why . . . why . . . ah . . . what do you mean?"

"You heard me." Del took a few steps into the room and set the lamp on a table.

"Well, I told him to . . . wait until the girl was gone, then see what . . . he could find out from her brother."

"What did you want to know?"

"How the Anderson woman got out of town, where she went and who helped her."

"I could have told you that."

"Then why didn't you?" Impatience drove through his usual caution when dealing with Del.

"You didn't ask me."

"I'm asking you now." Kyle tried to hide his apprehension behind an assertive manner.

"You better make sure that the next son of a bitch you send over to the Gateses' keeps his hands off Bonnie, because not only will I kill *him*, I'll come looking for the man who sent him there."

"I never told Miller to—"

"It's too late now to tell Miller anything." Del turned to the woman hovering in the doorway. "Good night, ma'am. I can find my way out."

"We'll talk when you get back from Bozeman, Del."

At the door Del paused. "I'll not be going to Bozeman. Not tomorrow anyway."

"Not . . . going? Why not?"

"I'm not going."

"Our deal was that you'd go and do the job for five hundred dollars." Forsythe's face had reddened considerably. He was mad clear through, but strove not to show it.

"Five hundred for killing a judge." There was a sneer in Del's voice. "I've been paid a thousand for killing a schoolteacher. But I said I'd do it and I will, but if you can't wait a week or two, get someone else."

There was a sudden stillness in the room. Del Gomer's expression never changed. His cold eyes held on to Forsythe for so long that Kyle thought his head would explode from the tension. Then the tall, quiet-faced man turned and left the room.

Kyle waited to speak until after he heard the soft click of the door downstairs being closed.

"Blow out the lamp. Look out the window and make sure that arrogant bastard is gone. The son of a bitch is so wild for that slut over at the eatery he's lost his reason. He doesn't need to think I can't find someone just as good with a gun as he is! There's plenty of gunmen who can blow him out from under that ten-dollar hat. Bastards! Give them an inch and they'll be pissin' on the dirt you're laying under!"

At the window Ruth listened to Kyle's ravings and was sickened by what she heard. *He had hired Del to kill a judge and sent that disgusting Cliff Miller over to beat up a crippled man.* She had known that Franklin Kyle Forsythe was ambitious, greedy, and ruthless, but she'd not known to what extent he would go to get what he wanted.

"He's gone."

Kyle flopped back down on the bed, angry that Ruth had seen his fear.

"Damn bunch of blunderheads. Well . . . are you coming to bed or not? I've not been pleased with your attitude lately, Ruth. What you need is a damn good smack on your bottom to remind you that you work here."

Kyle Forsythe scowled in the dark. *Yeah, it's what she needs.*

As soon as Ruth sank down on the bed, he pounced on her, rolled her over, pulled up her nightdress and began slapping her bare buttocks with the palm of his hand.

# Chapter Ten

$\mathcal{B}$uck struck a seldom-used trail and followed it to the ridges above Larkspur. The trail passed through a dense stand of aspen, then turned upward. He came out onto a small grass-covered plain dotted with bunchgrass and clumps of scrub oak. Twice, rabbits leaped up and scurried away. A hawk, soaring high above the treetops, watched for his chance to dive and carry off a luckless small animal for a meal. Buck rode on, the hooves of the big gray making no sound on the soft grass.

Cutting across a narrow meadow, Buck found what he had been searching for; fresh prints of a horse bisecting the trail he was taking. Turning the gray, he followed. In the meadow grass, the tracks were too indistinct to tell him much about the horse, but he didn't need to see the tracks to know where the rider was going. He was heading for the plateau above the trail leading to the ranch and was riding toward his objective in as straight a line as possible.

Wheeling the horse, Buck took off up a draw into the steeper hills, carefully scanning every open space before he crossed it. He knew only too well how little was required to conceal a man. A low bush, clothing that blended with the sur-roundings, and immobility were the essentials for remaining unseen.

When he was well above the trail behind the ranch buildings, he cut across and moved cautiously down through the trees. He studied the area, carefully examining each clump of bushes, each approach. These were uneasy days, for one of Forsythe's men could be waiting behind any rock or bush. He looked to see how the shadows fell, how the birds flew. Each might give an indication of where an enemy lay in waiting.

The wind shifted, rustling the leaves, and a faint scent of tobacco smoke reached him. He dismounted, ground-tied his horse, and moved silently through the shadowy woods. He was playing a high-stakes game with an unknown enemy and the prize was life. One wrong step, and he could lose. And he had only one life.

Each of the four days that Kristin had been at the ranch he had scouted this area. He knew that sooner or later Forsythe would become tired of waiting and send his henchmen. Each evening he had looked forward to returning to a house that had miraculously been turned into a home almost overnight. A welcoming smile and hot meal would be waiting. He would sit at the table over his coffee and watch Kristin move about *his* house, listen to her light chatter about things she had done, and watch her patient handling of Moss.

From the day he had first seen her she had never been far from his thoughts. Something within him, some feeling in his blood, some perception beyond the usual, told him that this was his woman. He wanted to be with her for the rest of his life, live with her here on the Larkspur, love her, provide for her and protect her. She would think, he was sure, that he wanted her for Yarby's land. That's what he would think if the situation were reversed. What would she think if she knew the truth about Yarby? Hell and tarnation! Why hadn't he told her right from the start?

*Because she might've insisted on going back to town, you stupid mule's ass.*

Buck stood stock-still in the thick growth, suddenly aware of how dangerous it was to let his mind wander. He attempted to wipe all thoughts of Kristin and Yarby and Larkspur from his mind. He had to concentrate on the man who was bent on killing him.

Buck's face, darkened by many suns and winds, was still, remote and lonely; it did not show the anger he felt at being hunted. Whoever stalked him planned to murder him, then ride down and kill a helpless old man and a woman. He stifled his rage. Anger could cloud his senses and cause him to make a wrong move.

His eyes scanned the slope below him. He studied each bush, each tree, each boulder. It was quiet; not even birdsong broke the silence. He started to step out and continue downward, then stopped and stepped back. Long ago he'd learned to trust his instincts. He didn't know why he hesitated, but suddenly things were not right.

He heard the shot and felt the wicked force of a bullet tear across the top of his shoulder and lose itself in the woods beyond. He hit the ground rolling and another bullet sailed over the top of him. He crawled quickly to the left, rolled to a downed log and stretched out alongside it. The shooter peppered with bullets the bushes where he had been. A bullet struck the log behind which he lay with an ugly *whap*.

He eased his gun out of the holster and waited.

Silence. Then he heard a voice shrill with excitement.

"Got 'em. If he ain't dead he'll soon be. I aimed true and got 'em. I seen it hit and I seen 'em fall. I heared the *whap* of that last bullet. Yessiree, we got that re . . . ward in our pocket."

"Lantz? You doin' *all* the shootin'?"

"Who else? Said I'd pay back, didn't I? He's 'round here some'r's. Got ta get me some proof ta take back to that high muckety-muck land man what thinks we don't 'mount to much."

*Lantz and the fat man.* Through a fog of rage, Buck's mind began to work.

Buck could hear the sound of boots crushing twigs as Lantz moved closer to the log, and he bunched his muscles to spring. He waited until he could hear breathing then lunged up practically in Lantz's face. Buck put three bullets in him in quick succession. Lantz fell backward with blood all over him.

"Damn you! Damn you to . . . hell—!" Lantz clawed at his chest and died.

Expecting to feel the jarring bullet from the fat man's gun, Buck spun in a half circle to see him frozen in place, a rifle dangling from his hand. With death looking him in the face, the fat man knew his only chance was to drop the gun and raise his hands. His face was a sickly yellow.

"Don't . . . don't shoot—"

"You sorry piece of horseshit!" Buck's finger tightened on the trigger and a bullet cut into a fleshy thigh an inch below the man's male organ.

He screamed, grabbed his privates, stumbled backward, and lost his balance. He fell heavily to the ground.

"Get up, you back-shootin' son of a bitch! Get up or the next one will be between your eyes instead of between your legs."

Buck stared at the fat man through a powerful red rage. His breath rasped in and out. Blood from the wound in his shoulder stained his shirt. Splatters of Lantz's blood shone on his face.

The fat man rolled to his knees and managed to get to his feet. Blood ran down his leg and spattered on his boot.

"Pick him up," Buck demanded.

Keeping his legs spread, the fat man waddled over to the bloody body of his friend.

"Take off his gun belt first and put his gun in it." He nodded toward the gun Lantz had dropped when Buck shot him. "Put it over there with the rifle, then pick him up."

After two tries the frightened man managed to stand with Lantz flung over his shoulder.

"Put him on his horse."

Buck followed the man as he staggered through the woods. One time his knees buckled, but he righted himself before he and the body he carried hit the ground.

The horses had been hidden in a copse three hundred feet from where the men had waited to ambush Buck. Buck noted that they had arrived at that point by approaching from two different directions; the only smart move they had made.

"Throw him over the rump of the gelding."

"That's my horse—" The man protested, but after a glance at Buck's angry face, obeyed.

"Mount up." The man went to take the reins of the blue roan tied near by, and Buck spoke again. "Leave it. The horse is mine now."

"You'd send me off without a gun? There's Sioux all over these mountains."

"Yeah. Maybe you'll run into some of Little Owl's kinfolk. The only reason I'm letting you go is that if I kill you, you and that other piece of shit will lie here, rot and stink up my land. I'm letting you take him out of here—but not back to Big

Timber. Head for Canada or California. If I see you again, or even hear that you're anywhere near the Larkspur, I'll come looking for you and shoot you down like a dog."

The horse was skittish. He smelled the fresh blood and felt the unfamiliar burden on his rump. Finally, the fat man was able to mount and when he eased himself down into the saddle, his face contorted with pain and he yelled. The frightened horse danced in place so that the fat man had to grab Lantz's belt to keep him from sliding off the horse.

Buck whistled for his horse, then mounted the gray and followed the fat man to the freight road that led to Helena. He wondered how long he would ride with the dead body of his friend. He didn't care where he was dumped, as long as it wasn't on the Larkspur.

After the first day, Kristin had not felt like an intruder in Buck's home. The man was an enigma. Kristin had no doubt that he was hard as nails, yet he was the soul of patience with his father. He was evidently proud of his home, but had furnished it as if he'd never lived in a house before. He told her the day they had come to an agreement that she was free to make any changes she wished in the kitchen as well as in the other rooms. He readily admitted he knew little about furnishing a house. He also shyly confessed that he had chosen the pieces from a catalog and had sent the order to Bozeman.

When he told her that, Kristin's eyes had darted to the green velvet chair, then smiled into his.

"It . . . looked different in the catalog," he said with a sheepish grin.

"It would be lovely in a parlor as would the globe lamp. Do you mind if I move the lamp to the other room?"

"Might as well. I've never used it in here." At that moment

there was something vulnerable and endearing about him. Kristin was to think about it as the days went by.

Buck was away from the house for most of the day. When he wasn't scouting, he was doing work he hadn't been able to attend to before Kristin came to watch Moss. One day he moved his horses to a higher meadow and hoped his men would return before they were found by rustlers or a roving band of Sioux who were unaware of the agreement he had with Iron Jaw.

He spent one day dragging deadfalls from the woods to the ranch yard, and for an hour or two each morning he chopped wood and stacked it along the south side of the house. Another time he worked on the ducts that brought water from the spring to the stock tanks inside the corral. In the evening he washed in the bunkhouse before he came to the warm, cozy kitchen where Kristin waited with a hot meal.

Kristin's days were spent cleaning while watching that Moss didn't wander out of the house. With an apron tied about her waist, she swept and scrubbed, rearranged the kitchen and the provisions, and washed the windows with vinegar water until they sparkled. After finding a roll of oil-cloth, she cut a length and put it on the table. In the center she set a handsome, newly polished cruet set she had discovered gathering dust in a far corner under the wash bench. She waited for Buck to mention it, but he never did.

Kristin was ever conscious of the danger of Forsythe's men coming out to the ranch. She had come to depend somewhat on Sam's giving a warning, but still, she scanned the horizon each time she went past a door or a window. Buck had warned her to be vigilant and fire the gun twice in rapid succession if *anyone* approached the house.

She entertained Moss much as she would have a small

child. He had become attached to her and followed her so closely that it was difficult for her to make a trip to the outhouse. Buck showed her the room at the end of the bunkhouse where he had put Moss when he had to be away. One time, when she needed to wash her monthly pads and hang them on the bushes out of sight behind the outhouse, she had put him in there and when she returned, he was sitting on the bunk crying. After that when it became necessary to relieve herself and Buck was not near, she went into her room and hurriedly used the chamber pot.

The days had passed so quickly that Kristin was surprised to discover that a week had gone by. She thought of this as she cooked supper for Buck, Moss and herself. She was adding another dipper of water to the pot on the stove when she heard Sam utter a welcoming bark. She went to the door to see Buck riding in on his big gray and leading a saddled horse. In her relief that Buck had returned once again, the significance of the horse without a rider escaped Kristin.

"Buck is back early today." She had formed the habit of speaking to Moss as if he understood what she said.

"I like tater dumplin's."

"You do?" Kristin turned with a surprised look at the old man sitting in the leather chair. "I like them too. I'll make you some."

Every so often Moss blurted out something that was familiar to Kristin. One day he'd said, "Trim and buck the tree first, Sean." She'd had an Uncle Sean who had died long ago. Another time he'd said, "It ain't nice to tease Anna." He pronounced the name *Onyah* the Swedish way. Kristin made a mental note to ask Buck if his father had been born in the Old Country.

Moss was content as long as his hands were busy. It was a

challenge to Kristin to think of things for him to do. She had taken a fancy knit coverlet from her trunk and given it to him to unravel and roll the yarn into balls. If she was still here when the weather turned cold, she would use the fine wool to make caps and gloves for herself and Moss. She didn't dare allow herself to think that Buck might appreciate a pair of knit socks.

Today she had made four loaves of bread. On the first day she had taken over the kitchen, she discovered Buck had put in a good store of provisions, but no yeast. She had made some by mixing flour, brown sugar, and a little salt. After boiling the mixture for two hours, she let it cool to lukewarm, then sealed it. Now three days later she had used some of it to make bread.

Kristin longed for milk and butter and eggs. A cow, chickens and a garden were essential, especially on a farm or a ranch. She understood why there was no garden. Buck simply hadn't had the time to plant and tend one. He had laid in a good supply of provisions: flour, sugar, cornmeal, rice, raisins, dried apples and beans. There was no shortage of beef or venison in the smokehouse. Tonight she had cut beef into strips, and boiled them until tender, then added potatoes and onions. She was counting on the fresh bread to give the meal some variety.

Moss had become bored with his work and had begun to move about the house. When Moss became restless it was usually because he had to go to the outhouse. He paced the floor then went to stand beside the door rocking back and forth. Kristin was afraid to wait longer for Buck to come in. She took the old man's hand and walked with him down the path to the necessary. Once there she slipped the galluses holding his britches off his shoulders and opened the door.

Thank goodness he was still able to tend to himself after she got him this far. The first time she'd had to do this, she had felt acute embarrassment for herself and deep pity for him. She still pitied him, but the embarrassment was gone. He was like a child, a very sweet, gentle child.

On the way back up the path toward the house, Moss tugged on her hand, pulling her toward the bunkhouse, where Sam lay beside the open door. The dog had grudgingly accepted Kristin after she had fed him cold biscuits.

"Mr. Lenning, are you in here?" The words had no more than left her mouth when he appeared in the doorway, bare to the waist, his hair wet and wild as if he'd dipped his head in a bucket of water. A wet bloody rag was thrown over his shoulder.

"Something wrong?" he asked curtly.

"No." She shook her head. "Moss—" She couldn't draw her eyes away from his bare chest where blood trickled down from the shoulder where the wet cloth lay near the curve of his neck. "You've been . . . hurt! Heavens!" She tried to pull her hand loose from Moss's, but he wouldn't let go.

"It's only a crease. I'm soaking my shirt in a bucket."

"It looks to me to be more than a crease, for crying out loud! Come to the house so I can clean it with vinegar water. That rag you've got on it looks none too clean."

"Wait till I wash my shirt."

"I'll take care of your shirt later. You have another one," she added sternly to hide her anxiety. She started for the house, pulling Moss along beside her. She looked back. He was still standing in the doorway. "Come on. I've seen a man's bare chest before. I have a brother, you know."

"The wolves and the cougers would've got him."

"Got who, Moss?" Kristin asked absently.

"Buck. Had to pull him with the horse on the snow."

She stopped and looked into the old man's face. For an instant she saw something there that could have been worry or concern.

"You did that, Moss?"

A twinkle came into his eyes.

"Flies in the buttermilk, skip to my Lou."

"Yes, of course. For a moment I thought—Well, never mind."

Inside the house, Kristin urged Moss to the chair and put the coverlet in his hand. Once he was settled, she moved a chair close to the wash bench, then hurried to her trunk to fetch clean cloth for bandages. When she returned, Buck stood in the doorway.

"Sit down," she said briskly.

"Something smells good."

"I baked bread today." She removed the wet cloth on his shoulder and dropped it in the washbasin. When she saw the red strip of open flesh on his shoulder so close to the base of his neck, she took a deep breath that quivered her lips. "An inch closer—"

"I was lucky."

Kristin turned quickly and tilted the jug of vinegar over the wash dish and soaked a piece of cloth. Without hesitation she placed it on the wound.

"Ohhh . . . That stings!"

" 'Course it does. Don't be a baby. Are you going to tell me what happened?" She tilted her head down to look into his face, her large eyes questioning. For a moment her eyes were lost in his intent gaze.

"Someone shot at me."

"I didn't think you'd shot yourself." Kristin fought to still her trembling.

"He was waiting on a shelf above the trail."

"I hope you shot back!"

"I did." He grinned a lopsided grin that crinkled the corners of his eyes.

"Were you a better shot than he was?"

Buck let her question pass as he watched the expressions flit across her face. She washed the wound again, then smeared it with a yellow salve she brought from her trunk. Her fingers were light and warm on his bare skin. He drew in a deep breath and held it while her hand rested on his shoulder as she patted a small strip of cloth over the salve.

"What's that?"

"Carbolic petroleum jelly. What do you use?"

"Pine tar."

"That's for . . . horses!"

His eyes sparkled with amusement. By jinks damn, she was pretty, soft as a woman should be, but strong. She wasn't a woman who had to be coddled even if she was used to all the comforts a town provided. He had a powerful urge to pull her down on his lap and bury his face against her breasts.

What would she do? Slap his face? Run to her room and bar the door?

"You killed him, didn't you?"

She was leaning down, looking into his face with her calm blue-gray eyes. Seconds piled on top of each other to make a minute before he could trust himself to speak.

"Yes." His throat was so clogged he could hardly utter the word. Would she turn from him now? Be repulsed? Think of him as a gunman? A killer?

She nodded her head ever so slightly and placed her hand on his naked shoulder again.

"You did what you had to do."

The warmth of her hand seeped into him and he went weak with relief. When she took her hand away, he desperately wanted to grab it and hold it against his chest. When she turned to empty the washbasin, he stood and went quickly to the room he shared with Moss and plucked a faded blue shirt from the peg on the wall. He pulled it on over his head and ran his fingers through his wet hair in an effort to tame it.

Buck Lenning had never been so unsure of himself in his life. He simply didn't know how to act around a woman like Kristin. He'd not been to town in a year . . . not that he'd have found one like her in town. It wasn't that he was lonely. He was used to his own company, and he'd had Moss and Gilly and an occasional visitor. It was just that he felt awkward and tongue-tied, although his tongue had been plenty loose the day she arrived. Anger at seeing a strange woman in his house had caused it. But the more he got to know her . . . yes, and to depend on her, the more self-conscious he felt when near her.

In the kitchen, Kristin was talking to Moss and gently tugging on a soft bundle of something that Moss was hugging to his chest.

"Who'er you?"

"Kristin. Supper's ready, Moss. You can work on this later."

"Are you my ma?"

"No. I'm your friend."

"I left my wagon and my mules."

"I was hoping this would keep you busy for a day or so. At this rate you'll have it all unraveled in another hour or two." She pulled the bundle from his arms, rolled it up and placed it on a chair.

"He's happy as a drunk hoot owl," Moss said, and looked at her expectantly.

"Then he must be very happy." Kristin took the old man's hand and led him to the washstand, where she dipped water from the bucket into the basin.

"Wash up, Moss."

Kristin threw a towel over his shoulder. Although he seemed to understand what he was to do when she led him to the privy or the washstand, he sometimes would continue to wash his hands until she pulled him away and handed him the towel.

"Milkin' cows is woman's work." Moss dried his hands and dropped the towel on the floor.

"It is, and if we had one, I'd welcome the chore." Kristin picked up the towel and hung it on the end of the wash bench. She reached for Buck's comb and ran it through Moss's hair.

"I'll get you one." Buck spoke from behind her. She turned quickly, and made an impatient motion with her hand.

"Oh, no. I was just talking to Moss. Besides, I may not be here long, and you'd be stuck with having to milk it. I doubt you'd like that. Men usually don't."

"Are you leaving?" Buck asked quietly.

"Not . . . immediately, unless you want me to."

"I thought we had an agreement."

"We do. I'll stay . . . until we get borders set for what's my land and what's yours." ·

"That may be hard to do. This house could be sitting right on the line."

To Buck's utter surprise and amazement, peals of Kristin's laughter filled every corner of the room. To him the sound was more beautiful than a church bell, more beautiful than the chimes on the clock. His smiling eyes narrowed and clung to her face. She was a wonder, tall and straight and shining. And when she laughed, the sound was like music, her eyes like stars.

"I'm putting in my bid for the back part of the house if we have to divide it," Kristin said pertly, still smiling broadly. "You have a cozy comfortable home here, but I like the kitchen the best, especially the stove. You can have the woodpile!"

Buck's mouth twitched, broke into a slow, uneven smile that sent creases fanning out from his shining green eyes and made indentions in his cheeks.

"You'll need firewood from *my* woodpile to burn in *your* stove."

"Maybe we can strike a deal. I'll bake biscuits if you furnish the stove wood."

"Fair enough."

"I guess we're stuck with each other for a while." She stepped around the table to take the coverlet from Moss's hands again. "After you eat." She gently pushed him into a chair.

"What's he wanting to do?"

"I gave him a coverlet to unravel. He seems to love pulling the yarn and rolling it into balls."

"There's a place where the trail twists around a boulder." Moss looked from Kristin to Buck and back again.

"What's a coverlet?" Buck's hand dropped to the bundle and felt the soft wool and raised his brows in question.

"A fancy cover to go on a bed."

"Did you make it?"

"A couple winters ago."

"It's . . . pretty."

"I've no use for it now. I can find a better use for good wool yarn."

"What will you make?"

"Mittens, caps, stockings, scarves."

"Who for?" He was desperate to keep her talking.

"I might even knit you a pair of sky blue stockings and a sky blue cap." A giggle that Kristin couldn't hold back came bubbling up.

"I'd be a sight in a sky blue cap, that's sure." He smiled. Lately it didn't take much to make him smile.

"I danced with a gal with a hole in her stocking."

Buck moved around the table to take his chair. As he passed Moss, he put his hand on his shoulder.

"I just bet you did, old-timer."

Kristin saw the gentle touch and wished that Moss knew how fortunate he was to have a son like Buck. Ferd would never have been so caring of their father. He would have shut him away somewhere out of sight, ashamed that he had lost his reason.

"I wish I'd known your father before." Kristin placed a stack of bread slices on the table.

"He was a very smart man. I guess I told you that."

"No, but you said Uncle Yarby was. Did Moss know him?"

"He knew him."

"You must have taken after your mother. You don't resemble your father at all."

"I've been told that."

"I guess I take after my Swedish parents. Both had light hair."

Buck liked looking at her, but he forced his eyes away, and cleared his throat before he spoke again.

"Forsythe bought the land next to a rancher about fifteen miles east of here. He's putting the squeeze on him to get his place. He rousted the man's steers out of the scrub and put his own brand on them. Ryerson hardly had enough to drive to market. He's got a couple of cows and some chickens. When Gilly gets back, I'll send him over to see if he's ready to sell."

"I hate to take advantage of someone's misfortune. Isn't there any way people can unite against Forsythe?"

"Some don't have the will to stand up against him. Some will stay and fight."

"Like you?"

"Like me and a few others."

"What a shame." Kristin clicked her tongue against the roof of her mouth.

"It happens out here."

"Something should be done about that . . . weasel."

"I've sent for a Federal marshal. I hope he gets here before there's an all-out war."

"That could happen?"

"Sure. Forsythe's careful now to stay off Indian land, but he'll get greedy. The Sioux will fight, and the army will be called in. 'Course, it'll be the Sioux who'll get the dirty end of the stick if it comes to that."

"What a pity."

# Chapter Eleven

$\mathcal{K}$ristin had been on Larkspur for a week. It had been the happiest, busiest and most satisfying week of her life. According to the calendar, it was Monday. Monday was wash day. Washing clothes in a tub with a scrub board was back-breaking work.

Buck had set up the big wooden tub on a bench outside the back door and had filled it with several buckets of water he drew from the well. Kristin added hot water from the cookstove. Under the workbench she found a large brown cake of lye soap, and the washing began.

When she told Buck to bring his dirty clothes, he had appeared embarrassed but had done so after she insisted. She understood his reluctance when she saw the unmended tears in his shirts, socks and britches.

"We really need another tub," she told him. "But I'll make do rinsing in a bucket."

"I took the clothes to the creek . . . except in the winter—"

She could not picture this big, wild-looking man washing clothes. But evidently he had—the scrub board appeared to be well used.

He left her then to fasten a rope to the end of the bunkhouse and tie the other end to the crossbar over the well that held the pulley. She had smiled her thanks and he disappeared behind

the buildings. That had been several hours earlier. Although
she had not seen him, she was confident that he was somewhere nearby. He had never failed to let her know when he
was leaving the homestead.

*What would Ferd think of his sister bent over the washtub?*

The thought brought a smile to Kristin's face as she
plunged her hand down into the warm soapsuds and brought
up Buck's shirt. She had soaked the bloodstain spots previously in cold water and now as she scrubbed them vigorously
on the ribbed board she made a mental note to mend the tear
on the shoulder made by the bullet as well as to fix the holes
in his socks where his clumsy attempts at sewing had left
lumpy ridges.

Back home in River Falls, Mrs. Jorgenson and her daughter had arrived every Monday morning at daybreak. In the
washhouse, set well back from the main house, they started
the wash water to heat in an oblong copper boiler long before
daylight. The wash was hung on lines stretched across the
back of the property. As soon as a garment or a piece of bed
linen dried, it was ironed, also in the washhouse. In the eight
years Mrs. Jorgenson had been the Anderson laundress, she
had never stepped foot past the kitchen door where she left
the baskets of freshly washed and ironed clothes.

Moss sat on the step playing with the toy Kristin had made
by looping a string through a large button. He seemed to be fas-
cinated with the toy and soon became quite adept at holding the
loop wide with spread hands and twirling the button over and
over until the two strings became entwined. Then by alternately
tightening and loosening the string, he made the button rotate
in alternating directions to produce a soft whirring sound when
the rotation was at top speed.

The sun was warm on Kristin's back, and little beads of

sweat dotted her forehead. She pushed the bright strands of hair back from her face with the back of her hand and picked up the last of her wash to carry to the line. Suddenly she heard Sam utter a low menacing growl. She set the bucket of wet clothes back down beside the washtub.

The dog had risen from where he lay in the shade of the oak tree. He stood on stiffened legs, his tail straight out, hair on his neck standing. He was looking toward the creek and making low growling noises. Kristin strained her eyes but could see nothing. Ears erect, Sam moved out to the edge of the house yard, his eyes still on some distant point. Kristin's heart picked up speed. She tried to calm herself; maybe Sam was seeing a small animal who had come to the creek to drink.

Then out of the woods beyond the creek came a group of horsemen. Sam let out a spate of furious barking.

"Buck!" The yell tore from Kristin's throat.

"I'm here." Buck came out of the shed with his rifle in his hand and quickly crossed to where she stood beside the step.

"Who? Are they . . . Forsythe's men?"

"No. The one on the buckskin is Gilly. The rest are Sioux."

"Are they . . . friendly?"

"The one next to Gilly on the Appaloosa is Runs Fast. He doesn't like me much. They've got women with them, so they're not up to mischief."

"Oh, dear! I've never been this close to wild Indians before."

Buck looked down at her and the corners of his eyes crinkled.

"Wild? They're not any *wilder* than we are. Their ways are different is all. They're just trying to hold on to what's been theirs for hundreds of years."

"What do you want me to do?"

"Nothing. Stay where you are. They've seen you, and if you disappear they'll think I'm hiding something."

"What will they think about Moss?"

"They know about him. The Sioux are very tolerant of the old and the sick. They call him Man-Lost-in-Head." With his eyes on the approaching horsemen, Buck said, "You'll be a curiosity. I doubt if they've seen a woman with hair like yours."

"I could tie a scarf over it."

"No. Stay here by Moss and don't act scared even if one of them wants to touch your hair."

"There are so . . . many of them."

After a word from Buck, Sam moved around behind him and hunkered down.

"Sam doesn't like Indians. It could be the smell. It could be that he knows they would eat him if not for me."

"Eat him?" Kristin felt her stomach quiver.

As the party of horsemen came thundering into the yard, Buck went out to meet them. The white man, dressed in buck-skins, got off his horse and shook hands with Buck. Full-bearded and brawny as a blacksmith, he had a huge head and a mane of black hair streaked with gray. His face was square and homely. She could not even estimate his age.

"Howdy. See somethin's been added since I left." Merry blue eyes darted to where Kristin stood beside Moss.

"Howdy, Gilly. Things go all right?"

"Right as rain. Lost a few, but what the hell. Iron Jaw says to tell his friend he'll watch his herd."

"What's Runs Fast doing here?" He glanced at the brave who had moved his horse out ahead of the others.

"Oh, he's just showin' off. He ain't goin' to do nothin'.

Iron Jaw's the subchief under Red Cloud. He don't dare go agin 'em."

Runs Fast was the only Indian to dismount. He stood at the head of his horse with his rifle in his hand. He wore buckskin britches tucked into knee-high beaded and fringed moccasins but was bare from the waist up except for the beaded armbands around his upper arms and the bead-and-tooth necklaces hung about his neck. His skin was smooth and shiny as if it had been oiled. Black braids entwined with thin strips of doeskin hung down over his chest. He was handsome, and he was arrogant.

Buck went to him with hand extended.

"Welcome to my lodge," he said in Sioux.

Runs Fast took his hand briefly. "I speak your tongue."

"And I speak yours." The two men stared at each other for a long, tense moment.

Runs Fast handed the reins as well as his rifle to another Indian and walked over to where Kristin stood beside Moss. He walked around her, looking her over from her head to her feet. Some inner voice told Kristin to stand still and look him in the eye. It took all her control to keep from cringing when he reached out and snatched the pins from her hair. The long silver braids slithered down her back.

Kristin was aware that Buck had moved over beside her.

"Whose woman?" Runs Fast demanded.

"My woman." Buck struck his chest with his closed fist.

"I will barter for her."

"No."

"Six ponies."

"No."

"Ten ponies."

"No."

"She's but a woman." The Indian's nostrils flared angrily. "Worth no more."

"A woman with silver hair is worth a hundred ponies."

Buck reached out and pulled one of the braids over her shoulder then left his hand there in a gesture of possession. The thumb of his right hand was looped in his belt over the gun that rested against his thigh.

"Ten ponies and two of my wives."

"No. I've seen your wives."

The Indian stamped his foot in fury.

"She make sons with hair like a cloud but she not worth a hundred ponies."

"The sons she makes will be my sons." Buck raised his voice to a level beyond the Indian's and struck his chest again with his fist.

In a lightning move the Indian's hand closed around one of Kristin's braids. He glared at Buck defiantly. Kristin kept her eyes straight ahead.

"I could take what you have."

"She is not worth the life of a brave warrior. She is weak. She cannot skin a deer. She is lazy. Only good for tending Man-Lost-in-Head."

Kristin could not believe her ears. Buck Lenning was talking about *her!*

Still holding the braid in his hand, Runs Fast seemed to consider what Buck had said.

"How is she on blanket?"

Buck's lips curled in a sneer as he gave Kristin a contemptuous look.

"She lies like a dead sheep. Use her and she wails the rest of the night."

Kristin gasped. Only the tight pressure of Buck's hand on her shoulder kept her silent.

"I take this from worthless woman and hang on my lodge-pole."

Kristin felt the sharp jerk on her braid and uttered a small cry of fright. Buck's hand lashed out and closed about the Indian's wrist.

"Cut my woman's hair, and I kill you."

Kristin sucked in her breath and held it. For what seemed to be an eternity not a sound was heard and not a breath taken. Then Runs Fast took his hand from her braid and stepped back, shoved his knife into his belt and crossed his arms.

Buck gently but firmly put Kristin behind him.

"I want no quarrel, Runs Fast. This worthless woman is mine."

"Bah!" the Indian snorted. "She old. Lazy. What woman can't skin deer? She not worth—" He spit on the ground.

"She is old. Lazy. She would be trouble in your lodge. Your wives would hate her because of her hair."

Buck calmly pulled a sack of tobacco from his pocket, thumbed a paper from a pack and rolled a cigarette. After he licked down the side to seal it, he put one end in his mouth and held the sack out to Runs Fast.

"Tobacco?"

The Indian's dark eyes were bright with anger. He snatched the sack of tobacco from Buck's hand and crammed it down into the waistband of his britches, then went to where Kristin had hung the wet clothes. She gasped as he jerked her white underdrawers off the rope line. She had tried to hide them between an apron and a dress. Runs Fast glared at Buck contemptuously, daring him to object. Swaggering back to his horse, he grasped the mane and leaped upon its back. Then with a defiant yell, he raised the underdrawers like a white flag, wheeled his horse and raced back toward the creek. All but six braves and two women followed.

Buck watched the departure, and when the yipping of the warriors was lost in the distance, he went to shake hands with each of the remaining Indians. They spoke for a minute or two, then walked their horses toward the knoll behind the ranch buildings. The women on ponies leading others loaded with supplies followed. Buck returned to where Kristin, seething with anger, was searching on the ground for her hairpins.

"You let him take my . . . take my—" She was so outraged she failed to hear the chuckle that came from the man called Gilly, but she saw the slow grin that lifted Buck's wide mouth and sent lines fanning out from the corners of his eyes. "I see nothing funny about it."

"I thought it a reasonable thing to do."

"The things you said. You insulted me. You said I was lazy, that I couldn't skin a deer. Let me tell you, Mr. Lenning, I could do it if I had to. You made me a . . . laughingstock, ridiculed me!"

"He had to save face, Kristin. It means much to a man like Runs Fast. He offered ten ponies and two wives for you. A big price for one woman. A man can usually get a wife for a couple of wild ponies. He can now say that my woman is worthless and lazy and brag that he took her drawers and I didn't fight him for them."

"Well, for crying out loud! I never heard of anything so . . . silly! I don't appreciate being talked about as if I were a . . . were a cow!" She lowered her head to hide her flaming face. "Did that savage take my hairpins, too? Gustaf brought them to me from New Orleans. I swear to goodness—"

"Moss picked 'em up, ma'am. Don't pay that Injun no mind. He's full a cussedness, but he ain't got no bite a'tall." Gilly pulled an old felt hat off his head when he spoke to her. "Buck did a fair job of gettin' him gone without a face-off."

"Hello." Kristin extended her hand. "I'm Kristin Anderson. Yarby Anderson's niece."

"Howdy." Gilly took her hand and gave it one downward dip, then released it. If he was surprised by who she was, he didn't show it.

"Where are the other Indians going? Are they staying here? Do I fix a meal for them?"

"No, ma'am. They'll set up their own camp, and they've got their women to cook for 'em."

Kristin took Moss's hand. He had closed his fingers around her hairpins and refused to open them.

"You rascal! Give me my hairpins."

"Milk early and shut up the calf with the cow," Moss murmured, and he held his fist tightly closed.

"What in the world am I going to do with you?" Kristin exclaimed. She picked up the button and string he had dropped on the ground. "I'll play with this if you're not going to."

She held on to each end of the loop and twirled the button until the strings were entwined before she pulled them back and forth. When the button was spinning at full speed, Moss dropped the hairpins and reached for the toy.

"Stage took the gold to Junction City," he blurted.

Keeping the rhythm going, Kristin patiently slipped the ends of the loops over his outstretched fingers. Gilly stepped closer to watch the button whirl.

"Now don't that beat all?"

"He catches on quickly to repetitive things he can do with his hands."

"Always was handier than a pocket on a shirt."

"Have you known him a long time?"

"Since I wandered in here four, five years back."

"Then you knew him before he took sick?"

"Yes, ma'am."

Buck's outstretched hand came between them. Kristin took the hairpins from him and put them in her apron pocket, leaving her braids to hang down her back. She knew he was watching her closely, but it would be a while before she'd be able to look him in the face after hearing him discuss her with the Indian. What in the world did he mean about being on the blanket like a dead sheep? Lord of Mercy! She hoped it didn't mean——It surely didn't mean that!

She picked up the bucket of wet clothes. With back straight, head high and flaming face, she crossed the yard to the line.

"Are you through with the washtub?" Buck called.

"I'm through washing, but don't empty the water. I'll use it to scrub the floor after the nooning."

"Haven't you done enough today?"

"A lazy, worthless woman would let all those good soapsuds go to waste. Is that what you're thinking I'll do? I'm not as lazy as you may think, Mr. Lenning. After I scrub the floor, *I'll* throw the water out, then *I'll* do the ironing."

"I don't have an iron."

"I have a small one. It'll do."

Both men waited until she was at the far end of the rope line before they spoke.

"She's got her back up good." Gilly took his hat off and scratched his head. "That part 'bout her bein' lazy hit a raw spot even more'n how she was on a blanket."

"She may not have understood the part about the blanket."

"Does she know about Moss?"

"No."

"How'd she get out here?"

"Caught a ride out on a freight wagon. Forsythe was putting pressure on her to sell."

"She's a right sightly-lookin' woman. 'Pears to be right strong-minded, too."

"And prouder than a game rooster."

Gilly chuckled. "And right now she's madder than a hive of stirred-up hornets. Hope it don't keep her from cookin'. I ain't had my feet under a woman's table since I went to town right after the thaw. I was so sick a eatin' meat all winter, I'd a et a rotten turnip could I find one." Gilly spat out a yellow stream of tobacco juice.

"I didn't know that. I'd a swore you was in a hurry to get to town to the whorehouse."

"That too, by gol!" Gilly's eyes went to Kristin at the line. "She stayin'?"

"For a spell."

"Moss likes her. Remember how he hated that Oglala squaw we got to watch him? First time we left him with her, he bit 'er." Gilly's chuckle was dry as cornshucks. "She got a hold a him and wouldn't turn loose. She was madder than a stepped-on snake. After givin' us both a cussin', she high-tailed it back to her tribe."

"He's going downhill fast, Gilly. Out a breath most of the time. Sleeps a lot, don't eat much."

"I could tell he's lost flesh."

"I got to decide soon—"

"Ya thinkin' she'd leave if she knowed?"

"Not leave, but she'd be put out because I didn't tell her right off."

"Why didn't ya?"

"I didn't know if I could trust her . . . then."

Gilly lifted his nose and sniffed the air like a hound dog.

"By gol, Buck. I'm thinkin' I smell somethin' mighty pretty. Jehoshaphat! It's fresh bread! Ain't it?"

"I thought you liked eatin' burnt Indian bread, stewed gooseberries and boiled prairie onions." Buck was fond of teasing Gilly, whose greatest pleasure in life was eating. They had spent many long winter evenings together and had weathered some rough times.

"It ain't bad if ya ain't et in a week and yore belly hole's dancin' up and down yore backbone."

"Kristin's a fine cook. I'd better warn you, though, she's a stickler for manners and such. She likes things nice. We got a cloth on the table and all that. Don't bring that stinking spit can in the house."

"Well I'll be dogfetched! Where'll I spit?"

"Outside."

"Ya mean get *up* and go *out?*"

"That's what I mean. And don't spit out the door where she'll step in it."

"Time's when womenfolks ain't nothin' but a ache in the arse, fer all their cookin'."

"You need to get housebroke, Gilly." Buck laughed at the sour look on the old mountain man's face and gave him a sound clap on the back. "Get a woman and raise a herd of younguns to take care of you when you get . . . old."

"Bullfoot!"

"It's good to have you back, Gilly. I've not had a full night's sleep since you've been gone."

"I found another one of them oil holes back up in the hills 'bout five miles this side of Crazy Peak. This'n shallower than the other'n. No more'n a couple a barrels of it seeped out in a basin."

"It'd be worth about twenty dollars a barrel if we could get it to a market. There's no way of knowing if the hole would fill up again. It would be more trouble than it was worth. We should get a bucket or two to use to grease wheels. It's not good for much else."

"We ort to get out there and fence it off, is what we ort to do. Them stupid steers would'a walked right in it up to their arse if I hadn't a spotted the sick-lookin' grass around it and a headed 'em off."

"I've had a chance to make a supply of fence posts while I hung around the place. We'll load the wagon and go out tomorrow."

"Had any trouble?"

"Two bushwhackers lay waiting for me yesterday. Had to kill one. Sent the other one packing with the body."

"Ort to a killed 'em both. It's what I'd a done."

"I was relieved to see the women with the Sioux. It meant they were going to set up camp and stay."

"Iron Jaw'll expect pay. He'd take yore woman. He ain't no young buck, but his bone is still hard enough to keep his womenfolk squealin' half the night."

Laughter left Buck's face.

"Iron Jaw or any other man that makes a move toward her will find himself laid out . . . toes up." He turned on his heel and walked away.

"Hummm . . ." Gilly spat again. "Things 'round here is a gettin' t'be mighty interestin'."

During the days that followed Kristin worked as hard as she ever had in her life. Every washday she scrubbed the floor;

and while it was drying, she pressed the wrinkles from the clothes with the small sleeve iron she had brought from River Falls. Lately, after the noon meal, Moss had curled up on his bed like a child and had fallen asleep.

While she worked, Kristin had plenty of time to mull over in her mind the events of the past few weeks and had come to the conclusion that she had a lot to learn about this land and its people, including Buck Lenning.

She had no doubt that he would have killed the Indian that day if he'd cut her hair. Life and death in this wild and unpredictable land hung on such a trivial matter. She had felt like a bone being fought over by two dogs. Yet it had been comforting, she admitted, having Buck's big, solid body next to hers, his hand warm and firm on her shoulder while the Indian fondled her hair.

*This woman is mine! The sons she makes will be my sons!*

Even thinking the words caused an unexplainable quiver in the region of her heart. She shoved the remark about being on the blanket back into the corner of her mind, not really understanding it and not wanting to think about it. It was Buck's way of protecting her, she reasoned calmly. Their deal was that she would cook, tend house and look after his father in exchange for his protection. He was just carrying out his part of the bargain, and that was all she must read into it.

Kristin decided that she liked Gilly Mullany, and would like him more if he would take a bath. He brought the odor of horse dung and woodsmoke into the house with him—not to mention stale sweat. It was a situation she'd have to work on very carefully. You couldn't tell a man that he stank and needed a bath—that is if you wanted him for a friend.

One of the first things she had noticed about Buck was that he was very clean and had kept Moss clean, too. He had shaved twice since she'd been here. Without the dark stubble on his cheeks he looked less sinister. She wondered how long it had been since he'd had a real haircut. It had to be at least a year. From the looks of it, he had chopped it off himself or Gilly had. He hadn't mentioned being in town since the posse had come for Uncle Yarby.

She wondered how Bonnie and Bernie had fared since her leaving Big Timber. Also Cletus and Mrs. Gaffney. She prayed that they hadn't gotten into trouble for helping her. Thinking of town brought another worry to the forefront of her mind. Gustaf had said that he'd come out to Big Timber in a few weeks. What would happen to him if he arrived and went to Mark Lee's office looking for her? Gustaf was used to dealing with rough men, but Forsythe's men were the worst kind, or they'd never have framed an old man like her uncle for murder.

She would have to ask Buck how to get word to Bonnie and Bernie to be on the lookout for her cousin and to tell him where she was.

*"Onyah."* Moss had come silently into the room breaking into her thoughts of Gustaf.

"You're awake. Did you have a good sleep?"

"I'm going far away, *Onyah.* "

There was a note of awareness and also one of sadness in his voice that Kristin had not heard before. A feeling of unease came over her.

"Where do you plan to go?"

"Honor thy father and thy mother, that thy days may be long upon the land which the Lord thy God giveth thee."

His voice, quoting one of the Ten Commandments, his hands clasped in front of him; eyes, faded now, as her father's had done after his long illness, brought back a sudden rush of

memories of her father when he lay on his death bed quoting
Scriptures.

"Ya did that, *Onyah.*"

With misty eyes Kristin saw the old man turn wearily away
and go back to his bed. Her heart thumped in sudden realization. Names Moss had mentioned came charging into her
mind; Anna, her mother's younger sister, Sean, her father's
brother. The breath she had been holding came out in a rush
as another coincidence occurred to her. Buck had never called
his father anything but Moss or old-timer. Never Pa or Papa—

"Oh, my goodness," she murmured in a stricken whisper.
Then, "Uncle Yarby?"

# Chapter Twelve

*The man Buck called Moss was her Uncle Yarby.*

Kristin's emotions ran from anger to sorrow to confusion. Why had he lied to her? What purpose did it serve? When she arrived, he had made it clear that he didn't want her here. He could have told her then that her uncle wasn't dead and that she had no claim to the land. She cringed inwardly when she thought back on the things she had said to him.

*Don't forget that you work for me now, Mr. Lenning.* She had made a complete fool of herself.

As she worked, Kristin went to the doorway from time to time to look at the frail old man sleeping on the bed. He had seemed completely lucid when he spoke to her. A few other times and only for an instant, she had believed him to be of sound mind. He was a small man as her father had been. Only the second generation of Andersons who emigrated from Sweden to Wisconsin were tall, and some, like Uncle Hansel's sons, brawny. Her brother, Ferd, was short like his father, but over the years he had put on weight. She could see no resemblance in either size or features between her brother and her uncle.

*Oh, Uncle Yarby, I would love to ask you why you made me your heir when you had so many others to choose from.*

As she prepared the evening meal Kristin came to the con-

clusion that she would confront Buck Lenning and tell him
that she knew the man he had passed off as his father was her
uncle and that she had every right to stay here and take care
of him, even if the house was not on his land. She was torn
between her anger at Buck for not telling her Moss was her
uncle and gratitude for the care the strange dark-haired man
had given him.

It was dusk when she heard Sam's welcoming bark and
Buck and Gilly rode into the yard. Before leaving, Buck had
assured her that the Sioux who had come to work for him
were perfectly reliable and would let him know if a strange
rider came within miles of the ranch house. She had no idea
how that was to be accomplished, but it was comforting to
know.

The light from the lamp on the table and the one in the
bracket over the work counter cast a warm glow over the
spotlessly clean kitchen. Before dishing up the meal, Kristin
went to the bedroom where Moss was sleeping. His breathing
was even. She touched his forehead. It was cool. She returned
to the kitchen as Buck came in the door.

"Your *father* is still sleeping."

"Is he sick?"

"Of course. You know that."

"I mean . . . sick."

"He isn't feverish if that's what you mean. He's a frail old
man, and his heart could give out at any time." Her mouth
clamped shut and she refused to look at him.

*She had given him yet another chance to say Moss was not
his father, and he had chosen to keep up the pretense.*

Buck noticed immediately her change of attitude and wondered what had happened since the noon meal that had put her
into such a disgruntled state.

"I'll go see about him."

"I just did. Sit down and eat."

Gilly came in with his hat still on his head. Kristin's frosty eyes fastened on it, then moved to the rack beside the door. He got the message, hung his hat on the peg and went to the wash bench.

After the men were seated, Kristin poured coffee and took her place at the table. She ate sparingly of the beef and rice she had prepared and made no attempt to enter into the conversation between Buck and Gilly.

Gilly talked at length about two pesky sinkholes on the land. It was his contention that a river of the stuff ran under Larkspur and they would be lucky if the messy black muck didn't pop up all over the land and spoil the grazing.

Buck asked the old drover about going over to a neighboring ranch to see if Forsythe was still putting the pressure on the owner to sell.

"Ryerson'll cave in," Gilly said with certainty.

"Tell him to hold on a little longer. If he promised to go in and sign as soon as he gets a count on his herd it would give him more time. Anything to stall. A Federal marshal will come as soon as he gets my letter—if he gets it."

"If'n Ryerson's got any gumption a'tall, he'll take his family and hightail it for Helena. Forsythe will take possession of his place, but I'm thinkin' he can't keep it if Ryerson don't sign it over. The courts will go ag'in' what Forsythe is up to."

"He might even have the judge in his pocket. He's got a lot at stake here."

"Dang-bust-it! It ain't right. Ryerson and his boys has put a lot of sweat in that place."

When the meal was over and before Kristin cleared the table, she took the table lamp and went to the other room, leaving the kitchen area only dimly lit by the bracket lamp over the workbench. She placed the lamp on the table beside the bed and bent over Moss. He had rolled onto his back, his eyes were open as was his mouth. He was gasping for breath.

"Buck!" She dropped to her knees beside the bed and took Moss's limp hand.

Buck was beside her in a matter of seconds. She looked up at him with both anger and anguish on her face.

"How could you? I'll never forgive you. Never!"

Buck's dark brows puckered. He didn't understand her anger, but now was not the time to question her.

"What's wrong with him?"

"I don't know!" She moved her hand over his face close to his eyes and he didn't blink. She lifted his hand and it fell lifelessly to the bed.

"Moss, can you hear me?" Buck put his fingers alongside the sunken cheek and turned Moss's head toward him.

There was no response.

"He's in a . . . stupor."

"Will he come out of it?"

"Not if it's apoplexy."

"I've heard of that. It means he can't move."

"My papa had it . . . at the end. So did Uncle Hansel. It's something to do with the blood going to the brain. The doctor said it paralyzes parts of the body. See . . . he can't close his eyes." Tears ran down her cheeks as she cried silently.

"What can we do?"

"Nothing that I know of." She pulled the blanket up around his shoulders.

"Might be it's fer the best." Gilly had come to peer over her shoulder. "Feller ain't ort to live out his days not knowin' nothin' like Moss's been doin'."

Kristin turned on him. "Best for who? Would you think it *best* if you were lying there?"

"Ya can bet yore buttons on it, ma'am. I'd a hoped somebody'd put a bullet in my head long 'fore now."

Buck brought a chair for Kristin, then moved to the other side of the bed. He stood for a long while with his forearm resting on the head of the iron bedstead. He had known this was coming. Moss was a mere shadow of his former self. Still, Buck wasn't prepared for the end to come so soon. He looked at the top of Kristin's bowed head.

*How long had she known?* She had been as patient and as loving with Moss as if he had been *her* father.

The wind came up and rattled the glass window and rippled the tin on the roof. It was as if it had come to carry the soul of the man away. It was a lonely sound—a death sound. Kristin shivered.

Buck left the room and went to where Kristin's shawl hung on the peg beside the door. He returned with it and gently draped it about her shoulders, then went back to the kitchen.

Her Uncle Yarby was dying. Kristin watched the breath going in and coming out of his open mouth. She reached up and gently closed his eyelids. People should not have to die with their eyes open and staring. Holding his thin hand between hers, she began to talk softly to him.

"Uncle Yarby, I wish I could have known you. You're an awful lot like Papa even though he didn't have white hair and a white beard. You really remind me of Gustaf. Gustaf is bigger, much bigger. But both of you have happy dispositions.

"When the letter came, telling me that you had left your land to me, I felt as if you were telling me to spread my wings, fly away and take charge of my life as you had done. Fly away, little bird. Gustaf said that. It's something you would have said.

"For the first time since Papa died I was given a chance to get out from under Ferd's thumb. Now I'll never be able to thank you properly. This Larkspur land of yours is a beautiful place. I promise you, Uncle Yarby, as long as I live, Colonel Forsythe will not have it . . . not legally anyway. It was despicable of him to accuse you of such a terrible crime. Surely God will punish him.

"I don't know why Mr. Lenning didn't tell me about you. I have to think that he had some reason that was logical to him. Even if you don't understand what I'm saying, I want to say it anyway. Thank you, Uncle Yarby. Already I've come to love this beautiful land and shining mountains."

Buck stood in the doorway. It didn't occur to him that he shouldn't be listening. She was hurting, and he wanted to be near her. In the far recesses of his mind, and knowing Moss as he did, he was sure the old man welcomed this release from life. The man he had been was no more—only an empty shell remained. He owed the little man his life. As long as there had been breath in the frail old body, he would have cared for and protected him. His only regret was that he hadn't trusted Kristin from the start, but, hell, how was he to know? He had lived for a year and a half trusting no one but Gilly and his Indian drovers.

Kristin was quiet now. Buck went to sit down on the other side of the bed. She didn't look at him. Didn't speak. She held on to Moss's hand, as if to assure him that he wasn't alone.

Time passed slowly. Buck heard Gilly put wood in the cookstove and open the oven door to allow the heat to take away the chill of the night, then the back door closed as he left to go to the bunkhouse.

When the clock struck midnight, Kristin realized the rasping sound of labored breathing had stopped. She looked quickly at Buck. He slipped his hand under the blanket and over Moss's heart. He met Kristin's eyes and slowly shook his head. She stood and carefully pulled the blanket up over the still face, then quickly left the room.

Buck stayed beside the body of his dead friend for a while. Without his realizing it, tears he hadn't known he was capable of shedding came to his eyes, and one rolled down his whiskered cheek.

"Good-bye, old-timer. You're the pa I never had, the brother I never had, the true friend few men ever find. I hope that wherever you are, you're the old mossback you were when we first met. It may be that you're with Anna, the woman you talked about the time you got drunk and I had to hold you to keep you from going out into a raging snowstorm to find her." Buck wiped his eyes on the sleeve of his shirt. "Don't worry about Kristin and the Larkspur, old-timer, I'll take care of her whether she wants me to or not. And I'll see to it that she has your part of the Larkspur. In a way she's a lot like you—gutsy and determined. It took grit for her to come out here by herself. You've put the world in my hand, old-timer, and I'll do my best to keep it."

When Buck went into the kitchen, he found Kristin filling the dishpan with hot water from the teakettle. He set the lamp on the table and carried the soiled dishes to the workbench. They worked together without speaking. She washed the dishes; he dried and put them away. Just before they finished, he put several pinches of dried tea leaves in the crockery pitcher, filled it with hot water and set a plate over the top so it could steep, as he had seen Kristin do.

Kristin slowly and meticulously cleaned the kitchen area.

When all was done, she hung the dishpan on the end of the wash bench and the wet towels over the string she had hung over the stove. She turned to see Buck holding two cups of tea.

"I'd rather go to . . . my room."

"Drink the tea. If you don't want to talk now, we won't. But soon you have to listen to why I did what I did."

"You deprived me of the few days I could have spent knowing him—as my uncle."

"I'm sorry for that." Buck set the two cups of tea on the table and waited until she sat down, then went to the other side of the table and straddled a chair.

"Why?" Kristin looked up from the cup that she bracketed with her two hands. His light eyes were unusually bright. She could almost believe they were teary.

"I didn't know you . . . and I had to be careful that no one but me and Gilly knew Moss was alive."

"I understand *that*. But later—"

"I was afraid that if you knew your uncle wasn't dead and that you had no claim to the land—you'd leave."

"You think I would have gone off and left you to take care of him when he was my kin and had thought enough of me to leave me his land?"

"Later I knew you wouldn't have done that, and I was waiting for the right moment to tell you. I had finally got up the courage and was going to tell you tonight."

"Did you start calling him Moss after I arrived?"

Buck almost smiled . . . remembering.

"I've always called him that. He called me the youngun, and I got to calling him an old mossback. That's how it started."

"I figure Uncle Yarby to be about sixty."

"Ten years ago he would have been fifty. I was just sixteen years old when I was shot and left to die by a man who wanted my horse. It was in the dead of winter, and I'd have frozen to death before nighttime. Moss's old dog, Sam's pappy, led him to me. I was too heavy for him to lift, so he made a sled out of pine branches and pulled me over the snow to that shack over there in the woods. He told me later I almost died on him a couple of times, but he'd not let me because the ground was frozen. He couldn't bury me and he didn't want to spend the rest of the winter with a stinking youngun."

Buck watched her intently. She didn't smile. Her face was set in a blank mask and her lashes veiled her eyes, allowing only a thin glittering line of blue to show between her gold-tipped lashes. She didn't speak for a long while, and when she did, her voice was a breath above a whisper.

"Who is the man in the grave at Big Timber?"

"I don't know. Gilly found him. There was nothing on him to say who he was. We got the idea to put something of Moss's on him and let someone else find him. If they found Moss dead, they'd stop looking for him. I had no idea that Moss had a will. I thought it would take a while to find next of kin and it would give me time."

Kristin stood, turned her back to him and went to the workbench. Her eyes burned with unshed tears. She had to believe in the man's sincerity. He had done what he had thought best. The small lie he had told was certainly overshadowed by the care he had given to her uncle. How many men would have gone to so much trouble to keep one old man alive?

"Kristin?"

She turned back. Buck was standing beside the table, his black hair tousled as if he had just come in out of a windstorm. His dark face was lined with concern.

"I was too quick to judge you. I think now you did what you had to do."

"Nothing is changed, Kristin."

"I know. For all practical purposes Uncle Yarby died a year and a half ago."

"You will stay?"

She lifted her hands in a futile gesture and her eyes filled with tears.

"I have nowhere to go."

Buck came around the table and gripped her shoulders with his hands. She was too proud to turn away and faced him with tears sliding down her cheeks.

"You have a place. This is yours now. All yours." His voice was smooth, but rough around the edges.

"Not the . . . house."

"It's all yours," he repeated. "If you want it. You like it here, don't you? You like the Larkspur?"

"Yes, but—"

"Do you like it enough to fight for it?"

Her legs trembled, and her voice wavered out of control.

"If I stay, I'll be another Anderson for you to take care of."

"No. We'll be partners . . . just like Moss and I were before he . . . took sick."

Even as he said the words, an inner voice was protesting. *No, not like that. I want you for my life's mate. It's unthinkable that I live my life without you by my side as my wife.*

Without conscious effort he was drawing her closer to him. Finally his hands slid behind her back and she was leaning against him, her head pressed against his shoulder. Buck turned his face into her hair.

"Please, Kristin. Please, stay here with me."

His words echoed to the core of her being. *What did he*

*mean?* She summoned all her determination to ask. Her voice came out thin and weak.

"As housekeeper?"

"That, and only that, if it's what you want."

"It's too soon for it to be anything . . . else."

She moved back to look at him. He didn't answer for such a long while that her eyes wavered beneath the intensity of his. Her lower lip quivered and, as she stared up at him, tears filled her eyes. He lifted a finger and wiped a teardrop from her cheek. Her skin was as soft and smooth as the down on a bird's breast.

*Lord help him to say the right words.* Happiness such as he never dreamed of having was right here in this sweet woman. He had lived his life among rough men while she had known only kindness and plenty. He had scrounged, fought, even stolen in order to eat. And he had killed to stay alive. He was rough, and at times brutal. Life had made him that way. Somehow he had to make her see him as a man who needed love and who had love to give—one who would stand between her and a stampeding herd of buffalo if it came to that.

"I'm trying to say the right words. It's too soon for you, Kristin. If you never want me *that* way, I'll understand. I'm not like the men you knew back in Wisconsin. I've never known a home with a woman in it. I've never even had a home until I built this one. I didn't even know what to buy to put in it."

"You . . . did fine—"

Buck felt a stirring of hope. His chest warmed with the quickening of his heart. He had to find a way to make her want him, not only his protection, but *him*. What would she think if she knew that each night since she came here he had lain in his bunk thinking of her? He had even dreamed that someday she would carry his name, have his children—

"If you say the word, Gilly will take you to Helena, or anywhere else you want to go. I'll stay here and fight for our land." The words were like ashes in his mouth, but words that needed to be said. "I don't want you to stay because you have nowhere to go. I want you to stay because you want to make the Larkspur your home, with me, or without me."

"Like you said, nothing has changed. I never came here thinking I'd meet Uncle Yarby. I'll try not to be trouble—"

"You'll be the sweetest trouble I've ever had!" he blurted and fear knifed through him that he had ruined everything.

*But she smiled.*

A great swell of joy washed over him. He felt a tremor run through him as if the floor they were standing on was shaking. Without thinking about it, he folded her in his arms gently, but securely.

"You won't be sorry." His words came from a tight throat.

"I know." Her words were muffled against his neck.

Kristin didn't know when his hands slid from her shoulders down her back to cross and splay over her rib cage. It seemed so natural to be standing there close to him, enfolded in his arms, leaning on his strength. Her hands moved, her arms went around him and she hugged his great, hard body to her. She felt the gentle pull of his beard when he bent his head, and pressed his cheek to hers. She heard the thump of his heartbeat, smelled the familiar smell of his buckskin shirt.

She wished that she could stop time and stay there with him forever. But deep in her heart she knew he was only being kind, consoling her in her grief.

# Chapter Thirteen

$\mathcal{B}$onnie set a pitcher of dark sorghum syrup on the table where a half dozen men were eating breakfast and a platter of flapjacks on the back table where two strangers were already on their second cups of coffee.

"Too gol-durn bad to end up like that. The old man was one of the first to settle here."

"Yeah. I liked to listen to the old bugger spin his yarns 'bout the olden days."

On her way back to the kitchen to bring in a platter of fried meat, Bonnie stopped beside the table, not wanting to believe they were talking about the old man who came every morning for his breakfast and who had become so dear to her and her brother. She had to ask:

"Who . . . are you talking about?" Bonnie glanced at the empty chair at the table. She knew before she heard the answer to her question and felt a sickness in the pit of her stomach.

"Old Cletus."

"Did . . . is he . . . hurt bad?"

"He was killed last night, ma'am. Thought you knowed that."

"Cletus Fuller?"

"Don't reckon I ever heard the Fuller part. 'Twas the old man who comes here to eat ever' mornin'."

"Oh . . . no! They wouldn't—" Bonnie's lips began to quiver.

Her hand flew to her mouth and her eyes filled with tears. "You . . . sure?"

"Yes, ma'am. He was pistol-whupped last night or worked over with a club. Hardly a bone not broke, but he had grit. He managed to crawl out to the yard and died there."

"Lady ain't needin' to hear that." A black-bearded railroad worker said crisply. "Can't ya see she's all tore up?"

" 'Tis what happened." After Bonnie went to the far end of the kitchen to lean against the wash bench, the one talking added in a low voice, "I could'a said some dirty, sonofabitchin' coward, too low-down to fight anybody but a old man, broke his leg, then beat his face to a pulp. Feller that found him said it looked like they was scared he warn't dead, went back, found him in the yard and caved in his skull."

"Why'd anyone do that?"

"Old Fuller was a damn good wheelwright in his day."

"Can't think he'd have any money to speak of, but could be somebody wanted what little he had."

"Town ain't what it was. I seen the time when all ya had to look out for was Indians. Nowadays a man's got to be mighty careful. Did they ever find out who busted up Bernie?"

Someone gave a derisive snort. "Ain't likely with the lawman we got."

"I ain't heard a word, and it's been over a week."

"That cold-eyed feller that usually sits at the back table ain't here this mornin'."

"Some say he's a hired gun."

"Might be. But I'm thinkin' beatin' a one-legged man and a old feller like Cletus ain't his style. He'd not want to get hisself dirty. Wouldn't doubt him walkin' up and shootin' 'em in the head."

Bonnie just faintly heard the murmur of conversation around

the table. She cried quietly for a few minutes, then washed her face with a wet cloth and dried her eyes. Tandy, the old camp cook they had hired to help out until Bernie was able to work again, carried a platter of meat to the table and then went to the cookstove and ladled out flapjack batter onto the iron grill.

The screen door opened and Mike Bruza, followed by a tall, thin, unkempt looking man, came into the eatery. Mike stood just inside the door while his small, narrow-set eyes traveled over each person in the room. They finally landed on Bonnie and traveled up and down her body like a searching hand.

"Mornin', darlin'. I'm here."

Bonnie's lips curled in a silent sneer before she turned her back. Sudden silence filled the room. Mike and the man with him sat down at the far end of the rear table occupied by the two strangers who were eating a stack of flapjacks from the platter Bonnie had set on the table.

Mike was in a good mood. He laughed too loud and talked too loud to the hawk-nosed man who wore his two guns strapped to his thighs.

"I like to eat my vittles served up by a purty gal. Ain't she just as purty as a speckled pup? Fry me up a half dozen eggs, darlin'. I'm hungrier than a ruttin' moose."

"You look like one, too." Bonnie's voice was loud and clear and filled with suppressed anger. She wrapped a rag around the handle of the coffeepot and refilled the cups on the front table.

Mike guffawed. Not a sound came from the other men in the room. Bonnie went back in the kitchen.

"Ya want that I wait on 'im, miss?" During the week Tandy had been working with Bonnie, he had become exceptionally fond of the troubled young woman. He scooped the flapjacks off the grill and filled the platter.

"No. I'll do it when I get around to it."

A red cloud of rage for what had been done to Cletus by Kyle Forsythe's bullyboys had settled over Bonnie. It calmed her and blotted out her grief, her fear and her common sense.

"Purty little split-tail," Mike bellowed. "Brin' my coffee. If I have to come get it, I'll get me a kiss for my trouble."

Bonnie ignored him and went to the strangers sitting at the end of the table.

"Can I get you something else? The sign says eat all you want."

"Nothin' more for me, ma'am, 'cepts maybe more coffee." The older man spoke with a distinctive Texas drawl.

"You, sir?" Bonnie looked from one man to the other thinking they could be father and son. She judged the young man to be near her and Bernie's age.

"The flapjacks were mighty good, ma'am. I'd be obliged for a few more."

"Guess ya can tell my friend here's just a growin' boy, ma'am." When the older man grinned, his leathery skin crinkled and the drooping gray mustache bracketed a wide, firm mouth.

"I'll tell Tandy to cook up another batch."

"Honey, I'm gettin' tired you ignorin' me." There was an edge to Mike's voice.

"Good," Bonnie retorted. "If I'm lucky, you'll get tired enough to leave."

The room was quiet. Not even the thump of a cup or the clink of eating forks broke the silence. Bonnie once again wrapped the rag around the handle of the coffeepot. She refilled the strangers' cups and turned to go back to the kitchen. Mike reached out and grabbed a handful of her skirt.

"I guess ya didn't hear me, sugartit. Pour my coffee."

"Turn loose my skirt, you sorry piece of *horse-dung!*"

"That ain't no way to talk to the man what's going to take old

Del's place. I'm thinkin' he ain't comin' back. But don't ya worry none, I'll see to it you ain't bothered by nobody . . . but me."

"Del Gomer doesn't have a place for you to take, you . . . pig-ugly dumbhead! You're stinkin' up my restaurant. Get out and take your two-bit friend with you."

"Whoa now, honey." Anger turned Mike's face red, but his voice was dangerously soft. "Yo're bein' a mite feisty. Old Del's not here to ride shotgun for ya. He took the train for Bozeman this mornin'. Yo're goin' to be needin' a man to look out for ya—"

"You rotten coward! I'd sooner be looked after by a rabid dog!" Bonnie spat the words as her anger took control. "Someday the decent men in this town will hang the likes of you who beat a crippled-up old man to death. Hang that land-grabbin' jackass, too."

"Watch yore mouth, gal. You better be knowin' who's boss in this town."

"It isn't you. Not even a mule's ass like Forsythe would put *you* in charge of anything. Now let go of my dress."

"Make me." He leered up at her.

"If that's the way you want it."

Bonnie swung the coffeepot around and tipped it. A stream of steaming hot coffee spilled onto Mike from his chestbone to his crotch.

He let out a roar, sprang to his feet and drew back his fist. "You . . . bitch!"

Eight men were on their feet, but Bonnie saw only Mike's hateful face. She swung the pot at his head and let go. He ducked. The pot hit the wall behind him and splattered his back with the hot liquid.

"Yeow!" His bellow filled the room and spilled out onto the street. He lunged for her.

"Don't . . . touch her."

Mike looked into the barrel of a Texas six-shooter held by the gray-haired stranger.

"Draw and I'll kill you." The Texan's young companion had moved swiftly and shoved the barrel of his gun into the ribs of the hawk-nosed man who crouched with his hands poised over his weapons.

"Godamighty!" Mike was dancing in pain. "Ya goddamn whore!"

The rest of the men in the room were on their feet. Those with guns had drawn them. Tandy stood at the end of the table with a long butcher's knife.

"Don't you dare call me that, you belly-crawling . . . snake!"

"Godamighty," Mike said again. "Ya've scalded me!"

"I'd like nothing more than to peel off your worthless hide!" Bonnie shouted. "You take pay from that thieving scalawag to push folks off their land, beat 'em up, and kill old men. You're cowards, lower than a . . . than a dung-eatin' worm and just as spineless!"

"Ya'd best shut yore mouth!" Mike's humiliation at being faced down by the girl and the strangers overrode the pain of the burns. He started for the door. When he neared Bonnie, he stiffened his arm and shoved her. Instantly the Texan's gun barrel was under his chin, pushing his face toward the ceiling.

"Where I come from we treat ladies with respect. Apologize."

"She . . . started . . . it—"

"*You* started it. You grabbed her dress and told her to make you let go. 'Pears to me she did just that."

Mike rolled his eyes toward Bonnie. He almost choked on the word, but he managed to murmur: "Sorry."

The Texan's young friend prodded the other man toward the door with his gun barrel.

"Put your guns on the counter. I never trust a man with two tied-down guns."

"Goddamn you—"

"Seems to me I've seen your face before. One as ugly as yours would stick in a man's mind."

The man carefully placed two well-cared-for Smith & Wesson pistols on the counter.

"I'll be back for these," he growled menacingly.

The Texan lowered his gun to allow Mike to go to the door. Before he went out, he looked first at the face of each man still standing at the front table.

"I ain't forgettin' this." He directed his next words to the Texan. "Ya made a mistake, mister. If ya got brains a'tall ya'll fork your horses and get outta this town . . . fast." His hate-filled eyes focused on Bonnie. "The cripple got off easy last time 'cause Del stuck his bill in. He ain't here now. Don't try to leave. I'll find ya wherever ya go."

After Mike Bruza and the other man left, Bonnie sank down on a chair at the end of the table as if her legs refused to hold her.

"I've got all of you in trouble. I'm sorry . . . I'm sorry—" She rested her face on her folded arms and silent sobs shook her shoulders.

*Thump, thump, thump.* The door was flung open and Bernie staggered in, the straps holding his stump to the peg loose and only half-fastened. He steadied himself against the counter with his good hand.

"What's going on? Who was yellin'?"

The voice coming from the swollen, cut lips was loud and strident. Both of Bernie's eyes were surrounded with dark bruises, even though it had been ten days since the beating. His battered face was almost unrecognizable to the men who knew him. The fingers on his right hand were spread and bound to small, thin boards.

Bonnie was on her feet instantly.

"I told you to stay in bed. How did you get down those stairs?"

"What did he do? I saw him come in and started putting on my peg."

Bernie spotted the two strangers and reached with his good hand for the pistol stuck in the waistband of his britches. Bonnie moved quickly between them and put her hand out to help her brother keep his balance.

"They're not . . . Forsythe's men. They stood up to Mike Bruza and his flunky."

Bernie looked hard at his sister, then nodded to the men. "I'm obliged. I'd shake your hand, but . . . well, you can see how it is. I'm Bernie Gates. You've met my sister."

"Name's Stark. This young buck is my sidekick."

The young man he mentioned still stood. He nodded to Bernie and picked up his coffee cup to drain it. He was tall and slim with a shock of light sun-bleached hair, clear blue eyes and a noticeable dent in his chin.

Bernie sank wearily down in a chair and mopped his brow with a handkerchief. When his sister brought him a dipper of water, he drank it thirstily. Tandy came from the kitchen with a mop and a rag to clean the mess made by the thrown pot. He straightened his bent back to look up at the tall Texan.

"I ain't much good now. But in my day, I'd a not stood by while a good woman like Miss Bonnie was put upon by the likes of Mike Bruza. And I ain't thinkin' the railroaders would'a hung back long if ya hadn't spoke up. We was glad ya was here, mister."

"Stark." The Texan held out his hand, and Tandy shook it vigorously.

"Things 'round here ain't been good fer quite a spell, Mr. Stark. Not since that land man come to town." Tandy picked up the plate from the table. "Young feller, I'll cook ya up another batch of flapjacks seein' how yores got all coffee-splattered."

"Thanks, but I've had plenty. I was kinda makin' a hog of myself anyhow."

Some of the men had sat back down to finish their breakfasts. Others were preparing to leave when heavy bootheels sounded on the boardwalk, and the door was pulled open with such force it hit the wall and bounced back. The man who stepped into the restaurant had a big tin star on his chest and a shotgun in his hand. Another man crowded into the room behind him.

"Back against the wall," he said to those paying for their meal. "The rest of you stand up and show yore hands."

The barked command came as a surprise. No one moved until the end of the shotgun swung in an arc around the room. All the men at the table got to their feet, except Bernie. The marshal stepped over and tapped him on the shoulder with the gun barrel.

"You! Get up."

Bonnie flew at him. "Get away from him . . . you fat . . . slob! Can't you see he's been hurt."

Marshal Lyster raised his forearm to hold her away. "Get this she-cat and hold her."

He flung the words over his shoulder to an ugly young man with feral features. He was thin and narrow-shouldered. When he made to grab Bonnie with long, bony fingers, the knife she had picked up on her trip to the kitchen appeared as if by magic in her hand.

"Touch me and I'll cut you."

"Well, well, this proves what Mike said."

"And what was that?" Bernie had struggled to his feet.

"Said your sister attacked him with a pot of hot coffee. He's at the doc's gettin' fixed up." Lyster's gaze settled on the two strangers. "Who'er you?"

"Name's Stark."

"Yo're the gunman that drew down on Mike when he tried to protect himself. Drop your guns. You, too." He jerked his head toward the younger man.

"I don't think so." Stark's voice was level and cold. He crossed his arms over his chest.

"What?" The marshal's face went blank with surprise, then livid with fury, his lips baring his big, uneven teeth. "Drop your guns or I'll open up with this shotgun."

"I don't think so," the Texan said again. "You might get off a shot, but it'll go into the ceiling as you're slammed into the wall. My friend will put a bullet right between your eyes while your brain is sending word to your finger to pull the trigger."

Marshal Lyster's jowls began to quiver. To be faced down in front of so many was humiliating, but not enough to challenge this calm, confident stranger.

"I asked you who you was."

"I told you."

"Get out of my town."

"You own it?"

"I'm the law here."

"Lawman!" Bonnie snorted. "He's one of Forsythe's boot-lickers! Ever'body knows that."

"Bonnie! Hush!" Bernie tugged on his sister's arm.

"I'm here to keep the peace." Lyster turned on Bonnie. "You'll go before the circuit judge—"

"Why not just take me to Forsythe? The judge is in his pocket, too."

"Miss Bonnie did what she had to, to protect herself." The black-bearded railroad worker spoke up.

"You goin' ag'in' the law?" Lyster glared at the man. "Watch yorself, or you'll be outta a job."

"What's right's right," the brakeman shot back.

"If you're so hell-bent on holding up the *law*"—Bonnie made the word sound so nasty she was in a hurry to get it out of her mouth—"why aren't you out trying to catch the one that killed Cletus?"

"Hee, hee, hee." Old Tandy laughed, then said with disgust, "He couldn't catch the clap in a whorehouse."

"You're gettin' a mite lippy, Tandy. Old men ort to mind their own business."

"Did Cletus get lippy?" The words burst from Bonnie with bitter sarcasm. "Is that why you or your so-called peace-keepers beat him to death?"

"Old man Fuller was killed by a thievin' Indian or a railroad bum."

"An Indian would cut a man's throat, not beat him to death," Stark said quietly.

"No one asked you to stick your bill in," Lyster snarled.

"Cletus is dead?" Bernie was visibly shaken. "Oh, my God! They killed him!"

Lyster's beady eyes continued to study Stark.

"I ain't through with you. I'll not put up with saddle bums comin' into my town and tryin' to take over. Is that understood?"

Stark ignored the question and asked one of his own. "How does a man get to be marshal around here?"

"By vote of the people. I was legally elected, not that it's any business of yours."

"The way I heard it every man that tried to run against you came up missing, or if they found him, he had a busted head or a broken leg." Bonnie continued to talk even with her brother trying to shush her. She turned to the Texans. "That's how *he* got the job."

"Somebody's goin' to have to take you in hand, gal. Yo're runnin' off at the mouth."

"My name is Miss Gates to you. Go back and tell the man who owns you that my brother and I are getting tired of being pushed around by his hired thugs. The next one that comes in here and lays a hand on me or my brother will get a belly full of buckshot."

When the marshal chuckled, his fat belly moved in an up and down motion.

"Does that go for Del Gomer, too?"

"It may surprise you to know that Del Gomer has never laid a hand on me, or been as insulting as others I could mention." She looked pointedly at the lawman. "Whatever else he is, he's been a gentleman when in my company."

"Is that so? How about on them walks from the church on Wednesday nights . . . in the dark?" he asked with an insinuating leer.

"Yes. Even then. But with your nasty mind you'd find that hard to believe, wouldn't you?"

"I shore would, honey. And I find it hard to believe he stands outside lookin' at yore window 'cause he thinks ya might fall outta it."

"Del will be interested to know that the town marshal is spying on him," Bonnie said sarcastically. "You may have to say that to his face."

"I ain't having no trouble with Del."

"Not yet. But you will after he hears you're so interested in his affairs that you follow him."

The marshal, wishing he had kept his mouth shut about the meetings at the church, screwed his hat down tighter on his near bald head and turned to the men.

"I'll let this go for now. But I'm keepin' my eye on all of ya. One wrong move and yo're goin' to jail. And that goes for you too, Bonnie. Break the law again, and you go to jail just as any man'd do."

"Ya'd put a woman in jail?" Tandy shook his head in disbelief.

"If she broke the law."

"Folks'd not stand fer it less ya had a damn good reason. 'Specially a woman like Miss Gates." The black-bearded railroader slapped a coin down on the counter.

"This is some town you got here, marshal," Stark said drily. "Never heard of it bein' against the law for a woman to defend herself."

"My advice to you is, keep your nose out of things that ain't yore business and get out of town."

"Where can I find Forsythe?"

The town marshal paused at the door and looked back at the Texan.

"What'd ya want him for?"

"That's my business."

"Then find him yourself."

# Chapter Fourteen

*T*he two men stood on the edge of the boardwalk and looked up the dusty street toward the swinging sign that said LAND OFFICE. They had been in towns such as this one many times. Dillon liked to refer to them as jackass towns. One main street and one jackass, like the marshal they had just met, trying to run things.

"What do you think, Cleve?"

"Think Buck had it spelled out about right. I want to find out more about the old man that was beaten to death. After we see Forsythe we'll slip back in and have a talk with the girl and her brother."

"I'm not sure I want to see the son of a bitch."

"Change yore mind? It's a long way to come to change your mind, Dillon."

"I haven't changed it."

Cleve Stark dropped his cigarette butt on the porch and smashed it with the toe of his boot. His hand rested for a moment on the shoulder of his young friend.

"Then it's best we find out if yo're goin' to be able to stomach him. I'm thinkin' we're in for a long haul before we can report back to that judge in Bozeman."

They went down the walk and at the end of the street turned the corner and headed for the livery.

"The first thing we'd better do is buy us a couple of good horses."

They had come up from New Mexico on the stage, stopped in Timbertown, Wyoming Territory, to visit Dillon's foster brother Colin Tallman and their friend T.C. Kilkenny, then had come on to Bozeman where they met Garrick Rowe, a lumberman friend of Colin's and T.C.'s. Rowe had taken them to see Judge James Williams. After telling the judge about the letter Stark had received from Buck Lenning, they took the train to Big Timber.

Arriving in Big Timber at dusk, they had looked over the town with experienced eyes before they checked into an old frame hotel near the rail station. It was shabby, but clean. The owner had assured them the place was as free of bedbugs as he could make it. The smell of kerosene was in the air, and they believed him.

At the livery, an old man sat in a chair tilted back against the side of the building. When the two men approached, he tipped forward and the two front legs of the chair struck the ground. He stood as they neared and nervously moved back away from the door. Two well-armed strangers could mean only one thing—Forsythe had hired more gunmen.

"Howdy," Cleve said. "Fine mornin'."

"It is."

"Got any horses for sale?"

"A few."

"We're in need of a couple."

"What I've got's in the pen yonder." The man motioned toward the pole corral attached to the livery barn.

"Mind if we take a look?"

"Help yourselves."

Cleve and Dillon ducked under the poles and entered the

corral. Fifteen minutes later they came out leading a buckskin and a sorrel, both big horses and the best of the lot. The liveryman stood where they had left him. They tied the horses to the hitching rail.

"Got saddles?"

"Inside."

They followed the short, bowlegged man as he limped into the barn. A peeled log set on crossbars held a row of saddles.

"Take yore pick. Comes with the horse. Warn ya, them horses come high."

"Expected it." Dillon shouldered an almost new double-cinched saddle. "This'll do for me."

"I'll take this one with the high back." Cleve pulled the saddle from the pole, carried it out and threw it on the back of the sorrel.

"Mind if we give them a try?"

"Couldn't do nothin' about it if I did."

The liveryman eyed them guardedly. He lifted his shoulders in a gesture of helplessness. His action told Cleve the man expected them to ride off and not return.

"How much?"

"Forty each."

First Cleve and then Dillon counted out the money and put it in the surprised man's hand.

"We'll be back in thirty minutes for a bill of sale or a refund."

"Fair enough."

The two men walked the horses to the edge of town, then trotted them to a road past the timber.

"H'yaw!" Dillon slapped the buckskin on the rump. "Let's see what you can do." The horse's muscles bunched. He sprang forward in a leap that left the sorrel behind. "H'yaw!"

The big horse moved out, running hard and free on the hard-packed road. Dillon looked over his shoulder to see the sorrel a length behind. He leaned over the saddle horn. "Go, boy! Go!" he urged. The powerful legs stretched, and a minute later they were more than ten lengths ahead of the sorrel. Dillon let go with a whoop of youthful laughter.

The men pulled the horses to a trot, turned and walked them back to town.

"By golly, Cleve, we lucked out."

"That buckskin likes to run."

"Danged if he don't! He wasn't even winded when I pulled him up."

As they rode toward the livery barn they saw the proprietor with his back to the building and two men standing rather close to him. One of them was the hawk-nosed man who had been in the eatery with Mike Bruza.

Cleve and Dillon pulled the horses to a stop behind them.

"Give 'em the money back," the hawk-nosed man demanded, and jerked his head toward Cleve and Dillon. "We had our sights on them horses. Told ya we'd be back."

"They bought 'em, fair and square—"

"I ain't carin' 'bout fair and sqaure, ya old crippled-up pile a shit." He took a fistful of the liveryman's shirt and shoved him against the barn.

"Whoa now!" Dillon stepped down from his horse. "Let go of him. He had horses to sell. We bought 'em. You got a thing to say, say it to me."

The man ignored him and spoke sharply to the old man, emphasizing his words with a slam against the wall.

"Give back the money or I'll wring yore scrawny neck."

"Maybe your ears are plugged up." Dillon's voice was equally sharp. "I said back off."

The man spun around in a crouched position. His face resembled that of a snarling wolverine. His hand hovered over the gun on his thigh. He only had to bend his elbow to grasp the butt.

"Ya stickin' yore nose in, *boy?*"

"You might say that, *shithead.*"

"Ya know who I am?"

"Reckon I do. Just now figured it out. You're a two-bit gunslinger named Greg Meader. Seen that ugly face of yours on a poster down in Oklahoma Territory not more than a week or two ago."

"You wantin' to try me, *boy?*"

"No, but reckon you're itchin' to try me. So make your move."

Meader bent his elbow. Before his hand grasped his gun butt he was looking into the business end of Dillon's gun. He choked with surprise and fear. He stared blindly at the tall, light-haired man and waited for the bullet that was sure to come. It was beyond belief how fast he had drawn the gun. Meader had outdrawn every man he had ever challenged—until now.

"You got a horse here?" Dillon asked calmly.

Meader nodded, his mouth so dry he couldn't speak. He didn't dare take his eyes off Dillon.

"Get on it before I change my mind. I don't like your face and I don't like you. You're nothing but a cocky little bully who picks on a smaller, weaker man. Ride out, or I'll kill you and collect the reward."

"What's . . . what's stopping ya?"

"The crooked marshal, Lyster. The money would go in his pocket unless I hang around for a month or two to collect it. And I'm not doing him any favors."

"Get the horses," Meader said over his shoulder to the other man.

"Do they owe you for board?" With his eyes still on Meader, Dillon spoke to the liveryman.

"Two bits."

"Pay up."

Meader tossed a coin into the dirt at the man's feet.

Cleve and Dillon watched the two men mount tired, underfed horses.

"I ain't forgettin' you." Meader's eyes glowed with pure hatred.

"You'd better not if you want to live. I'll be coming to collect that reward."

"What's yore name?"

"Bertha Mae Sutton."

"Bertha Mae Sut—? That's a woman's name."

"Yeah. I'm a woman dressed up like a man. Ain't that a lark? You've been outdrawed by a woman. I'll spread the word that Bertha Mae backed down Greg Meader. You'll be the laughing-stock in every saloon in the West."

Spitting on the ground at Dillon's feet, Meader put his heels to his horse's flanks and gigged him cruelly. The tortured animal squealed in protest, then took off at a run.

The liveryman's eyes went from the stubble of whiskers on Dillon's chin down his six-foot, muscular, rock-hard frame. Then the old man began to chuckle.

"Ah . . . shoot!" He slapped his hat against his thigh.

Dillon grinned. "Throws 'em off every time."

Cleve removed his hat, wiped the sweat from his brow with his sleeve and slapped it back on his head.

"I'm getting too old for this, Dillon. I just got a couple hundred more gray hairs."

"You hadn't ort to a worried. He was just a show-off." Dillon laughed, then said, "A man with two guns is usually a lefty. His left holster was more worn than the right. I was watchin' his left hand."

"Do you get many like them?" Cleve asked the liveryman.

"Lately I do."

"Meader was in the eatery this morning with a man called Mike Bruza. Know him?"

"He's a mean 'un. Got about as much sense as a loco steer. Just right, though, fer what he's used fer."

"We didn't aim to cause you trouble," Dillon said. "But I wasn't giving up this horse. He's a beaut." He rubbed the buckskin's nose and the horse nuzzled his shoulder.

"Feller gets used to trouble these days."

"Did you know the old man who was killed last night?" Cleve asked. "We heard talk about it this morning."

"Ever'body knew Cletus Fuller. He was a old-timer 'round here. Give ya the shirt off his back if ya asked for it."

"It was a mean way to kill a man in order to rob him."

"Bullfoot! Cletus didn't have nothin' to be robbed of."

"Someone must have had it in for him."

"Mister, there be two sides in this here town. A man's either for the big muckety-muck or ag'in' 'im. Me, I be doin' my dangest to straddle the fence."

"Good idea."

"You plannin' on stayin' long?" the liveryman asked hopefully.

"Long enough to buy some land. Who do we see?"

"Harrumpt! Ain't but one man to see. Forsythe."

"Is he the only land man? How about the banker?"

"Banker don't go to the outhouse without askin' Forsythe.

There ain't a lot of sellin' goin' on, 'cepts *to* Forsythe. He's buyin' up ever'thin' in sight."

"Must have a lot of ready cash."

"Don't need a lot at what he's payin'."

"Where can we find him?"

"He's got a land office up over the bank. What I hear is he does most of his business at home."

"Where is that?"

"A street over. Big house with two brick chimneys. Fanciest house in town. Ya can't miss it."

"You got a couple of stalls we can rent?"

"Ya bet. Bring 'em on in."

After leaving the livery, Cleve and Dillon walked back up to the main street, crossed over and headed for "the fanciest house in town."

In the fanciest house, Kyle Forsythe stood before Marshal Lyster and Mike Bruza, who were seated in two wooden chairs next to the wall of his study. Forsythe was at his best when he was on his feet looking down at his underlings. His anger was directed at Mike.

"Goddammit! I told you to leave the Gates girl and her brother alone. As soon as Del's back is turned, you're over there. What the hell did you do to her?"

"I asked for coffee. She threw the pot at me."

Kyle's lips curled. "I suppose that was all there was to it."

"All that mattered." Mike grimaced when his burned back touched the back of the chair.

"I doubt if Del will think it was all that mattered." Kyle sat down in the swivel chair by the rolltop desk, leaned back and laced his fingers over his abdomen. "You know what happened to Cliff Miller."

"That killer shot him in the back."

"You're wrong. He got it right between the eyes where you'll get it if you bother Bonnie Gates. Del's got a hard-on for that woman."

"Goddammit! It was her fault. I'll be walking spraddled for a month. If I hadn't moved back when I did, the bitch would'a ruint me."

"What a pity. You'd have to give up screwing that skinny whore down at Flo's."

"The closer the bone the better the meat, I always say. A man takes his pleasure where he can get it."

"Don't expect me to interfere when Del comes looking for you."

"I can handle 'im."

"Like you handled old Fuller?" Kyle's hands went to the arms of the chair and he sneered at Mike.

"I didn't do that."

"Who did?"

"Greg Meader. I told him to find out what the old man knew about where that Anderson woman went. He got hisself carried away and went too far."

Kyle looked at Mike without speaking for so long that the man began to fidget. Finally he spoke to Lyster.

"What about the two gunmen at the café?"

"They won't give no trouble. I told 'em to get outta town."

"Who were they?"

"Texans riding through, I think."

"I don't pay you to think."

Lyster's jaws turned red under the rebuke.

"They're gone. I saw them ride out."

Kyle lifted the lid of his cigar box, let it fall and shouted: "Ruth!"

"Yes." The woman's voice came from outside the door.

"My cigar box is empty."

"I'll get another one."

A minute later, Ruth DeVary came into the room, keeping her back turned to the men in the chairs, she set a box of cigars on Kyle's desk. He looked up at her and smiled.

Ruth left the room quickly, her eyes down, her head turned to the side. Both she and Kyle failed to see Mike's elbow nudge Lyster.

"All right." Forsythe left the word hanging and lit a cigar. "What do we have?"

Mike answered. "Fourteen men waiting over near Cedar Bend. With me, Greg Meader and Lyster, seventeen."

"If I ride out to the Larkspur who'll keep peace here?" Lyster blustered.

Forsythe ignored him. "We'll wait till Del gets back. He's worth ten of your so-called gunmen."

Mike's face reddened and he ground his teeth. "If he don't have his mind on pussy," he muttered.

The loud clap of the brass door knocker sounded. Forsythe gave Mike a disgusted look and shouted:

"Ruth, see who it is." Then, "You two get out of here. And stay away from the Gates woman and her brother. I don't want any trouble with Del. It seems I'm going to have to depend on him to get things done."

Dillon's mind was too occupied to notice and appreciate the deer heads etched in the thick beveled glass of the double door. He was searching his memory for information about the man he was about to meet.

"The bastard!" Dillon muttered.

Cleve looked at him sharply. "Want to back out? This isn't something you have to do."

"Hell, no! I want to see the son of a bitch."

"Don't forget the job we have to do."

"I'll give nothing away . . . yet."

The door opened. A neatly dressed woman stood there. Both men were startled to see that she had a dark bruise on her cheekbone and the corner of her eye was swollen shut. However, she smiled and greeted them politely.

"Good morning."

"Mornin', ma'am." As Cleve spoke, they took off their hats. "We'd like to see Mr. Forsythe about buying some land."

"Won't you step in. He's busy at the moment, but you can wait here in the foyer and I'll tell him you're here."

Ruth opened the door and stepped back to allow them to enter. Cleve and Dillon shared a questioning look. After closing the door she walked down the hallway that divided the lower floor of the house and stopped at an open doorway. She hesitated, evidently waiting for her presence to be acknowledged.

"Someone to see you about buying some land, Colonel."

"Send them in. These *gentlemen* are leaving."

The woman beckoned. Dillon and Cleve walked down the hall and were about to step into the room but the doorway was blocked by Marshal Lyster. Mike Bruza stood behind him.

"Hello, again," Dillon said pleasantly. Then to Mike, "How are your burns? That hot coffee didn't get to your little old peanut, did it?"

"None a yore goddamn business!"

"Well, then, how about your back?" Dillon raised his brows.

"Listen to me, you smart-mouthed—"

"I thought I told you fellers to get outta town." Lyster interrupted with a rasp of authority in his voice, his eyes darting to Forsythe, who was still seated in the swivel chair.

"Ya *advised* us," Cleve said calmly. "Is it against the law not to take yore advice?"

"We don't put up with slick gunmen in this town."

"We understand that, marshal," Dillon replied, with his hands at his waist. He teetered back on his heels and grinned down at the shorter man. "That's why we ran Greg Meader out of town for you. Did you know that his face is on a wanted poster?"

"Not on any poster I've got."

"Too bad. There's a two-hundred-dollar reward—dead or alive."

"Then why didn't you kill him?"

"You'd a liked that. When the reward came in a couple months from now you'd a had yourself a high old time on money I earned."

"I'll be keepin' my eye on both you fellers," Lyster said threateningly, and moved to go out the door. "One wrong move, and I'll lock you up."

"You'd better get ya a better jail than what you got."

"It'd hold you."

Cleve knew Dillon continued to bait the marshal because he was nervous about facing Forsythe.

"I'd not mind a bit being locked up with Miss Gates. You goin' to put us both in that little old cracker box?"

"What about Miss Gates?" This came from the colonel, rising from his chair. "You threatening to jail Miss Gates?"

"Naw. He's . . . just shootin' off his mouth, Colonel."

"Get out . . . both of you. I'll see to you later if Del don't beat me to it."

Cleve's eyes honed in on Forsythe. He saw only a faint re-semblance between this man and the Yankee captain who had been in charge of the troops assigned to guard Judge Van Winkle some eighteen years ago when his train joined the freight-wagon train crossing Indian Territory. Forsythe was heavier now; his hair was thinner on top and gray at the temples, as were his mustache and short beard. Cleve doubted if the man remembered him. At that time Forsythe had considered himself far above the freighters and had paid them scant attention.

Cleve glanced at Dillon. He was looking at everything in the room, *except* Forsythe.

"Name's Stark." Cleve held out his hand. "The young feller here is my sidekick. He and Bruza didn't hit it off too well this mornin'."

"Glad to meet you, Mr. Stark. You, too, young man. Have a seat."

Dillon was staring out the window and never offered his hand. He remained standing while Cleve took the chair vacated by Lyster.

"The marshal told me about the set-to at the café. Bruza gets to feeling his oats at times."

"Where we come from ladies are treated with respect."

"And where is that?"

"We came up from Kansas."

Kyle glanced at Dillon standing beside the window and frowned.

"I invited you to sit down."

"I choose to stand." Dillon bit out the words, turned and stared at Kyle with hard blue eyes.

"Then suit yourself."

"I usually do."

Kyle looked at him for a moment with a look that had intimidated men much older than this one. It didn't work. Dillon stared back. Kyle shrugged and turned to Cleve.

"My housekeeper said you wanted to buy land. What do you have in mind?"

"What's available?"

"It's a big country out there."

"Do you have a map?"

Kyle went to the far wall and loosened the strings that held a rolled-up canvas. When let down it showed a large map of central Montana Territory. Cleve moved closer to study the map, but Dillon backed away from the colonel. Anger and resentment ate at him. Here in this room was the man he had despised from the moment he had learned about him. He ached to slam his fist into that arrogant face. Cleve's voice came from across the room, and Dillon tried to focus on the reason he and Cleve had come here.

"Point out the sections not already taken."

"Any of this area. The bank will finance, but with a sizable amount of money down."

"Where is the land set aside for the Sioux?"

"There's not many Sioux in the area. They've moved out since the Little Big Horn battle in '76."

"How about the section called Larkspur?"

"It's no longer available."

"That's a big section. Looks like it was owned by two parties." Cleve put his head close to the map and squinted to read the small print.

"Fellow named Anderson had most of it."

"Who owns the part that extends up into the mountains? 'Pears to me this land is boxed in by Anderson's."

"Fellow named Lenning owns this chunk. He'll be giving it up when the new owners take over the Larkspur."

"Who are they?" Cleve asked casually.

"A group of investors here and in Bozeman."

"I may go see if they're interested in selling. I'm fronting for a Kansas City banker who's sending up a herd of longhorns."

"Good grazing land over around Miles City. Land is opening up north of Helena, too."

"He wants an area here along the Yellowstone. Are you sure the Larkspur isn't to be had?"

"Not a chance. New owners will be taking possession in the next few days."

"How about Lenning? Will he sell?"

"That land would be no good for what you want. You'd have to cross the Larkspur to get to it. Besides, Larkspur controls the water."

Cleve turned away from the map to see his young friend's eyes riveted on Forsythe and decided they had better leave before Dillon exploded. Not that it mattered much now, but it would be helpful if they could keep up the pretense a little longer.

"Well, that's that. Thanks for your time." Cleve prodded Dillon ahead of him out the door and down the hallway, aware that Forsythe was close behind them.

"Sorry I couldn't help you." The colonel opened the door and stood aside.

Dillon paused, turned, and looked at Forsythe with an expression of searing contempt.

"I just bet you are."

"What did you say your name was?" Kyle asked, puzzled by the dislike evident on the young man's face.

"Didn't say."

"Why not? You ashamed of it?" Kyle's temper began to simmer.

"Proud of it. Just didn't think it any of your goddamn business."

"Then get out of my house and don't come back."

"Oh, I'll be back, Colonel! You can bet your sorry life on it."

Dillon followed Cleve out the door. He had no more than cleared it when Forsythe slammed it so hard the doorframe shook.

"Goddamn, rotten, sonofabitchin' piece of horse-dung," Dillon muttered.

"Cool down, son. He ain't worth gettin' all het up over."

"I wanted to knock that smirky, superior look off his face. I wanted to break his . . . rotten neck."

"If things work out right, we'll get him where it really hurts. Let's nose around and see what we can find out."

"Impudent young pup!" Forsythe snarled. "If I had him under my command for a month or two, he'd learn some manners. He'd learn to treat his superiors with respect. Ruth!"

"I'm here, Kyle." Ruth came halfway down the open stairway and stood beside the railing.

"What are you doin' up there? Hiding?"

"I'm not exactly proud of my face, Colonel."

"Then take care that you don't provoke me again. What did they say when they came in?"

"Who?"

"Stupid bitch! The two men who just left."

Ruth's face flamed. Pride kept her from cowering.

"They said they wanted to see you about some land."

"Is that all?"

"That's all."

"Go get Lee."

"You want me to go out on the street? People are sure to ask what happened to my face."

He looked at her for a full minute. She refused to look away.

"Get that idiot that hangs out back in the carriage house. Tell him to be damn quick. Another thing, Ruth. I've seen you sneaking him plates of food out the back door. He's been eating as good as I have. It's going to stop."

"I wasn't sneaking. You don't pay him, Kyle. He works for his board."

"Then throw him a bone once in a while."

Kyle Forsythe flopped down in the swivel chair. He had an uneasy feeling about Stark and the insolent young pup. Their story didn't ring true. If a Kansas City banker was interested in bringing a herd of longhorns up here, he would have heard about it.

*They were hired guns. But who had hired them?*

# Chapter Fifteen

On his way back from the bunkhouse where he had shaved and put on a clean shirt for the burial, Buck paused to look at the black scarf tied to a nail beside the door. It was but another reminder of the differences between him and the lady who lived in his house. It would never have occurred to him to put the symbol of death on the door. But Kristin had thought it proper and had put it there out of respect for her uncle.

Even though he had cared deeply for Moss and was grieving for him, Buck would have simply wrapped him in a blanket and buried him. It was Kristin who had insisted that he be washed and dressed in black britches and a freshly ironed white shirt. She had combed his hair and placed his hands on his chest.

During the night Gilly had put together a burial box out of old wagon plank. The box had been lined with a blanket before Moss was placed in it. The coffin was now in the wagon Gilly was bringing around to the back of the house.

"Kristin, we're ready to go."

Dressed in her black skirt, her white blouse covered with a black wool shawl, Kristin came out into the sunlight clutching a Bible. Her face was pale and her eyes, dark-ringed from the sleepless night, were clouded with fatigue. She had wrapped her shiny braids into a crown and pinned them atop her head. She was so pretty, even in her sorrow, that Buck's eyes were continually drawn back to her.

"I don't have a black hat," she said, and looked as if she would burst into tears.

"Moss would be glad. Remember how he liked to touch your hair?" Buck gently gripped her elbow and guided her toward the wagon.

"Is it far?"

"Not really, but it's too far for you to walk today. You're worn-out. We'll ride here on the tailgate."

He lifted her to sit on the end of the wagon, then sprang up beside her. When the wagon moved past the bunkhouse and the corrals, on a grassy plain beyond the ranch buildings the Sioux came into view. Several women had stopped work to watch them. Two small children squatted in the area between the two cone-shaped, hide-covered shelters. A cradleboard was propped against a tepee pole.

Kristin waved at the women. They watched, silent and still.

"Is it not their custom to wave?"

"They are a little . . . ah . . . suspicious of you," Buck explained.

"Why? I am a woman just as they are."

"They're shy. I doubt that they've seen a woman with hair like yours. And I think they admire the way you stood and didn't cringe away from Runs Fast when he was going to cut your braid."

"I was able to do that because you were beside me."

The wagon wheels bumped over the uneven prairie ground. The grass was so high that it almost reached the bottom of the wagon, and their feet, hanging from the tailgate, sliced through it. The wagon headed for a knoll back of the ranch buildings where a lone pine tree stood as a silent sentinel. At first light, Buck and Gilly had gone there to prepare Moss's final resting place.

"Why did you choose this place?"

"Someone else chose it for a burial ground. Not long after I came here, Moss and I found a small grave covered with stones. We figured it was the child of a settler passing through. A few years later we buried one of our drovers here, and right after that a fellow who had been shot came in. We never did know who shot him or how he managed to stay on his horse. Guess he was determined not to die out there in the mountains all by himself."

"Was the drover you buried here an Indian?"

"No. The Sioux take care of their own dead. He was a drifter who happened by and worked for his board. At the time we couldn't afford to hire drovers."

"You get along well with the Indians."

"Yes. By and large they are good people trying to hold on to their way of life. But there are bad ones among them just as there are bad whites."

"Tell me about Uncle Yarby . . . back then."

"Moss was small, quick and wiry. Always good-natured. He could outwork a larger man and liked doing it. When I was sixteen, I was taller and heavier than Moss and had to struggle to keep up with him.

"He could spin a yarn that would last an hour; and even though you knew he was making it up as he went along, you didn't want it to end." He looked directly at Kristin. "I learned about the world outside this territory from Moss's tales."

Buck felt a pang of guilt. Moss was lying dead in the box behind him, and he was enjoying this short time with Kristin. He had never talked much, being one to hold his thoughts to himself, but it was so easy to talk to her that the words just continued to flow from his mouth.

"I could read only a little when I met Moss, or rather when he found me. He shoved newspapers, books, catalogs and even wanted posters under my nose. He forced me to read until I got to where I liked it."

The wagon stopped. Buck hopped down and lifted Kristin to the ground. The sun was shining brightly and a slight wind moved the branches of the pine tree. The men placed two ropes on the ground beside the gaping hole and set the box on them.

"Bury him facing the east, please."

The box was carefully turned; then, with a rope in each hand, the men gently lowered the box into the ground, removed the ropes and stepped back. When Kristin opened the Bible, they removed their hats.

She stood at the head of the grave and read a Scripture from the Bible, then closed it and held it to her breast while she recited the Lord's Prayer in a low, trembling voice. When she finished, she raised her face toward the sky and began to sing.

*"Jesus, Lover of my soul, Let me to Thy bosom fly, While the nearer waters roll, While the tempest still is high—"*

Her eyes were on the blue sea of the sky, and she was unaware that the big man with the wild dark hair was blinking tears from his eyes.

Sunshine made her hair a bright halo around her face; the wind teased it with its fingertips, and sighed in the grasses around them. Her voice was clear and sweet, full of love and pain. It had an unearthly quality and floated over the grassy knoll like the song of a bird. Buck had never heard anything so beautiful.

Even Gilly, filled with awe and wonder, watched and listened.

There was a moment of utter silence when her song ended. She stooped, picked up a handful of soil and dropped it on the wooden box. Then she stood by, wordlessly, while Buck and Gilly filled the grave. It seemed symbolic that, at that moment, from the forest behind them came the lonely, plaintive call of the mourning dove.

Buck put the shovel back in the wagon and came to stand beside her.

"We'll bring up a load of rock and cover it."

"Do you suppose we could make a marker?" She looked around at the other stone-covered unmarked graves.

"I'll burn his name in a board."

"Someday I'd like to plant larkspur on his grave."

"You can do that in the spring."

There appeared to be no question in the mind of either of them that she would still be at the ranch in the spring.

Gilly climbed up onto the seat.

"No matter what happens now," Kristin said, as Buck lifted her again to sit on the back of the wagon, "Uncle Yarby will stay on his Larkspur until the end of time."

The rest of the day was filled with a strange quiet. Kristin prepared the noon meal. When Buck and Gilly came in to eat, hardly a dozen words were spoken during the meal and none of them were directed to her except to thank her when they left the table. While she was cleaning up after the meal, Kristin saw Gilly leaving the homestead. One of the Indian drovers rode behind the wagon on a spotted pony.

To Kristin it did not seem fitting that she plunge into the cleaning or other household duties on the day a beloved relative had been laid to rest. At home in River Falls only the most essential chores would be performed and the rest of the day spent in remembering.

After wandering about the quiet rooms for an hour, she put on her shawl and left the house. She walked out to the corral and looked at the horses. They appeared to her to be wild and rangy; not at all like the stocky, well-fed horses back in Wisconsin. As she stood there leaning on the top railing, an Indian with shoulder-length hair and a doeskin band wrapped about his head moved among the more than a dozen animals. It was impossible to tell his age. He was short, his face scarred, and his legs bowed. He tossed a rope around the neck of one of the horses, led it through the gate, grabbed a handful of its mane, leaped up onto its back and rode away.

The Indians here were different too, Kristin mused. Back home they had not appeared to be so uncivilized. Here they were more like the country they lived in: wild, fierce and unbroken. Not one time, as far as Kristin could tell, had the Indian looked at her, but she had the feeling that he was aware of every move she made even when she lifted her hand to shoo away a large fly that settled on her cheek.

At the end of the bunkhouse she leaned against the wall and looked toward the mountains. A thin trail of smoke came from the Indian camp. The cone-shaped tepees looked small from this distance. She would like to go there and talk to the women but feared that she would not be welcome. One of the women bent over a campfire, another pounded something with a wooden mallet. The third woman worked on the carcass of an animal that hung by its hind legs from a tree branch. Kristin wondered if they intended to live in those flimsy shelters when winter came.

Beyond the barn stretched a long slope of meadowland,

backed by the woods from which the Indians had come that day. Kristin began to move through the knee-high grasses.

Beautiful monarch butterflies flitted restlessly to and fro. A black ladybug with bright orange dots clung to a blade of grass. When Kristin reached to touch it with her fingertip, the clever little beetle spread its tiny wings and flew, reminding her of an old rhyme.

*"Ladybug, ladybug, fly away home. Your house is on fire and your children all gone."*

She was suddenly overcome with homesickness for Cousin Gustaf, the smell of the river and the rich, black Wisconsin soil.

She paused.

Instead of seeing the grassland leading to the mountains, she saw the road that wound between her father's farm and Uncle Hansel's. It had deep triple ruts made by wheels and hooves and was lined with a thick border of wild plum bushes. It passed the schoolhouse where purple iris bloomed. Tall bushes of lilac grew beside the door and a vine of wild yellow roses climbed the stone chimney.

At the farm, Cousin Lars, the eldest of Uncle Hansel's boys, would be in the open shed beside the barn working at the forge. The sharp smell of singeing hooves would be in the air as he shod the Anderson family horses or those of a neighbor. And Gustaf, her childhood playmate, would come to meet her and tease her with a long, slimy worm or a warty toad.

Unaware that her feet had continued to move, Kristin reached the creek and looked down into the clear water racing over the stones.

"Where are you going?" she murmured. "And where did you come from?"

She walked along the bank of the creek, not thinking to

look back or to note how far she had come from the ranch house. The sun was warm on the top of her head, the air sweet and clean. She stooped to pluck a tiny blue blossom that struggled to survive amid the grass that grew along the creek bank. She held it to her nose and glanced across the stream.

Her heart did a crazy little dance of fear.

Not a dozen yards away, the Indian called Runs Fast sat on his horse watching her. Where had *he* come from? *Why had she not heard him?*

He was bare-chested as before: fringed leggings, beaded armbands around his upper arms. A shiny metal amulet hung from a thong about his neck. Today his braids were entwined with a strip of red cloth and white feathers hung from the ends. He held a rifle in his hand, the butt resting on his thigh. His raven black eyes were fixed on her face as he moved his horse toward her.

*Keep calm. Show no fear.* Buck's words rang in her ears.

It took all Kristin's willpower to stand still. She didn't dare glance over her shoulder to see how far she was from the house. Common sense told her that she would never be able to outrun him no matter how close she was, and it would be better to try to bluff him. So she waited, head up, heart pounding, her face expressionless.

The Indian came close to her, so close, she could have reached out and touched his foot. She stood her ground, hugged the shawl tighter around her and hoped that he could not hear the pounding of her frightened heart. He looked her up and down for a long moment. It took all her control not to cringe when he reached out and snatched one of the pins from her hair. When he reached for another, she stepped back.

"No!"

"You not Lenning's woman."

"I am."

"Not," he hissed angrily. "You not sleep in his blanket."

"How . . . how do you know?"

"I know."

"You don't know."

"You say I lie?"

"I say you are mistaken."

"Mis . . . take-on? What that?"

"Means you *think* you know, but you don't."

"I know. I see it in my dream."

"That's foolish."

"You talk too much. I not like my woman talk back."

"I'm not your woman, and I'll talk any way I please."

*Buck! Buck, where are you?*

Her heart was pounding heavily, and she could not seem to swallow, but she continued to look at Runs Fast squarely, remembering Buck telling her not to cringe.

He lowered the rifle and in a lightning move poked at her crotch with the end of the barrel. She jumped back.

"You got white hair there, too?"

It was a moment before she realized what he meant, but when she did, a hot flood of anger washed over her.

"You . . . you . . . low-down, loathsome creature! You've got the manners of a . . . a hog!"

Her anger had no effect on him. He urged his horse to take another step toward her.

"You no wear white drawers when you my woman. Up," he snapped and swiped her skirt with the end of his rifle. "I want to see."

Kristin gasped in outrage.

"Get away from me, you uncivilized lout! Buck Lenning will kill you when—"

Her words ceased when she saw the Indian's inky black eyes go beyond her. She dared to turn her head in hope that Buck was coming to her rescue.

Renewed fear coursed through her.

Not more than a hundred feet away the Indian who had taken the horse from the corral was motioning with his rifle toward the woods, plainly telling Runs Fast to go.

*What did it mean?*

Runs Fast yelled something and his face creased in an angry scowl. He jerked his head in a negative reply and gestured wildly for the other man to leave.

Kristin turned her back and as if going for a stroll, began to walk toward the ranch house. Runs Fast jumped his horse in front of her.

"You stay."

She stared into eyes as dark as midnight. His handsome face could have been chiseled from stone. The commanding voice of this arrogant savage plucked at her taut nerves, and only a momentary burst of common sense prevented her from yelling vicious words at him. After taking a deep breath to calm herself, she lifted her chin and returned his gaze with one of cool superiority. When she spoke, it was with much more confidence than she felt.

"The next time we meet, I will have my gun. And if you bother me . . . I'll shoot you."

He looked at her with fathomless eyes.

"You name White Flower."

"I suppose you got that from a dream, too."

"It is name," he insisted.

"My name is Kristin Anderson, but call me whatever you like. Just get out of my way!"

"You stay. We talk."

"Get away from me!"

"BOOM!" The sound of a gunshot blasted the silence and echoed in the hills beyond.

Runs Fast looked over his shoulder, then back down at Kristin.

"I come again." To her surprise, he wheeled his pony, crossed the creek and sped into the woods.

Kristin turned to see Buck, on his big gray-spotted horse, coming across the grassland at a dead run. He was hatless, his black hair whipping in the wind. He had fired a warning shot and was shoving his gun back into the holster.

At the sight of him, Kristin's feet moved of their own accord, and she ran toward him. She had held her fear in check, but now tears of relief filled her eyes and blurred her vision. She stumbled as she ran. Her shawl fell from her shoulders and floated to the grass. Buck jumped from the horse before the animal had completely stopped and came to meet her.

They came together, her arms locked around his waist. He held her tightly to him.

"Did . . . he hurt you?" he whispered in anguish.

"No. But I thought . . . he would!"

"I'll kill him if he comes near you again." Buck's relief had turned to anger.

"No." Kristin rolled her head back and forth, her tears wetting his shirt. "It's my fault. I'm sorry—"

Buck wanted to beat the damn Indian to a bloody pulp. Runs Fast already had three wives. He wanted Kristin because it would add to his prestige to have a woman with silvery blond hair and because he believed that she was the woman of a man who had once beat him in a footrace. If the Indian persisted, he would make a trip to the Sioux camp and have a talk with Iron Jaw.

"You told me to stay close to the house, and I didn't obey you."

"It's all right. It's all right." *Pretty woman. Sweet woman.* The wind blew her skirt around his long legs and a strand of her hair across his face. It was like a caress. His heart almost stopped beating when she turned her face, and he felt her warm breath on his neck.

He gently stroked the head of silky blond hair pressed to his shoulder. She had dominated his thoughts since she had come here. At night he lay flat on his back, his chest tight, his face hot, and his manhood tenting the covers. During the day he was alert to her every move, every glance in his direction.

He became aware that she was no longer crying and was standing quietly in his arms. He trembled with the desire to crush her to him, to move his hands down her back to her buttocks, to press her against the aching arousal that tormented him when he was near her. His fingers itched to caress the softness of the breasts pressed against his chest, and he longed to kiss her until she wanted him as much as he wanted her.

*Good Lord! What was he thinking?* He cursed silently to himself. She wasn't for the likes of Buck Lenning, a man who had no idea who his parents were, a drifter, scrounger, and at times a thief.

She had endured more than any woman should since she had come alone to this place and today that arrogant bastard had nearly scared the life out of her. How could she ever accept *him,* the rough, uneducated wanderer her uncle had taken in out of the cold? His arms loosened. He moved back until the delicious softness of her breasts was no longer touching his chest.

"I was praying you'd come," she said in a breathless whisper, and looked up at him with tear-wet eyes.

"I came as soon as I heard the signal."

She moved farther back, but held on to his shirt with both hands as if afraid to let him get away from her.

"Signal?"

"Red-bird whistles. Bowlegs was keeping an eye on you. We keep in touch by birdcalls. It's such an old, well-known trick that hardly anyone pays attention to it anymore."

"You asked him to watch me?"

"Only if you . . . decided to wander off."

"I'm sorry, Buck. I'm sorry to be so much trouble."

"You're talking twaddle. You've been a great . . . help." His voice was rough, his hands on her shoulders gripped hard.

"I'll not be so thoughtless again."

He walked away from her and picked up her shawl.

"I'll give you a ride back to the house."

She stood still as he wrapped the shawl about her shoulders.

"I've never been on a horse."

"Never been on a horse?" he echoed in surprise.

"Not many women ride horses in River Falls. We rode in a wagon or a buggy."

Without being conscious of the action, Buck reached for her hand. When she put hers in it, and laced her fingers with his, he was elated.

"I'll . . . walk with you."

"I'd like to ride the horse . . . if you promise not to let me fall off." She smiled up at him and his heart did a stupid dance in his chest.

"I'll guarantee it."

He took the reins of the ground-tied horse and swung into the saddle. He commanded the big gray to stand still, then removed his boot from the stirrup and told Kristin to step on his foot. When she did, she was pulled swiftly up to sit across his thighs. She gave a small cry of surprise. A strong arm encircled her while the horse shifted restlessly in protest at the extra weight. Another sharp word from Buck and the animal stood still again.

"I'm so heavy!"

"You're not heavy."

"I'll hurt your shoulder."

"Naw. That little cut is mostly healed."

He settled her on his lap and laughed happily as she wrapped her arms around him and clung. Holding her tightly to him with one arm, he used the other hand to handle the reins. The horse responded to the gentle touch of Buck's heels and moved into a slow walk.

"Don't worry. I'll not let you fall."

Kristin's heart pounded with excitement. *She was high off the ground on a horse!* That in itself would have been enough to set her pulses racing, but being held close in Buck's arms was almost more excitement than she could handle. The nearness of him was something she hadn't anticipated. She could feel every nerve in her body respond to his lean hardness. He was warmer and stronger than she imagined a man to be. She felt her hair catch on the whiskers on his chin and snuggled her face in the curve of his neck. A great load of weariness dropped away from her.

"Scared?" he asked huskily.

"Noooo—" She pressed closer to him. His powerful arms not only held her safely in front of him, but also controlled their lively mount.

"I'll find a gentle mare if you want to learn to ride." His voice was deep and soft, close to her ear, and it trembled just a little.

"I've always thought it would be grand to get on a horse and ride away into the forest. Do you think I could?"

"Not alone, but you could with me. You'd have to rig up something to wear."

"Would it be . . . outlandish if I wore a pair of Uncle Yarby's britches?"

"Not at all. I was going to suggest it."

"I'm sorry I wandered away and caused you to have to come after me."

"Don't worry about it."

"Runs Fast said he'd be back." Kristin tilted her head so she could see Buck's face. His wild, dark hair was blowing in the wind. She just managed to resist the urge to touch it. "I don't understand why he's so determined. What man would want a woman who didn't want him?"

"He's not been turned down before. It hurt his pride."

"He says I'm not your woman. He saw it in a dream."

"He's vain and has more pride than brains. Because Crazy Horse took another man's wife, he thinks he can, too."

"But . . . I'm not your wife. Oh . . . oh—"

The horse tossed his head protesting the slow walk. Buck's arm tightened around her.

Kristin dared not look up at him again. She pressed her face to his shirt and kept it there. She was aware of the smooth easy stride of the horse as he carried them easily across the open ground and of the wind that stirred her hair. When she finally lifted her head to look down, her fear was gone in the sheer exhilaration of the ride. Her eyes, bright with excitement met his.

God help him. The full realization of what had happened to him hit him with the force of a thunderbolt! He loved this woman with all his heart and soul. *You fool! You miserable fool!* He would hold the secret in his heart and never tell her, for he'd not be able to endure her scorn if she knew.

With anguish Buck realized that he was what he was, and she was what she was. Out here on the Larkspur she was grateful for his protection. In town she would be ashamed of his rough looks and rougher ways. She deserved a preacher, a banker, or even a merchant. No way on God's green earth could the two of them hitch for the long haul; he'd better get that piece of business out of his mind.

The best way to put an end to it would be to go to Billings and get himself a strong woman of childbearing age. He'd wait until he'd settled with Forsythe and Kristin was in her own house on her land. She'd have plenty of suitors to choose from.

Her laugh was a soft, husky sound. She tightened her arms around him, hugging him, her face nestled against his strong body.

"I think I like riding a horse. I might turn out to be another Martha Jane Canary, the woman they called Calamity Jane."

Buck closed his eyes. He had heard of the notorious Calamity, but right now the scent of Kristin misted through his brain like a fog, and he wished the ride might never end.

# Chapter Sixteen

$\mathscr{A}$t the edge of the porch he lifted her down from the horse. Even though he was careful to set her gently on her feet, it was as though she were no more than a sack of grain being delivered to the door. Then without a word he turned his horse and went to meet the Indian he called Bowlegs. The two of them talked for a short while, then disappeared behind the ranch buildings. Kristin waited to see if he would wave, but he didn't and she went into the house.

Had she been mistaken or had his heartbeat pounded in rhythm with hers as he held her tightly to him? And was it wishful thinking that caused her to believe she felt his face in her hair, and the trembling of the work-roughened hand that held hers? Kristin felt a hot flush of embarrassment that she had been so foolishly happy and chided herself for being a love-starved old maid.

Puzzled by his sudden coolness, she roamed restlessly about the house. Then she went to the porch and looked across the grassland to the road she had traveled on the freight wagon. Lonelier than she'd ever felt in her life, she went back in the house. Finally, she sat at the table and looked through a stack of old, well-worn newspapers but saw nothing there to catch her interest. Needing something to keep her hands busy, she picked up the wool coverlet and began pulling on the yarn.

Time passed slowly.

At dusk she lit the lamp, shook down the ashes in the cookstove and added a handful of kindling and a stick of wood. She put the teakettle on for tea and sliced the boiled potatoes left over from the noon meal into a skillet. With supper warming on the stove and the table set, she sat in one of the big chairs to wait for Buck to come in.

Life was not simple. Kristin massaged her temples with her fingertips. She didn't understand how she could have *feelings* for Buck Lenning. She didn't even know the man. Heavens! He could have run off and left a wife and children, or he could be an . . . atheist!

*Land a livin'!* she scolded herself. Buck had come here at age sixteen—if what he had told her was true. That ruled out leaving a wife and children. Was he being kind and protective of her because he needed her land to get access to his? That worked two ways. She needed him in order to hold on to hers.

Buck felt responsible for her. It was an extension of the obligation he had felt toward her Uncle Yarby for saving him and tending to him when he was young and helpless.

At age twenty-three Kristin had given up hope of finding a man whom she could love and who would give her children. She wanted a special man who would share her dreams of building a strong, loving family like Uncle Hansel's. A man she could turn to in the night and into whose arms she would go eagerly when he reached for her. She had not met a man she could think of as *husband*—until now, and she had not detected a single clue that he wanted her in that way.

Supper was a silent affair. Buck greeted her when he came into the kitchen, then washed and ran the comb through his hair. His facial features reflected none of his thoughts. His big work-hard body demanded nourishment, and he ate with a hearty appetite. He didn't linger when the meal was over as he sometimes did. After thanking her for the supper, he went out the door and closed it firmly.

Kristin was so lonely after he left that she wanted to cry. It was the first night since Buck started sleeping in the bunk-house that she would spend without getting up a couple of times during the night to see about her uncle. After she put the kitchen in order, she carried the lamp to her small room and prepared for bed. The cloth she had hung over the glass window gave her privacy, so she stripped and washed, wondering if ever again she would climb into a tub of warm water for a treasured bath.

At length Kristin stretched out on the bed. She felt an ache in each muscle, a stiffness in her bones, and a heaviness in her heart.

Forsythe met Mark Lee at the door and together they went down the hallway to the study. Once inside, Kyle closed the door.

"Ruth is upstairs, but I'd not put it past her to come down and listen at the door, so talk low. The fewer who know about this the better."

"I hope to God *nobody* knows about this but you and me!" Mark took out a handkerchief and wiped his face.

"Why are you sweating? Who'll know and what could they do about it if they did." Kyle went to the other side of the desk and sat down. "I've already put out the word to that tight-ass banker that she's signed the Larkspur over to me. Let's see what you've got."

Mark took a sheet of paper from his leather case and placed it on the desk.

"I traced the signature several times on this thin paper."

"How did you get the book away from the hotel desk clerk?"

"I told him I had to compare a signature on a legal document to be sure the person was who *he* said *he* was."

"Let's see what you can do."

Mark placed the signature sheet of paper over a blank page and carefully traced Kristin's name with a pencil. When he finished, he held up the blank page and showed Kyle the indention made by the pencil.

"I'll trace this with the pen and ink and it will be just about perfect."

"Damned if it isn't!" Kyle was pleased. "Sign the paper giving you power of attorney, and we'll get it up to the territorial capital."

Thirty minutes later the papers were signed and back in Mark's leather case. They toasted each other with Kyle's best brandy and settled back to enjoy a cigar. Business was never far from Kyle's mind.

"Did you find out anything about this Stark fellow who claims he's here to buy land for a Kansas City banker?"

"Not yet. I sent a wire to a friend of mine in Denver. He'd know of any herds coming up from Texas."

"That smart-mouthed kid with Stark needs his ass busted. I'd like to have him under my command for a few weeks. I had some like him in the army and know how to take the sass out of them. The more mouthy they are the easier they are to back down."

"He didn't back down from Greg Meader. According to the old man at the livery, he outdrew him and sent him packing with his tail between his legs. Bruza was raising hell at the saloon because Meader left town without telling him."

"Where did he go?"

"Up to the camp, I imagine."

Kyle shrugged. "Where's Stark and that kid hanging out?"

"Saloon mostly. Ate a couple of meals at Gates' Café, so Lyster tells me."

"Getting chummy with them?"

"Hard to tell yet."

"Del will put a stop to it if they are." Forsythe puffed on his cigar. "Stark's story didn't hold water. He seems mighty interested in the Larkspur."

"It's going to take some doing to bust Lenning away from that place."

"A couple dozen men should do it."

"Don't forget Lenning has Sioux drovers, and that old fool Ryerson is dragging his feet about selling. He could team up with him."

"Once Lenning is gone, Ryerson'll buckle under."

"Do you think the Anderson woman went out there?"

"She didn't take the train. I believe that she went to Larkspur on a freight wagon. Someone helped her to get to the freight yard. If it wasn't Cletus Fuller, then who?"

"It was probably Cletus," Mark said slowly. He was uncomfortable. The killing of Fuller had shaken him. When Mark had teamed up with Forsythe, he hadn't known the man was so . . . ruthless.

"Could have been Bernie Gates. I'm keeping an eye on him and his sister. I'm thinking a fire at the café would run them out of town before Del gets back."

"A fire could burn down the whole town!" Mark exclaimed in alarm.

"As long as that woman is around, Del will have his mind in her drawers and not on the job I'm paying him to do."

"What if the Anderson woman comes back to town and claims she didn't give me the power of attorney?"

"She won't. We'll manage for her to be found scalped. A patrol will find that blond hair hanging from a lodgepole."

The colonel spoke so matter of factly and so coldly that chills went up Mark's back. Feeling a sudden urge to get away from the man, he stood and placed his glass on the sideboard.

"I need to get back to my office and finish the letters to go out on the train in the morning." It was the only excuse that came to Mark's mind. Forsythe had often kept him there until the wee hours of the morning, drinking and talking about *himself*.

The colonel walked with Mark to the door. He put his hand on his shoulder.

"You've done a good job, Mark. When I'm governor of this state, you'll have the job of attorney general. It's good to work with a man I can trust."

"Thank you, Colonel."

The two men shook hands. Forsythe waited in the doorway until Mark was out the gate and walking toward town before he closed the door and headed for the stairs.

In the upstairs bedroom, Ruth DeVary stood before her bureau brushing her hair. She looked at her face in the mirror. The large bruise on her cheekbone was fading. How had she come to this degrading state? Two years ago she had thought she was lucky to secure a position with this well-situated man. She had entertained the thought that he might fall in love with her and marry her; then the struggle to support herself after her husband had been killed would be over.

That would not happen now. In the beginning she had refused to sleep with him, then after a few months she had relented even though she had suspected the meanness that lurked beneath his well-bred facade. Several weeks ago it had erupted, and now the slaps were almost an everyday occurrence. One reason, she realized, was that it was difficult for him to be the stallion he once had been and, of course, he blamed her.

"Ruth!" he bellowed. "I'm coming up. Get down here and close up the house while I'm getting ready. Then get your clothes off and get into bed."

She heard him bellow her name and dread settled like a knot in her stomach. Merciful heavens! The slight affection she'd had for him had turned to loathing the first time he struck her. All she had left was her looks and her pride, and he was doing his best to destroy both.

"What am I to do?" she asked herself as she hurried out of the room.


Cleve Stark rapped three times on the door of the shed attached to the back of the restaurant, a signal previously arranged with Bernie Gates. When Bonnie opened the door, he and Dillon slipped into the darkened room. After the door was firmly closed, she struck a match, lit the lamp and looked at Cleve.

"We were afraid you weren't comin'."

"We waited until we were reasonably sure we could get here without bein' seen."

"I've got to get my sister outta this town before I blow Mike Bruza to hell," Bernie blurted. "They'll hang me and she'll be left to fend off the likes of Del Gomer."

"We'll go, Bernie, as soon as you're able to travel." Bonnie moved over and placed her hand on her brother's shoulder.

"Fat lot of good that'll do. Trouble will just follow," he replied with resignation.

Cleve and Dillon squatted on their heels beside the door.

"I knowed right off ya was lawmen." Tandy, sitting on a three-legged milking stool, spat tobacco juice in the can at his feet.

"It's bound to come out. We want to find out as much as we can about Forsythe before that happens."

"He was here when we got here less than a year ago," Bernie said. "It didn't take us long to learn who was runnin' thin's in this town. The merchants, the banker, all kowtow to him. Lyster gets his orders from him. Guess you could tell that. Most folk go along and keep their mouths shut. But christamighty! Killing old Cletus Fuller was a purr-dee mean low-down thing to do."

"Why'd they do it?" Dillon asked.

" 'Cause he helped a woman, who had inherited from her uncle, get out of town before they could force her to sign over the Larkspur."

"Bernie helped her, too. Forsythe sent a man to beat him up. They'd have killed him if not for . . . if not that I came home from church."

Bernie snorted. "Del Gomer came in and killed him. Not because the man was beatin' the hell outta me, but because he'd put his hands on Bonnie."

"I didn't know that you knew that." Bonnie tilted her head, the better to see her brother's battered, rugged, almost primitive-looking face.

"I might'a been a bloody mess, Sis, but I heard every word he said," Bernie retorted.

"It doesn't surprise me that the coward would hire bullyboys to do his dirty work." The dislike Dillon felt for the man was reflected in his voice.

"What do the townfolk think of him?" Cleve asked.

"He puts on a good face. Gives to the church and the school." Bernie rubbed the stump of his leg as he continued. "He's a shyster. Men have left town with broken arms, legs, heads cracked. None of that is tied to him. There's been several murders and he has *generously* offered to buy the land from the widows. His hired gunman left on the early westbound for Bozeman. I'd bet my last dollar that Forsythe sent him to kill someone."

"You don't know that, Bernie," Bonnie chided.

"I know it and you know it. That's why Mike Bruza was so brave that morning. He'd not have done what he did if Gomer had been in town." He spoke to the others. "That killer watches Bonnie like a hawk. Between him and Bruza, she's like a bone being fought over by two wild dogs."

"Has Gomer a . . . been disrespectful?" Cleve asked.

"Not one time," Bonnie said firmly. "I liked him before I found out what he was. He helped me with Bernie when he was beat up."

"—He did it for you, not me," Bernie added.

"Why didn't you get on the train and leave?" Dillon asked quietly.

"He would have followed," Bernie said. "I tell you, he's wild for my sister!"

"Is that his *real* name?" Cleve asked.

"I don't know."

"What do you know about Buck Lenning?"

Bernie shook his head. "I've never met him. Cletus Fuller trusted him. The old man who owned the biggest part of the Larkspur ranch, Yarby Anderson, was accused of raping and killing a woman. Cletus said he'd known Anderson for years, and it was a put-up job to get old Anderson's ranch. Anyway, Lenning got Yarby out of the country. A year later they found him dead in the woods. Something was funny about that. Cletus knew and liked him, but he didn't go to the burial."

"Where did the Anderson woman go?"

"To the Larkspur. Cletus said she'd be better off with Buck Lenning than here if she refused to sell to Forsythe. I've not heard that they've hurt a woman yet, but I'd not put it past them."

"How did she get out there?"

Bonnie spoke up. "Bernie took her out to the freight camp in our buggy. Cletus had made arrangements for her to ride on a freight wagon."

"The talk in the saloon was that she sold the Larkspur to Forsythe and had gone back East."

"That's a lie!" Bernie said harshly. "I was the last to see her and she hadn't signed nothin'. She was afraid they were going to force her."

"The best place fer these two is out at the Larkspur, where Miss Anderson went." Tandy spat in the can again. "I be here to tell ya that Buck Lenning ain't a man to be messed with. 'Sides he's in tight with the Sioux. Heard he saved Iron Jaw's youngun from a grizzly. I'm a-thinkin' they'd not stand by and see him run out by Forsythe."

"Miss Anderson said we'd be welcome." Bernie glanced up at his sister. "What do you think, Bonnie?"

"I'd rather know what Mr. Stark knows about Buck Lenning." Bonnie's brown eyes fastened on Cleve. "I know Cletus liked him, but I want to be sure we're not jumping out of the frying pan and into the fire."

"I know him pretty well. Stayed with him and Moss—the

name he called Yarby—for a few months. It was dead winter. Horse slipped and fell on my leg. Damn near busted it. Buck is a rough man, but pure hickory. He sent me a letter weeks ago telling me about Forsythe. That's why I'm here."

"We'd have to go before Del gets back." Bonnie shook her head. "Bernie can't ride horseback all that way. He's just barely able to walk and it's been a week since the beating."

"Ya got the buggy," Tandy said. "Aint't it and the horse still in Mrs. Gaffney's shed? I'll go along an' ride shotgun. I'm thinkin' that marshal'll be ridin' my tail from now on. I ain't never learned to keep my mouth shut."

"Ah . . . Tandy—" Bonnie reached over to grip his shoulder. "I was so proud of you for standing up to that tub of lard. Now I'm afraid for you. Are you sure you won't mind taking us out to the Larkspur?"

"Not one dang bit. Buck Lenning just might be glad to have a couple more rifles to stand off that bunch a buzzards. I ain't braggin, but I ain't no slouch when it comes to shootin'." Tandy spat again. "Won a sack a sugar once in a turkey shoot down in Arkansas after the war."

"Goodness! Do you think it'll come to that?" Bonnie's dark eyes questioned Cleve.

"Soon as I get the lay of the land, I'll send word to Fort Kearny. I know a captain stationed there. I don't think Forsythe will want to go up against a platoon of soldiers. There's a judge in Bozeman that's been told about Forsythe. He might get us some legal help outta Helena."

Cleve stood. "Dillon and I will try to get you out of here. Let it be business as usual tomorrow. On the sly, gather up what you want to take with you, put it here in the shed and plan to leave out about this time tomorrow night if we can arrange it. If not the next night. Tandy, do you know the way out to the Larkspur?"

"With my eyes shut."

"Good. Dillon and I will be here for meals tomorrow. I'll have a message for you to take to Lenning."

Bonnie blew out the candle. Dillon opened the door a crack and looked out, then silently he and Cleve moved out into the darkness.

"What do you think, Bernie?"

"It's our only chance of getting away from here. We go openly for the train and Gomer would be behind us in a week."

"He'll come to the Larkspur."

"But we'll not be alone. We sure as hell can't expect any help here in town."

"He's right, missy." Tandy's voice came out of the darkness. "They'll kill Bernie next time."

"I guess you're right. It's just that I hate taking our troubles to someone who has plenty of his own."

# Chapter Seventeen

*T*wo mornings later the tension between Buck and Kristin was even more intense than it had been the day of the encounter with Runs Fast. Buck came to the house shortly after he had seen the light in the window and smoke coming from the chimney.

"Mornin'," he muttered.

"Morning." Without looking at him she slid a pan of biscuits into the oven.

He placed an armload of wood in the box beside the stove, picked up the waterbucket and went out again. When he returned, Kristin had warm water in the washpan and a fresh towel waiting for him. His eyes caught hers.

"For me?" he asked.

"Of course."

He usually washed in cold water—it was a luxury to splash the warm water on his face, and then dry it with the clean, fresh-smelling towel. He had never had anyone do for him what she had done—darn his socks, sew up the holes in his shirts. It was hard to get used to.

Buck stood beside his chair and waited for Kristin to be seated before he took his place at the table. Kristin was impressed. Ferd, even though he'd been taught manners, seldom did that.

The meal was half-finished before either of them spoke. For the life of her, Kristin could not think of anything to say. Each time she glanced at him he was looking down at his plate.

"I'll not be here for a noon meal." Buck's words dropped into the silence.

"But you will for supper?"

"I plan to."

There was a curious stillness between them—a waiting, uneasy silence that deepened as the meal drew to an end. Although only the quickness of her blue-gray eyes and the faint color that lay across her cheeks betrayed her nervousness, Buck sensed her unease.

"You'll not be alone. Bowlegs will be here."

"That's supposed to make me feel better?" she said in a chiding tone.

"No one will get within five miles of the ranch without him knowing about it. If that should happen, do whatever he tells you to do."

"I wouldn't be able to understand him."

"Just go with him if he wants to get you away from here."

"I'm not completely helpless. I have Gustaf's gun."

Despite the wintry expression on her face, something like a smile crossed his. He studied her thoughtfully.

"You'd best leave the gun where it is until I can teach you how to handle it."

"Gustaf showed me," she said defiantly, beginning to be irritated by his attitude.

Buck endured her hostile look with no betrayal of the tension swirling through him.

"Pardon me," he said as he stood and went to take his hat from the peg beside the door.

Kristin looked up at him. Surely he meant to say, "excuse me." She got up quickly.

"Do you mind telling me where you're going?" Her throat was dry. She was embarrassed that her voice cracked, and she couldn't keep the tremor out of it.

"I'm driving some of my horses into the mountains."

"Where they'll be safe?"

"Safer than here."

"Do you think they'll come?"

"Yeah, I do. When Forsythe gets all the cards stacked in his favor, he'll come to take over."

"With men and guns?"

"That's the size of it."

"I'll fix some meat and biscuits for you to take for a noon meal."

She met his downbearing gaze with the same air of resignation she had maintained during the night Moss died and later at the burial.

"Don't go to any . . . trouble—"

"It's no trouble." Her hand fluttered toward the pan on the stove.

With tension drawing his nerves tight, he could only think that her voice was sweet and low like the music of a brook. Her eyes had come from the sky and looked into his, clouded with uncertainty. Her skin, golden from the sun, and her hair, bright, shiny and thick, was heavy with small tendrils dancing around her face. She was soft, pretty as a mountain lily, calm, sensible and compassionate.

Buck had no name for the feelings that flooded him as he looked into her face. She was the total sum of everything he'd ever dreamed of having, and without her life would have little meaning. *The thought scared the hell out of him.*

Unaware that his feet had moved or that he'd taken a step toward her, he dropped his hat, placed his hands on her shoulders and pulled her to him. Before she had time for more than an indrawn breath, he had bent his head and placed his lips gently on hers in the sweetest of caresses.

He lifted his head, looked at her mouth, then covered it again with his. The kiss was hard, hungry and frantic. For an endless time he held her clamped to him, hurting her with his desperate hunger to feel every inch of her and to kiss her as he had wanted to when they were riding the horse. Just this one time, he told himself. When he released her, he stooped and picked up his hat. Then shook his head as if to clear it.

"I'm . . . sorry," he whispered miserably, and hurried out the door.

Kristin's heart throbbed under her ribs in a strange and urgent way that alarmed her. Almost unconsciously, she raised the back of her hand to her lips still warm and tingling from his kiss. She knew now why her eyes had constantly sought him, why she felt so terribly alive when she was with him. How had she fallen in love so quickly with this wild-haired man? It was incredible. She had simply handed her heart over to him, and he had not even asked for it.

Merciful heavens! Had her longing for him been so evident on her face that he had felt sorry for her and decided to give the "old maid" a thrill? She groaned aloud at the humiliating thought. *She had stood there like a dunce while he kissed her.* He had said he was sorry and hurried out as if he was ashamed of what he had done.

Afraid that she would be tempted to stand like a lovesick calf and watch him leave, she went through the house to the porch that stretched across the front. She leaned against a peeled-pine post that supported the roof, looked out over the grassland and listened to the silence. Now that she knew the sweet touch of his lips, she would forever long to feel them again.

Kristin relived the kiss over and over in her mind while she went through the house like a whirlwind, cleaning, cleaning, until not a speck of dirt could be found anywhere. She swept down the walls, cleaned the ashes from the fireplace and emptied the ash box on the cookstove, then rubbed the surface of the iron range with a greased cloth until it shone.

The tall oak clock on the mantel was one of Buck's prized possessions—she could tell by the way he carefully wound the spring and set the pendulum in motion. The tick-tock was a friendly sound in the silence. If this were *her* house, she thought as she wiped it with a soft cloth, she would place pictures of her mother and father on the mantel and perhaps someday there would be a . . . wedding picture to display beside the clock. She shook her head at the foolish notion and moved on to dust the desk.

It was a beautiful piece of furniture. The top displayed a pair of butterfly hinges, and was finished with thumbnail molding. A four-inch drawer ran the width of the desk and had a brass pull knob. She ran the soft cloth lovingly over the polished surface. She had never lifted the lid or opened the drawer beneath it. Feeling a pang of guilt, she did that now.

With the top leaning against the back wall, she looked down at the few papers and account books stacked neatly to one side and at the pigeonholes. They were nearly all empty, but a few of them held envelopes.

Kristin was about to close the lid when she saw a small clipping which appeared to be cut from a newspaper. She picked it up and carried it to the window so that she could see to read the small print.

*Manners of a gentleman.*

1. Remove your hat when entering a house although you may leave it on if in a place of business.
2. Never sit while a lady is standing.
3. Allow a lady to go through a doorway first.
4. Say EXCUSE ME when leaving her presence.
5. Say PARDON ME when bumping into her or treading on her feet.
6. Grasp her elbow to help her into a carriage. Never, ever touch her derriere to give her a boost or you will invite a slap.

Kristin's eyes scanned the list down to the things a gentleman should *not* do, and for the first time that day, she smiled.

10. Do not spit on the floor.
11. Do not pick your nose at the table.
12. Do not scratch your groin, your armpits or suck on the ends of your mustache.
13. Do not let wind in her presence—even silently. The stink will give you away and she will know that you are not a gentleman.
14. Do not swear, or make reference to bodily functions.
15. If you must sneeze at the table, turn your head away from the lady.
16. Do not slurp your coffee from a saucer. Hold it with both hands and tip it toward your mouth.

Kristin stopped reading.

She understood now why he had said, pardon me, this morning. With a feeling of compassion for the poor little boy who'd had no one to teach him manners, and for the man who realized the need, she placed the clipping back in the desk and hoped that he never would learn that she had read it.

The day seemed endless.

On one of her trips to the outhouse, she saw a party of Indians riding single file along the edge of the woods. One trailed behind the others looking toward the ranch. She couldn't tell if it was Runs Fast. From a distance the Sioux all looked the same. An uneasy feeling came over her, and she hurried to the house.

At noon she sat at the table, nibbled on a biscuit and drank a cup of tea. Later she made a cobbler out of dried apples and extravagantly added a handful of raisins. The brown beans she had put to soak the night before were simmering on the stove. For want of something to do, she began knitting a muffler out of the sky blue yarn.

It was late afternoon when Kristin heard Sam's welcoming bark and knew that Buck had returned. Her heart picked up speed as she hurried to the back door in time to see him and two of the Indian boys ride into the yard. Bowlegs appeared and opened the corral gate. While Buck unsaddled his horse the Indian talked to him and gestured toward the east. Buck shaded his eyes with his hand, the better to see across the grassland, then spoke again to Bowlegs, who mounted his pony and rode away as Buck turned his face toward the house.

Kristin stepped back away from the door. Not for anything did she want him to know how glad she was that he was back safe and sound. How would he act toward her when he came to the house? Would he apologize again or ignore what had happened between them?

More nervous than she'd ever been in her life, Kristin waited for Buck. Surely he would come in before suppertime. She looked around the room with a critical eye. Buck valued his home. It was as neat and as clean as she could make it. She sank down in the chair and picked up her knitting again, but after having to remove several wrong stitches, she sat quietly with the work in her lap.

With her eyes tightly closed she pictured his face, unreadable as one on a stone sculpture. She wondered if he would ever share his innermost feelings with anyone. She longed to see his firm lips spread in a smile, his green eyes laughing, his stoic features relaxed, and, above all, she wanted him to feel the happiness of knowing he was loved and wanted.

Jarred from her musing by another spate of Sam's barking, Kristin went to look out the window. A wagon with a cow tied on behind was pulling into the yard. Heavenly days! A cow meant milk, cream and butter!

She grabbed her shawl and went out the door. The wagon had stopped beside the corral. Her breath caught in her throat and her hand caught at the porch post for support. Getting down from the wagon was a man with a jaunty bill-cap on his blond head.

"Gustaf!" The name tore from her throat as she began to run. "Gustaf! Gustaf!"

Gustaf opened his arms and she ran into them. With a whoop of laughter, he grasped her around the waist, swung her around before he sat her on her feet and kissed her soundly on the mouth.

"Hello, little cousin. Told ya I'd come out to see this grand place Uncle Yarby left ya."

Tears flooded her eyes, and she hugged him as if she would never let him go.

"How did you know where to find me?"

"Well, now, I figured you'd be at the Larkspur. It was a

stroke of luck to meet Gilly. Now don't ya be bawlin'," he said gruffly.

"I've so much to tell you—"

"I already heard some of it from Gilly."

"How did you get here? Where did you meet him? What all has he told you?"

"Wait, wait a minute!" Gustaf laughed. "My backside is numb from ridin' on that wagonseat and my ears are tired from listenin' to Gilly. He said you wanted a cow. This one is 'bout as sorry a cow as I've ever seen. She's goin' to calf any day is why it took us part of last night and all day today to get here."

With her arm about his waist and his about hers they went to the end of the wagon where Gilly was untying the cow. She was reddish brown with a white streak down her face, and pitifully thin except for her bulging belly.

"She's beautiful." Kristin patted the side of her face. "And so tired," she added. "Don't worry," she crooned to the cow. "You'll get plenty to eat if I have anything to say about it."

"Ya'll have all to say 'bout it," Gilly said. "I ain't havin' nothin' to do with no cow!"

Kristin laughed happily. The sound reached to where Buck stood just inside the corral. He had heard her shout and saw her fly off the porch to meet the agile blond-headed man who sprang down off the wagon to meet her. This was the cousin she was always talking about. He saw the look of happiness on her face and heard it in her voice.

A sickening feeling began to grow in the pit of his stomach. Was the good-looking man more to her than just a cousin? Cousins sometimes married. Hell, Moss had said it was done all the time in some backwater places. They had idiot children. Even knowing that, would it stop a woman from mating with a man if she loved him?

For less than a minute he contemplated getting on his horse and riding back up into the mountains. She didn't need him now. She had her *Gustaf* to look after her. The moment passed. This land was his and Moss's—hers now. The house was his. He'd worked his ass into the ground building it and, by God, he was not giving up any part of it. He jerked his saddle off the fence and carried it into the barn. She had her damn cow and from the looks of the crate in the back of the wagon a rooster and a couple of hens.

"Where ya gonna put this sorry pile a hair and bone?" Gilly, leading the cow, stuck his head in the barn door.

"In here, for now." Buck lifted a bar from one of the two stalls and led the cow inside. "We can stake her during the day."

"*We?*" Gilly said irritably.

"Where did you run onto . . . him?"

"At Ryerson's. Ryerson's boys came in—riding the rails. He was with them. They hopped off the train and came cross-country."

"Ryerson going to stay?"

"Him and his boys is goin' to stick it for a spell. The boys took his woman and the girls to his brother's in Billings. Most a his stock's been run off."

"Hell of a note, isn't it?" Buck filled a bucket of water from a barrel and set it in the stall with the cow.

"Yeah. But he's a tough old coot. He kept one cow. Sold me this'n and the chicks for six dollars. Hell, the meat'd brin' that much in town."

"See anything of Forsythe's men?"

"Naw. Met up with Glazer. He asked how Miss Anderson was doin'. Said he hoped ya wasn't put out cause he brought her here. Cletus Fuller asked him to do it. Said he heard the old man was killed right after. Somebody beat him plumb to death."

"Son of a bitch!" Buck exclaimed angrily, then bowed his head for a moment. "Do they know who did it?"

"They know, but ain't nothin' been done 'bout it. Takes some kind a man to beat up a crippled-up old man who couldn't walk but with a cane."

Buck stared off toward the mountains. Knowing of his fondness for Cletus Fuller, Gilly was quiet for a moment before he spoke again.

"Glazer's goin' to start freightin' outta Dumas Station," Gilly said. "It ain't but a wide spot in the road, but he ain't wantin' to go to Big Timber what with all the ragshags driftin' in. He's had to hire more fellers to ride shotgun. What ya want me to do with the chickens?"

"Turn 'em loose. I'll spread some feed. They'll not go far."

"Ya betcha they won't. Sam'll have 'em before their feet hit the ground."

"I'd forgotten about Sam. Leave them in the coop till morning."

"Ya've stalled long enough. Ya better get on out and say howdy to the cousin."

Buck frowned at Gilly. "Who's stallin'? He's got a right to come visit Kristin."

"Visit? Horse-hockey! He be here to stay. 'Sides, it ain't her place nohow."

"Drop it, Gilly."

"Why was ya lookin' daggers at him, if'n he's got so much right?"

"What the hell you goin' on about?" Buck snarled.

"He ain't a bad feller, as Swedes go. Good talker. Tells some tall tales 'bout far-off places. He's been all up and down the big river. Clear down to the ocean. Got a real fondness for Kris. That's what he calls her. Kris."

"Hell," Buck said with disgust. "I need another tenderfoot to look àfter like I need my guts strung from here to Boze-man."

"Ya didn't 'pear to mind lookin' after . . . her."

"Mind your own business."

Buck strode out of the barn as if he was going to do battle. Kristin and Gustaf were standing by the porch. She was cling-ing to his hand. Buck ground his teeth in frustration.

"Buck," she called. "Come meet Gustaf. He's the cousin I've been telling you about. I was telling him that if he'd got-ten here a few days ago, he would have met Uncle Yarby."

Gustaf stepped forward and held out his hand.

"Howdy. After what Gilly said about you and from what Kris has been sayin', I expected ya to be somethin' more than a mortal man."

Buck accepted the firm handshake.

"Gilly's been known to stretch things a bit. And as for Miss Anderson, she don't know me none a'tall." Buck's eyes, mere slits of green between his dark lashes, flicked from Kristin and away.

"If I'd a known what was going on here, I'd never have let her come out here alone."

"Even without Forsythe, this is hard country. Some men would kill for a woman like her. It was foolish of her to come here, foolish of her menfolk to let her. She was lucky to have met some decent folks in town that helped her. It may have cost one of them his life."

"Thank God things turned out all right."

"Not yet they haven't."

"What . . . do you mean? Who has lost his life?"

"Cletus Fuller."

"Oh, no!" Kristin's hands flew to her cheeks. "Oh, merciful heavens! Do you think . . . it was because of me?"

"Who knows?" Buck saw the distress on her face and wished he hadn't mentioned Cletus. "Someone might have thought he had money."

"Gilly filled me in a bit," Gustaf said, throwing his arm across Kristin's shoulders to comfort her. "The Andersons owe ya debt for what ya've done for Uncle Yarby and now our Kristin."

"Forget it! The Andersons don't *owe* me a gawddamn thing," Buck spoke with a voice as hard as iron.

"I never dreamed Gilly was going to get a cow," Kristin exclaimed hurriedly. "And chickens. Oh, I've missed hearing a rooster crow."

Gustaf's sharp eyes were going from his cousin's flushed face to the face of the big dark-haired man who stood with his feet planted firmly on the ground and his thumbs hooked in his belt. Both of them were edgy. Neither one looked directly at the other. He knew his cousin well enough to know that it wasn't fear of the man that was causing her anxiety. That, at least, eased his mind.

"He won't do much crowing if Sam gets him," Buck commented dryly and turned to look at the shaggy dog lying on the ground, his eyes on the chicken coop.

A little cry of distress came from Kristin. "He would eat them?"

"He hunts for his food," Buck said crossly. "He can't be blamed if he takes what's handy."

"I understand that but—"

"Keep them penned. I'll explain matters to him in the morning. Make yourself to home," he said to Gustaf. "I've things to do."

"I'll lend a hand." Gustaf stepped off the porch.

"No. Visit with your cousin."

"Supper will be ready in a little while." Kristin's voice seemed to have shrunk.

Buck nodded. He walked away, grinding his teeth in frustration.

"This is Buck's house," he heard Kristin say and automatically slowed his steps. "He built it all himself. He's been kind enough to let me stay here because Uncle Yarby's house is not in very good—"

Her voice was lost to him when she and her cousin went into the house.

# Chapter Eighteen

Kristin took pride in showing Buck's house to her cousin, a fact that was not lost of Gustaf.

"He built it himself. Uncle Yarby may have helped him some. He said he learned about carpentry from Uncle Yarby. Did you notice how tight the logs were on the outside? No chinking in this log house. Buck said that the logs were smoothed with a broadax and laid face-to-face. The boards on the floors are two inches thick." She flipped up the table covering. "He made this table, the wash bench and the—" Her voice faded when she glanced at her cousin's grinning face.

"Does he put the moon to bed at night and get up ever' mornin' and hand out the sun?"

"Oh, Gustaf!" A beet red blush rushed up her neck to flood her cheeks. "Stop teasing!"

"Ya don't have to sell him to me, love. Gilly already done that."

"I wish you could have seen how he was with Uncle Yarby." A wistful look came over her face. "He was so gentle with him. He hid him away when the posse came to hang him and has been taking care of him all this time—"

"Gilly told me. And he told me he thought the man was sweet on ya—said he'd taken to shavin' ever' two or three days and was mindin' his manners."

"Forevermore! Gilly talks to hear his head rattle. He passes the time with flummadiddles. I learned right away that he says things without giving any thought to them."

"Well?"

"Well, what?"

"Have ya fallen in love with him?"

"Good grief!" Kristin plunked the teakettle down on the stove with such force it made a clanging sound. "What a thing to say. I've only known the man a few weeks. He's been very . . . kind to me, just as he was to Uncle Yarby."

"I don't like ya bein' in the middle of all this, Kris. I ain't forgettin' that I went against Ferd and helped ya get here. Now, if somethin' happens—"

"Nothing's going to happen. Buck will take care of things. I'm here, and there doesn't seem to be much we can do about it at the moment."

"From what Ryerson told me, Buck will have his hands full holding on to this place. I think ya should leave until it's settled. Ryerson sent his wife to Billings—"

"—That's fine for Mrs. Ryerson," Kristin interrupted. "I understand she has small children. I'm not going anywhere unless Buck asks me to leave his house. And if he does, I'll go through the woods there"—she flung her hand toward the grove—"and live in the house Uncle Yarby left me."

"If somethin' happened to ya, love, it'd kill me."

The door opened and Buck stepped into the kitchen with an armload of stove wood. Gustaf's arm lay across Kristin's shoulders, his fingers were beneath her chin. Buck paused and looked from one to the other, but didn't speak until he'd put the wood in the box. He felt almost sick to his stomach.

"Do you need anything from the smokehouse?"

"Not for supper, but I'll need some of that side meat for breakfast."

"I'll get it in the morning."

Buck picked up the waterbucket and went out. He was perfectly miserable. *If somethin' happened to ya, love, it'd kill me.* It looked like the cousin was about to kiss her. The man had deep feelings for her and she for him. It couldn't be any plainer than that. The knowledge was so painful that it lay like a rock in his tired heart.

*Kristin and her cousin loved each other.* How could he have been so stupid, even for that short time, to think a rough bastard like him had a chance with a woman like her? A man wouldn't come all the way from Wisconsin unless he loved her. Damn it to hell! No one could take better care of her in this country than he could.

Coming back across the yard from the well he met Gilly.

"Ryerson said there's a gang hangin' out at that old Skelton place up in Creek Canyon."

"Has he had trouble with them?"

"Not yet. He's thinkin' they be gatherin' to ride in on us and him to take over when Forsythe gives the word."

"How many?"

"Dozen or two. Says they come and go."

"Wish there was some way I could get Kristin out of here."

"She . . . et! Where'd she go? If she went to Billings, he'd track her down and make her sell or do away with her. Same if she went to Bozeman. To my way a thinkin' old Cletus was right. She's better off here . . . less'n she *wants* to sell the Larkspur to the mangy polecat."

"She doesn't want to sell. She's made that clear. If she did, I'd buy it if there was a way I could raise the money with half my stock run off."

"If ya wed up with her, ya'd have it all, an' ya wouldn't have to buy it."

Buck turned so fast that water sloshed out of the bucket. Gilly jumped back.

"I'm not weddin' any woman to get what she's got or to keep what I've worked for."

"Ya don't have to get yore back up 'bout it."

Buck stepped up onto the porch and flung open the door. Kristin turned from the stove to look at him and wondered what had happened to make him so angry.

Buck and Gilly left the house as soon as they finished supper. Kristin was disappointed. Buck had not said much during the meal. Thank goodness for Gilly's curiosity. He had asked Gustaf question after question about Wisconsin and his travels on the Mississippi River. She had hoped that Buck and Gustaf would like each other. She didn't know of anyone except Ferd who *didn't* like Gustaf.

"Is Lenning always so down in the mouth? He's not at all as Gilly described him." Gustaf carried the plates from the table to the work counter.

"He's got a lot on his mind."

"I'll make it clear to him that I'm not here to mooch a living. I'd make a poor cowboy, but I'm a damn good woodchopper."

"I feel like I'm pushing Buck out of his house," Kristin said sadly.

"When I mentioned fixing up Yarby's old place and staying there, he looked at me as if he'd like to run me through with a saber."

"You've not seen Uncle Yarby's place. It would take more

than a little fixing up. Besides, Buck said there was plenty of room in the bunkhouse."

"I got that part. I think he feared I expected to stay in here with you."

"Land sakes, Gustaf! Your imagination is running wild."

When the cleanup was done, she and Gustaf moved to the parlor end of the kitchen. Kristin threw her shawl around her shoulders before she sat down in one of the big chairs. Away from the cookstove the room was cool. This time of year nights were cold, but not cold enough to light the fireplace. She looked around the cozy room and thought about Buck sitting in the dreary bunkhouse. This was his home. This is where he should be.

Suddenly he was.

The door was flung open and he bounded into the room. Kristin jumped to her feet.

"Put out the light!"

He grabbed his coat from the peg beside the door and threw it around Kristin's shoulders just as Gustaf turned down the lamp wick throwing the room into total darkness.

"What's hap . . . pening?" Kristin stammered.

"Someone's coming." Buck hustled her out the door.

"Where are we going?"

"You're going to that room I built for Moss. Stay there till I come for you."

"But . . . I didn't get my . . . pistol—"

"You don't need the damn pistol." With his hand firmly attached to her elbow, he urged her into a run across the yard. At the door to the room he pushed her inside. "Do as I say. Stay here."

"What shall I do, Lenning?" Gustaf asked.

Buck shoved a rifle into his hands.

"Can you shoot?"

"Damn right."

"Get over there by the woodpile. If anyone comes to this door beside me or Gilly, shoot him."

Gustaf disappeared in the darkness.

"Buck . . . ? Who's coming?"

"I don't know. I got the signal from Bowlegs. It could be someone coming to burn us out. If so, I don't want you in the house. That's the first place they'd torch."

"Burn . . . our house!" Kristin wailed.

"Shut the door and drop the bar on the inside. There's an escape door in the back. If I come for you, it will be from the back."

"Be careful—"

Inside the dark room, Kristin held the door open a crack so that she could look out. All she could see was the shape of the house that she had come to think of as almost her own.

*Dear God in heaven, please don't let them burn Buck's house.*

Buck positioned himself on one side of the house and Gilly on the other so that anyone approaching would be in the cross fire. Bowlegs and two of his drovers were out there somewhere. The others had been sent to protect their women and children and hustle them off into the mountains if it came to a fight. He wished that he'd had time to get Kristin to a safer place.

He checked a pair of Smith & Wessons. One he had in the holster, the other one tucked in his belt. Buck strained his ears for a foreign night sound or the absence of a normal one. Night lay like a dark blanket over the grassland. Usually a million stars twinkled in the sky but tonight they were hidden by an overcast sky.

On the breeze that came from the south was the smell of sun-ripened grass that stretched like a pale gold carpet from the foothills to the mountains. This was lonesome country. His country. Here the large herd of buffalo had roamed for hundreds of years. Here the rawhiders had come to slaughter them by the thousands. Here the Indians had had to give up their land and move west.

*Standing at the corner of his house Buck Lenning swore that he would not give up an inch of it.*

For a while all the sounds he heard were those of a squirrel scampering around in the tree overhead, birds getting resettled, and an owl sending out its lonely call. Then faintly his ears picked up the slight jingle of harness and the swishing sound as a wagon or buggy cut through the tall grass.

The enemy would not come in a buggy or a wagon. Unless . . . to bring a barrel of kerosene to burn him out. Angry and tense, he waited. Now he could hear the heavy wheezing of a tired horse. The shape of a buggy loomed out of the darkness.

"Hel . . . lo, the house—"

Buck waited. He was quite sure he'd not heard the voice before.

"Hel . . . lo, the house."

"Who are you?" Buck called.

"Bernie Gates. I've got a message from a man named Cleve Stark."

This could be a trick. Someone might have intercepted a letter to him from Cleve. The name, Bernie, had a familiar ring. He was the man who took Kristin to the freight camp. Was this him or was it a Forsythe man pretending to be Gates?

"What did you say your name was?"

"Gates. Bernie Gates. My sister, Bonnie, is with me. A man named Tandy is with us. He's been shot."

Buck knew an old geezer named Tandy Williamson. The old trail cook, a friend of Moss's, had spent a week or two here a couple winters ago.

"Bernie! Is that you?" Kristin came running across the yard.

Muttering a string of curses, Buck raced after her. He grabbed her around the waist with one arm and dragged her back behind a large oak.

"Goddammit to hell, Kristin! Are you trying to get yourself killed?" he whispered angrily.

"It's Bernie and Bonnie. They're my friends. They helped me get out of Big Timber."

"Kristin! It's me, Bonnie." The feminine voice sounded close to tears. "Let us come in. We're so . . . tired and Tandy's been shot."

"Come on in," Buck shouted. "Gilly, get a lantern." Buck's arm was still around Kristin, holding her tightly to him. "I could beat your butt. You scared the living hell out of me. It could've been Forsythe's men out there. Don't you understand that they'd like nothing better than to see you dead? Dammit, next time I tell you to do something you'd better do it . . . or I'll shake the puddin' outta you."

"I'm sorry, Buck." She touched the side of his face with her palm before she pushed herself out of his arms. "Bernie risked his life to get me to the freight camp. I couldn't let you turn them away."

"I wasn't going to turn them away. I had to be sure who they were."

The buggy moved past them as he spoke. They followed it to the yard behind the house, where Gilly waited with a lantern. The tired horse slowed to a stop and stood with his head hanging, his sides heaving.

The three people on the buggy seat blinked against the light. An old man's head lolled against Bonnie's shoulder.

"Please . . . help him—"

"Oh, Bonnie! Are you all right?"

"Yes, but Tandy and . . . Bernie—"

"Oh, my—" It was all Kristin could say when she saw Bernie's face. Without Bonnie's being with him, she would not have recognized him as the man who had driven her to the freight camp only a few weeks ago.

Bernie held Tandy on the seat while Buck lifted Bonnie down to stand on shaky legs. When Gustaf reached for the old man, he groaned and cried out when he was moved.

"Where's he hit?"

"In the back. Sonsabitches shot him in the back," Bernie said.

"I'll be careful, mister, but it'll hurt ya some." As Gustaf lifted Tandy in his arms he glanced questioningly at Buck.

"Take him to the bunkhouse. It's warm in there. Kristin, fetch hot water and rags."

"I'll go with Tandy—" Bonnie moved to follow the men.

"Come help me, Bonnie." The tired girl's steps faltered, and Kristin took her arm.

Bonnie waited at the door. Kristin groped for the matchbox, touched the flame to the wick and turned to Bonnie. Her hair had come loose from the pins and was hanging in strands. Her face was dirty, her dress torn and bloody, but it was the hopeless, tired look in her eyes that tugged at Kristin's heart. Her memory of Bonnie had been of a spunky girl with sass in her voice and an angry sparkle in her eyes.

"Sit down, Bonnie. I'll get the bandages."

"I can't sit until Tandy's tended to." Tears flooded her eyes. "He'd got down to water the horse and they shot him. We didn't know anybody was about."

Buck came into the kitchen, walked past the women and into the room at the front of the house. He returned with a box in one hand and a bottle of whiskey in the other.

"We need cloth for bandages, Kristin. Do you have more of the salve you put on my shoulder?"

"I'll get it and cloth and vinegar. There's hot water in the teakettle." When she came out of her room, she touched his arm briefly as she handed him a bundle of cloth and the salve. "Is it bad?"

"Can't tell. He's got a bullet in his back. I'm thinking his heavy coat helped to slow it some."

"Do you need me and Bonnie?"

"No. We've got to cut the bullet out. It's not something you need to see. Fix a meal for Gates and his sister. They haven't eaten today."

Gustaf appeared at the door. Kristin gave him the teakettle and the jug of vinegar.

"Careful with the teakettle. The water is almost boiling," she cautioned as the men stepped off the porch.

The bullet had gone up under the shoulder blade. Bernie explained that Tandy was bent over when he was shot. Buck was puzzled as to how to get the bullet out until Gustaf took from his pack a rolled-up doeskin that contained a small razor, tweezers, a tin of salve, a bottle of laudanum, a length of linen thread and several needles.

"Never go anywhere without this kit. Pulled out many a splinter and sewed up many a cut after a fight. Meanness comes out in some folks when they ain't doin' nothin', but watchin' the shoreline go by. All it'd take is for somebody to look at 'em crossways and they're up and rarin' to go at it."

"Was ya the doc?" Gilly asked.

"No, but a lot of fellers kept a eye out so nothin' happened to me in case somethin' happened to them." Gustaf grinned. "Worked out pretty good. If I got in a fight, I had plenty a backup."

"See what you can do," Buck said. "Tandy deserves better than what I can do for him."

"Can't say that I can do better, but I'll give it a try."

The men watched as Gustaf scrubbed his hands with lye soap and poured water from the teakettle over the tools he would use. Tandy yelled when he cut his flesh with the razor. He yelled again when the bullet was removed with the tweezers. The Swede was skilled when it came to doctoring, Buck had to admit. After Gustaf stitched the wound he gave Tandy a few drops of laudanum and the tired old man went to sleep.

Sitting on one of the bunks, Bernie took off his boot and handed a folded paper to Buck.

"I wasn't sure we'd make it and didn't want Forsythe's men to get their hands on it."

Buck moved close to the lamp, read Cleve's message and put the paper in his pocket.

"Well?" Gilly was never one to hold back when he wanted to know something. "Air we gettin' help or not?"

"Cleve says a judge in Bozeman is looking into Forsythe's affairs and that they've claimed Miss Anderson sold out to them. He says for us to hold on here while longer and keep an eye on Kristin. It'll be her testimony that'll cook Forsythe's goose."

"There's rifles and ammunition in the ba . . . ck of the

buggy. And some grub. We ain't aiming to put ya out any more than we have to." Bernie's voice cracked.

"Take a swig of this." Buck held out the whiskey bottle. "You look like you could use it."

After a few minutes Bernie began to talk.

"We left Big Timber about two in the morning. Noon the next day we stopped at a creek to water the horse. Bonnie and I had gone down to drink when Tandy was shot. We got him behind a dirt bank. I'm thinkin' they hadn't seen me and a few minutes later two men rode in bold as brass thinkin' to take Bonnie. I opened up with an old buffalo gun, shot the horses out from under both of them. Hit one in the leg pretty bad. The other'n was carryin' him on his back when they made for the woods."

"Did they follow you from town?" Buck asked.

"I don't think so. I think we were as much of a surprise to them as they were to us. But they knew who we were. Bonnie says one of them was in the café with Mike Bruza. We waited until dark to leave that place, then run that poor horse almost to death to get here."

"They'll get back to town and Forsythe will know you're here."

"I'm sorry to come in on you, but Stark seemed to think it was the thing to do. They'd of killed me in another day or two, and God only knows what would've happened to my sister. I'll tell you one thing, that killer that's so crazy for her will be here sooner or later."

"Are you planning on going up against him?"

"If he tries to take her, I'll have to." Bernie shook his head. "The man's a puzzle."

The men in the bunkhouse listened intently while Bernie told about Del Gomer's obsession with Bonnie.

"He's a cold-blooded killer. He'll shoot a man in front or back and not bat an eye. When he finds out Bruza put his hands on Bonnie, he'll kill him. As bad as he is, at times I was grateful for his protection."

"Who killed Cletus Fuller?" Buck asked.

"I don't know for sure, but I'm thinking Mike Bruza had something to do with it. He takes orders from Forsythe."

Buck went outside and spoke with Bowlegs. The Indian was satisfied that the buggy had not been followed. It was decided that his drovers would take the first two watches and Buck and Gilly the early-morning shift. Bowlegs trotted away and Buck went back to the bunkhouse.

Kristin and Bonnie were sitting at the table when Buck brought Bernie to the house.

"How is Tandy?" Bonnie asked anxiously.

"He'll be all right unless blood poisonin' sets in," Bernie replied. "The Swede is quite a doctor."

"I'd forgotten about that," Kristin said quickly. "Back home Gustaf even set some arms and legs when the doctor was down sick." She glanced at Buck's quiet face and away. "Sit down, Bernie. I'll get you some coffee. Do you want some, Buck?"

"No. I've things to do." He went to the door and stopped when Kristin called his name.

"Buck." She set a cup of coffee on the table and took her shawl from the back of the chair. "Bonnie, will you dish up some supper for Bernie?" Looking up into Buck's puzzled face, she asked, "May I speak with you for a minute?"

He hesitated, and she thought that he was going to refuse. Then he held the door open. She went through and he followed her onto the porch.

Kristin walked out into the yard toward the well. When

they were well away from the house she stopped and turned to him. Her heart was racing like a runaway prairie fire, and she was having trouble getting enough air into her lungs, yet there were things that had to be said.

"Before I knew how things were out here"—she took a deep breath hoping to steady her voice—"before I knew that Uncle Yarby hadn't really left me a house to live in, I invited Bernie and Bonnie out to stay with me after I found out that they were having trouble with Colonel Forsythe's men."

She placed her hand on his arm. He stepped back as if she had burned him, and her hand fell to her side. She was grateful for the darkness so that he'd not see the tears that sprang to her eyes.

"I'm sorry that because of me these people have come in on you—the Gateses, Mr. Tandy and Gustaf—" She almost choked on the words, and pretended to cough.

"It isn't like any of you will be here forever." The voice that came out of the darkness was low-edged with sarcasm.

"I plan to stay. Oh, not in your house," she added quickly. "In one of my own. I appreciate your letting me stay here, but I feel that because of me you're being pushed out of your house."

"No one pushes me anywhere I don't want to go."

She could feel his unrest and it made her nervous. She could also feel his hard eyes on her face. He radiated energy, strength. He was the most confident person she had ever met. The silence between them stretched into frozen moments of time.

"Have I done something to . . . offend you?" she asked softly.

It seemed an eternity before he answered.

"Why do you say that?"

"You've . . . been different lately."

"*Things* are different lately. A few weeks ago it was just me and Gilly and Moss. Then you came. Now people are cropping up all over the place."

"When I came, you were forced to take me in. Now the others have come here because of me. We've disrupted your life, taken over your home. I'm going to ask Gustaf to start fixing up Uncle Yarby's old place—"

"Are you wanting to move over there . . . with him?"

"It's a matter of not wanting to impose on your hospitality any longer than necessary," Kristin said quietly.

Buck rocked back on his heels; and when he spoke, it was with more anger than she had heard from him before.

"Where will he get the lumber, Miss Anderson? The nails? The tools? And when it's tight enough for winter, what will you sleep on? Cook on? Do you think Forsythe will sit still for you to haul what you need from town?"

"Gustaf could go to town. He's not known in Big Timber. He could take the wagon. I've a little money—"

"No! You're staying right here in my house where I can keep my eye on you." His hands came out to grip her shoulders. "Gustaf is not fixing up that shack, Kristin. You're staying where you are until this thing with Forsythe is settled. It could rock on until spring. By then you'll have had your fill of this country and will be begging your cousin to take you back to Wisconsin."

"You're wrong, Buck. I love it out here. I don't care if I never go to town or see River Falls again. This is my home now . . . here on the Larkspur. I'll find a way to stay here—"

"In the meanwhile Gustaf will stay in the bunkhouse, but he'll work for his keep," he said as if she hadn't spoken.

"He expects to . . . stay in the bunkhouse," she said defensively. "And he will work. Gustaf's not a moocher."

"He'll have to help defend this homestead."

"He's not a coward, either. I can shoot, too, for that matter. We're not going to hide behind you. We'll help any way we can."

"You could have gotten yourself killed tonight. You'll do what I tell you . . . next time. And there will be a next time, you can bank on it."

"I know. And I'm sorry about tonight, Buck. Truly I am. I put *you* in danger, too."

"Bullfoot!" he scoffed. "I've lived with danger every day of my life. It's not new to me."

His hands gripped hard. He drew her closer to him. His face was close to hers. He could feel her breath on his lips. Nothing in his life had prepared him to love a woman. It was gut-wrenching to see her day after day and know that she could never be his. From time to time, he had thought about it as he went his lonely way, but always as something that happened to other men.

"Do you love . . . him?" he asked urgently. "Do you?"

"Love Gustaf? Of course I do, but not—"

Buck suddenly remembered that his hands were on her shoulders. He dropped them as if he gripped a red-hot stove and moved away from her.

"Go back to the house."

He walked quickly toward the barn.

She watched him leave with tears blurring her vision.

# Chapter Nineteen

*A*fter Bernie and Bonnie left town, Cleve and Dillon moved to a boardinghouse suggested by the black-bearded railroad worker they had met at the café. The railroad men were not pleased that the restaurant was closed, and uneasiness was filtering through the town's population.

In the saloon the talk was about the marshal harassing Bonnie Gates and threatening to put her in jail for defending herself against Mike Bruza. The men quietly speculated among themselves about the killing of Cletus Fuller and the cowardly beating of a one-legged man. They feared that what had happened could easily happen to any one of *them.*

Cleve and Dillon heard no sympathy expressed for Greg Meader and Shorty Spinks, who had come into town riding on one horse with Spinks full of buckshot from an old buffalo gun. No one believed that Bernie or Tandy had deliberately opened up on them as they claimed.

For the most part the Big Timber residents kept their opinions to themselves. They were merchants who depended on trade from small ranchers and townfolk connected with the railroad. They were not equipped to stand against a man who controlled the city law enforcer and who had a crew of hired guns.

One morning Cleve sent a wire to a friend in Kansas City

telling him that all large sections of land in the area of Big Timber had been taken up, and added, "no reply necessary." He knew his friend would understand the coded message. He and Dillon lingered in the depot and read the papers that had come in on the morning train.

Just as they expected, a man came in, opened the cage door and spoke in low tones to the telegrapher. After a moment or two he was given a sheet of paper. Dillon followed the man when he left.

Cleve spoke to the telegrapher.

"You on Forsythe's payroll?" he asked bluntly.

The man was so surprised that he almost choked on the wad of tobacco in his jaw. His lips worked, and his frightened eyes darted first to the window and then to the door before he answered.

"Why . . . why do you ask that?"

"You gave the man a copy of my wire."

"Mister, I have to live here."

"Tell me about it."

"I've got a wife and five kids. Does that tell you anything?"

"Plenty."

"When asked, I tell some of what they want to know, but not all. That way I keep my family safe and my pride intact."

"Good idey."

"I'd appreciate it if you wouldn't hang around here. They'll get the wrong idea."

"The word's out, huh?"

"Reckon it is. It seems you and your friend are on the wrong side of the fence."

"I won't ask what wires they've sent or received about me."

"I wouldn't tell you if you did."

"I've got to trust you enough to tell you that I'm a United States marshal, and I'm tryin' to break the hold the man's got on this town and on the land surrounding it."

"Good luck to you. You'll need it."

"I'll be back in a day or two to send a wire down to Fort Kearny. At the same time I'll send one to a friend over at Trinity. When they ask, give them one or both. It's up to you."

"I hear you." The man turned his back.

Cleve joined Dillon on the street in front of the meat market.

"Went straight as a string to Lee's office," Dillon said as they passed the dressmaking establishment and crossed the street to step up onto the boardwalk that fronted one of the two mercantiles.

The inside of the store was cool and dim. Both walls were lined with shelves. On the dry-goods side were bolts of cloth, a J. & P. Coats thread case, ribbons, ready-to-wear and medicines.

On the other side, a long greasy counter sat directly in front of the grocery shelves stacked with canned goods. At one end stood the lord of the counter, the mechanical cheese cutter. One turn of the wheel moved the golden disc of cheese around to a "nickel's worth." One stroke of the handle sliced it off. Flanking the cheese counter were barrels of rice, beans and crackers. Over the cracker barrel the sign said: "ONE HANDFUL, ONE NICKEL."

Dillon headed for the cheese counter. He rounded a corner and bumped into a lady wearing a large-brimmed hat covered with a thin veil that floated down over her face. The encounter tilted her into the table holding chewing tobacco, snuff, cigars, vanilla extract, baking powder and epsom salts. A package slipped out of her hands.

"I'm sorry, ma'am." Dillon gripped her arm to steady her but released it quickly when he heard a little cry of pain. "Did I hurt you? Golly-bill, I'm sorry." He stooped to get the package she had dropped. "I was in a hurry to get to the cheese," he finished lamely.

"I'm all right. Don't fret. I . . . should have been looking where I was going." She stepped around him and hurried out the door.

With a slab of cheese in one hand and crackers in the other, Dillon joined Cleve, who was paying for his purchases: a cigar and a needle and spool of thread to sew up the holes in his socks. Dillon dropped two nickels on the counter.

"Who was the woman in the black hat? She just bury somebody?"

"Mrs. DeVary, Colonel Forsythe's housekeeper." The clerk's voice was barely above a whisper.

"Some of her folks die?" Dillon asked with a mouthful of crackers.

"She don't have no folks that I know of."

"Then why the black cloth over her face?"

The clerk lifted his shoulders indifferently and turned to replace the needle packet on the shelf. When he turned back Dillon and Cleve noticed a muscle jumping in his jaw and his eyes darting toward the door.

"Listen. I don't ask questions. The lady has taken to wearing the veil lately. If she don't want her face seen, that's her business."

"We saw the lady when we first came to town. A week ago, wasn't it, Cleve? She had a bruise on the side of her face and one of her eyes was swelled almost shut. Somebody had beat on her. I'm thinkin' it was that bastard she works for."

"Young fellow, if I were you, I'd keep my mouth shut about

Colonel Forsythe and his affairs . . . unless you *want* your hide full of holes."

"That bad, huh?"

"Worse."

"Why do folks stand for it?"

" 'Cause, well— You're about to find out."

Three men had come into the store. One was a husky young rowdy they had seen in the saloon. Still in his teens, he was loud-mouthed, swaggering, and because of his size, intimidating to some.

A second man looked as if he had been in a hundred barroom brawls. His nose was off-center, and a deep scar ran from the corner of his eye down into the whiskers that covered his cheeks. His eyes were red and watery.

The other man was a short, mustached Mexican, one of only a few Cleve and Dillon had seen in Big Timber. He wore a black, round-brimmed hat with a snakeskin wrapped around the crown.

The older man stopped just inside the door. The young one swaggered up to the counter as if he owned the store and tried to elbow Dillon out of the way.

"Gimme some chawin' tobacco, and be quick about it," he demanded of the clerk, and pushed his hand down on the stack of crackers Dillon had placed on the counter.

Dillon planted himself solidly on the floor, taking the big kid's elbow in the ribs. He decided right then that he was going to hit the cocky bastard. One reason he was going to hit him was that the kid needed a lesson in manners, but mostly it was because he'd wanted to hit someone since he first came to this one-horse town.

"The clerk's waiting on us, you stinkin' pile of shit. Take your turn."

The kid spun around. He looked like a riled-up bull ready to charge. His small dark eyes focused on Dillon and he bent his elbow as if to reach for the gun that lay against his thigh.

"What did ya—"

He never completed the sentence. Dillon's fist lashed out and struck viciously. The blow landed flush on the side of the kid's face. He hit the floor, full-length, like a poleaxed steer.

Dillon looked across the fallen man to the other two who were with him.

"You dealing yourselves in?"

"We're studyin' on it," the scar-faced man said.

"Make up your mind . . . fast."

"Ya hit hard, *Señor.*"

Dillon's eyes flicked to the Mexican.

"I can hit harder." He answered in fluent Spanish. "Be glad to show you."

"It is not necessary, *Señor,*" the Mexican said with raised brows.

"What ya jabberin' 'bout?" the scar-faced man snarled.

"About the *gringo* on the floor," the Mexican said in English. He knelt down beside the unconscious man on the floor and muttered in Spanish as if to himself. "Yi, yi, yi, they come to kill you, *Señor.*"

Lounging against the counter, Cleve watched the scarred man's hands when he turned to confront Dillon.

"So you can hit hard. How are you with a gun?"

Dillon didn't answer immediately. He looked the man up and down, then stepped away from Cleve and the clerk.

"You're wearing one. If you want to know, you'll have to pay to find out."

There was a long quiet. Neither man moved. Dillon let his gaze travel over the man with a deliberateness that was blatantly insulting. The air was charged with tension. Suddenly the scar-faced man knew that this blond-headed cowboy from the south would kill him if he made a move.

"Just askin'." The careful way the man spoke revealed his awareness of the tight spot in which he'd found himself.

There had been no movement from the kid on the floor. Dillon poked him with the toe of his boot.

"Is he dead, *Señor?*"

"Naw," Dillon said in Spanish. "Head's hard as a rock and full of horseshit."

"*Sí, Señor,* it is so."

The Mexican lifted the kid's head and let it fall back to the floor with a thump. After he had done that several times, the kid blinked, groaned, rolled over and sat up.

"Take his gun," the clerk said. "Sonofabitchin' kid's got no sense a'tall. Thinks he's all balls and rawhide."

"Let him keep it," Dillon said. "He pulls it on me, there'll be one less shithead in town."

The Mexican helped the kid get to his feet. He stood swaying with his hand to his jaw and tried to focus his eyes. Suddenly he remembered and looked at Dillon.

"If you've got a mind to use that gun, get at it, or get the hell out of here."

Jerking his arm out of the Mexican's grasp, the kid stumbled toward the door, the scar-faced man close behind him. The Mexican followed, but turned and winked at Dillon.

Dillon went to the door and watched the trio walk down the street toward the saloon. Cleve saw the clerk slip a shotgun back under the counter and looked at the man with a little more respect.

"You don't take much pushin'," the clerk said when Dillon returned to pick up his slab of cheese.

"Not from a mouthy asshole who smashes my crackers."
He fetched another handful of crackers from the barrel and
dropped a nickel on the counter.

"Not this time." The clerk pushed the coin back. "Thanks.
I've been listening to that jackass bray ever since we came
here. Next time I'll break his damn neck or the neck of the
bastard he works for."

Cleve was grinning and shaking his head.

"Who's tickled your funny bone?" Dillon snarled. "I 'bout
busted my fist on that hardhead."

"I'd swear, Dillon, that you're more like John Tallman
every day."

"I'm John Tallman's son, dammit to hell! Don't you or anybody else forget it."

The clerk watched them leave, wondering what had made
the young blond giant so angry at being called John Tallman's
son. Even up here in the Montana Territory folks had heard
about John Tallman and his legendary father, Rain Tallman.

Well, well, well. John Tallman's son was in Big Timber and
had been here for a week. How come he'd not heard about it?
*Tallman and his friend were keeping that information under
their hats.* Had the older man let it slip on purpose? If he had,
the clerk mused, *he'd* not be the one to spread the news, that
was certain.

Two ladies on the porch moved hurriedly out of the way as the
groggy young man was helped down the steps. They fearfully
eyed the two men who minutes later came through the door.
Cleve and Dillon tipped their hats, then went to stand at the
edge of the porch. The women scurried into the store.

As Cleve bit the end off the cigar he had purchased and

struck a match on the porch post, his sharp eyes scanned the dusty street. The three men were not in sight.

"I've seen the Mexican somewhere before." He held the flame to the end of his cigar.

"It's the first I've seen him in town. You heard him warn me the ugly one wanted to kill me."

"I heard that."

"I'm getting sick of this town."

"As soon as we find out what Forsythe is goin' to do, we'll hightail it out to the Larkspur."

"I don't understand why he's so dead set on getting that particular section of land. He's takin' a risk using a forged deed and framing an old man for murder to get him out of the way."

"Buck will have the answers to all that. There's more to this than just a land grabber out to make a dollar. Buck has lived with the Sioux and speaks their language. They'll back him if Forsythe's men try to take over the Larkspur. There'll be killin's. It could start up another Indian war and kill hundreds of homesteaders like what happened in Colorado after the Sand Creek Massacre."

"The bastard must know that! He doesn't care."

"Got to have some hard evidence against him before we can arrest him. I'm counting on him presenting that forged deed to do it. I told Buck in my letter to keep his eye on Miss Anderson. If she's killed, it will be hard to prove the signature is not hers."

"How'd it go with the telegrapher?"

"I think he's a good man, but he's scared. The engineer will send my message to the fort from up the line."

A wagon with a man and woman on the seat and three children in the back rolled down the street. In front of the hotel several men stood talking. On the surface Big Timber was a calm and peaceful town.

In a room at the hotel, Colonel Forsythe was talking to a man in a wrinkled brown suit. He took the envelope the man had placed on the bed and put it in the inside pocket of his coat.

"I knew that oil out there would be a gold mine," he said gleefully, and patted his breast pocket. "This proves it."

"Depends on how much there is of it."

"I'm told there's sinkholes all over the place."

"In that case I won't have to go all that deep to tap in on it."

"How long will it take to set up the rigs?"

"Give me two months to set up after I get in there and decide where to drill. And in another two months we'll be shipping oil."

Forsythe rubbed his hands. "I can't wait to announce to the world that oil, and not sheep or cattle, will be the making of Montana." A knock sounded on the door. "Here's Mr. Lee with your check."

"Morning." Mark Lee shook hands with the man, then handed him an envelope.

"Thank you, gentlemen. I'll keep you advised. If you'll excuse me, I'll get a few hours sleep before I catch the 3:40 back to Bozeman."

Mark went to the door and closed it behind the man. He waited until he heard the closing of a door down the hall before he spoke.

"How soon can he start?"

"Two months."

"The deed to the Larkspur will be recorded in a week or two."

"Why that long?"

"I didn't want to take it to Helena myself and draw attention to it. I wanted it to appear like a normal transaction and so I mailed it." Lee fidgeted nervously. "I'm afraid that damn woman is going to show up."

"Don't worry about it. If she's at the Larkspur, all the better. As soon as we get the recorder's stamp on that deed, the men will ride out and take over." Forsythe looked around to see if he had left anything in the room before he went to the door. Lee followed.

"What's this about Meader and Shorty Spinks getting shot?"

"They met the Gateses and that old man that works for them about twenty miles out on the old freight trail. Meader said before he knew who they were they opened up on them with an old buffalo gun. Spinks is shot up pretty bad."

"Where could they be going but to the Larkspur?"

"Good. We'll be rid of her, and Del will stick to business."

"I don't like the thought of killing—"

"Then don't think about it."

The harshness that always alarmed Lee was in the colonel's tone. The man was cold as a stone, and Lee was aware that he would turn on him in a second if it were to his advantage. He had wished a hundred times over during the past few weeks that he had never met the man. He knew with a certainty that now he was in so deep that he had to go along, or . . . be killed.

They walked through the hotel lobby, came out the double doors to the boardwalk and came face-to-face with Cleve and Dillon. Forsythe stopped.

"Mornin, Mr. Stark." He ignored Dillon. "Have you found any land for your Kansas City investor?"

"No, but I'm still looking."

"You won't find any. If there was a piece of land that hadn't been filed on between Billings and Bozeman, I'd know about it."

Dillon stood on spread legs, his thumbs hooked in his gun belt. Despite his easy pose, the skin at the corners of his intense blue eyes had tightened, narrowing his gaze, and his mouth had thinned. Wanting nothing more than to destroy the arrogant man in front of him, he clamped an iron control over his impulse to reach out, fasten his hands about the man's neck and choke the life out of him. A bullet would be too quick.

"Well, howdy, Mistah Colonel, suh." Dillon spoke with an exaggerated Southern accent. "Ya had any old men killed yet this mornin'? Have ya beat up any ladies? Oh, 'scuse me for askin', suh. I done forgot. It ain't noon yet."

Forsythe's cold eyes passed over Dillon and settled on Cleve.

"You'd better put a rein on this mouthy piece of horseshit before he gets his head blown off."

"He's his own man. I don't tell him what to do or say. But I'll tell you this. If you set him up for killin', you'd better be sure your gunman gets both of us, because I'll come looking for *you* and you'll die Apache-style. I think you know what *that* is."

Forsythe felt a chill travel down his spine. He tried to pierce the surface of Stark's inscrutable eyes, and failed.

"You're playing a dangerous game, Stark."

"That's the way the cards fall sometimes."

"Let's go, Colonel. We'll be late for our meeting." Mark Lee tried to steer Forsythe around the men, but Dillon sidestepped, barring the way. He gave Mark Lee a dour grin as he pulled a paper from his shirt pocket.

"The next time you want a copy of a wire we've sent, ask us. You'll find the dumbhead you sent to fetch it in the alley behind your office with a split lip. He didn't want to be sociable."

Dillon swept the high-crowned hat from Lee's head, shoved the paper inside, slapped the hat firmly back down on the startled lawyer's head. He patted the top with his open hand.

"There ya go, little feller. Golly-bill, Cleve, ain't this hat somethin'? The only man I ever heard who wore one like that was old Abe Lincoln."

Forsythe glanced at the men standing along the porch. A few were smiling; a few were trying not to. To be made a fool of by this smart-mouthed fly-by-night was more humiliation than he could endure.

"Who are you?"

"A *man,* Colonel, suh. A man who doesn't hit women, kill old men or cheat poor homesteaders out of their land." Dillon had more to say. "Do *ya* know what *ya* are, Colonel, suh? *You're* a low-caliber *crook* and nothin' more!"

Forsythe's fury burst forth in a strangled shout.

"Stay away from me, you stupid son of a bitch, or you'll end up in an alley with a bullet in the head."

In a lightning move, Cleve grabbed Dillon's arm before he could draw his gun.

"Wait," he said urgently. "Wait—"

At that moment, Cleve was one of only two men in the world who could keep Dillon from killing Forsythe for those words. The other man who had that power was John Tallman. Cleve prodded the angry man until their backs were to the building. They watched Forsythe and Lee hurry across the street and go up the stairs to the land office.

"Reckon I've tore it?" Dillon asked, his voice choked.

"Naw. Might be for the best. Get a man mad and he makes a mistake. He'll not send his pack against us while we're in town. Too many people heard the threat. There's more men here against him than for him. You caused a few grins."

"Gawd, I hate that son of a bitch! Sometimes I think the hate is eating me up."

In the office above the bank, Forsythe flung his hat down on the desk and paced the floor.

"That sonofabitching kid wanted to kill me! What the hell have I ever done to him?"

"It could be that one of his relatives was Ellington, Spencer, Gottworth, Johnson or any of the homesteaders we've forced off the land."

Mark Lee's uneasiness about his association with Forsythe had escalated steadily since the killing of old Cletus Fuller. Forsythe ordered a killing as casually as he ordered a meal at the restaurant. Lee had no doubt that if the land deal blew up, Forsythe would throw the blame on him and come out of it with a little scandal attached to his name, but nothing that would prevent him from starting up another scheme in a few years.

"What the hell did he mean—hitting women?" Forsythe blurted as if suddenly remembering Dillon's words. "If Ruth has been shooting off her mouth, I'll break her damn neck. I'll tell you another thing"—he was working himself into a full-blown rage. The face he shoved close to Lee's was fiery red.—"I'll have another job for Del Gomer when he gets back. Nobody, and I mean nobody, talks to me like that and gets away with it. Damn kid'll not think he's so smart with a bullet between his eyes."

# Chapter Twenty

"*O*h, look, it's suckin'."

Bonnie stroked the head of the tired cow, who had been too exhausted to get up after giving birth to the calf at daybreak. Gustaf and Bonnie had prodded and coaxed until finally the cow had stood on shaky legs to munch on the fresh-cut grass Bonnie offered.

"Gustaf says we can wean her in a week or two. It will be nice to have milk again." Kristin gave the cow an affectionate pat on the rump. "I'm going in, Bonnie, and start a batch of bread."

Kristin couldn't work up much enthusiasm for the new calf. Her thoughts were constantly on the widening gulf between herself and Buck. Three days had passed since Bernie and Bonnie had arrived, and Kristin had sunk deeper each day into her private misery. Buck came to breakfast and supper, which she prolonged, if possible, until she saw him ride into the yard. Each morning she wrapped biscuits and meat in a clean cloth for him to take for a noon meal.

This morning, after he had muttered his thanks without looking at her, her temper had flared.

"Why thank me? It's your food. I didn't pay out a penny for it."

He had looked at her then. Kristin was too angry to notice that his eyes softened and briefly caressed her before he shook his head slowly and that closed-in look pulled all feeling from his face. When he spoke, even the tone of his voice closed her out.

"Your *work* here amounts to pay. I'm not wearing socks with lumps where I've tried to sew up the holes. You cook the meals and . . . this house hasn't been this clean since the day it was built." His glance fell away and he shoved his hat down on his head. "Don't wait supper for me."

"As you just indicated, my job is to cook. Your meal will be waiting . . . whenever you get here," she said stiffly.

Her shoulders slumped as his footsteps crossed the porch. She felt as if she had been physically mauled. She had always been proud of her abiding strength, and now it was beginning to fail her. She sank down on a chair and planted her elbows on the table. Keeping the land her Uncle Yarby had left to her was no longer her all-consuming passion. Perhaps she and Gustaf should leave. They could go across country to Billings, the route he had taken to get here.

*If I meant anything to Buck at all, he would come for me . . . sometime.*

"Ya love him, don't ya?" Bonnie stood in the kitchen door. Kristin had not even heard her cross the porch.

"What makes you say that?" She got to her feet and took a clean cloth from underneath the wash bench.

Bonnie laughed and came into the room. "Ya don't look at each other or say anythin' that amounts to much. Ya either love each other a powerful lot or hate each other a powerful lot. I ain't thinkin' it's hate that's makin' ya sad."

"That's experience talking?" Kristin covered a pan of bread dough with a cloth and began to carry soiled dishes to the dishpan.

"I was in love once, or thought I was. It ain't somethin' a body can do anythin' about."

"A body can do what she has to do if she sets her mind to it. Let's get the kitchen cleaned. What're we going to name the new calf?"

"You name her. She's yours."

"She's Buck's. I named the cow Dolly Madison. She didn't have a name when she got here."

"Gustaf thought the name Andora would be fittin' for the calf."

It began as a nervous titter, then a nervous laugh, the first Bonnie had heard from Kristin since they arrived.

"Leave it to Gustaf."

"What's so funny about naming the calf Andora?"

"It's my brother's wife's name. She's very pretty and very useless."

"You and Gustaf don't like her?"

"Not much."

Kristin washed the dishes; Bonnie dried them and put them away. The two women worked well together. Isolated in her brother's house, Kristin had never had a woman friend like Bonnie. During the past three days they had talked about everything . . . except the strained relationship between her and Buck. It was too painful for Kristin to speak of it with her newfound friend.

Her pride in Buck's accomplishments had been reflected in the way she had bragged about how well he had built this sturdy cabin and painstakingly crafted some of the furnishings. She told Bonnie how he had cared for her Uncle Yarby, who had been as helpless as a young child.

"I don't know if Gustaf would have had the patience to care for Uncle Yarby like Buck did. Buck not only tended to him, but he also protected him from a posse that came here to hang him."

Bonnie listened to Kristin's warm praises of Buck Lenning

and hoped the man was smart enough to realize that she was in love with him.

"Gustaf says that Tandy is a lot better." Bonnie stood the broom in the corner after sweeping the room. "He and Bernie are takin' turns standin' guard. Mr. Lenning wants one man besides the Indian drover here at the house at all times."

Kristin didn't bother to tell Bonnie that this was something she had heard discussed at the dinner table. She sensed that Bonnie's curiosity about Gustaf was the reason the girl had brought his name up so often the last few days.

While cleaning the lamp chimneys, Kristin talked about herself and Gustaf being born on the same day a mile apart and growing up almost as twins. During their childhood he had been her closest friend and was to this day. Bonnie understood that. Their mother had died giving birth to her and Bernie. They had been raised by their father and grandmother. After both of them passed away, the twins had only each other.

In his early teens Bernie had been knocked down by a horse and his leg run over by a freight wagon. The bones were so badly crushed that the doctor had amputated it below the knee. Bernie had adjusted to the loss of his leg amazingly fast, and together he and Bonnie had worked at a stage station in northern Wyoming cooking meals and making beds. Bernie had taken care of feeding the stock and repairing the harnesses. The burly station owner had hooked up the lively teams to the stages. When the station closed, the twins had gone to Big Timber and put every penny they had saved over five years into the restaurant.

"I don't know what we'll do when we leave here, but we'll get along. We always have."

"When this is settled and I get title to my land, I'll have to sell off a piece of it to get started. Gustaf will help me, and if I can afford it, I'll give Bernie work. If not, maybe Buck will."

"Bernie likes Mr. Lenning. He said that he doesn't make him feel any less a man because he has only one leg."

"I saw him leave this morning. That horse he was on was kind of . . . frisky."

"Mr. Lenning fixed a stirrup for Bernie's peg. My brother is happier than he's been in a long time. He never really liked being in town." Bonnie pulled on a worn coat of her brother's. "I can smell fall in the air. Winter will be here before we know it. I'd better go see about Tandy. I'm afraid I'm getting fond of that old coot."

"Why afraid?"

"Something usually happens to people I'm fond of. Our father and our granny died. Cletus was killed. Then my brother was beat so bad, I thought he'd die. And a man I could have loved turned out to be a hired killer."

Kristin watched Bonnie cross the yard. As much as she enjoyed her company, she was grateful to have a few minutes alone. The thought that perhaps she and Gustaf should leave clung to her mind like a burr to a dog's tail.

Buck's attitude toward her had changed drastically since the day the Indian, Runs Fast, had caught her down by the creek. She was sure that he longed to have his home to himself again and be rid of the responsibility of watching over a houseful of tinhorns, as Gilly called them.

Tonight she would talk to Gustaf about it.

Three Indians rode out of the trees and toward the Sioux camp behind the ranch buildings. The women in the camp glanced at the horsemen and then went on with their work. Whatever the men wanted had nothing to do with them. One of the drovers, not much more than a boy, but one who took the responsibility of guarding the camp seriously, came from the farther tepee and stood with arms crossed over his chest.

Two of the horsemen sat their horses a distance away and one rider came on, heeling his mount to a stop a few feet from the boy. He sat for a moment and stared arrogantly down at him.

"Where Lenning?"

The boy waved his hand toward the north.

"Where?"

"North."

"North is big," the Indian retorted angrily.

The boy lifted his shoulders. He did not like this man whose tongue was not straight.

"Where Lenning? I bring message from Iron Jaw."

"How I know that?" The boy was enjoying this brief interlude of authority.

"You say I lie?"

"I did not say you lie."

"Do I go back and tell Iron Jaw that a *boy* who has not yet performed his *hanblecheyapi* and entered into manhood refused to warn Lenning?"

The barb was so personal that it shook the boy's confidence and when he spoke, his voice trembled.

"Warn Lenning?" He had a great fondness for the *Wasicun* who had trusted him to do a man's job.

"Lenning must be told that bad white man make camp on Billy Creek. Iron Jaw send warrior to tell Lenning."

"Why did you not say that? Lenning go to Wheeler Creek."

"When?"

"Morning."

"Daylight?"

The boy nodded and was relieved when the Indian whirled

his mount and rode toward the trees. The others followed. As soon as they were out of sight of the camp the warrior stopped, held up his hand and gestured toward the north.

"Lenning go Wheeler Creek. It long way. Go. See he not come back long time."

"How we do that?"

"Stupid crow! You are but cow dung!" Runs Fast snarled. "Have you nothing in your head? Frighten herd with brushfire. Lenning not come back soon."

"Brushfire?"

"It is what I said, stupid one. A warrior does what he has to do." Runs Fast wheeled his horse and rode to the top of a hill where he could look down on the ranch buildings.

The two young warriors who, until now, had been impressed by the older man's flamboyant ways and had begun to copy his actions, moved their ponies deeper into the trees before they stopped.

"It is wrong to start fire," one said softly and looked over his shoulder.

"Runs Fast one crazy Indian. Lenning kill man who start fire."

"Iron Jaw kill him, too."

"Brushfire enemy of all people."

"Spirit wind bring fire down mountain to Iron Jaw camp. It is bad. Very bad. We should go long way from crazy man who asked it."

"He will be very angry."

"Not as angry as Lenning when Runs Fast takes his woman." The warrior turned his pony toward the mountains and the other pony followed.

On the hill, Runs Fast surveyed the ranch with a spyglass, hoping to get a glimpse of the woman he called White Flower.

He had seen her in his vision and believed that she was not of this earth. Her hair was sunlight itself. She was the sun, a flower blossoming in a pure day. He could no more walk away from her than he could cease to breathe.

When she was his, he would be the only warrior in all this vast land with a wife with silver hair. He would bury his manhood in the silvery nest between her legs and beget sons that would lead the Sioux to retake their land. She would be his talisman. With her beside him, he would be immortal.

The Indian smiled. The Gods were pleased with him. He had persuaded Iron Jaw to send Bowlegs as his representative to grieve for a subchief at a camp on Porcupine Butte. The grieving ceremony would last two days. All who remained at the ranch were wet-eared drovers who would be at their sentry posts, a cripple and a light-haired *Wasicun* in a silly hat. Old Gilly usually went to the bluff over the road, and the dog was used to Indian smell.

All was ready.

Gilly was the first to come in to supper. The men had been eating in shifts since the Gateses and Gustaf arrived. Gilly would relieve Gustaf. Then Gustaf would relieve Bernie.

"There isn't a reason in the world I couldn't take one of the watches," Bonnie said, and dished up a large dish of bread pudding for Gilly after he'd finished off a plate of fluffy dumplings that had been cooked with the meat of a young rabbit he had brought to the house that morning.

"Fine and dandy with me, missy. Ya can take mine. It's five miles out on the bluff." Gilly liked the spunky girl and liked to tease her. "Only thing is, thar's a nest a rattlers on that bluff. Don't reckon they'd bite ya though. It'd be dark, and they'd think ya was me."

"Gilly, you're the biggest storyteller I ever heard of. You'd put the devil hisself to shame when it comes to lyin'."

Kristin watched and listened to Bonnie and Gilly and wished that she could be that lighthearted. A half an hour later when Gustaf came to supper, she noticed that Bonnie made sure that she waited on him.

After Gustaf washed, he threw his arm across Kristin's shoulders.

"You look worn out, love."

"I'm not. Bonnie cooked most of the supper."

"She did? Goshamighty! I'm hungry as a starved wolf and was plannin' on havin' me some *decent* vittles."

Kristin's glance slid quickly to Bonnie. She had picked up a wooden spoon and rapped Gustaf smartly across the knuckles. They were laughing at each other as if they were the only two people in the room. *He likes her!* Oh, I'm glad. Maybe he'll want to stay here and make his home in the West with . . . Bonnie.

"You don't get any bread puddin' for that remark." Bonnie filled a plate with dumplings while Kristin sliced the fresh bread.

"Kris, did I hear somebody say *bread* puddin'?"

"You sure did, and in a couple of weeks, if we're still here, you can have milk with your bread puddin'."

"If we're still here? Ya think Buck is goin' to run us off?"

"We are a bother to him, Gustaf," Kristin replied.

Bonnie stood at the end of the table looking from one to the other with large, brown, serious eyes. She shook her head.

"Buck will never ask you to leave, Kristin."

"I know. He's too nice a man for that. He feels responsible for me because of Uncle Yarby."

Gustaf almost choked on a mouthful of dumplings. His eyes caught Bonnie's and held.

"Some folks are blind as bats, huh, Bonnie?"

"Yeah. And they've got cousins that are dumb as stumps."

"Well, now. I wonder who that could be."

Bonnie was quiet for a long while after Gustaf went out.

"Your cousin is a flirt," she finally said, then added with a sigh, "some men are born flirts."

"I never considered Gustaf a flirt. He has a sunny disposition and gets along well with everyone. He has a serious side, too, and takes his responsibilities to heart. That's why he came out here to see about me. He encouraged me to come here and collect my inheritance."

When Bernie came in, it was easy to see that he was tired. He washed and came slowly to the table.

"Smells good," he said, and smiled at Kristin.

"You're almost too tired to eat, aren't you, Brother?" Bonnie soothed the hair at the nape of his neck.

"Almost, but not quite. I'm hungry as a bear."

"Gustaf was hungry as a wolf," Kristin said. "He would have eaten all the bread pudding if we hadn't held some back for you and Buck."

"Buck didn't think he'd be back until after midnight."

"That late?" Kristin set the hot coffeepot back down on the stove. "Heaven's sake. Where did he go?"

"Up north someplace. He said he'd give the signal when he rode in so we'd not shoot him."

"Let me take your watch, Brother. You need some rest."

Bernie's head came up and he glared at his sister.

"Don't ever suggest that, Bonnie! I'm warning you. I'll be madder than hell if you do. I can carry my own weight. I may not be able to run as fast, but I can do anything else a man here can do."

"I know that . . . but just a few days ago you could hardly climb out of the buggy. I worry—"

"Don't. Gustaf will take the first watch. He'll wake me when it's my turn."

The evening dragged on. After Buck's supper was in the warming oven and the kitchen was put to order, Kristin sat in one of the big chairs and knitted on the muffler she was making. After an hour she put it down.

"I think I'll make my nightly trip to the outhouse, then go to bed."

"I'll go with you."

Kristin threw her shawl around her shoulders and lit the lantern while Bonnie went to their room for her coat. They walked out into the cool autumn night.

"This place must be higher than Big Timber. I didn't notice it being so cool nights."

"It's that time of year. The stars seem brighter tonight."

"That's because there's no moon. I love to look at the sky at night." The woman walked down the path to the outhouse. "This is a nice place," Bonnie said. "Some outhouses in town aren't this nice."

On the way back to the house, Gustaf's voice came out of the darkness.

"I could sure use more a that puddin'."

The women stopped, looked at each other and laughed.

"Gustaf, where are you?"

"Blow out the lantern, Kris. You can see that light a mile away."

Kristin blew out the lantern. "Where are you?"

"On top of the barn."

"You're no such thing. Stop teasing."

"I know where he is." Bonnie took Kristin's hand and they walked toward the woodpile. They found him sitting on a log, a rifle beside him.

"How did you know I was here?"

"If you're goin' to do any sneakin' around, you'd better cover that light hair with a cap."

"Stay and keep me company."

"Do that, Bonnie. I'm going to bed."

"How about it, bonny-Bonnie, brown eyes?" Gustaf tugged on her skirt.

"Just for a while. But if you get smart-mouthed—"

"I'll not get smart-mouthed, but I might get fresh."

"Just try it. I know how to handle mashers."

"I think you've met your match, Cousin Gus," Kristin said. "I'll leave the lantern on the nail on the porch."

When they were alone, Bonnie became almost tongue-tied. She sat on the log leaving a foot of space between her and Gustaf. Even Gustaf's wit seemed to have dried up.

"Your cousin's feelin' down in the mouth." Bonnie finally thought of something to say.

"It's Buck. She's in love with him and he's too dumb to know it."

"He likes her, too. I've seen him watchin' her when she wasn't lookin'. Do you approve?"

"Hell, I don't know. Kris has never been courted that I know of. She doesn't know much about . . . that sort of thing."

"But you do. I suppose you're a regular textbook on courtin'."

"I've done a little . . . now and then. Here and there."

"Probably more than a little."

"Well . . . what can a feller do when so many girls follow him that he has to carry a club to hold them off?"

Bonnie began to laugh. "I'll swear. You act like you're the only rooster in the henhouse."

"And you're a pretty little brown hen. Would Bernie let me court you?"

"You'll have to ask . . . him." Suddenly Bonnie couldn't draw enough air into her lungs.

"What about that feller in town that's got his sights set on you?"

"Did Bernie tell you about him?"

"Said he was crazy about you."

"I don't understand why—"

" 'It lies not in our power to love or hate. For will in us is overruled by fate.' Those lines are from a poem by Christopher Marlowe."

"Who's he?"

"An Englishman who died a couple hundred years ago. Kris gave me a book of his poems, and I've read them all a hundred times."

"I don't know much about poems—"

"I didn't either until I started reading his. This is the one I like best.

> *Come live with me and be my love,*
> *And we will all the pleasures prove*
> *That hills and valleys, dales and fields,*
> *Woods, or steepy mountain yields.*

"Do you like it?"

"It's . . . pretty. But I don't understand it."

"You have to think about it for a while. But enough of that.

Tell me about this man who's so crazy about you. Does he force his attentions on you?"

"He's never been disrespectful. I'm not afraid of him for me or for Bernie, but I don't know about anyone else—" Her voice trailed. "He's dangerous. Very dangerous."

"Tell me about him," Gustaf insisted. He moved and narrowed the space between them.

Bonnie told about meeting Del Gomer when she and her brother first came to Big Timber. She confessed that she liked him a lot at first. When she found out he was a killer for hire, she felt a fool for liking him and told him she wanted nothing more to do with him. He took the rejection calmly and still came to the restaurant.

"I think I feel sorry for him." Bonnie's voice was hardly above a whisper. Her face was turned toward him but it was all darkness and he could see nothing of her expression. "There is a total lack of feelin' in him for everythin' but—"

"—Everything but you."

"Yes. And I don't understand it," she said again.

A low growl came from Sam, and Gustaf jumped up. The dog lay a short distance away. He lifted his head, looked toward the grove west of the house, growled again, then lay back down.

"What is it?" Bonnie whispered.

"Maybe a fox thinkin' to get in the chicken coop." Gustaf sat back down, but watched the dog. He appeared to be going back to sleep.

Time passed quickly. The wind stirred, a faint breeze. The night was wide and still. The stars hung like lanterns in the sky. A quail sent out a questioning call. Again, Gustaf cocked his head to listen. It was not the signal. He looked down at the warm hand clasped in his and wondered how long it had been there.

# Chapter Twenty-one

When Kristin entered the house, she struck a match, lit a candle and blew out the lamp. She had tried to use Buck's lamp oil sparingly and chided herself for leaving the lamp burning while she and Bonnie went to the outhouse.

The house was lonely and quiet. She left the candle on the table and went into Buck's room. He had slept there the first few nights after she came here, then moved out to the bunkhouse when she insisted on taking over the care of Moss at night in order to give him some rest. His clothes hung on the pegs and his extra pair of boots sat on the floor beneath them.

She ran her hand over the foot of the iron bedstead. Bonnie probably wondered why she was sharing Kristin's bed when this bed was unoccupied. This was Buck's bed. The sheets had been washed and sun-dried, the feather pillow fluffed. It was ready for him when he came back to take possession of his home.

Kristin felt a desperate loneliness. How could she love a man who had so little feeling for *her*? Was she doomed to go through life without the loving husband and family she'd dreamed of having?

On the way to the door, Kristin touched the clean, mended shirts she had hung on the pegs. If there had been a bureau, she would have folded them and put them in one of the drawers. His heavy sheepskin-lined coat hung on the wall. She rested her face against it for a moment. It smelled faintly of woodsmoke.

She sighed heavily as she lifted the bar on the door, opened it, and went out onto the porch.

A cool breeze was blowing down from the mountains. Kristin hugged her shawl closely about her and looked up at the blanket of stars. She wondered if Buck, wherever he was, was looking at the same stars. He would be hungry when he got home. He was a big man—

The hand that came out of the darkness cut off her thoughts and the air going to her lungs. She was jerked off the porch. The arm about her waist was like an iron band. The hand over her mouth tightened, a thumb and forefinger squeezed her nostrils.

Fighting for breath, feeling her heart was about to burst, Kristin struggled, flailing with her feet, aware she had been lifted off the ground and that her arms were pinned to her sides. Her last conscious thought as she plunged toward an enormous black pit was: *Buck . . . I love you.*

With Kristin over his shoulder, Runs Fast ran swiftly through the woods. He was more convinced than ever that it was his destiny to have this woman. The Great One had cleared the way for him to take her. He had not had to send an arrow into the heart of the *Wasicun* beside the woodpile. He had not needed to go into the house or to kill the *Wasicun* woman who slept in the house with his talisman. White Flower had opened the door and come to him.

When she stirred, the Indian stopped, laid her on the grass and waited for her to take great gulps of air into her lungs. Then before she was fully conscious, he put his hand over her mouth and pinched her nostrils until she was quiet again. He picked her up and continued his journey to where his horse waited. By sunup they would be far away and by midday at the place where his other wives waited with the skins for his lodge, his horses, and warriors who admired and followed him.

Runs Fast felt good. It was over. Now he felt purified in mind as well as in body. The Great One would be pleased with him this night.

*He had taken Lenning's woman.*

Bonnie was sure that she had never been happier in her entire life. Sitting in the dark, she and Gustaf seemed to be enclosed in a small world all their own. They talked of many things. At times they teased; at other times they spoke of serious thoughts and dreams.

Gustaf confessed that, even though he had not expected to, he liked this wild country. This was a place where a man was judged by his deeds and not by his assets. He was seriously thinking of spending his life here. Of course, he had no intention of staying *here* on the Larkspur unless Kristin needed him to help her get started. Then he would strike out on his own.

"Bernie would like to work on engines," Bonnie confided, knowing her brother would not care. "He thinks engines will be on most carriages in a few years, and they'll even be pulling water up out of a well and plowin' fields. 'Course he couldn't make a livin' doin' that yet. There aren't enough of them. We'd still have an eatery and make our living that way."

Time passed so quickly that Gustaf almost forgot to pull the heavy silver watch from his pocket and light a match to see what time it was.

"An hour after midnight. I can't believe we've been sitting

out for almost four hours." Bonnie stood. "Bernie will be put out if you don't wake him for his shift. He's so afraid of not doing his share."

"He don't need to worry about that. Your brother is more of a man than many I've met who have two good legs but not much between the ears."

"He's got more than his share of pride . . . and temper, too," she added with a nervous little laugh. "I was glad to get him out of Big Timber. At times I was so worried—"

Gustaf threw his arm across her shoulders much in the way he did when with Kristin.

"You don't have to worry by yourself now. You and Bernie have friendships. *Friendships multiply joys and divide grief,*" he quoted.

"Did that Marlowe fellow write that, too?"

"No. A fellow named Bohn said it."

"Have you been to a university?"

"Good Lord, no! I've been on the river since I was fifteen years old. When I wasn't there, I was working on my brother's farm. My mother and sister are there. I go back every once in a while to help out. It's my way of paying my share of their keep."

Bonnie had walked with him to the door of the bunkhouse. He stuck his head in and called softly to Bernie, who replied immediately.

"Be there soon as I get my peg on. Damn," Bernie swore as he dropped the peg on the floor.

"Ya ain't needin' to be so quiet," Tandy's voice came out of the darkness. "I ain't asleep. All I done been doin' is layin' here on my backside and sleepin'. Damn girl won't let me up," he grumbled.

Gustaf was walkin' *the damn girl* to the house.

"Will Bernie be sore cause you stayed out here with me?"

"I don't know why he should be. We give each other credit for good sense. Besides, he likes you."

"Thanks for the company. It made the time go fast. I would've stayed out there all night as long as you stayed with me."

Bonnie felt her heart jump out of rhythm. She tried to cover this feeling of elation with sassiness.

"That's fine for you, but what about me? I'd have been dead on my feet tomorrow and still would have had to help cook and wash your dirty clothes."

"I might be able to find some socks for you to darn."

"Oh, you—"

Bonnie opened the door. A draft coming through the house almost sucked the flame from the candle on the table. It flickered and hissed as it swayed into the melted wax. Bonnie closed the door.

"She left a candle burning," she whispered. "It's burned down to almost nothing."

"There's a door or window open." Gustaf was suddenly uneasy. "Light the lamp."

When a flame was safely behind the glass chimney, Gustaf put out the candle and a spiral of smoke lifted toward the ceiling. With a worried frown, he went to the front of the house, where the door stood wide-open. He looked out at the starry sky, then closed it.

"Bonnie! The door was open. Don't they usually keep it barred? See about Kristin!" He hurried back to the kitchen as she came out the door of the small room.

"She's not here!" She went to the mantel and carried the lamp back to Kristin's room. "She . . . she hasn't been to bed.

It's still made up and her nightdress is there—folded on top of her trunk."

"Oh, my God! Where can she be? Maybe she went out the front door to the outhouse." Gustaf ran to the back door and leaped off the porch. "Kris!" he called as he ran.

Bonnie hurried after him and took the lantern from the nail beside the door, brought it to the kitchen and lit it. She went out onto the porch and shouted: "Kristin!" Seconds later she moved out into the yard to meet Gustaf when she saw him running up the path.

"She's not there! Kris!" he shouted, then again, "Kris!"

"What the hell is going on?" Bernie came out of the bunkhouse carrying a rifle and pulling on a coat.

"Kristin's gone. We can't . . . find her." Bonnie was near tears.

Gustaf took the lantern from Bonnie's hand and went to the barn. They could hear him shouting for his cousin as he passed through and circled the bunkhouse. Bonnie explained to her brother what had happened.

"They must have taken her. They came in right under our noses."

"Didn't you hear anythin' at all?"

"The old dog raised up once and growled, then lay back down. If he'd a smelled or heard anythin' strange, he'd of raised a ruckus, you know that."

Bernie put his arm around his sister while they waited for Gustaf. He came around the side of the pole corral, the light from the lantern bobbing as he trotted toward them.

"Nothin'. She ain't here! Oh, my God! If they hurt her, I'll kill ever' damn one of them!"

"If they hurt her, Buck will beat you to it." Bernie headed

for the bunkhouse. "I'll tell Tandy. He got all excited when he heard you yell."

"Gol-durn right I got excited. I might be old, but I ain't dead." Tandy had pulled on his britches and boots and with a blanket wrapped about his shoulders met Bernie at the door.

"You shouldn't be up, Tandy," Bonnie scolded, as the old man sank down on the bench beside the door.

"What should we do?" Gustaf was almost in a state of shock.

"Buck will be back soon. It's past midnight."

"—But what if he doesn't come back till mornin'?"

"Call in them Indians and Gilly, is what ya ort to do," Tandy said.

"How'll I do that?"

"Fire three fast shots. Gilly will hear, so will Buck if he's in five miles a here."

"I'm not sure it's a good idea," Bernie said. "Maybe the only ones that'll hear it will be the one's who took Kristin."

"What'er ya carin' if they hear?" Tandy said crossly. "Gilly will hear. The sound'll bounce off them mountains and travel down the valley. Fire the shots."

Bernie took the handgun from his holster, pointed it upward and fired three shots in rapid succession.

Buck was bone-tired. He slumped in the saddle and let the big gray horse choose his own pace. He could have sent one of the drovers to see about the cattle in the secluded canyon near Wheeler Creek, but it gave him a reason to spend the day away from the house. He needed to think.

The trail he followed crossed a clearing and when he looked up at the sky, he saw that a cloud bank had appeared in the southwest with a promise of rain before morning. The box canyon where he had driven a small herd was in need of a good rain.

A coyote spoke to the sky, his shrill cries mounting in crescendo, then dying away in echoes against the canyon walls. Always cautious, Buck turned abruptly, rode a short distance and waited, listening. He heard no hoofbeats or other sounds of travel. There had been no sign of an enemy, yet he took no chances. After a while he walked his horse on down the trail and rode into grass-covered country scattered with tall pines.

For the first time in his life, Buck was letting another man call the shots. Cleve Stark had said for him to sit tight and guard Kristin. Without her, there would be no way to prove that Forsythe and Lee had forged the document that gave Lee the authority to sell the Larkspur to Forsythe.

What Cleve didn't understand was that Kristin had come to mean so much to him that without her he didn't care what happened to the Larkspur. When this was over, if it ended in their favor, he would give her his land, his house, and take himself out of the country. Buck wanted nothing more than to grab her up and take her someplace where she would be safe—but that was out of the question. She'd go nowhere with him. He was just an ignorant cowboy reaching for the stars.

He had crossed Sweet Grass Creek and was coming through brushland when he heard the three pops echoing down the valley. He pulled the gray to a quick stop and listened. There was no sound except the scraping of stiff dry branch as the wind passed through them.

"Kristin." He spoke her name into the silence. He said her name a second time, louder, this time with rising fear.

He slapped his mount on the rump, and the gray was off and running, heedless of obstruction. He darted around turns in the trail the first quarter mile until he came to the open field, then Buck urged the gray into an all-out run, knowing that with one misstep he and the gray would go down.

It was the longest twenty minutes of his life. As he neared the ranch buildings, he saw lights. He pulled the blowing horse to a stop, put his fingers to his mouth and whistled. Seconds later he heard the answering signal and urged the tired gray to move on.

A group of people waited in front of the bunkhouse. His eyes searched for blond hair but saw only that of Kristin's cousin. Gilly, Bernie and three Indian drovers stood with him. Bonnie sat on the bench beside Tandy.

"What's happened? Where's Kristin?" The words were out of Buck's mouth even before the horse came to a complete stop.

"She's gone—"

"Gone?" Buck stepped from the horse. "Goddammit! What do you mean . . . gone?"

"Just that," Gustaf said. "Bonnie and I were sitting out here by the woodpile, and when Bonnie went in, Kristin was gone. The front door was open—"

Buck grabbed him by the shirtfront. "Damn you! You were to watch her! If she's hurt, I'll break every bone in your worthless body." Buck shoved Gustaf from him. His mind was so clouded with worry he could hardly think. "Gilly, where's Bowlegs?"

"Iron Jaw sent for him this mornin' right after ya left."

"Godamighty! Why didn't you send for me?"

"Thought there'd be no problem. We ain't seen hide nor hair of them hired riders. Ain't nobody even been scoutin' 'round. They ain't so brainless they'll come in without scoutin', is they?"

"Mr Lenning, ah . . . Buck, if it's anybody's fault Kristin's gone, it's mine." Bonnie stood wringing her hands.

"There's no time to be laying fault. When did you last see her?"

"After supper we went to the outhouse. And"—sobs came up in Bonnie's throat—"and we came back here and saw Gustaf at the woodpile. I stayed with him for a while . . . and Kristin said she was goin' to bed."

"How long were you here?"

"Three hours or . . . more," she answered in a low voice.

"Three hours? Dammit to hell! Sonofabitch! Gawddamn bunch a tinhorns with shit for brains!" A string of obscene words spewed from Buck's mouth. "She could be anywhere by now. That is if they let her live. Get me a fresh horse," he barked to one of the drovers.

"Buck, hold up jist a dad-burn minute." Gilly's voice stopped Buck as he strode toward the house. "Wait up an' listen 'fore ya go off half-cocked."

"Listen to what? More muddleheaded excuses. She's gone!"

"Me an' the boy here's got us a idey." The boy, who had been left to guard the Indian camp hung back behind Gilly. He had never seen the *Wasicun* so angry.

"Say your piece," Buck snapped.

"Beaver Boy come an' told me when I came in to noonin', that Runs Fast had been to the drovers' camp an' asked where ya was. He told the boy a bunch of bad men was camped up on Billy Creek and Iron Jaw sent him to tell ya 'bout it."

"Runs Fast lied. Iron Jaw knows the people camped on Billy Creek are a preacher and his boys. Tinhorn Bible-thumpers is what they are."

"There be somethin' else. Gus said old Sam lifted his head once and growled, then calmed down and went back to sleep.

If a strange *white* man had been within smellin' distance of
Sam, he'd a raised old Ned. But that dog's been hangin' 'round
the drovers' camp and is used to Indian smell. Might be he paid
it no mind."

"You think Runs Fast got her?"

"The door was open. I'm thinkin' that she went out for a
breath o' air and Runs Fast was waitin'. There ain't been no
riders on the trail a'tall. And them hired riders ain't goin' to circle 'round to come in from the other side and risk gettin' their
hair took."

"Have you looked for tracks?"

"No, an' I told 'em to stay clear till ya could look."

Buck and Gilly took the lantern and went around to the front
of the house. The group by the bunkhouse stood quietly waiting, relieved that Buck was here, even though his anger was
frightening.

"Stands to reason a Injun took her," Tandy said. "Ain't
many white men that I know of what can sneak up on a body
like one a them redskins."

"Oh, Lord. I don't blame Lenning for being angry. Bonnie
and I were talking, but I swear I never heard a thing. I was de-
pending on the dog, and I shouldn't have. What if we don't
find her? This is such a big . . . gawddamn country—" Gustaf
finished lamely when Buck and Gilly returned.

"Found moccasin tracks,"'Gilly announced. "I'd bet my hat
it was that stuck-on-hisself Runs Fast that's always struttin'
'round like a rooster. He had his eye on Kristin's blond hair
from the start. Remember, Buck? He stole her drawers right off
the line."

"He'll regret the day he set eyes on her when I get through
with him."

The Indian had warned Kristin that he would be back and

she had believed him, but Buck had thought it just a brag. He wished now that he had taken the threat more seriously and gone straight to Iron Jaw's camp and had it out with Runs Fast.

A drover came from the corral leading a long-legged sorrel with Buck's saddle on its back.

"Ain't ya better wait and rest up a bit?" Gilly said. "Ya been in the saddle since mornin'."

"I'll rest when I get Kristin back, and not until."

"Bonnie, run get him a canteen of water and something to eat on the way." Bernie gave his sister a little nudge toward the house.

"I'm going with you, Lenning," Gustaf said.

"No, you're not."

"It was on my watch that she was taken, and she's . . . my cousin."

"You're not going," Buck said emphatically. "I don't want to have to be looking out for you. I'll have my hands full as it is. I doubt he'll take her to Iron Jaw's camp, but that's where I'll have to go to find out where he might have taken her."

Buck spoke to the Indian boy in the language of the Sioux.

"You did good telling Gilly about Runs Fast coming to your camp. By doing so we may find the *Wasicun* woman quickly."

He hung the canteen over his saddle horn and tucked the cloth-wrapped food in one of the deep pockets of his coat. Before he mounted, he spoke to Gilly, who came from the bunkhouse with extra rifle shells that he dropped in one of the saddlebags.

"Stay here at the house. Have the drovers watch the stock so they aren't run off. I'll not be back until I have Kristin." He swung into the saddle and put his heels to the fresh mount.

# Chapter Twenty-two

ℬuck was almost sick with worry.

He rode toward Iron Jaw's camp feeling as if he had rocks in his stomach. An hour from the homestead he had taken a few sips of water and had tried to eat a few bites of the food in the pack, but it had stuck in his throat.

It had been some comfort to learn that it was Runs Fast who had taken Kristin and not Forsythe's men. They would want her dead. The Indian wanted her for a trophy. He would be cruel to her if she did not comply with his wishes, but he would not kill her. Buck wondered if Kristin might not rather be dead than suffer the indignity of being raped by the Indian.

All he could think of was how frightened she must be. He didn't allow himself to think of what may have already been done to her. He didn't believe the Indian would rape her . . . yet. He would want to be sure she was not carrying the *Wasicun's* child and would have one of his women examine her. He cringed inwardly at the thought of how humiliated she would be to be held down and have her legs spread.

When Buck was within five miles of the Sioux camp, he looked for a place where he could bed down until daylight. He knew better than to approach the camp in the dark. He also knew that he needed his strength for what lay ahead, and that meant rest now for him and the horse. He got stiffly down from his mount and led him into an area sheltered from the wind by a thick growth of pines. After unsaddling and picketing the horse, he threw out the bedroll he always carried behind his saddle.

Buck lay down, his handgun and his rifle by his side. It was a cold night. He pulled a blanket up over his shoulders and lay still, hearing the slow heavy beat of his own heart. He tried not to think of Kristin, but his mind returned to her again and again. He saw her running toward him the day Runs Fast caught her down by the creek. That day he had felt like he had the whole world in his arms . . . for a while, until reason took over.

Was she cold? Had that bastard hit her and knocked her senseless before he carried her away? She wasn't strong like an Indian woman. But she had spunk, she would fight him and not give in to him until her hope of being rescued died. She must know that he would come for her . . . or die trying.

*I'm coming, sweetheart! I'll be with you as soon as I can.*

Sleep overcame Buck suddenly. More than twenty hours in the saddle had taken a toll even on his great strength. He slept soundly. When he awoke it was just as suddenly. He was fully alert. Birds were chirping in the branches overhead and the light of dawn streaked the eastern sky. He rolled up his bedroll, then moved around to get the stiffness out of his joints.

After relieving himself, he drank from the canteen and ate one of the biscuits from the food pack. He talked to the sorrel while he saddled him.

"You're a good boy. I know you're thirsty. We'll find a creek up ahead and you can drink your fill."

Before he mounted, Buck checked the handgun and the rifle. Satisfied that they were ready, he stepped into the saddle. The sorrel was eager to go. Perhaps he understood the promise of water. Ten minutes later, Buck knelt beside a stream and splashed water on his face while the horse drank.

While still several miles from the Indian camp, Buck was aware that his presence had been observed. At one point, he lifted his arm to a sentry who stood on a bluff. The warrior lifted his rifle in response. Buck thanked God that he was known and liked here. He would have to convince Iron Jaw that Kristin was his *wife* and had not gone willingly to Runs Fast's lodge.

The Sioux respected marriage. Divorce, however, was not uncommon, for no one could hold a Sioux to anything against his wishes. Divorce was particularly easy for the woman. The tepee was hers and any time she was dissatisfied with the husband she was free to throw his possessions out into the village as public notice that she was done with him.

It was also easy for a man to throw his wife away. If she displeased him, he usually got a give-away stick, carved to mean a giving, and threw it at some man who might at least take care of the hunting and the protection of the woman until another man wanted her.

The warrior might take a second wife and even a third, but he usually consulted his wives before adding to their number. Buck doubted the arrogant Runs Fast would do that.

A Sioux maiden learned early in life how to use a knife. She carried one in her belt, ready for work and for defense. She would defend herself at all cost against attack, against any who would violate the chastity rope of soft doeskin she always wore when away from the lodge. Such attacks were rare. Any such attack was punished by being forced to live alone and camp outside of the lodge circle.

The smell of woodsmoke and cooking meat filled the air as

Buck rode down the line of lodges to the large one at the center of the camp. An old man stood in front of it with his arms folded across his chest. His face was wrinkled, his hair gray, but his back was straight and his eyes sharp.

"How do, friend Iron Jaw?" Buck held up his hand, palm out.

"How do, Lenning? Come." Without further ado, he went into his lodge.

A boy appeared to lead Buck's horse away. Buck dismounted and followed Iron Jaw into the lodge, leaving his rifle in the saddle scabbard, for to remove it while among friends would have been an insult.

Iron Jaw seated himself on a blanket across from a man Buck did not know. Between them was the morning food: Indian bread, a dish of boiled lamb and onions, and stewed gooseberries.

"Sit and eat," Iron Jaw said, helping himself to a large slab of the Indian bread. "When word came you were coming, I sent for Black Elk. He is cousin to Crazy Horse, nephew to Red Cloud."

Buck looked at the handsome face of the Indian. Black Elk stared back. Seated on Iron Jaw's right, he was evidently a man of importance. Buck remembered Gilly saying a group of Oglala Sioux from the south were joining Iron Jaw. Then suddenly it came to him where he'd heard the name.

"I have heard of Black Elk from his sister, Little Owl. Did her leg heal straight?"

"She is walking with two sticks." The Indian spoke perfect English.

"I am glad."

"It was much you did."

Buck shook his head. "It was only what I hope would be done for my sister."

"Is your sister good to look upon?" A smile flicked across the Indian's face and was gone.

Buck forced a smile. "I have no sister, but if I did she would not be as sightly as Little Owl."

Courtesy demanded that he eat the meal before he spoke of his reason for being there. It was hard to wait. He talked of the herd he had driven onto Indian land, and told Iron Jaw about the death of Man-Lost-in-Head. He referred to Kristin several times as his *wife*.

"I not know you take wife, Lenning."

"We married and signed a paper long time ago. I was but a lad. She stayed with her family until now."

"It is so with our people." The old man nodded his understanding.

"Runs Fast came to my ranch and wanted to take her away. She would not go. Now she is gone. I must find her. She may be carrying my son in her belly."

The old Indian's sharp eyes fastened on Buck's face.

"You say Runs Fast took your woman?"

"I say she is gone. He came to my house while I was at Wheeler Creek and spoke to Beaver Boy. She is gone. I see moccasin prints." Buck shrugged indifferently.

"Runs Fast much trouble here. He says he sees vision from the Great Power. He take warriors who follow him and go west to Little Big Horn."

"Do you know the way he would go? If my wife went with him willingly, I will divorce her and she can stay with him. If not, I want her back."

"You will fight for her?" Black Elk asked.

"Of course. Wouldn't you fight for your wife?"

The Indian nodded. "I fight for what is mine. I show you the way."

When Buck came out of the lodge, he saw Little Owl. She stood with a group of maidens and smiled as Buck came toward her.

"Hello, man from Larkspur."

"Hello, Little Owl."

"My leg will not be crooked and I will not limp as I feared."

"That's good, Little Owl. Mighty good."

"Did bad men try to kill you?"

"They came on my land and tried. I killed one. The other went far away."

"That is good."

The boy brought Buck's horse and he mounted. Black Elk appeared on a fine spotted horse. A half dozen warriors were with him.

"Good-bye, Little Owl."

"Good-bye, man from Larkspur."

Buck joined Black Elk and they rode out of the camp. The maidens with Little Owl began to chatter.

"He is the one?"

"You never said he was handsome for a *Wasicun.*"

"Will he be back?"

Little Owl watched the horsemen leave and hoped that he would.

Del Gomer got off the morning train and walked rapidly up the street to the hotel. In his room he took a gun from a canvas bag, loaded it and put it in a shoulder holster beneath his coat. He checked the load in the gun on his thigh and put extra shells in his coat pocket.

He worked quickly. The expression on his face did not reflect the rage that burned within him. Del had been gone a
week on what he called a wild-goose chase. The judge he had
gone to kill was not in Bozeman. Del was told that he was
away in Helena but that he would be back any day. Del
waited, pretending to be a traveling man, keeping his ears
open for news of the judge's return. Every day he was away
from Big Timber he became more concerned for Bonnie.
Forsythe suspected she and her brother had helped the Anderson woman get out of town. Bonnie needed him, whether she
realized it or not.

Del had decided the day he arrived in Bozeman that he was
not going to trail the judge to Helena and kill him there, so on
the sixth day, when the man had not returned, Del boarded the
train for the return trip to Big Timber.

A man whom Del had seen at Bonnie's restaurant made a
point of speaking to him at a water stop between Bozeman
and Big Timber. The man, a brakeman, deliberately sought
him out and told him that Mike Bruza had gone to the restaurant and had been less than respectful to Bonnie. The marshal
had threatened to jail her for pouring hot coffee on Bruza
when he grabbed her. The brother and sister had closed the
restaurant and left town.

"Guess we'll have to find another place to eat, huh, mister?
Damn shame a decent woman has to put up with the likes of
Mike Bruza and a half-ass marshal. Well, I got to get aboard.
Thought you'd like to know, seein' as how you took your
meals there."

*Bonnie, Bonnie. My sweet Bonnie. If they've hurt you, I'll
kill them. I swear it.*

The words echoed in Del's mind as he left the hotel and
went down the boardwalk to the marshal's office. No one was

there. He continued on to the restaurant. The curtains were drawn. A sign on the door said CLOSED. He looked in and saw that the furnishings were still there. Bonnie's apron hung on the nail beside the wash bench.

Del stood in front of the restaurant for a long moment. The town was wide-awake and going about its business. When he moved, it was to the alley and over to the next street. His long legs quickly ate up the distance to the big house enclosed with a white picket fence.

Colonel Forsythe was seated at the large dining-room table. Ruth moved between kitchen and table, serving coffee or hot bread. A mass of blue bruises and red welts marked her face. Her cheek was swollen, as was the side of her mouth. Her hair was perfectly groomed as usual. A freshly ironed apron covered her dress. She held her head proudly, looked Kyle in the eye and refused to cower. That, more than anything, irritated him enough that he vowed to break her spirit.

When a sharp rap sounded on the beveled glass of the door, Forsythe got up to open it. Del stepped inside without being invited and closed the door behind him.

"Mornin', Del. Had breakfast? Ruth," the colonel shouted without waiting for an answer, "set a place for Del."

Ruth came from the dining room. She looked directly at Del Gomer. He removed his hat.

"Hello, Mr. Gomer. I'll be glad to set a place for you." Ruth spoke barely moving her mouth. He looked at her steadily, but not a flicker of expression crossed his face at the sight of hers.

"I didn't come to eat, but thank you, ma'am." He turned his colorless eyes on Forsythe.

"Have coffee then," the colonel hastened to say. "Ruth, get

Del some coffee." He cleared his throat. "Business over with in Bozeman?"

"As far as I'm concerned it is. I don't want coffee. Please excuse us, Mrs. DeVary."

Forsythe rubbed his sweaty hands. He always felt a chill in the presence of this man.

"I'll get the rest of your money."

"You owe me nothing more."

"No . . . no. My word is my bond. I said I'd pay you—"

Without warning Del reached out, grasped the colonel's starched shirt front, whirled him around and slammed him against the wall.

"Where are Bruza and Lyster? I want some answers and I want them now. What happened at the restaurant? Where did Miss Gates go?"

"Calm down, Del, and I'll tell you." Del loosened his hold on the colonel's shirt front. When free of the man's grasp, Forsythe moved away.

"Start talking."

"I knew you'd be upset about that, Del. The girl is all right. She and her brother went out to the Larkspur. I've given strict orders that they are not to be bothered in any way. Mike got a little angry when she spilled coffee on him. Lyster, in his stupid way, was merely trying to do his job. Hell, the people of this town wouldn't stand for him jailin' a woman like Miss Gates. He knows that."

"Where is he? Where is Bruza?"

"Mike and Lyster went out to the old Taylor place. Greg Meader is out there . . . raisin' hell. I told them to straighten him out or send him packing."

"Are they going to ride on the Larkspur?"

"Not on orders from me," Forsythe said quickly. "Hell, I'd

not put those brainless fools in charge of cleaning out a shit-house. We were waiting for you."

"When did Miss Gates leave?"

"A couple days after you did. Some fellers saw them on the freight trail heading north. They wouldn't have gone on to Helena alone. They must have stopped at Lenning's place."

Del went to the door. Pinpoints of light glittered in the cold depths of his eyes.

"You better be right, Forsythe."

Del walked out the door, closing it behind him, crossed the porch and went down the steps. Forsythe's lackey, the boy with the crooked back who lived in the carriage house and tended the yard, was hoeing a flower bed along the fence. As Del passed, the boy said, "Sir, don't look at me. He's watching."

Instantly alert, Del stopped, pulled a cigar from his pocket and struck a match on the wooden gate. He took his time lighting the cigar.

"Miss Ruth say men ride on Larkspur *today*. Told to kill all."

"Obliged to you." Del flipped away the matchstick, walked on down the street and headed for the livery.

*That lying, cowardly son of a bitch had been beating on that woman!* That in itself was reason enough to kill him.

Del had been sure that Forsythe was lying. What surprised him was that Ruth DeVary would take the risk of warning him. Why didn't she shoot the bastard as he slept or cave his skull in with a club? Del drew deep on the cigar. When he was finished with Lyster and Bruza, he would do it himself—for her. He surprised himself for thinking this.

Del rode out of town on a tall, strong roan he kept at the livery. An hour out of town he met a rider, a Mexican he had seen hanging around with Forsythe's men. He nodded and rode on. His business was with Lyster and Bruza, and he expected to settle with them at the Larkspur ranch.

He seldom indulged in self-analysis. He did so now as he realized that lately he had undergone a subtle change. For five years he had been a destroyer with hand ever ready to grasp his gun. At first he had suffered pangs of conscience when he killed; but the second time it was easier, and, by degree, he had become contemptuous of his victims and had killed casually.

He knew that he could never go back to what he once had been. He had to find words to reach the woman he loved. He must make her realize that what he did for a living had nothing to do with his love for her and that his profession earned him a tidy sum that would permit him to give her most anything she wanted. Her brother was dear to her. Del couldn't understand that, but it appeared to be a fact. He would set him up in a business if it would make Bonnie happy.

To speak of love was not easy for a man like Del, when the feeling was deep and strong. Somehow he had to convince her that he would spend his life providing for her, protecting her. He thought of many things to say to her, but they formed no logical order in his mind.

The one thought that stood foremost was that without her, the future seemed empty and meaningless.

It was midafternoon when Cleve and Dillon rode into town and stopped at the livery. They had ridden out to a place along the Yellowstone River where, it was said, two Englishmen planned to build a bridge. Cleve had thought to get some information that could be used against Forsythe, but only a camp of tree cutters was there.

"A Mexican was here lookin' fer ya, Mr. Stark." The liveryman came from the barn.

"Yeah? What'd he want?"

"Didn't say. Horse he was on was lathered and 'bout wore out. Reckon he'll be back." The liveryman looked beyond Cleve. "Dang my hide if he ain't comin' now."

*"Señores!"* The Mexican's short legs pumped as he hurried toward them. "Yi, yi, yi, you choose hell of a time to leave town." He spoke in rapid Spanish.

"What's on your mind, *amigo?*"

"Men ride on the Larkspur," he said in Spanish, and looked at the liveryman.

"Who are you?" Cleve asked.

"Yi, yi, yi, it does not matter now. Pablo Cardova." He doffed his wide-brimmed hat and wiped his forehead with the sleeve of his coat. "Colin Tallman, my good friend, say come keep eyes on little brother Dillon Tallman. So I come. Find out plenty more if they do not know I friend. Smart, huh?" He grinned, showing a gold tooth.

"Where did you see Colin?" Dillon demanded. "I can take care of myself without any help from him."

"At Timbertown, *Señor.* He know who is here. Papa Tallman, Mama Tallman, all know and worry—".

"Well, for cryin' out loud! You'd think I wasn't dry behind the ears yet!"

"We can sort this out later," Cleve said. "What about the men riding on the Larkspur?"

"More than a dozen, *Señor.* They want me to go. I say I sick in the bowels. Smart, huh?"

"When did they leave?"

"Two, three hours. Kid with stone head, the ugly one, the marshal and one named Mike. He take charge. Mean man, that Mike. He said leave no one to say anything. He want to kill lady with crippled brother. Forsythe say kill lady with light hair named Anderson. Marshal don't want to go, Forsythe say him go to say they serve papers. It . . . one big . . . bad thin' they do, *Señores.*"

The liveryman had not understood á word that had been said. Cleve explained.

"Forsythe's men are riding on the Larkspur—"

"—Goin' to burn 'em out! By jove, that son of a jackass ain't fit to shoot."

"Yo're right about that. Water and feed the horses. We'll be back in twenty minutes. I'll go send the wire to the fort and to Judge Williams. He was due back in Bozeman today. Dillon, how about checkin' around to see how many of Forsythe's men are still in town."

"I can do that, *Señor.*"

"You're in this for the long haul?" Cleve asked.

"Of course, *Señor.* I go with you to Larkspur." Pablo's dark eyes shone with mischief as he looked up at the tall, blond Dillon. "How else I keep eyes on little brother?"

"She . . . et! If you're goin' to get along with me, you pepper-eater, you'd better cut that out."

# Chapter Twenty-three

*B*lack Elk manifested all the qualities of a leader. He treated his warriors respectfully, but issued orders firmly. He was proud, but not vain. It was easy to think of him as brother to Little Owl, who had been so courageous with a broken leg.

Buck liked him.

They set a steady pace through the passes of the Crazy Mountains. Black Elk would stop and look at tracks, especially if they came to an open place where several animals had crossed the trail. No words were exchanged.

Buck could read the trail as well as the Sioux. Runs Fast was leading a horse. At one time Kristin had fallen off. A blond hair had caught on a bush, and an indention marked where her bottom had hit the ground. He kept this knowledge to himself, not wanting Black Elk to think he was wanting to share the leadership.

At times Buck's anger almost choked him as he thought of what Kristin was enduring. *Please God, if you're up there, and I think you must be—don't let him rape her.*

They rode for several hours before they came out onto a grassy plain. By the time they reached the foothills of the next rise of mountains, the sun was directly overhead. Black Elk stopped when they reached a small stream of clear water coming down from a sheer rock wall. He spoke to one of his warriors who rode on ahead.

"Not far now, Lenning," Black Elk said as they watered their horses. "Your woman has hair like a cloud? It is not tied and catches on bushes."

"Yes. Her people come from over the sea. Her hair is very light."

"All *Wasicun* come from over the sea."

"That is true. I had not thought of it."

"Is this woman of your heart, or was she chosen for you?"

"She is of my heart. I will know no peace until she is with me."

The Indian nodded gravely. "One of my wives is of my heart. The other I took with her permission to help her because she is not strong. I do not bury my manhood in my second wife. It is reserved for the wife of my heart."

Buck was surprised the Indian revealed so much about his private life.

"Do you have sons?"

"Yes." A smile came over the handsome face. "A big, strong son." The smile faded quickly. "He is the cause of my wife's weakness. The medicine woman say she get stronger and in time we will have more sons."

"Runs Fast will not want to give up my wife."

"If you have not divorced her, he has no right."

"I will kill him if he has raped her." Buck looked the Indian in the eyes to judge his reaction.

"It is what I would do," he said simply.

A half hour later, Black Elk's warrior returned. Buck understood enough of what he said to know that Runs Fast, with six braves and three women, was camped up ahead. The women were taking down the tipis and preparing to move. A *Wasicun* woman lay on a blanket. Other women kicked her as they passed.

It was not surprising to Black Elk that the women would be angry when their husband brought in another wife, without consulting with them first.

*Sweetheart, you've been through hell. I'll be there in just a little while and will get you out of there or die trying.*

Buck wanted to start for the camp immediately; it was hard to wait and let Black Elk take the lead. After the warrior had watered his horse, Black Elk gave the signal to mount up. They rode single file until they came to the clearing where, in haste to depart, even the warriors were helping load the packhorses. Buck moved up beside his Indian friend.

Runs Fast stood waiting for them, a rifle in his hand. Buck had never seen him so untidy. Gone were the decorations, the fancy leggings, the beaded moccasins. The look of hatred on his face caused Buck to drop his hand toward his gun butt because it would take only a slight move for the Indian to tilt the rifle and fire.

Black Elk moved out ahead of Buck and slid from his horse.

"You would shoot your Sioux brother?"

"I will shoot the *Wasicun*, if he tries to take the woman."

"It would be foolish. You would no longer be welcome in the Sioux camps. The woman is his wife. He has a right to her."

"She is not his wife. She does not sleep in his blankets."

"It is not the *Wasicun*'s way for a wife to sleep in her husband's blankets when she is bleeding. You have stolen the man's wife. Will you give her back or fight to the death of one of you?"

Runs Fast looked beyond Black Elk to his well-armed, seasoned warriors, and then to his own who were not. He did not want to die here. He called on the Great One to help him find a way to keep the woman and to appease his Sioux brother. He had spent the night and the morning getting here and he was tired. The damn woman had wailed half the night. At one time she shouted for Lenning, and he'd had to stop and put a rag in her mouth.

"I will think on it," he said to Black Elk.

Buck dismounted, and keeping his eye on Runs Fast he headed for the blanket where Kristin lay. The Indian moved between them and stood over Kristin.

"No! I have not yet decided."

Buck's temper exploded. He jerked a knife from his belt and prepared to spring.

"I've decided, you stinkin' pile of cow dung." Buck moved the two-edged blade back and forth. "Touch her and I'll rip you wide-open."

Black Elk moved in. "It is time to smoke and talk while Lenning speaks to his woman."

Runs Fast reluctantly moved away with Black Elk. Buck knelt down on the blanket, turned Kristin and lifted her up in his arms. His lips moved in silent curses as he looked at her face. It was scratched, dirty, and there were dark smudges beneath her eyes. Her hair had come loose from one of the braids and hung down over her face in strands dampened by her tears. The other braid hung over her shoulder. She shivered from the cold.

"Kristin . . . honey, are you all right? What did that bastard do to you?"

Kristin opened her eyes. There was a strange singing noise in her head. She thought she had heard Buck's voice and called to him.

"Bu . . . ck—?" At first her voice came out in a croaking sound. Then became stronger and she called frantically, "Buck!"

"I'm here. I found you . . . love—" It *was* Buck's voice, close to her ear.

She moved her head and her eyes began to focus. She saw his face, the dear face she had seen behind her closed lids all through the long, dark and torturous night. This Buck's cheeks were covered with several days growth of beard.

*It's . . . you?* Her lips formed the words, but she didn't say them.

Their faces were so close she could see the amber circle around the irises in his eyes. She was being cradled in strong arms against a warm chest that smelled faintly of woodsmoke. *Let it be real. Please let it be real.*

"Buck? It's you? Really?" Her mouth trembled, her eyes flooded until she could no longer see his face. She lifted her hand to his cheek.

"Yes, sweet girl. It's really me. We'll be going home soon."

"I prayed you'd find me." Her arms went around him and held him with surprising strength.

"I'd have crawled on my belly through a valley of rattlers to get to you. I kept telling you that I was coming."

"I heard you. I swear I heard you."

"Darlin' girl. Sweet, sweet woman of my heart."

The hoarsely whispered words came out on a breath. Kristin wasn't quite sure if she heard them or if she just hoped that she had. She buried her face in the warm flesh of his neck and savored his nearness, his strength, his warm breath on her cheek. Every bone in her body throbbed with pain and her back felt as if it was about to break, but a wondrous spurt of happiness flooded her heart.

"Can we go home now . . . to your house?"

"First . . . I must know if he hurt you."

"He . . . hit me once and . . . pinched my nose to cut off my air. I thought I was going to die. He was angry because I couldn't stay on the horse—"

"Did he . . . rape you?" The words came croakingly from his tight throat.

Kristin leaned back so she could see his face. His stern profile was outlined against the blue sky. Her hand came around to cup his cheek.

"No. He didn't touch me that way."

"If he had . . . I would kill him now."

"He said if you came he would kill you. I wanted you to come . . . and I didn't want you to."

"I never thought he'd go as far as steal you away."

"When can we go home—"

"Soon. First I have a few things to settle with him. Don't worry. We have friends here from Iron Jaw's camp. Can you stand up, love?"

"Oh, Buck, am I your . . . love?"

"I think of you that way. I'm not good with words, especially when I'm with you. I get all tongue-tied and afraid I'll say the wrong thing."

"We talked about a lot of things when I first came to the Larkspur."

"That was before I realized that you're the most important thing in the world to me. I think about you all the time. When it's settled with Forsythe, I want you to have all the Larkspur, the house, all I have—"

"Sshh—" She put her fingers on his lips. "It would mean nothing without you—nothing. I know that I'm dirty and look ugly, but would you kiss me—" Tears rolled once again from her eyes and down her cheeks.

"Ah . . . little love. You're the most beautiful woman I've ever seen. You will never look ugly to me . . . not even a hundred years from now." His voice was choked with emotion.

"Then hold me, kiss me—"

A flood of tenderness washed over him when she turned her lips to his. He was anxious to settle with Runs Fast and leave this place, but the temptation to kiss her sweet lips was too great. He pressed his lips to hers, gently, sweetly, not caring who was watching. He lifted his head and looked down at her. Then put his lips close to her ear.

"The Sioux honor marriage. I have said that you are my wife. I've told them we were married long ago and that you stayed with your family until now."

"Buck . . . I wish it were true. Oh, I wish it were true."

"Ah . . . sweet girl. I'm not half good enough for you. We must talk about it, but first we've got to get away from here. I may have to fight Runs Fast—"

"No! Oh, God! No!"

"If I do, stay close to Black Elk. He is the one with the blue stone hanging from a cord around his neck. He is our friend. If anything happens to me, he will see that you get back to the Larkspur. Now, stand up if you can. Hold up your head like you did that day Runs Fast stole your drawers. Act haughty and proud." He kissed her ear and pulled her to her feet. She leaned against him and lifted her face.

"I thought I might never see you again," she whispered. "I couldn't bear to lose you again. Will you think me shameless, without pride, if I say . . . I love you?"

With his arms around her, conscious of a dozen or more pairs of eyes watching them but not caring, Buck bent his head and pressed gentle kisses on her lips.

"Ah . . . sweet woman. No one has ever said those words to me. It'll take some getting used to. Promise you'll say them again . . . when we're alone."

"I'll say them every day for the rest of our lives . . . if you want me to."

Buck closed off his mind from this strange and wonderful thing that was happening. He had to deal with the present danger and could not afford any distractions. He turned to Black Elk and Runs Fast seated before a small fire. Runs Fast's wives waited beside the packhorses, his warriors beside their ponies. Black Elk's men waited patiently, one held the reins of Buck's sorrel.

With Kristin walking beside and slightly behind him, Buck approached the fire.

"Sit and smoke," Black Elk invited.

Buck shook his head. "I'll not smoke with the man who stole my wife."

Runs Fast snorted angrily, but Black Elk nodded his understanding and got to his feet. Runs Fast followed and stood scowling.

"My Sioux brother says that he had a vision," Black Elk explained. "The Great One told him to find a woman with silver hair to be his talisman. With such a woman by his side, he would be able to do great things for his people."

"Let him find another woman to be his talisman," Buck said firmly, and moved so that Kristin stood behind him. "This one is my woman."

"There is a way for Runs Fast to hear the voice of the Great One without the woman—"

"—There is no way," Runs Fast interrupted angrily. "Have I not told you that—"

Black Elk turned on Runs Fast and spoke harshly. "Can you not make your tongue be quiet in your mouth?"

"I would hear of this way," Buck said, and was pleased to see the arrogant Indian's face reflect his embarrassment at being rebuked.

"It is the hair and not the woman that speaks to Runs Fast

through the Great One," Black Elk said. "He can take the hair to the faraway mountains, but leave the woman with her husband."

"No!" The word exploded from Buck's mouth and he reached for the knife in his belt. The image of a bloody scalp flashed before his eyes.

Black Elk moved over to where Kristin stood beside Buck, and touched the braid that lay on her breast.

Kristin had not understood a word spoken. But remembering Buck's words the day Runs Fast came to the ranch, she did not cringe away from Black Elk's hand.

"I do not suggest taking the scalp, Lenning. Only braid to hang in his lodge until he finds the woman of his vision."

"What did he say, Buck?" Kristin asked anxiously.

"He wishes to give Runs Fast your braid."

Buck looked at the handsome face of his newfound friend and began to understand. Black Elk was a diplomat and was trying to solve the problem without a fight. Buck knew that if he fought Runs Fast it would be a fight to the death. The Indian would accept no less.

"Is that all? Then we can go home?"

"I'll not ask you to cut your hair and give it to the man who stole you away from your home and put you through a night of hell."

"Take it, for heavens sake!" Kristin held out the braid to Black Elk.

"Not without the permission of your husband. And he must cut it from your head and give it willingly to Runs Fast."

"Do it, Buck. Cut it off. It'll grow back."

"It's askin' a hell of a lot, honey, for me to give it to him willingly."

"Please—" She held the braid out by the end that was tied with a string. She didn't understand why her light hair was important to the Indian. Back home there were so many Swedish women with light hair that it went unnoticed. "I would shave my head and give it all to keep you from fighting him."

"I see why this is the woman of your heart, Lenning." Black Elk's eyes admired Kristin before he turned his attention back to the sullen Indian who stood with arms crossed. "Is it not enough if Lenning gives you his woman's hair?"

Runs Fast looked off toward the mountains. He remembered Lenning defeating him in a footrace several summers back. His humiliation had been great. Lenning was larger, stronger; and while Runs Fast considered himself skilled with a knife, Lenning would have the advantage because he had not gone for more than a day without rest as Runs Fast had done.

By taking the woman's hair, he would save face with his warriors and his wives would be glad to be rid of the hated *Wasicun*. He looked at his women now through different eyes. They were good to look upon and they did not wail or fight him as the *Wasicun* had done. They were strong, admired him greatly, and in time would bear him many sons.

His camp had been in an uproar since he had arrived with the *Wasicun* several hours ago. He had not thought his women would resent another wife so much, but they had screeched and yelled insults and threatened to divorce him. When he was rested, he would call them all to his blankets and let them give him pleasure.

"What is your word on this?" Black Elk thought he had given Runs Fast sufficient time to make a decision.

"I will take the hair, but I will cut it."

"The hell you will," Buck said heatedly.

"It is the husband's duty to give his wife's hair." Black Elk nodded for Buck to proceed.

Buck pulled his knife from his belt. Kristin held on to the

braid close to her head and Buck took the end. With it stretched tightly between their two hands he sawed back and forth with his knife until it came loose in his hand.

Holding it by the bound end, he held out the foot-long braid. Runs Fast reached for it and snatched it from his hand.

"Come near her again, you mangy son of a bitch, and I'll kill you," Buck muttered.

"It is done. We go." Black Elk walked quickly to his pony and sprang up onto its back.

Keeping himself between Kristin and Runs Fast, Buck urged her to where the warrior held the reins of the sorrel. One side of her hair hung down her back, the other side swung loosely over her shoulder. He boosted her into the saddle and mounted behind her.

Black Elk set a faster pace on the return trip to Iron Jaw's camp. The days were getting shorter and dusk came quickly to the mountains.

During the long ride they stopped only one time to water the horses and to let the scout behind them catch up and another scout go ahead. Buck could almost think Black Elk had had military training.

Kristin rode astride in front of Buck. She had been uncomfortable, at first, because her dress came only to her knees. Buck whispered to her that their companions were not shocked at the sight of her black-stockinged legs. He explained that men and women often bathed together in streams. She drew in a shocked breath.

"Without . . . clothes?"

Buck chuckled. "As bare as the day they were born."

"My goodness gracious!"

Buck opened his coat, drew her tightly against his chest and wrapped the coat around her. His tired body took on new life. Here in his arms was everything he ever wanted. That she was safe and back with him was a miracle. Now he had to figure out a way to get her to a safe place until the business with Forsythe was over.

While he was at Wheeler Creek he had decided to send her away with Gustaf. His arms tightened around her at the thought. When she was rested, he must talk to her about it, even though it would almost kill him to let her go.

"I saved bread pudding for your supper."

He groaned. "Don't tell me. Bonnie gave me some biscuits to eat on the way, but I was so worried I forgot to eat them."

"How did you find me?"

"At first I thought it was Forsythe's men. I'll tell you about it later. Are you warm?"

"Warm and happy."

After a few more whispers she fell silent, and he realized that she had gone to sleep.

Smoke from supper fires hung over the camp when they reached it. Buck followed Black Elk to Iron Jaw's lodge. The Indian dismounted when the old man came out. He listened to what Black Elk had to tell him, then came to where Buck sat his horse holding Kristin, who was still sleeping.

"It is good that Runs Fast gave up the woman without you having to kill him."

"I'm not so sure I would have. He is strong and clever."

"But you fight for your woman," the old man said. "You would have been the victor."

"Black Elk has my thanks for finding a way to prevent the fight."

"Runs Fast will go far away and look for his foolish vision.

He is vain and thinks only of what is good for him, not for our people." Iron Jaw spoke bitterly.

"I regret he has taken some of your young warriors. If you need the drovers you lent to me, I will send them back."

"They learn much from you. Black Elk says Buck Lenning is a man he could call brother."

"I say the same about him. I have long admired the Sioux and been ashamed of the treatment they have received from my people."

"It is enough that you say this."

"Thank you. My wife will also thank you when she awakens."

"When Man-Lost-in-Head first came to these mountains, he have hair like this." Gnarled fingers stroked the bright hair that had escaped from beneath Buck's coat. "Then his name White Cloud."

"Man-Lost-in-Head was my wife's uncle."

"I can see that it would be so. Long ago when first I see you, in Man-Lost-in-Head's bed, you cry with pain. I call you Crying Boy." The old man chuckled. "You mad, say bad words, want to fight." He placed his hand on Buck's knee in a gesture of affection. "No longer Crying Boy. Lenning is much man now."

"If that is true, I owe it to you, Iron Jaw, and to Man-Lost-in-Head."

"Be gone, my son." The old man waved his hand. "Black Elk will take you to a tepee where you can spend the night. Tomorrow will be time enough for you to return to the Larkspur."

# Chapter Twenty-four

Kristin awakened when Buck lifted her from the horse. She was dazed with fatigue and her legs were numb. He held her until she was able to stand alone, then led her into the tepee where a small fire burned in the center, the smoke going out the hole in the top of the cone-shaped structure.

"Stay here where it's warm. I'll unsaddle the horse."

He had thrown the stirrup up over the saddle to unfasten the cinch when she appeared beside him, shivering from the cold.

"I'll stay with you—"

He slipped out of his coat and put it around her shoulders. When he carried the saddle into the tepee, she was right behind him. The boy who had taken his horse that morning appeared and spoke to Buck, his dark eyes stealing glances at Kristin.

"Iron Jaw say take Lenning's horse."

"What's your name?"

"Three Toes. Soon I bring water and food."

"We would thank Three Toes for water that is warm so that we can be clean."

"Iron Jaw has commanded that I do that."

After the boy left Buck explained to Kristin what had been said, then took his bedroll from behind his saddle and rolled it out on a pile of furs beside the fire. Kristin watched him.

Her hair was a tangled mass framing her white face, her blue eyes clouded with fatigue.

He went to her and grasped her upper arms. In the dim light of the flickering fire he could see the tired lines around her eyes. He didn't want to add to the distress that had already been heaped upon her, but there was a thing he had to say.

"We must spend the night here . . . together. They believe we are man and wife. You're not to worry that—that I'll—"

"I want to sleep with you—"

"Sit down, honey. The boy will bring water for you to wash in and some to drink. He'll bring food." He eased her down to sit on his bedroll.

"You don't want to sleep with me." She said it in a resigned tone of voice.

He knelt down beside her and began unlacing her shoes.

"I want to sleep with you. God, how I want to!" He could not look at her for fear she'd see the longing in his eyes. "But I don't want you to do something tonight because you're worn-out that you'll regret tomorrow."

As he was removing her shoes the boy came with a kettle of water. He set it beside the fire and went out again. Buck opened one of his saddlebags and removed a cloth and a small slab of soap.

"I always carry this. I never know when I'm going to fall in a mud hole," he said in an attempt to lighten her mood.

He wet the cloth in the kettle, handed it to her and sat back on his heels to watch her. Her hair, her beautiful hair, was short on one side and jagged where he had cut her braid with his knife, the other side was snarled and hanging down her back.

She wiped her face with the warm cloth and groaned with pleasure.

"Oh, it feels so good."

When she finished, she rinsed the cloth in the warm water and, on her knees beside him, she ran the cloth lovingly over his rough cheeks, his forehead and into the corners of his eyes where dust had gathered. Dark lashes hid his eyes, but she knew they were on her face. He remained perfectly still as a long-buried memory of someone washing his face with loving hands came tumbling through his mind. *Was it the mother he had long forgotten?*

When she was finished, Kristin placed soft kisses on his forehead as if she were comforting a small child. Then with her arms around him she drew his head to her breast. With her lips in his wild dark hair and her eyes tightly closed she prayed:

*Dear God, please find a way for me to be with this man for the rest of my life. I will be a good wife to him. He is so deserving, and he has been so long without anyone to love him.*

The boy came in with a basket, set it down and left without their noticing he had been there. She continued to hold Buck and stroke his head and his cheeks.

He closed his eyes and gave himself up to this wonderful moment. He could hear the steady beat of her heart against his ear. He turned his head so that his lips were against her soft breast. He gloried in the scent of her woman's body. It was heaven—it was hell not to wrap her in his arms and blurt out his love for her.

When he moved, her arms fell away from him and she sat back down on the bedroll.

"I'll go out if you want to undress and wash all over."

"No! Don't go." She reached under her skirt, and rolled off her stockings and rubbed her tired feet.

Buck wet the cloth and lifted her feet to rest on his thighs.

He washed one gently with the warm cloth, then did the same to the other foot. Kristin's love for him grew. Never had anyone risked so much, or tended her as gently as this man she had known for only a few short weeks. She had not imagined there was a man like him and now he was woven into the fabric of her life, making her depend on him, making her love him.

"Maybe I was hasty taking off your shoes." His voice was husky with emotion. "If you need to go outside, I'll slip them back on."

"Will you go with me?"

"Sure."

"Let's go then." Kristin slipped her bare feet into the shoes. Buck draped his coat around her.

"I had my shawl last night. It got lost along the way."

"Can you make another out of that blue yarn?"

"The sky blue? You're afraid I'll knit socks for you out of that yarn," she teased.

They walked out into the darkness. Behind a thick fir tree, Buck stopped.

"You'll be all right here. I'll not be far away."

"Don't leave me. I don't care if . . . if you stay." Her voice was a mere breath of a whisper.

"I'll be just a few steps away. Call me."

"Don't go far." Kristin fumbled with her clothing, squatted down and quickly relieved her swollen bladder. She stood and called out to him even as she rearranged her clothing. "Buck."

"Here I am." His hand reached for her. She went to him eagerly.

With his arm holding her securely to his side, they went back to the warm shelter. Buck closed the door flap and put more sticks on the fire. He brought the food basket to the bedroll.

"You may not care for Indian food, but you should eat. We've got miles to travel tomorrow."

"Do you like it?"

"I'm used to it."

The basket held cold roasted grouse, flat Indian bread and a food Buck told her was *wasna,* a pemmican made with dried meat pounded with chokecherries and stuffed into sack casings instead of a buffalo bladder as was done in days of old. There were also wild plums and grapes.

"A feast," Kristin said, and smiled.

"It is. The only thing lacking is Indian turnips, cane shoots, mushrooms, boiled onions and a hindquarter of . . . ah . . . meat."

"What kind of meat?" Kristin pulled away a piece of the grouse.

"You don't want to know." His eyes smiled into hers.

"Yes, I do. This meat is very good. What kind of meat?" she asked again.

"Dog." He watched her, his eyes shining with amusement.

"Did you say—?"

"Yes."

"Like . . . Sam?"

"Yes."

She raised her brows and her mouth formed a silent O. Then she took a deep breath and smiled.

"I can't let it spoil my supper. This *wasna* isn't bad. It's kind of gritty though."

"That's the chokecherry seeds in it. Very little in the way of food goes to waste."

The fire had burned low by the time they finished eating.

Kristin wiped her hands on the wet cloth, then offered it to Buck.

Into the silence that followed Kristin asked, "Do you think everything is all right back . . . back home?"

"If not, wouldn't your cousin have told you?"

"I mean at Larkspur. Wisconsin is no longer my home."

"Your cousin wants to take you back there."

"He hasn't mentioned it because he knows I wouldn't go. He knows my heart is here now."

"You love him?" The question was so important to him that he couldn't look at her.

"Yes. I love him the same way Bonnie loves Bernie. He is almost my twin. After my mother died, he was the only person who cared about me. My brother, Ferd, took me into his home because it would have looked bad if he hadn't, but he never really cared for me. Maybe it was because we had different mothers."

After another long awkward silence, Buck said, "I'll put out the fire if you want to take off your dress and lie down."

"You don't have to put it out."

Kristin's fingers worked at the buttons on the front of her dress. She averted her eyes in sudden confusion.

"Reckon I'll step outside," Buck got to his feet.

She didn't ask him to stay or if he would be nearby. She followed him with large questioning eyes. When she was alone, she stood, removed her dress and her drawers, leaving only her thin shift covering her body. Feeling wanton and scared, but determined, she lay down on the bedroll, turned on her side and pulled Buck's blanket up over her.

After a while she began to feel a little fluttering sensation in her stomach. Would he come back? He had said they must stay together tonight. He had not answered when she asked if they would sleep together. He would have come to take her from the Indian out of loyalty to her Uncle Yarby. That was the kind of man he was. But had she misread his intentions when he called her his love? Honey? Sweetheart?

Tears of frustration and confusion were trickling from between her closed eyelids when she heard him enter the tepee. Regardless of her doubts, her resolve was firm. She would have this night with him. She opened her eyes and saw him squatting beside the fire.

"Come to bed. I know you're tired."

"Kristin—" His voice was strained. "I'm too dirty to sleep there with you."

"Not if you . . . take off your clothes."

"Oh, Lord—" Could he endure the gut-crushing agony of losing her if he was unable to control his desire for her and she was repulsed by him?

"Come." She folded back the blanket in invitation. "What harm is there in us sharing these blankets?"

The hunger to be with her, sleep with her in his arms, was too great. He stood and pulled off his shirt. Kristin could not pull her eyes away. His dark hair, wild as usual, matched the mat on his chest that tapered to his navel. By the dim light of the dying fire she could see that his shoulders were broad, heavily muscled and that his skin was darker than hers and smooth.

He sat down on the end of the bedroll and removed his boots. He was as still as a stone for a full minute as if trying to come to a decision. His big, shaggy head turned toward her.

"These . . . britches are filthy—"

"So was my dress."

He stood, worked at his belt and stepped quickly out of the heavy duck pants. She had seen the knee-length underwear he wore when she washed his clothes. It looked different now on his magnificently sculptured body than it had when she hung it on the line. She held her breath at the wonder of being here with him like this.

He slid under the blanket. A moan escaped him when his arms closed around her, and he pulled her into the curve of his big, hard body.

"Ahhh—" she breathed joyously, and tugged the blanket up and about his naked shoulders. She was safely ensconced against his firm, wide chest. She felt the sigh that went through him before she heard it.

"This feels good—"

"More than good—wonderful," she snuggled against him and whispered against his shoulder.

"More than wonderful. Much more."

For an endless time he held her clamped to him, desperate in his hunger to feel every inch of her, breathing hard into her hair. She tilted her head. His lips unerringly found hers. They caught and clung, released and caught again. They laughed together, low, intimate, joyous. Her moist breath on his neck preceded her lips that fastened and made little sucking movements reducing him to a quivering mass of pleasure.

"Humm . . . I'm so warm," she murmured and giggled happily. "I didn't know you had . . . hair on your chest."

"I wish I had shaved."

"I don't mind." Her fingertips went to his cheeks, to his lips. She laughed again, her face in the curve of his neck.

"I'll scratch your face."

"I have so many sore spots, one more won't matter."

"Where? Where do you hurt?" His arms loosened. "Am I hurting you?"

"No." Her arms tightened about him. "Buck? Do you think I'm a . . . bad woman for wanting to be with you like this?"

"Why would I think that? I wanted it, too. I wanted it so bad my insides were tied up in knots."

"We can be together like this . . . all night long." She yawned. "I wish I wasn't so tired."

A great wave of tenderness washed over him. She was wonderful, magnificent, and had stood up far better than most women would have under the circumstances. If he had nothing else, he would have this night with her to remember. The niggling fear that she might not want him after they returned to the Larkspur and she was with Gustaf again lingered in the back of his mind.

"Go to sleep, sweetheart," he whispered with his lips against her forehead.

"Will you sleep, too? Oh . . . I'm so comfortable. Are you? Are you warm?" She tucked the blanket closer about his shoulders.

"I could sleep on a pile of rocks with you in my arms."

"What a lovely thing to say! Will you tell me that in the morning?"

She sighed. Her head was pillowed on his arm, her legs interlaced with his, her breasts pressed to his chest. The feelings they had for each other were wholly without passion. More than thirty-six hours of physical and mental stress had taken a toll on their young bodies.

Kristin was first to fall asleep. The man holding her wanted to stay awake in order not to lose a minute of this time with her. But after two days in the saddle with a scant two hours of sleep, his body demanded rest.

He awakened several times in the night. Once was when Kristin turned, and pressed her back to his chest and her firm, round buttocks to his groin. He settled her head on his arm and went back to sleep. Another time he awakened to find his hand cupping her breast and her hand on his holding it there. His face was buried in her hair. He sighed with contentment and went back to sleep.

"Mornin', sleepyhead."

Kristin opened her eyes. Buck was leaning over her. Firelight flickered over his tousled hair, his face, and down over the mat of hair that covered his chest. His eyes held hers in a sensuous embrace. Her arms lifted to encircle his neck, his arms closed around her.

"Is it morning?"

"Uh-huh."

He tucked silky strands of her hair behind her ear and stroked her cheeks with his fingertips. Relaxed after her deep sleep, Kristin lost all touch with rational thinking. Her eyes moved lovingly over his smiling face. Her fingers spread and her palm rubbed in a circular motion against the rough hair on his chest. He seemed to be as mesmerized by her as she was by him. It was as if the world had suddenly fallen away, leaving only the two of them.

Buck knew the instant she became aware of the aroused part of him that pressed tightly to her hipbone. He searched the depths of her gaze for her reaction.

*She didn't cringe away from it.*

He lowered his head slowly until his lips were a fraction of an inch from hers. The sweet scent of her breath, the tangy smell of her skin, and the firm warm flesh of her thigh between his were a wild and powerful drug that started a craving for fulfillment deep in the center of his being.

Small puffs of air came from between her lips. Her hand

slid up his throat, then to the back of his neck. The core of passion that had long lain dormant within her flared into life, and, driven by her love, strong and pure, she fastened her lips to his.

The arms that held her to him were rock-hard, yet his response to her was so strong that they trembled. He deepened the kiss. She quivered at the heady invasion of his mouth and ran the tip of her tongue over the sharp edge of his teeth in welcome.

"Kristin, sweet—" He spoke thickly, his breath coming in even gasps that matched hers. In spite of himself he pressed and rubbed his hard aching flesh against her. "Tell me to go—"

"Do you want to go?"

"No, my darlin' girl . . . no! But I will—"

She pulled away from him a little and pulled her chemise down to her waist.

"I will never tell you to go, my dear, sweet man. I love you and, right now . . . I want to feel my breasts against you."

The tenderness of her tone caused a wild, sweet singing in his heart. His mouth moved over hers, gentle at first and then hard. She felt the tremor that shook him when the softness of her breasts touched the hair-roughened skin of his chest.

For a long while he loved her with his hands and his lips and his murmured words. "Kristin . . . my Kristin." A deep longing compelled her to meet his passion equally. She kept her eyes tightly closed, not wanting to come out of the dreamlike state. Suddenly the driving force of feeling took her beyond herself into a mindless void where there were only Buck's lips, Buck's hands, Buck's hard demanding body covering hers.

Without hesitation, their bodies joined in mutual, frantic

need. She heard sounds of his smothered groans, as if they came from a long way to reach her ears. Incredibly, there was no awkwardness, no hesitation, and she felt only a few seconds of discomfort when he entered and filled her. Then their pleasure rose to almost intolerable heights.

Kristin had never felt anything like the sensations she was feeling now. Her hands moved over the smooth muscles of his back and down to the smoothness of his buttocks. Aware of his tense excitement, listening to the heavy beat of his heart, she knew the excruciating joy of mating with her man. She moved against him, clutching at his back while he pressed into her. She wrenched upward and tensed, wanting to know and have every little bit of him. His weight pressed her into the bedroll, and her arms tightened about him as they rode out the storm of their emotions.

When it was over, neither one of them moved. Kristin could feel tiny aftershocks of climax in the heated sheath that enclosed him. Gradually their hearts and lungs regained their natural rhythms. His head rested on her shoulder, his lips touched the spot beneath her ear. They lay still, sharing the sweet aftermath of their loving.

"Kristin, sweet one. I'm sorry . . . if I was rough. I wanted you so , . . bad—" The soft ragged whisper came to her ear.

"You were not rough. I'm not fragile. I liked what we did and how we did it." She shifted her legs slightly to cradle his hips more comfortably between her thighs.

Buck lifted his upper body and supported it by both elbows. There was a seeking look in his eyes.

"Kristin?" Her name was a murmured, husky whisper. "You know what I am. I've not had much schooling and my manners are not what they ought to be. I've got a spot of land and a small herd of steers. Not much to offer a woman like you. But Kristin . . . sweet, would you . . . consider marrying me?"

"I don't need anything but you." She framed his face with the palms of her hands. "You're the sweetest, kindest man in all the world. If you hadn't asked me to marry you, my heart would have broken right in two. I want to be with you forever. I'll be so proud to be your wife."

She caught her breath as his face was transformed with love and happiness. If she didn't know better, she would have thought the glistening she saw in the brilliant green eyes was caused by tears.

"We'll plant our roots on the Larkspur, my darlin'. We'll have sons and daughters to bring us grandchildren. And when we're old, we'll sit on the porch and look at the mountains. Oh, Buck. I'm so happy, I think that . . . I might even like Runs Fast . . . a little!"

His lips moved to hers. Gently and tenderly he held them captive in a long, lingering, trembling kiss. When he would have moved his lips away, she followed with her own, and his sigh was a mingling of pleasure and need as he flexed his hips and she flexed hers in a welcoming response.

He was sure that he was the luckiest man alive.

# Chapter Twenty-five

*I*t had been a day of anxiety at the Larkspur.

Bonnie cooked meals, and the men came silently to the table to eat them. Gustaf had such a look of anguish on his face that it was difficult to believe that he was the cheerful man he had been a few days ago. He blamed himself for allowing the Indian to come in and steal Kristin away.

Bonnie felt guilty because she was here and Kristin wasn't or could be dead. There were many *ifs* in her mind. *If* she had gone into the house with Kristin. *If* she hadn't been so wrapped up in her visit with Gustaf, she might have heard something. *If* she and her brother had not come here in the first place.

After the noon meal, Bonnie went to see about the new calf and fed a few of the remaining biscuits to Sam. The dog gobbled the treat and hurried back to the bunkhouse, where he figured to get another bit of food from Tandy. During the last few days he and the old man had become fast friends. Sam lay beside the bunk for hours at a time while Tandy's fingers stroked his bristly head.

By late afternoon a fresh, cool breeze blew down from the mountains. Bonnie stood on the porch. In the evening light the vista as far as she could see was an arcadia of peace and beauty. The blue-gray of the mountains was a background for the pale gold grasses and the dark green of the cedars. She drew in a long breath of the fresh air and permitted herself to enjoy the view before she went back into the house to put the supper on the table.

Even Gilly was quiet during the evening meal. Bernie encouraged him to talk about Buck and his friendship with the Sioux, but after a few grunted responses the conversation died. Bonnie set a pan of rice pudding on the table and turned to get the coffee pot when the Indian lad, known as Beaver Boy, opened the door and said two words that caused a flurry of action.

*"Wasicun* come."

Chair legs scraped the floor as the men got to their feet. Gilly picked up his rifle and headed for the front of the house. The others followed. Two riders were coming out of the woods at the north side of the house.

"It's Marshal Lyster. He doesn't have authority out here," Bernie said. "I don't know the other fellow."

"I do. He was with Mike Bruza the morning I poured coffee on him. Two-bit gunslinger is what Mr. Stark called him."

Marshal Lyster rode up to within a few yards of the porch.

"Evenin', folks. I could smell your supper a mile out. Smelled mighty good."

"If yo're expectin' an invite to supper, yo're outta luck," Gilly said bluntly. "What'd ya want here?"

"Come to see Lenning. Got some papers to serve." Lyster shifted his weight to get off the horse, but after Gilly spoke again he settled back into the saddle.

"Nobody invited ya to get down."

"Ain't ya the hired hand here?"

"Ya might say that."

"I know the gal and her brother, but who're you?" Lyster's eyes focused on Gustaf.

"Name's Gus. Who are you?"

"Marshal Lyster."

"Of Big Timber, not out here." Bonnie's voice was fringed with sarcasm. She ignored the grinning, rat-faced man on the other horse who was leering at her as if he'd never seen a woman before.

"Still mouthy, ain't ya, gal."

"Her name is Miss Gates." Gustaf spoke sharply to the big pot-bellied man on the horse. "You're sadly lacking in manners for a public official."

"Ya think so, huh? And you tinhorns have big mouths. Well, are we gettin' an invite to supper or not?"

"I cooked it. I'd give it to the buzzards first."

"My, my." The marshal leaned on the saddle horn and leered at Bonnie. "Somebody's goin' to have to take you in hand and knock the sass outta ya, gal. It just might get done before the night's over."

"I'd be right glad to do the job fer ya, marshal." Greg Meader leaned forward, a wolfish grin on his face.

"Just try it, you weasel-faced mule's ass, and I'll spread your rotten guts all over the territory!" Bonnie used her voice to cut as deeply as her words, but Meader only laughed.

"Wheee—! Ain't she a caution?"

"Buck ain't here, so be gone," Gilly broke into the conversation.

"Is Miss Anderson here? Miss Kristin Anderson, old Yarby's kin."

"I know who she is. She ain't here either."

"Off some'r's ballin' with Lenning. Huh?"

"Drop your guns." The voice came from behind.

Bonnie spun around to see Mike Bruza in the doorway, two six-guns in his hands.

"Took ya long enough." The marshal swung down from his horse.

"An Indian kid was hangin' around the back. Had to wait till he left," Bruza said. "I'd a shot the little bastard, if not for the racket it'd a made."

Meader dismounted and swaggered up onto the porch. He jerked the rifles from the hands of Gustaf and Gilly and lifted the gun out of the holster Bernie wore.

"We know Lenning ain't here. Had a feller watchin' the house all day. We figure to wait for him here where it's warm and we got somethin' to pass the time with." Bruza spoke as if he and not Lyster was in charge. "Meanwhile"—he gave Bonnie a nudge with the end of his gun—"put some supper on the table and . . . be careful with that coffeepot, or I'll put a bullet right between yore brother's eyes." He swung the gun around and pointed it at Bernie's head.

The marshal led the way into the kitchen; the men followed, knowing that Mike had his gun in Bonnie's back.

"Sit down on the floor," Lyster commanded. He cut the line Kristin had strung over the stove to dry the dish towels. While Meader held his gun on the men, the marshal bound their hands behind their backs. "Now scoot back against the wall. Behave and nobody'll get hurt. It's Lenning and the Anderson woman we want."

"Speak fer yoreself, marshal. I'm wantin' me some a that." Meader spoke with his beady eyes on Bonnie.

"Ya'll have to stand in line after me," Mike said. "This bitch *owes* me. She damn near ruined my whacker. It's all right now," he said as if to reassure her. "I tried it out a couple of times down at Flo's." Mike gave Bonnie another shove. "What's that in the pan?"

"Rice puddin'. I let the dog pee in it."

Meader laughed uproariously. "Ain't she somethin'?" he said between guffaws. "I like a woman with sass."

Mike was not amused. "What I said about that brother of yores goes." He poked Bonnie in the back again with the gun. "Get some grub on the table and keep your mouth shut." He was almost shouting by the time he finished.

Bonnie added wood to the firebox and moved the stew kettle to the front of the stove. She added a couple of dippers of water and several pinches of salt. From beneath the work counter she took a jar, opened it and reached in for what looked like a handful of dried leaves.

"What's that?" Mike was behind her touching her shoulder with his chin.

"Sage. I had to water down the stew to make enough." She shrugged her shoulder away from him, dropped the leaves in the pot and stirred vigorously with a long wooden spoon.

"I don't like sage."

"Too late, it's in there." Bonnie replaced the lid and shoved the jar back under the counter. As she turned her head, her eyes caught Gilly's briefly.

The marshal settled down in one of the big chairs. Meader roamed about the room. He pulled down the lid on Buck's rolltop desk, pawed around and then closed it. He went into the room shared by Bonnie and Kristin and came out with Kristin's hairbrush. Long blond hairs were entwined in the bristles!

"She's been here."

"Hell, we know that!" Mike snatched the brush from

Meader's hand. He gave Gilly a vicious kick on the thigh. "Where is she?"

"How the hell do I know? Her'n Buck rode off some'er's. Buck said somethin' 'bout Helena."

"Helena! Ya lyin' bastard." He threw the hairbrush against the wall. "No woman'd go to Helena and not take her hairbrush." He squatted down beside Gustaf. "What're ya doin' here, pretty boy?"

"Thank you, sir, for the compliment," Gustaf said pleasantly. "Just passing through your beautiful country. I was invited to stay a spell and rest up. And here I am."

"Here you are," Mike echoed. "Tinhorn, you stopped at the wrong place."

"I didn't think so at the time. Folks gave me a fine welcome. Now . . . I'm not so sure."

"Who . . . gave you the welcome?"

"Mr. Lenning and his Indian wife."

"I've not heard that Lenning took a squaw." Marshal Lyster spoke up.

Gustaf shrugged. "I only know what they tell me. Her people are"—he looked at Gilly as if seeking confirmation—"did he say Iron Jaw, or something like that? I think they're camped not far from here. You might go ask them."

"I don't like you, pretty boy!" Mike struck Gustaf across the face with the back of his hand.

"It'll be a shame to put a torch to this place." Meader stood before the mantel. "Always did want me a clock like this. I could live here like a gawddamn gov'nor. I'd get me a couple of squaws to do fer me. Yes, sir. I'd sit here and listen to that clock tick-tock, tick-tock, tick—"

"Shut up!" Mike shouted. "Get outside and make sure there ain't nobody sneakin' round."

"Why've I got to do that for? Ya got half a dozen out there a watchin'. Ya'll know it if Lenning rides in."

"Half a dozen rattle-headed saddle tramps is what I got out there. Go take a look around, ya horny goat, and get yore mind off gettin' in that woman's drawers. Plenty of time for that later."

Meader went out the door; Bruza moved to the window and peered out.

"Dish up a bait a that stew, gal." Marshal Lyster seated himself at the table. "I ain't had nothin' since early mornin'."

Bonnie filled a large bowl for Lyster and another for Mike and carried them to the table.

"Your supper is ready, *Mister* Bruza." Anger made her voice shrill.

Bruza continued to look out the window, turning every few seconds to glance at the men sitting on the floor. Bonnie sliced bread and watched anxiously as the marshal wolfed down the stew. After shoving the platter of fresh bread at him to divert his attention, she went to her brother and placed one hand on his back, the other on his forehead.

"Get away from him!" Mike barked.

"He's been sick. I'm seein' if he has a fever." The knife up her sleeve slid down Bernie's back. He grasped it in his bound hands.

"It ain't goin' to matter pretty soon if he's sick or not. Get away from him."

Bonnie backed away. Bruza came to the table. He had placed his gun beside the bowl of stew and had started to sit down, when a thump sounded from the porch. He looked at the red-faced marshal who, still eating the stew, hadn't seemed to notice the sound. Mike's eyes darted to the men on the floor, then to Bonnie. Quick as a cat, he was behind her, with his gun in her back.

"Open the door! Call out to Meader. Tell him supper is ready."

Bonnie did as she was told. Her voice came out squeaky.

"Meader, supper is ready."

"It will be impossible for him to eat with his throat cut." The voice came out of the darkness.

"Who's out there," Mike demanded. "Speak up or I'll gut-shoot this woman."

"You know who I am, Bruza. I've come to kill you as I told you I would if you as much as touch a hair on Bonnie's head."

Del Gomer's figure emerged out of the darkness at the end of the porch.

"Forsythe said you was in Bozeman."

"Forsythe is a lying son of a bitch, just as you are. Let go of Bonnie and you'll die easy. Hurt her and I'll burn your eyes out before I cut the flesh off your bones."

Bonnie could feel the panic in the hand that gripped her shoulder. Mike tried to pull her backward into the kitchen. She dug in her heels to make it as difficult as she could.

"Get back or I'll shoot her!"

Del continued across the porch, his eyes on Bruza, his hand gripping the gun at his side. When he was a couple of yards away, Mike moved the gun around and fired under Bonnie's arm. She saw Del stagger and a cry of alarm escaped her. She threw herself back and to the side to give Del a clear shot. Mike fired again. As she hit the floor she heard three shots. Three bullets slammed into Mike and drove him back into the room. She hastily got to her feet. Del hung on to the side of the door, the smoking gun in his hand.

"Bonnie . . . did he . . . hurt you?"

"No! But he hurt you. Oh, Del—" Bonnie glanced quickly at Mike on the floor, then at the marshal whose head had dropped to the table. The larkspur weed had either killed him or rendered him unconscious. She went to Del and put her shoulder under his arm. "Get inside so I can close the door. There's others out there."

Leaning heavily on her, he managed to get to a chair. Bonnie slammed the door shut and dropped the bar. She grabbed a big knife and hurried to cut the bonds of the men on the floor. Bernie had freed himself with the knife she had slipped to him. He cut Gilly's bonds.

As soon as Gustaf was freed, he jumped to his feet, grabbed the marshal's hair and lifted his face. Lyster was still alive and gasping for air. Gustaf uttered a few angry words in Swedish and shoved the marshal's face down hard in the bowl of stew.

"Eat, you bastard!"

Bonnie hurried to Del and tried to remove his coat. He was holding his hand tightly to his side.

"Don't, my love. It's no use."

"Don't say that!"

"I came as soon as I . . . knew." His voice was raspy.

"Bernie, help me get him to a bed."

Gustaf and Bernie carried Del to the little room and placed him on the bed. Bernie covered the window with a blanket and Bonnie brought the lamp from the kitchen.

"Is the marshal dead?" she asked.

"I hope so. What did you put in the stew?"

"Dried larkspur. Kristin said it would kill cattle so I thought it would kill buzzards, too. She said Buck cautioned her about it. He kept the jar to use to kill lice on furs— Oh, Bernie, we've got to do something for Del." Bonnie opened Del's shirt and gasped at the amount of blood. "Take off his shoes. I'll get towels and water."

In the darkened kitchen, she was careful to step around Mike's body when she went to Gilly, who was watching out the back window.

"Do you think they'll come?"

"Ain't sure, missy. One thin' sure, that feller saved our bacon. We'd a been done for when Bruza got a look at the marshal, all keeled over."

"Is he dead?"

"If the larkspur didn't kill him, Gus drowned him in that stew."

"I was thinking they'd all eat at one time."

"Worked out just dandy. Ya done good, girl. Marshal might'a shot us all when he saw Bruza go down. I hope Tandy stays put in the bunkhouse," he added worriedly.

"We could open the door and yell across to him."

"Don't do that. They may not know he's there, missy. Gus is watchin' out the front. We'll know if the bastards get close with a torch."

Bonnie gathered up towels and hurried back to Del's bedside. Bernie had taken off his shirt and his shoes. He looked at his sister and slowly shook his head.

"Maybe Gustaf can do something."

"I'll send him in."

Bonnie pressed a towel to the wound almost in the middle of Del's stomach. It was immediately soaked with bright blood. She placed another on top of the first one. All the time Del's eyes followed her.

When Gustaf came in, he lifted the towel to look at the wound below Del's ribs then covered it quickly and added another towel. Del appeared to be oblivious to Gustaf and the pain he must be suffering.

"Is this . . . your bed, Bonnie?"

"It's where Miss Anderson and I slept."

"It's . . . I'm . . . getting it all bloody."

"Don't worry about it. It'll wash."

"Mister." Gustaf knelt down beside the bed. Del's silver eyes turned to him. "I'm not a doctor, but I've seen quite a few gunshot wounds. I don't think there's a thing we can do for you. You're bleeding inside. If I were in your place I'd want someone to be straight with me."

"It's . . . what I . . . thought. I got rid of a couple out in the grove. The one that came out . . . is at the end of the porch. Don't let them get Bonnie." He gasped for breath, then added: "Shoot her . . . if you have to. I know what they'd do—"

"We thank you for what you've done. They were going to kill us and . . . do worse to Bonnie. We'll . . . take care of her now."

Bonnie knelt down beside Gustaf and took Del's hand. Tears rolled down her cheeks. She never knew when Gustaf left them and she was alone with the dying man.

"You . . . cryin' for me, Bonnie?"

"It was dumb of you to keep comin' when you knew he'd shoot you."

"I . . . knew he'd not shoot the one . . . shielding him. That's all I . . . cared about." It was difficult for him to breathe, but he continued to talk. "I heard what happened at the café. I'm glad you . . . burnt him."

"Del." She held his hand to her cheek. "I wish I could have loved you after . . . after I knew—"

"You loved me before?"

"Yes. And . . . still a part of me loves you."

"It's all . . . right. Don't cry . . . sweetheart." His eyes remained glued to her face. Blood came from his nose and streaked his cheek. She gently wiped it away.

"I'm the way I am and you're the way you are—"

"This is more than I . . . expected. It's a good end for a man . . . like me. I'm here with the woman I love, in her bed and . . . she's cryin' over me." He smiled; one of the few smiles she'd seen since she had met him.

"I never thought it would end like this."

"There's always an ending. See a man in Bozeman named Joseph Long. I made a will while I . . . was there last week. I had a feeling—" His voice was weaker, his skin almost yellow as his life's blood seeped away. "You won't have to work . . . so hard."

Bonnie held back the words of protest that came to her mind.

"How did you know I was here?" she asked.

"Forsythe. He's . . . crooked as a snake. He beats that nice woman he lives with." His voice trailed and his eyes drifted shut, but opened quickly. "She got word to me that . . . he'd sent Bruza and Lyster . . . here." He gasped for every word. "I was afraid . . . I'd be too late. 'Bout rode that horse to death."

Bonnie stroked the hand she held in hers. It was not the hand of a laboring man. It was smooth, the fingers long and slender, the nails cut close. The fingers had pulled the trigger . . . how many times? How many men had they killed? She could feel his calm, silver eyes on her face like caressing hands.

"Why me, Del? You're a handsome man. Well-mannered, well-dressed women must have been after you."

"They weren't you. You didn't want anything. Your smile was the same for me as it was for old Cletus, for a little kid, or Mrs. Gaffney. I love . . . your laughing eyes, your sweet mouth, your loyalty to your brother. I . . . never knew what it was to . . . have a sister . . . or a brother." His voice picked up strength as if he were determined to say what he had to say. "Bon . . . ie, Bon . . . ie. I love to say your name."

Each time he closed his eyes, she wasn't sure he would open them again. She leaned over and soothed the hair back from his forehead with her fingertips. Then pressed a gentle kiss on his lips.

"Thank you . . . for loving me," she murmured. "You saved my life and my brother's life back in Big Timber and again here."

"I . . . could do no less . . . for the woman I love."

"I'll remember you . . . always."

"Will you kiss me . . . again?" His eyes were beginning to cloud. Bonnie wiped away the blood that came from his nose and pressed her warm lips to his cool ones.

"Bon . . . nie, remember . . . me—"

He closed his eyes, but almost immediately they opened and fastened on her face. His hand continued to grip hers.

Minutes passed. After a while Bonnie realized the eyes staring into hers had not blinked and the hand she held lay lifeless in hers. She felt grief, loss . . . pity. She sat beside him for a long while. Then she heard the clock strike the half hour.

"Good-bye, Del. I'll not forget you," she murmured, and gently closed his eyes. With a wet cloth, she washed his face, the long slender hands, and covered his face with the sheet.

Bonnie blew out the lamp and sat down in the chair beside the bed. What had caused a man, handsome and educated, to become a hired killer? What had caused him to love her, to give his life for her? She couldn't despise him, and she couldn't love him. But what she had said to him was true, a little part of her would always care for him.

She sat beside him, wondering if he had a family somewhere who loved him. What kind of childhood had formed the man who killed for money? There were two men inside the handsome body of Del Gomer: the cold-blooded killer, and the gentle, lonely man who was capable of loving and willing to die for the one he loved.

She would never know the answers to the questions that would haunt her for the rest of her life.

When she left the room, she closed the door. In the kitchen, a flickering candle set beneath the table gave just enough light so that she could see her brother at one window and Gustaf at the other.

"It's over." Her words fell into the quiet.

After a pause Gustaf's voice came from the parlor end of the room.

"His guts must have been on fire. Some men would have been screaming their heads off, but I never heard a peep from him. He really loved you, Bonnie."

"Yes, and I don't want to hear one bad word about him." Bonnie's voice choked.

"You'll not hear it from me. The man knew what he was doing when he walked right into that gun."

"He was a strange man," Bernie said quietly. "I hated him for wanting Bonnie and . . . he gave his life for her."

They were silent while the clock struck midnight. Four hours had passed since they had sat down to supper. So much had happened.

Gilly came from the other room.

"I been on the porch listenin'. Somethin' goin' on out there. Heard a couple horses take off on the run. Could be that

Bowlegs got back and cut their horses loose or else Buck come home. If he did, he'll give a whistle."

"Oh, I hope he did. I hope to God he's got Kristin."

Gilly opened the back door. The repeated whistle of the redbird was followed by the call of a squalling hawk.

"I ain't never heard that call before. It ain't no Indian. It ain't Buck either." Gilly was plainly puzzled. The call was repeated, then silence.

"Do you think someone's tryin' to fool us to get in here?" Bernie asked.

"I ain't knowin'. Ain't that someone callin'?"

"Buck! It's Stark! Cleve Stark!"

"That's a relief. We know Mr. Stark."

"We ain't knowin' fer sure it's him." Gilly was cautious. He stuck his head out the door and yelled, "How'er we knowin' that?"

"That you, Gilly? Dad-blameit, ask Bernie if me and Dillon met with him and his sister in the back of the restaurant one night last week."

"It's Stark." The twins spoke at once.

"Come on in," Gilly yelled.

Three men walked their horses into the yard and up to the back porch.

"Lord, Gilly, it was easier to get through that bunch waitin' to burn you out than to get in here. Where's Buck?" Cleve stepped down from his horse.

"Gone. What happened . . . out there?"

"Nothin' much. We played a few tricks on them and they decided to head for Wyoming."

"Light the lamp, missy." There was a tired, but relieved tone in Gilly's voice. "Come on in. We got us some talkin' to do."

"We heard shots a hour ago, then the lights went out. Figured ya come out on top, or Bruza would've called in his dogs."

The Mexican looked down at Bruza, who lay where Del's bullets had slammed him.

"Yi, yi, yi. He was a bad one, *Señores*."

"This is Pablo Cardova. He rode with Bruza and his bunch for a while—"

"Then what's he doin' here?" Bernie's voice had a belligerent tone.

"It's a long story. He's really here . . . for another reason. Fellers out there thought he was on their side. Who's that?" Cleve asked, jerking his head toward the man who sat at the table with his face in a bowl, the contents of which were slopped out onto the table.

"Marshal Lyster of Big Timber," Gilly said with a grimace. "He's eatin' his supper."

"Somebody's been busy. Found three men outside with their throats cut." He stepped over Mike. "Got coffee?"

"Got plenty of coffee, but don't touch the stew." Bonnie shook down the ashes and added more wood to the cookstove. "I'll have to dump it in the outhouse to keep the dog from eating it."

"That bad, huh?"

"Ask Marshal Lyster. He'll tell you."

# Chapter Twenty-six

Kristin and Buck left Iron Jaw's camp at sunup. As they were preparing to leave, Black Elk and his sister, Little Owl, came to where Buck was saddling his horse.

"Is all well with your wife, Lenning?"

"She is good."

"Little Owl has a gift for her."

Black Elk urged his sister forward. She came awkwardly, using a forked stick as a crutch. Shyly, she held out a pair of elaborately beaded moccasins.

"For woman from Larkspur," she said in halting English.

Kristin accepted the moccasins, looked at them closely, and hugged them to her breast. The smile she gave to Little Owl was radiant.

"Thank you. Oh, thank you! They're beautiful. Did you make them?"

Little Owl's large questioning eyes went to Buck.

"You make?" he asked slowly, then to Kristin. "Speak slow and she'll understand."

"I make. Give to Lenning's woman."

"I want to put them on." Kristin looked at Buck. He nodded. She sat on the ground and unlaced her shoes. With the moccasins on her feet she stood, lifted her skirt and looked down. "Oh, my. They are so comfortable and . . . pretty." Her pleasure was so obvious that Little Owl began to smile. Kristin reached out and clasped her hand. "Thank you. I wish to be your friend."

"Friends," Little Owl repeated.

"Can she come to the Larkspur sometime, Buck? Oh, I wish she could. I'll make her a gift . . . out of that sky blue yarn." Her eyes laughed into his.

"You are welcome at the Larkspur," Buck said to Black Elk as he put Kristin's shoes in one of his saddlebags. "My home is your home. My wife would be friends with your wife and your sister."

"Soon we leave for lands in the West. It is a long journey to the Larkspur. My wife is not strong. My sister's leg has not healed."

"Can we come back, Buck?" Kristin asked. "I'd love to come back before they go."

"We'll see."

He placed his hand at the back of her neck and followed the one long braid down over her shoulder. Early that morning he had watched in fascination as she pulled her hair to the side and wove the short strands in with the long hair to make the braid. She showed him how she would wind the braid around her neck and pin it until the cut side had grown out.

"The braid is not quite so fat," she had told him, "but no one will know . . . but you and me."

When they were ready to leave, he took his coat from her shoulders, slipped it on and lifted her up onto the horse. He stepped into the saddle and settled her in front of him. With her back against his chest, the coat and his arms around her, they waved good-bye to Black Elk and Little Owl.

"Thank you for helping to find me, Black Elk. And thank you for my lovely moccasins, Little Owl," Kristin called as they rode out of the Indian camp. She felt Buck's lips moving on the side of her face and her heart pounded with a happiness she never dreamed would be hers.

"A month or so ago I found Little Owl down on Sweet Grass Creek with a broken leg. I'll tell you about it sometime."

"She's very pretty."

"Not as pretty as my . . . wife."

"I love hearing you say *that*. How could something that started off so terrible, have such a grand ending? Buck, I'm so happy, I may burst open at the seams."

"Don't do that, love."

His arms tightened. He had just spent the most wonderful night of his life. It was almost beyond his understanding that this lovely creature could love him and want to spend her life with him.

"What's grand is that you're mine, and I can hug you and kiss you . . . and touch you"—his hand slid under the coat and cupped her soft breast—"whenever I want to."

"Only when we're alone, my love." She pressed his hand with her own. "Feel my heart pound?"

"Is that your heart? I thought a scared bird had got caught in there." He chuckled, his breath warm puffs against her ear.

"Will you want to kiss me when I'm old and gray . . . and have no teeth?"

"By then I'll have whiskers down to the knees and won't be able to get up out of my chair."

"That'll be all right, my love. I'll sit on your lap so you can kiss me." Their happy laughter mingled.

Although the sorrel was a powerful animal, it was carrying double weight. Buck wanted to reserve the horse's strength should they need it in a hurry, and he stopped often to give it a rest. During these times they stood close together, her arms around his waist, his arms and the coat wrapped around her. This new freedom to touch her, to know that she loved him, filled Buck with indescribable joy and contentment.

The sun was past the high point in the sky when they rode onto Larkspur land.

"I hope everything is all right at home." Kristin spoke as they came down from the upper mesa and entered the valley.

Until now the thoughts of Forsythe and his plans to grab the Larkspur away from them had been shoved to the back of her mind. The discovery that Buck loved her made all else pale in comparison. With or without the Larkspur, they would be together from now on. That was all that mattered to her.

"We'll know soon."

Buck's eyes moved constantly from one side of the trail to the other. Out in the open they scanned the edge of the woods. He had not smelled woodsmoke since leaving the Indian camp and was reasonably sure his homestead had not burned while he was away.

At the edge of the woods, just beyond the creek and with a good view of the house, Buck stopped the horse. His sharp eyes discerned that there were more horses in the corral, a lot more, than should be there. The possibility existed that Gilly and the others were being held hostage by Forsythe's men until he returned. The Indian camp behind the homestead appeared to be deserted.

Out of rifle range and with a clear escape route behind him, he put his fingers to his lips and whistled.

"There are sheets on the line. I wonder why Bonnie washed. Do you think something is wrong?" Kristin asked fearfully.

"I don't know, sweetheart. I'm not riding in there with you until I'm sure it's safe." He whistled again.

A minute later a group of men and Bonnie came out the kitchen door and into the yard. It was easy to identify Gilly's white hair and Bernie's peg leg when he came from the bunkhouse. Sam came running, barking a welcome. Still Buck waited for Gilly's signal that it was safe to come in. When it came, he put his heels to the sorrel and they crossed the grassland to the ranch house.

"Our house, Buck. Our beautiful house. I was afraid I'd never see it again."

"Wave to Bonnie, honey. They're anxious to know if you're all right."

"Are you still blaming Gustaf for letting Runs Fast take me?" Kristin asked as she waved.

"No. He's not wise to our ways, and Runs Fast knew all the tricks. I'm kind of mad at Sam. But I guess he got used to the smell of Bowlegs and the other drovers and didn't pick up on Runs Fast's smell."

Gustaf was there when they rode into the yard, as were three strangers and Gilly, Bonnie and Bernie.

"It's Cleve Stark, honey. Remember me telling you I had sent for a Federal marshal?" Buck murmured the words in Kristin's ear.

"Kris! Thank God you're all right." Her cousin was there when the horse stopped. She put her hands on his shoulders and he lifted her down. "Hellfire! I've been so scared I haven't spit for two days." He hugged her. "I'm downright sorry I let that Indian carry you off—"

"—And I'm so sorry I didn't go into the house with you," Bonnie said, and grasped her hands. "Lordy, but we've been worried. Gilly kept sayin' that Buck would find you and bring you back. Goodness, I've so much to tell you." Words rushed from Bonnie's mouth.

"I've got lots to tell you."

As she spoke, Kristin's eyes rested lovingly on Buck. He was shaking hands with one of the men. Another man, much younger, stood nearby and pumped Buck's hand vigorously when introduced. A swarthy bowlegged Mexican with a drooping mustache watched, then shook hands with Buck.

"Kristin, come meet Cleve Stark, Dillon Tallman and their friend, Pablo." Buck held his hand out to her. "We're going to be married as soon as we can get to town and find a preacher." He made the announcement proudly while looking over Kristin's head at Gustaf. To his surprise, her cousin's face broke into a huge smile.

Blushing prettily, Kristin shook hands with Cleve Stark, then the handsome young blond giant, who gave her a devilish grin.

"Pleased to meet ya, ma'am. And . . . this bowlegged, grinnin' jackass beside me waitin' his turn to hold your hand ain't no friend a mine."

"*Señora,* pay no mind to the kid. He love me." The Mexican clasped her hand warmly, then backed away and grinned up at Dillon.

Kristin felt Gustaf's hand on her arm. He pulled her close and hugged her.

"Best news I've heard in a month of Sundays, little cousin." Gustaf was genuinely pleased. It was what he'd hoped for. She deserved the best. "How'd you get Buck to propose, love? Did you poke needles under his fingernails? Why else'd a man propose to an ugly old thing like you? And, Buck, as her almost-twin, I give my blessing. Glad to get her off my hands and turn her over to you."

"Gus! Stop teasing!"

"Keep her pregnant, Buck," Gustaf chortled happily. He was enjoying himself and had more to say. "Get a dozen cows for her to milk, put her behind a plow, switch her once in a while with a willow switch and she might make you . . . ah . . . a fair-to-middlin' wife."

Kristin hit him on the forearm with her fist. She tried to present a picture of outrage, but her laughter burst from her lips. Her shiny blue-gray eyes sought Buck's, as they had done a hundred times that day and found them resting lovingly on her face.

"Excuse my cousin, gentlemen. Sometimes he acts like he doesn't have a lick of sense. And excuse me, too, I need to wash and get into some clean clothes. And . . . I'm starving—"

"Don't eat any of Bonnie's stew." Gustaf spoke loudly from behind his hand and winked at Bernie.

"It ain't fit fer a dog to eat, and that's a fact," Bernie added.

Kristin noticed the glances that passed between her cousin and Bonnie's brother. She was pleased to see that a bond of friendship had been forged while she'd been away.

"Shame on the two of you for teasing her. I'd let them cook their own meals, Bonnie."

"I hate to admit it but this time, they're right. There's hot water on the stove, Kristin. You men stay out here for . . . at least a half hour," she tossed the orders back over her shoulder as she and Kristin walked toward the house.

Bonnie asked and received permission from Buck to bury Del Gomer on the plot of ground above the ranch buildings where Yarby Anderson had been laid to rest.

"He has no friends in town. He has no friends . . . any-where. I can't bear the thought of him being loaded in the wagon with the others . . . and being hauled away . . . like he didn't amount to anything. He was a man, a bad man, but he had a good side, too."

To some it may have been sacrilegious to read a passage from the Bible and to sing a hymn over a hired killer. On the knoll, beneath the towering pine, it didn't seem to matter what he had been in life. When the brief services ended, those whom Del Gomer had saved, along with Buck and Kristin, stood by while Cleve and Dillon filled the grave.

When they had finished, Bonnie placed a sprig of evergreen tied with a scrap of ribbon on the mound of fresh soil.

"Good-bye, Del. And . . . thank you," she murmured, and turned away.

Earlier, Cleve and Gilly had taken Buck to the barn to view the bodies of six men laid out in one of the stalls. The stew had been wiped from Marshal Lyster's face but was still visible on his shirtfront.

"Hell, the larkspur that spunky gal fed him might a got to him 'fore he drowned in the stew. I ain't knowin' or carin'." Impatience made itself known in Gilly's tone. "The bastard was gonna kill us. There ain't a mark on him. Nobody can prove we done in a marshal."

Cleve had already showed Buck the papers they took from Lyster's body—papers that said Kristin Anderson had sold the Larkspur land to Forsythe Land Company.

"They were desperate to get rid of Miss Anderson," Stark said. "Without her alive to deny she signed the papers, they would have had no one to dispute their claim."

"I may be indebted to Runs Fast," Buck said, a muscle twitching in his whiskered cheek. "How did they get this close to the house?"

Gilly answered. "Luck, I guess. You and Bowlegs were gone at the same time."

Bonnie and Kristin took the sheets from the line and re-made the bed Del had died in. The bloodstain on the kitchen floor would remain there. No amount of scrubbing would re-move it completely.

"Don't fuss, Bonnie. I'll cover it with a rag rug."

Kristin refused to let anything put a blight on her happi-ness. She was back in the house she loved, with the man she loved and, miracle of miracles, he loved her. Her friends and her cousin had come through a terrible time and were unhurt. God had been good to her.

After supper, with all present including Tandy, Cleve talked of getting Buck's letter and what he had learned about Forsythe's affairs.

"Judge Williams of Bozeman was going to Helena to check the records of people who had signed intent to take up land, or bought it outright and later had willingly sold out to Forsythe. He had a tight grip on the town. The marshal, the banker and the only lawyer in town were in cahoots with him. He had money inherited from his wife to work with, and a siz-able number of thugs working for him. That number was re-duced by six last night, and the dozen we scared off are probably in Wyoming by now."

"What scared 'em off?" Gilly asked. "Ya said ya played some tricks—"

"Pablo was able to walk right up to them because they thought he was one of them. Dillon's brother, Colin Tallman, sent him up here to keep"—Cleve paused when he heard a low growl come from Dillon—"to help us. He threw in with Bruza's bunch when he got to Big Timber to see what he could find out. Last night he sidled up to each one and told of the Sioux uprising. He said they were out to avenge Sand Creek—"

"But . . . that happened in '64," Buck said.

"The dumbheads didn't know that. Pablo told them that Iron Jaw had two hundred warriors on the other side of the ranch and after they burned it and massacred everyone in it, they were heading for Big Timber."

"And they believed it?" Buck chuckled.

"All but one, *Señor,*" Pablo said with a wide grin. "Big ugly one in the barn. I had to tickle his ribs a bit with my knife."

"We're going into town tomorrow, honey. Are you up to it?" Buck squeezed the hand he held under the table. The words of endearment dropped naturally from his lips without hesitation.

"I'm ready. I want to get this all behind us."

"Bernie and I will go back to the café . . . if it's still there."

"Bowlegs'll be back tonight to keep a eye on thin's here, I jist might mosey on in with ya and visit Flo." Gilly sent a teasing glance in Buck's direction.

"I didn't know you had a lady friend in town," Kristin exclaimed. "You've not mentioned her before."

Bonnie rolled her eyes to the ceiling and, after an awkward silence, leaned toward Kristin.

"Flo's a whore," she whispered.

Kristin's face turned a fiery red. Her eyes, large and round, went to Gilly and quickly away.

"Oh! Well, my . . . goodness," she stammered. She turned and hid her face against Buck's shoulder. She could feel the silent laughter that shook him. When she got over her embarrassment, she began to giggle. Her hand went to Buck's neck and she pinched him. *"You're* not going there! I'm telling you that right now!"

*   *   *

After their guests had bedded down, Kristin and Buck sat in the big chair beside the hearth. The only light came from the fire. She rested in his arms, her head on his shoulder. His lips touched her forehead, his cheek lay against her hair.

"I don't want to go to bed without you," Buck whispered.

"Can we be married tomorrow as soon as we get to town?"

"It will depend on how things go, honey. We'll visit the preacher before we leave, that's certain."

"Bonnie knows him."

"Cleve's plan is to keep Forsythe from finding out you're there until the judge arrives from Bozeman. He sent a wire to him before he left to come to Big Timber. He's planning on him arriving on the afternoon train."

They sat in quiet contentment, Kristin's head on his shoulder. Time assumed a dreamlike quality. No unnatural noise intruded on their privacy, and the moments were filled with the simple pleasure of being together. The past twenty-four hours had been bliss for them. Buck had never loved, felt or enjoyed so deeply as when he held her in his arms.

Such happiness, he mused thoughtfully, came to only a few men. He prayed to God it would last. But there were a few details that needed to be aired; he wanted no secrets between them when they wed.

"I wish I knew why Uncle Yarby named me in his will." Kristin's whispered words broke the silence. "There are so many others that he knew better than me."

Buck was quiet for a long time. His hand stroked her arm, then took her hand and pressed it to his cheek, now free of whiskers.

"I'm sure it had something to do with Anna, the woman he loved. He spoke of her now and then."

"She was my mother's sister. I remember Mama saying that she was sick and came to live with us. She died shortly after I was born."

"Honey, Moss had a wooden box he always kept with him. He said it was the one he brought his possessions in when he came from Sweden, as a boy. When he went out of his mind, I put it in the attic."

"My papa had a box, too . . . with heavy iron hinges." Kristin raised her head to look at him. "I'd love to look into Uncle Yarby's box sometime."

"I did . . . after Yarby was gone."

"Why didn't you tell me? We could have done it together."

"I thought about it. But I was afraid there might be a later will in the box. A will that left the Larkspur to me, or to a male member of his family. If that were the case, you'd have no reason to stay here . . . and I couldn't let you go."

"I wouldn't have cared if he'd left it to you." She rubbed his cheek with her palm. "I'm going to sign it all over to you anyway. It will be best all around if the land's in my husband's name."

"There was no other will, honey, but there were letters from your mother."

"I knew she kept in touch with him. She was fond of Papa's younger brother."

Buck took a tight hold on his resolve and doggedly continued.

"She wrote of Anna's death. She told him that *his* daughter was the spitting image of Anna and that Anna had loved him until the end."

The calmly spoken words dropped into the stillness. Kristin's eyes searched his face.

"I didn't know Uncle Yarby had a daughter," she said

slowly. "Mama never mentioned her. Are you saying that he and Aunt Anna were . . ."

"They loved each other, but her father wanted her to wed another. Yarby came West, thinking that if he wasn't around, Anna's life would be easier. When she refused to wed the man her father chose for her, he turned her out. She went to her sister. Your mother and father welcomed her and cared for her until she died."

"How sad. If the daughter lived, she would be the heir. Buck?" Her hands went to his shoulders, a puzzled frown on her face. She shook him and spoke very quietly. "I'd like to read the letters. Do you think he mistook me for his and Anna's daughter?"

"Sweetheart, he made no mistake," he said gently. "When we get back from town, you can read the letters. Your mother wrote to him every year or so and told him how pretty you were and how well you did in school. Then, what a lovely young woman you were. The last one was when you were fourteen."

Kristin's face was still. Her eyes searched his.

"Are you trying to say . . . that sweet little man was . . . really my father?"

"Honey, since I found out, I've been trying to figure out a way to tell you. Your mother wrote to him as if you were his daughter. Are you disappointed?"

"Nooo . . ." she said slowly. "I don't think so. It will take some getting used to. My mother's sister and my father's brother loved each other, but they couldn't marry." She repeated the facts slowly as if to put them in order. "Why didn't Anna just go away with him? It's what I would have done."

"We'll never know."

"I was raised by my aunt and uncle," she said in an awed tone of voice. "Does Gustaf know?"

"I've no idea. I'd not discuss this with anyone but you. Nor would I allow anyone to go into Moss's things without your permission."

"Of course." She stroked his cheek with her fingertips. Still looking into his face, she said, "It's possible that Ferd knew, or suspected. It would account for his dislike of me. He would have been fifteen when I was born. He never liked me or my mother."

"Was he . . . mean to you?"

"Not while Papa was alive. Papa believed more in education than his brothers. Their sons worked on the farm, Papa sent Ferd to a boarding school. Ferd's mother died and he married Mama while Ferd was away. On second thought, I don't believe he knew or he would have thrown it up to me." She rested her head against his shoulder again. "It doesn't change anything. I don't feel any different. I loved Moss, even when I believed that he was *your* father."

"At times I'd see Moss watching you with a smile on his face. I thought it was because you're so pretty. Now I wonder if far back in his mind he was remembering Anna."

"He called me *Onyah* a couple of times. That's Swedish for Anna."

"Honey, I wanted you to know about this *before* you looked into the box. I thought it would be less of a shock to learn you had a different set of parents. Moss treasured the letters your mother wrote. They look as if they've been read many times."

"I'm glad he had you, Buck."

"He was father, mother, all my kin rolled into one. I grew to be a man with Moss. I never knew my folks."

"Don't you even know *of* them?"

Buck was glad of the opportunity to get her to think of something else.

"I heard that the Lennings came from New York State, a place called Middlecrossing. One of the Lennings, a bad one named Stith Lenning, came as far as the Wabash and got himself killed. His younger brother, Silas, came on west to a place on the Missouri River called Kanesville. He *could* have been my grandpa. My Pa's name was Roy Lenning. That's all I know about him. I know nothing of my mother."

"Where did you grow up?"

"In Wyoming with first one homesteader and then another—whoever would take me. I always knew I didn't belong to the family I was with. My name was Buck Lenning, my pa's name was Roy. I grew up knowing only that. I was about eleven years old when I signed on to do a man's work with a freighter carrying supplies to a mining camp. After that, for probably five years, it was root-hog or die. Then I met Moss, or rather Moss found me. My life started that day."

Kristin's fingers moved up to comb through his wild, dark hair.

"Poor little boy. I'll make it up to you. I'll love you so much, you'll never again think of growing up alone and unloved. We have a lot to thank Moss for."

"Are you hurt or disappointed about him being your father?" he asked anxiously.

"No. And for some reason, I'm not as shocked as I should be. I know Mama loved me and Papa doted on me. It doesn't seem important to me that Mama didn't give birth to me. I've wondered why she never had other children because most all the Andersons had big families. There were eight children in Gustaf's family. There may have been some physical reason Mama couldn't have babies."

The clock on the mantel struck midnight. It was late, but she didn't want to leave him.

"As soon as I got the lawyer's letter I knew I was coming here. And as soon as I saw the land, this house, I loved it. I felt that it was where I belonged. Do you think . . . what you've told me had anything to do with that feeling?"

"I don't know the answer to that, sweetheart. But I do know that you'd better go to bed. We're leaving before daylight, and you and Bonnie will have to pack some food for us to eat on the way."

"Buck, I want lots of children," she said suddenly. "I hope there's nothing wrong with me like was wrong with Mama."

"Anna had you, remember?" He kissed her forehead.

"That's right. It's hard to think of Mama not being Mama. I wish we could start right now." She tilted her face to his and turned his cheek so that their lips could meet. The kiss was long and sweet, his lips soft, then firm and demanding.

He lifted his head. "Much more of that, and I'll carry you off to bed and make a loose woman of you," he growled.

"I'm already one, remember. Once, twice . . . three times in the tepee." She laughed at him. "It's grand being a loose woman."

"The next time you'll be Mrs. Buck Lenning, and I'll not have to be careful of how much noise I make when I love you."

"We'll come right back home, won't we?"

"Ya betcha—"

"I'm going to get curtain material while we're in town. And—"

"Whoa, right there. You can get what you want, but now you're going to bed." He helped her off his lap and walked with her to the door of the room she shared with Bonnie.

"Night, sweetheart." His kiss was gentle on her lips.

"Night. I'll miss you. Did I tell you how wonderful it was to sleep in your arms?"

"Kristin! You're stalling. I just might have to take Gustaf's advice and get a willow switch."

"You wouldn't!"

"You're only going to get a couple hours of sleep, sweetheart. Now scoot." He opened the door and gently urged her inside.

Kristin undressed in the dark, so happy that she doubted she would sleep a wink. What Buck had told her about her parents was important to her, but not important enough to crowd from her mind the wonderful feeling of being loved by Buck Lenning, the dark-haired man of Larkspur. She giggled happily.

When she slipped into bed, Bonnie roused and moved from the middle of the bed to the far side.

"What are you doin' in here? Why aren't you in there with your man?" Then with a yawn, she murmured, "Crazy woman!"

# Chapter Twenty-seven

$\mathscr{A}$n hour before daylight the procession left the Lark-spur and headed for Big Timber. The morning was clear and cool. Gustaf drove the buggy with Bonnie between him and Kristin. The wagon carrying the dead bodies followed, with Gilly driving and Tandy on the seat beside him. Five mounted men, including Bernie, rode alongside.

"I'm glad you insisted on drivin' the buggy so Bernie could ride with the men." Bonnie's voice came softly out of the darkness.

"It was pure selfishness on my part, my bonny-Bonnie," Gustaf said cheerfully. "I get to sit close to a pretty girl and besides that, Bernie's much better at straddling a horse than I am."

"It's important to him to be treated as if he can do anything any other man can do."

"Hellfire. He'd be a man to be reckoned with if it come down to a fight. He's got guts he ain't used yet. Your brother does as much on one leg as some men do on two."

"He didn't make many friends in Big Timber. We'd put everything we had in the café or we'd have pulled out after the first month. People there are so tied in with Forsythe they wouldn't give newcomers a chance."

"I'm glad you didn't go." After a silence, he asked, "Are you warm enough?"

"Plenty."

Kristin listened to Bonnie and her cousin whispering together and realized that not only had Gustaf become close friends with Bernie, but something had blossomed between him and Bonnie.

She wondered what her cousin would say when she told him the news about Aunt Anna and Uncle Yarby. It was puzzling to her how her mother and father had been able to pass Anna's baby off as their own. Kristin yawned. That it didn't seem to matter to her, was another thing that she didn't understand. *I'll always think of Papa as Papa and him as Uncle Yarby—* This was Kristin's last thought as her head drooped against Bonnie's shoulder and she slept.

When they stopped to rest and water the horses, Buck came to the buggy and lifted Kristin down. His eyes searched her face for lines of tiredness. He drew her apart from the others and opened a canteen he took from his saddle. She drank deeply.

"That was good."

"We're making good time," he told her while he adjusted the heavy shawl about her. "The horses don't get so tired when it's cold. Have you been warm enough?" His face was close to hers, his eyes anxious, his wild, raven black hair held down by a wide-brimmed hat.

"Yes, and I even slept a little."

He tilted her chin with his finger so that he could look into her face. Oh, God! He loved her so much. His mind almost fluttered to a stop when he thought of losing her. It weighed heavily on him that he was taking her into town where Forsythe wanted her dead.

"Would you mind if I kissed you? It's gotten to be a habit lately."

"I don't care if the others see you kissing me."

"I wasn't sure—"

She lifted her hand to caress his cheek. It was warm and rough and his whiskers scraped gently against her palm. It came to her that he had been lonely for a long, long time, just as she had been. He turned his head so that his lips touched her fingers and a wave of tenderness washed over her.

"Do you want one long one, or two quick ones?" She wanted to make him smile and he did . . . a little.

"I'll take anything I can get," he said as he bent his head. His kiss was warm and sweet and over far too soon.

"Are you worried about today?"

"A bit. Cleve says this judge is an honest one. A friend of his over at Trinity, a fellow named Garrick Rowe, had nothing but good things to say about him. But I'll not feel easy until it's over and we're back at the ranch."

For an endless moment their eyes held. His black brows were drawn together, his eyes anxious.

"Don't worry so." Her fingertip traced his brows in an attempt to smooth away the frown.

"I'm not a town man," he said with jaws tightly clenched as if it was something he was determined to say. "I might embarrass you."

"Oh, Buck!" Her hands moved down to clasp his arms. "Why do you think that? I'll be so proud to be at your side."

"I've not been with people much. Especially a judge. By myself, I wouldn't care, but with you—"

"Do you think I care if your manners are not perfect? Good heavens! My brother, Ferd, knew all the correct things to do, and he was a bigoted, selfish know-it-all. All he thought about was his station in life and making money so that his friends would be envious." Kristin's voice quivered with sincerity. "I fell in love with dark, wild-haired Buck Lenning, who is the kindest, sweetest, bravest, most honorable man in the world. I adore Buck Lenning. I wouldn't change one thing about him for the whole world!"

"Sweetheart—I don't deserve you." His voice was a husky whisper.

"Yes, you do, my love. And I deserve you."

He looked into her face for a long moment, then bent his head and kissed her mouth, softly and reverently.

"If the judge doesn't believe me when I say that I never sighed the paper selling Forsythe—if we lose the Larkspur, I'll go with you wherever you want to go, if it's to . . . China. Nothing is as important to me as spending the rest of my life as Mrs. Buck Lenning."

"If he rules against us, sweetheart, I'll not go away like a puppy with its tail between its legs. I'll take you to a safe place, then I'll fight for what Moss worked for and for what he wanted you to have. The man that takes over that land will never have a peaceful night's sleep again. I know how to fight, and I'll fight dirty if I have to."

"That's *my* Buck talking now." She smiled at him, then leaned her forehead against his chest for a moment. She looked up at him and whispered, "Don't change, my love. Don't ever change."

Buck looked beyond her to where the horses were being brought up from the creek.

"Cleve will go on ahead with Dillon and Pablo. They can get to town a couple of hours before we do by cutting across country. Bernie is going with them, but he'll bypass town and go to Rose Gaffney's and let her know that you and Bonnie will be staying there. I expect bringing six bodies into town and one of them the marshal will create quite a stir."

"Be careful. I hope the men who were scared away are in Wyoming by now."

"I doubt that even they were dumb enough to believe that story after they thought about it. Don't worry. Cleve will know what we're up against by the time we get there."

Cleve and Dillon rode directly to the telegraph office, and Pablo went to the saloon to see what he could find out there.

"Any messages for me?" Cleve stood at the end of the telegrapher's booth.

"Two." He took them from beneath a thick book that lay on the desk.

"Anybody else seen these?"

"Nobody's even asked."

"How about yesterday?"

"I showed the one you sent to Trinity."

"I'm obliged to ya."

"Good luck."

Cleve and Dillon moved to the end of the waiting room and Cleve read the wire from Judge Williams.

"He'll be here on the 4:20. That'll give us some time to set things up before Buck gets here."

The second message from Lieutenant Collier was longer.

"The lieutenant and his men were to arrive this morning. He'll set up headquarters. His orders from the territorial governor are to stay until Federal or territorial law can be established here."

"That was fast."

"Shows ya what an influential man like Garrick Rose can do. He went straight to the governor." The men left the depot and mounted their horses. "I'll go look up Lieutenant Collier," Cleve said. "I want to be sure he and his men are on hand when Buck comes in with the bodies."

"I want to be on hand myself. I can't wait to see the look on the face of that puffed-up jackass when he sees his marshal and his gunmen piled in that wagon like a load a meat goin' to a butcher shop."

"Why don't you nose around and make sure that little weasel of a lawyer is still in town. I'll meet you back here when the train comes in."

Dillon left his horse at the livery and walked up the street to the building where Mark Lee had his office. He took the outside stairs two at a time and threw open the door at the top.

Lee looked up from his desk, and a man in the rough clothes of a railroad worker turned to look at him, too.

"Howdy," Dillon said cheerfully.

"What do *you* want?" Mark Lee's tone made it clear that he was not pleased to see Dillon.

"Nothin'. Nothin' a'tall. I'm just makin' sure the little weasel is still in town. Don't want ya goin' off someplace and gettin' lost."

Lee's face turned beet red and he stood. "Get out!"

"I'd be careful about doin' business with the little weasel." Dillon addressed the railroad man. "He's got more tricks than a dog's got fleas 'bout how to get in your pockets. He'll make it seem like he's doin' ya a favor to take your money."

"Get out, or . . . I'll get the marshal."

"Now . . . that'd be quite a chore. *Adios, amigos.*"

Dillon backed out the door and went down the stairs chuckling. An angry man makes mistakes . . . it's what Cleve said, and nobody, except his pa, understood the nature of men as Cleve Stark did. On the way to the saloon, Dillon met Pablo coming toward him. He turned into the mercantile and Pablo followed.

"Any talk of the uprising?" Dillon went straight to the cheese counter and turned the wheel. With a slab in one hand, he dipped into the cracker barrel with the other.

"Nothin'."

"You reckon they don't know that two hundred Sioux are ridin' this way?"

"Ain't nobody worryin' about it."

"The brave men didn't even stop by to warn the town. Bet they were scared Forsythe'd shoot 'em."

"The deputy and four others are here. But not to worry, *Señor.* Pablo is here to take care of little brudder." Pablo said this as two women came down the aisle toward them.

Dillon ground his teeth in frustration and waited for the ladies to pass.

"You little warthog! Someday I'm goin' to shove that hat down your throat."

"Why you do that, *Señor?* This good hat."

Dillon went to the counter and dropped two nickels. The clerk scooped them up and put them in the till.

"Don't it beat all about the soldiers being in town. Lieutenant come in with a letter from the captain out at the fort. The army will pay for any supplies the lieutenant needs. Hope they'll be here for a long time."

"What'er they doin' here?"

"Ain't knowin' that. Some of the town folks is glad, some not so glad. I'm hopin' they stay and clean out that bunch that's been hangin' round."

"Wish I'd be here to see it. I purely do."

"You leavin'?"

"In a day or two."

"Wish you'd hang around. Big Timber needs folks like you and that friend of yours."

"Big Timber needed folks like Yarby Anderson and Buck Lenning, but they sat by while Forsythe tried to run them off."

"Well that's the way folks do at times. There wasn't anybody who'd step up and go against the colonel."

"Cletus Fuller did."

"Yeah, well—"

"I'll have another hunk of cheese and be on my way." Dillon tossed another nickel on the counter and headed for the cheese wheel.

Several men got off the 4:20 train and went into the depot. None of them looked like a judge. Cleve and Dillon leaned against the depot wall.

"Might be gettin' off the cattle car," Dillon said.

"Doubt that."

A man in worn boots, wearing a range hat and a leather vest came out of the depot, set a well-worn valise down by a bench, and watched the train pull out. When the last car passed he walked over to Cleve.

"Howdy. You Stark?"

"You . . . Judge Williams?"

"Been James Williams for fifty years. Judge Williams for ten."

Cleve held out his hand. "Glad you're here. This is my friend, Dillon Tallman."

"Tallman. That's a name to reckon with in the West."

"You've heard of 'em, way up here! Well ain't that somethin'?" Dillon grinned as he shook hands with the judge. "Pleased to meet you. You don't look like any judge I've ever seen."

"Don't look judgy enough for you, huh? Wait till I get duded up in my suit and bow tie. I'll look judgy."

Dillon decided then and there that he liked Judge Williams a lot.

An hour later in the judge's hotel room, Cleve stood and put on his hat. Dillon had rapped on the door and said Buck and the wagon were coming into town.

"That's about the size of it. Miss Anderson will be here to swear she never signed the paper or accepted any money for the Larkspur."

"Then what we've got is fraud and forgery."

"Is that all?"

"All we can prove."

"We might scare the hell out of Mark Lee, Forsythe's lawyer. He'll want to save his own hide."

"Let's see how it plays out."

"After Buck gets here with the bodies, I'll serve notice on Forsythe that he's to appear in your courtroom in the morning. By the way, I've arranged with the hotel for you to use the dinin' room. They were glad to oblige after I threw in the governor's name a time or two."

The judge put on his hat. "I think I'll go along and see the show. I'll keep my distance from you, but point out Forsythe if you see him."

Colonel Forsythe was showing Mark Lee to the door.

"Don't you have any guts? You're as nervous as a whore standing at the Pearly Gates. Can't you stand up to that mouthy kid?"

"He knows something—"

"What could he know? I'm expecting the marshal and Bruza

back anytime. No one knew the men were riding out there except you and me."

"What about Del Gomer?"

"He was here and tossed around a few threats. He's so lovesick he's probably holed up in his hotel room, and tomorrow he'll take the train to Helena. That's where he thinks that slut and her brother headed."

"Not to the Larkspur?"

"How the hell do I know? If he went there, he's dead meat by now. Bruza'd shoot him in the back or have someone else do it." Forsythe opened the door, hoping Lee would leave.

"Why have the soldiers come to town now?" Lee stood in the doorway.

"They've been here before from time to time. You know that."

"Someone could have called for them."

"Who? Not me, and I'm the only one in town that knows the captain at the fort or the governor well enough to ask for them." Forsythe was becoming exasperated. "Let me tell you something, Lee. To get through this life and get what you want, you run a bluff every day. Act guilty of something, folks think you're guilty of something. Put up a confident front, and folks think you're a smart, upstanding fellow. Now get that hangdog look off your face and get the hell out of here."

Lee went down the street to Mrs. Barlett's rooming house.

"Supper will be ready in a little while, Mr. Lee," the woman said as he came into the foyer.

"I think I'll lie down, Mrs. Bartlett. I'm not feeling so well."

"Sorry to hear it. I'll save something back for later if you feel like eating."

Lee went up the stairs to his room, took off his coat and tie and stretched out on the bed. The feeling of doom had hovered over him since the colonel had sent his men to the Larkspur to kill Lenning and the woman. He lay staring at the ceiling, unaware of the event taking place on the main street of the town he was so anxious to leave.

The sun had completed its journey across the sky, but it was not dark enough for the lamps to be lit when Buck walked his horse in front of the team pulling the wagon into town. He approached from the north and came down the main street.

*He hated this place. Lord, how he hated it.* The odor of rotten food and outhouses hung over the town. He wanted to get this business over so that he could get back out into the wideopen spaces where he could breathe. He was never comfortable among so many people.

At first only a few people on the street paid attention to the rider and the wagon. Then, as if his name had been carried on the breeze, people came out of stores to stand on the boardwalk and gawk. Up ahead Buck's sharp eyes caught sight of Dillon's blond head, and standing not far away was the Mexican, Pablo. From a side street, Bernie fell in behind the wagon.

Buck stopped the horses in front of the saloon. He sat for a long moment looking at the hostile faces staring back at him. No one spoke or even nodded a greeting. He had expected none.

"Who's the law here now?"

A broad-chested man, dressed in a wrinkled black suit, and with a full black mustache and chin whiskers stepped off the porch. A shiny tin star was fastened to a coat with sleeves much too short for his long arms. He strutted out into the street and stood on spread legs, his coat pulled back, his thumbs hooked in his belt.

"I'm in charge. Marshal Lyster is outta town."

"No, he isn't. He's in the back of the wagon."

At Buck's calm words the deputy's mouth dropped open, and quiet fell over the crowd.

"You say the— Gawddamn!" The deputy went to the back of the wagon and yanked on the tarp that covered the dead men.

"What the hell!"

His explosive words brought the men rushing from the boardwalk. Within seconds there was not an inch of standing room around the wagon.

"That's Mike Bruza!"

"By gawd! Greg Meader."

"Ain't that Shorty Spinks and Squat Jones?"

"And that ugly bastard they called Heinz? Looks like he got it in the ribs with a pigsticker."

"Jesus! They all been whittled on with a knife. Don't see a gunshot on any of 'em."

"Ain't no blood a'tall on the marshal."

"Somethin' else is on the front of his shirt. He puked from the looks of it."

"Cover 'em up," Gilly yelled over the murmur of voices. "They stink!"

The deputy moved through the crowd to where Buck sat his horse, leaning his forearm on the saddle horn . . . waiting.

"Mister, you better get to talkin' . . . fast."

"Not to you. Where's the undertaker?"

"Here." A man in a black coat stepped forward. "Who's payin'?"

"Forsythe. They're his men."

"Now see here." The deputy puffed out his chest and tried to speak with authority. "Yo're actin' mighty high-handed. Yo're that Lenning feller from the Larkspur, ain't ya?"

"You know damn good and well who I am, and you know damn good and well what those men were doing out at my place last night."

"Yeah, I know that. The marshal went to serve papers to get ya off Mr. Forsythe's land." An angry grumble came from the men surrounding the wagon.

"He couldn't'a killed Bruza and Meader by hisself," someone yelled.

"He could've if he snuck up on 'em an' cut their throats."

"It's what he done. Ain't nobody dumb enough to face Greg Meader with a gun. He's the fastest I ever seen."

"He ain't gettin' away with killin' a marshal," a man shouted.

"Ya fellers is jist a-blowin' wind!" Tandy yelled.

"What's old Tandy doin' with that Larkspur bunch?"

"Hadn't we ort to go get Colonel Forsythe?"

"Not yet," the deputy said. "We'll handle this."

"Then, goddammit, get to handling it," Buck said loudly and in a manner calculated to insult. "I'm not sitting here all day. Gilly, take the meat wagon to wherever the man wants it."

"Hold on!" the deputy shouted. Encouraged by the crowd behind him, he pulled his gun and pointed it at Buck. "Get off that horse. You're goin' to jail."

Buck eased his horse forward, then suddenly jumped him. His booted foot lashed out and kicked the arm holding the gun. It flew out of the deputy's hand. He stumbled back, lost his balance and hit the ground.

"Don't point a gun at me, you hairy jackass, unless you're intendin' to kill me."

"'Ary a man draws, this shotgun goes off," Gilly stood in the wagon and shouted.

"This'n too." Tandy pointed his gun at the crowd. "Ain't a

man-jack among 'em got guts enough to skin a cat . . . by his-self."

Buck's attention was on the deputy, who was picking him-self up out of the dirt, and he didn't see Cleve and Dillon pushing through the crowd to reach him.

"We ort to hang the lot of 'em." The voice came from the back of the crowd.

"What's going on here? Stand back!" An officer came down the walk with several men marching behind him. His voice rose up over the murmur of the crowd and rang with authority. "I said what's going on here!"

"The marshal's there in the wagon, dead." The deputy picked up his gun and shoved it down in the holster. "This man killed him and *five* of his men. I'm takin' him to jail."

"Because a man brings in a body doesn't mean he killed him."

"Well, gol-damn," a man shouted. "Even you soldier boys ort to know murder when ya see it."

"Sergeant Burton, clear this area."

"Yes, sir!" A burly sergeant and four men lined up with ri-fles at the ready. "Back up on the walk. Ya be quick 'bout doin' it."

"If ya need help with this bunch of grizzly ba'ars, soldier boy, give me n' Tandy a holler," Gilly yelled.

"Thanky kindly, gents. But I ain't thinkin' we be needin' help with the likes of them. They be a bunch a pussy cats."

The deputy felt his authority slipping away fast. With Lyster dead he had a chance to be the marshal if he acted fast.

"Who be you?" he demanded of the lieutenant. "Ya ain't got no right to give orders in this town."

"I'm the law here until a territorial marshal arrives. Give me the keys to the jail. If you're going to argue about it, you'll be my first arrest."

The lieutenant glowered down at the shorter man. His iron gray hair and his demeanor was evidence of many years in the military.

"If'n you're goin' to arrest somebody, it ort to be this killer here," the deputy stammered.

"Do you have evidence that he murdered these men?"

"Ever'body knows the marshal and some men went out to his place to serve papers. They ended up dead. 'Course he killed them."

"That's not for you to decide." Collier reached out and plucked the tin star from the deputy's coat. "You'll not be needin' this. Move the wagon," he motioned to Gilly. "Take the bodies to the back of the furniture store." He waited until the wagon pulled out and the crowd had thinned before he spoke to Buck.

"Mr Lenning," he held out his hand. "Lieutenant Collier." He continued in a low voice. "Federal Marshal Stark advised me of the situation here. My advice is . . . stay off the street tonight and keep an eye on Miss Anderson. Should you need help, send word to the hotel; that's where I'll be until suitable quarters can be arranged for me and my men."

"I'm obliged to you. I will take that advice." Buck tipped his head and put his heels in the horse. He rode on down the street and turned into the alley. Bernie rode up beside him.

"Let's leave the horses at the livery and go into the back of the café. If anyone's interested, they'll think you're sleeping there. When it's dark we'll slip on over to Mrs. Gaffney's."

# Chapter Twenty-eight

𝒟arkness had settled on the town by the time Cleve and Dillon turned down the street where the Forsythe mansion occupied an entire block. Cleve was pleased with the way Buck handled himself when faced with the angry crowd. Judge Williams had been impressed, too, and commented that Buck would make a good lawman if he ever decided to give up ranching.

They were walking alongside the picket fence when Cleve spoke about the problem at hand.

"You plannin' on devilin' the man some more? If this wasn't so serious, it'd be fun."

"It'll be fun. I've waited a long time for this. I hope he gets so riled up he wets his drawers," Dillon said.

"So yo're goin' to tell him who ya are?"

"I thought I'd let you do that."

"I do it for you, *Señor.* I tell him plenty." Pablo came up suddenly behind them. "You no hear me comin'," he said proudly.

"I heard ya." Cleve said. "I knew ya were there."

"Dammit to hell! Can't I go anywhere without you taggin' along?"

"Got job to do. Colin say look out for little br—"

"Say it, you bowlegged clabber-head, and that mustache'll

be ticklin' your tonsils." Dillon stopped and drew back his fist.

"That's enough. You two can jaw all you want after the job here is done."

"He's not goin' in!" They were walking up to the front steps.

"No, he's not. Pablo, stay here on the porch."

"*Sí, Señor.* But Pablo come runnin' if little brudder—"

"Hush up!"—Cleve lifted the knocker on the door—"Or I'll bust your nose myself."

After a few minutes the door opened. Forsythe looked from one man to the other.

"What do *you* want?" he asked bluntly.

"A word with you," Cleve said.

"I conduct business in my office, not my home."

"Ya'll see us now." Cleve gave the door an unexpected shove, pushing Forsythe back out of the way.

"Thanks," Dillon said pleasantly. "We'll come in, but we can't stay to supper."

Forsythe backed up even more when the two big men crowded into the foyer. Something in the face of that damn kid who had been needling him caused his bravado to waver. Stark was taking something from his pocket and attaching it to his coat.

"What authority do you have for pushing your way into a man's house?"

"None, when it comes right down to it. I'm a Federal marshal."

"I knew you weren't what you claimed," Forsythe sneered, eyeing the badge. "What's a Federal marshal doing here?"

Cleve ignored the question.

"—And my friend here is Dillon Tallman of New Mexico.

His father is John Tallman, the well-known scout, trader and rancher."

Forsythe's eyes went to the tall blond man, and the color drained from his face.

"You're . . . you're—?" was all he could say before his voice dried up.

"John and Addie Tallman's son. How do, Mr. Kirby Hyde. Isn't that what you called yourself down in Arkansas?" Dillon's eyes were as cold as his voice.

Before Forsythe could recover from the shock of hearing the name he had used more than twenty years ago, Dillon's fist lashed out and landed on his chin. The blow sent the older man back against the wall. He hit it with a force that stunned him. He slid down the wall to the floor and sat there, shaking his head to clear it.

"That was for a lady named Addie Faye Johnson." Dillon hauled Forsythe to his feet and pinned him to the wall with one hand and slapped him across the face with the other. "That was for runnin' out on her down in Freepoint, Arkansas." He slapped him again so hard, the man's eyes crossed. "That was for marryin' her under a false name so you could get her in bed. And this—"

Cleve stepped in and took Dillon's arm. "Don't knock him out until I can serve the papers."

"I won't knock him out. And this"—he slapped Forsythe hard and repeatedly on first one cheek and then with the back of his hand on the other—"is for all the work she did during the war to keep her son from starving."

Dillon grasped Forsythe's upper arms and banged his head against the wall.

"Since the day my mother told me about you, I've wanted to kill you. But killin' would be too quick an end for a piece of horseshit like you." He held him against the wall and spat in his face.

Forsythe took the insult with a stunned expression on his bloody face and stared back at him with spittle running down his cheek.

"Mama said you were a sorry excuse for a man. Now that I've seen you, I know you're not worthy to be called a man. You're nothin' . . . but shit."

Dillon backed away, wiping his hands on his britches as if touching Forsythe had left something offensive on them.

Blood from Forsythe's nose ran down over his white mustache and onto his shirtfront. His face was beet red from the blows and his eyes blazed with hatred. He pulled a handkerchief from his pocket and held it to his nose.

"If I'm shit, what does that make you?" he sneered.

"Nothin' that's got anythin' to do with you. Any rotten, gutless male, even a cur dog, can spill a seed. It takes a *real* man to tend that seed. My pa, John Tallman, saw to it that I had everything I needed to grow into a man." Dillon reached over and grabbed Forsythe's shirtfront. "Don't ever, in any way, word or deed, link me to you or I will kill you!"

"Get out!"

"Not yet." Cleve drew a paper from his pocket and held it out. Forsythe ignored it until Cleve waved it in his face, then he snatched it from his hand.

"What the hell is . . . this?"

"It's a notice to appear at nine o'clock tomorrow morning in the courtroom of Judge James Williams. Bring all the papers you have concerning any land deals you've made during the three years you've been here."

"The hell I will! Everything I've done here has been according to the law."

"Killin' old men legal now, Cleve?" Dillon asked. "Hell. I didn't know that."

"Get out!"

"We're goin'."

Cleve went to the open door and tried to prod Dillon out ahead of him, but he held back for one last word.

"You're a rotten no-good son of a bitch! You're like a cancer sore eatin' away at everything that's decent in this town. But not for much longer, *Colonel* Asshole." He slammed the door behind him.

"Feel better?" Cleve asked as they went across the porch and down the steps.

"Not as good as I thought I would. He's nothin' . . . but shit. Just stood there and took it. Hell, he's less than nothin'."

"Ya needed to find it out for yourself."

"Ya didn't need me, *Señor?*"

Dillon turned on the Mexican. "Why in hell would I need a stunted little pissant like you? If ya breathe one word of what ya heard in there, I'll break both of yore bandy legs, cut off your balls and make a geldin' outta ya! Hear?"

"Ohhh . . . ahhh—" Pablo grabbed his privates. "That'd hurt, *Señor!*"

Cleve walked on ahead. The fact that the man who had sired him had deserted him and his mother had been eating away at Dillon for years. Maybe now that he had shown his contempt for that man face-to-face, he would settle down and forget there ever was a Kirby Hyde or a Kyle Forsythe.

John Tallman, Cleve's friend of many years, had told him to take Dillon with him to the Montana Territory and let him confront the man. When he had expressed the hatred he felt, he'd put it behind him and it would no longer be of such importance to him.

From the sound of the lighthearted bickering between Dillon and Pablo going on behind him, it seemed that John was right.

In the Forsythe mansion, Kyle paced the floor, holding a wet towel to his face. Ruth had not been in the kitchen when he went there to get the towel. She had not gone upstairs . . . unless she had slipped by while that son of a bitch was hitting him.

His bastard had grown up to be quite a man. Even so, if he'd had a gun, he would have killed him. He had felt that there was something familiar about that kid. Now that he thought about it, he had Addie's hair and eyes.

Well, what the hell! He probably had a dozen other by-blows scattered from Tennessee to Arkansas to New Mexico and into the northern territories. They meant no more to him than a fart in a whirlwind.

He pulled the paper Stark had given to him out of his pocket. It was a printed form with time and place written in. What was going on? Lee had sent the correct papers to Helena to be recorded; the paper supposedly signed by the Anderson woman giving Lee the authority to act in her behalf and the papers turning the land over to him for the sum of three thousand dollars. Someone there in Helena must have begun wondering about how much land he was acquiring and contacted Judge Williams.

The judge had a reputation for siding with homesteaders and others who signed to use government land. Forsythe had known that if trouble came, it would be from him. That was why he'd sent Del to Bozeman to kill him. If the lovesick bastard had done his job, this wouldn't be happening. It should be all over out at the Larkspur by now. Bruza, Lyster and the men would be returning soon. *He had plans for Del Gomer when they got back.*

Forsythe continued to walk back and forth, holding the wet towel to his face. Everything had been done legally . . . according to Lee. If the axe should fall, it would not be on him, it'd fall smack-dab on the one who had claimed to have the authority to sell him the land and who had collected the money—Mark Lee. He had made sure a check had been issued to Lee, cashed, and the money put back in his account. It paid to have the banker indebted to you. Forsythe would have laughed, but his jaws were too sore.

He went to the foot of the stairs and yelled.

"Ruth!"

"I'm here." Ruth came from the kitchen.

"Where were you?" he demanded.

"Out on the porch."

"All the time?"

"Most of it. I didn't want anyone to see me."

Her once-lovely face was bruised and swollen, her lips almost twice their normal size. Her neck, and chest to the neckline of her dress, showed marks of a beating.

"You only have yourself to blame for the beatings. You've become arrogant, so damned arrogant I can hardly stand the sight of you. You're a servant here, Ruth. Just because I sleep with you, doesn't give you special privileges. I want you to go get Lee. Tell him to get over here and fast."

"Kyle, you know I don't like to go out alone at night. All those men that hang around—"

"Hush up!" he said harshly. "I don't care what you don't like! Goddammit, do you have to argue every time I tell you to do something? You're a stupid bitch, Ruth. A stupid bitch! I've fed and clothed you these past two years. You're no better than the lowest-paid whore down at Flo's. At least they can give a man satisfaction."

Ruth turned to go get her shawl. She knew the signs. He was in a rage. The boy (his son, from what she'd overheard) had worked him over. She had listened with glee to every blow that landed. While shivering on the porch she had made up her mind that she'd not take another beating without fighting back.

"Don't turn your back while I'm talking to you," Forsythe shouted.

"I'm going to get my shawl."

"You heard, didn't you? 'Course you did. You heard every word the bastard said. You nosy bitch! You can't wait to spread it all over town."

Forsythe moved toward her. She backed up and sidestepped along the wall toward the kitchen. He stalked her, his eyes bright, his nostrils flaring. This was a game he liked to play. She sidled toward the dining room; he continued to stalk her. She moved around the table and he followed. When she made the break for the door, he pounced, caught her, and pushed her up against the wall.

As Dillon had done with him, he held Ruth with one hand against her chest and with the other hand he slapped her back and forth across the face. The first blow bloodied her nose. The second one whipped her head around so hard she blanked out for a second or two, but she refused to cry out. *It would only excite him more.*

"Bitch! Bitch! Bitch!" he shouted as he struck her time and again.

It excited him to hit her. Already he was getting aroused; he wanted to throw her to the floor and plunge his stiffened member into her. Since he had discovered this treatment of her aroused him, he'd taken her on the table amid the supper dishes, on the stairs, on the back porch in plain sight of the carriage house where the stableboy could watch, and a time or two at night, in the dirt of the flower bed.

He thought constantly of ways to humiliate and degrade her.

"Get on the floor," he commanded.

The instant he moved the hand holding her to the wall, Ruth kicked at his groin. When he jerked back, she ran to the kitchen. He was so startled that she would dare to fight him, that seconds passed before he went after her.

"Ruth," he shouted. "I'll beat the livin' hell out of you. Slut! Whore! Get on the floor and spread your—" Words and breath left him when he swung back the kitchen door.

Ruth was there. She had a crazed look on her bloody face. Her lips were drawn back over her teeth and she looked like what she was: a woman possessed. In her hand, raised high over her head, was a long kitchen knife.

"Nooo . . . !" she screamed and dived at him. "Nooo . . . ! Nooo . . . !"

Her voice rose, bouncing against the walls of the room, echoing throughout the house and spilling out into the still, dark night.

Before he could recover from the shock of seeing the usually cowered woman so wildly distraught, she was on him and plunged the knife into the base of his throat. Blood spewed like a fountain. His eyes widened, his mouth opened, his hands lifted to ward her off as he crumbled to the floor.

Crazed and screaming, Ruth fell to her knees beside him and plunged the knife again and again into his chest.

*       *       *

It was near midnight. Gustaf sat on Mrs. Gaffney's porch with his rifle across his knees. He had been given the responsibility of protecting Kristin, and he was determined that no one would slip past him this time. His mind, however, drifted from time to time to Bonnie.

Bonnie Gates was quite a woman. It had taken courage to poison the stew with the larkspur. Not one woman in a hundred would have thought of it. He liked her attitude about the money Del Gomer had left to her. She swore that she'd not take a cent of it for her own personal use. The money, she declared, would go to an orphans' home, or if there was enough of it, to establish a new one.

His thoughts were interrupted by Kristin. She came to the porch every few minutes to ask Gustaf if he'd heard anything.

"Stay in the house, Kris. Buck said that he and Bernie would come as soon as they thought it safe."

Gustaf, too, was worried. It had been hours since Buck had led the wagon carrying the dead bodies into town. But if there had been trouble at that time, he reasoned, they would have heard of it by now.

Gustaf was happy that Kristin would have a man like Buck Lenning to look after her. It was obvious that the man was wildly in love with her. Just looking at his rough exterior, it would seem that he was an unlikely choice for his cousin, but Gustaf knew men. He had learned from his travels up and down the river to separate the ones who dreamed and created from the ones who raped and destroyed.

"Don't come out, Kristin," he said when he heard the door squeak, behind him.

"Let her come out." The voice came out of the darkness beside the porch. Gustaf sprang to his feet with his rifle ready. The voice came again, quickly. "It's me, Buck."

"Buck! Oh, Buck! I've been so worried." Kristin came flying out the door and threw herself into his arms. "I never want to go through such a night again. Are you all right?"

"I'm sorry you worried, honey." Buck spoke with his arms tightly around her. "Things have come to a head. Let's go in, and I'll tell you about it. Come on in, Gus. Bernie should be along soon."

Rose Gaffney greeted Buck warmly and led them to the brightly lit kitchen.

"We saved you and Bernie some supper," Bonnie said. "I'll warm it up when he gets here."

Buck looked at the expectant faces waiting for him to relate the news and plunged right in.

"Forsythe is dead. His housekeeper killed him."

Kristin was the first to react. "Oh, my goodness!" Then, "Mrs. Gaffney may not have heard—"

"I heard," Rose said. "I hear when I want to. All I've got to say is, she did the town a favor."

"Sit down and tell us." Kristin took his hat from his hand and hung it on a hook on the wall, then sat down close beside him.

Buck told them everything that had happened from the time they stopped the wagon in front of the saloon. He told about the crowd's reaction when they saw the dead men and about Lieutenant Collier's being the law until a territorial marshal arrived.

"Dillon came to the room behind the café to tell us that the judge was there and that court would be held in a room at the hotel at nine o'clock tomorrow morning. He and Cleve were on their way to serve the papers on Forsythe. Later, just when Bernie and I were getting ready to come here, Dillon came back with the news that Forsythe was dead."

"She seemed like a nice lady," Bonnie said sadly.

"According to Dillon," Buck said, "Forsythe had been beating her. It had gone on for several weeks, maybe longer. He and Cleve had seen her with marks on her face."

"She stopped coming to church a few weeks ago," Rose said. "She and her man had been here only a few months when he up and died on her, leaving her nothin'. She had to work for her keep."

"The lad that worked there and slept in the carriage house heard her screaming. He went to the kitchen door and found her sitting on the floor . . . all bloody, and Forsythe dead. He ran up to the main street and got the sergeant in charge of the men on patrol. After he saw what had happened he reported to the lieutenant who was in the hotel lobby with the judge and Cleve."

"Poor woman. What will they do with her?"

"I don't know. But it would seem to me that a lady has the right to defend herself. Dillon said the preacher's wife and some other ladies are with her."

"Folks liked Ruth DeVary even if she did sleep with that no-good Forsythe. Women ain't got it easy makin' their own way," Rose added.

They heard the thump of Bernie's peg as he came up onto the porch. Gustaf hurried to the door to let him in. He came to the kitchen and sank wearily down in a chair.

Bonnie pressed her hand on Rose's shoulder when the older woman would have gotten up.

"I'll fix them some supper, Rose."

"I guess Buck's told you the news," Bernie said, rubbing his stump. "The only new thing I can add is that Forsythe's thugs are high-tailin' it out of town. Mark Lee is in jail, and the banker has orders not to leave his house. That judge is a pisser!"

"Bernie!" Bonnie turned and glared at her brother. "Watch your mouth."

"I meant it in a good way, Sis. He don't let any grass grow under his feet—"

"Don't worry, Bonnie." Kristin was holding Buck's arm with both her hands. "I'm getting used to the colorful language of the West. After I've lived here a few years, I'll probably be using it myself."

Buck tilted his head so that he could look at her. His face was wreathed in smiles, and his eyes shone with happiness. Kristin laughed, hugged his arm, and rested her cheek against it. Buck's heart swelled with pride and pleasure.

"Cleve said court will still be held tomorrow morning. They'll deal with the lawyer and the banker. They need Kristin to swear that she never signed the paper giving Lee authority to sell and that she didn't get any pay for the land. Hellfire," Bernie scoffed. "We all know that. She wasn't in town long enough. Wish old Cletus knew that Forsythe got it the way he did."

"That old bugger's sittin' up there laughin' his head off." They all looked at Rose. She could hear every word that was said. "Flitter! I got in on a lot of thin's with folks thinkin' I couldn't hear. Even heard the preacher fart and nearly died, wanted to laugh so bad."

Kristin looked up at the man smiling down at her to see how she was taking the plain talk. When she spoke, it was evident her mind was on other things.

"We'll get married tomorrow and go home?"

"Now I've been thinkin' about that," Gustaf said, and all eyes turned toward him. "While you're with the judge, the rest of us can make arrangements with the preacher. I want to get this thin' done before Buck changes his mind."

"Oh, you!" Kristin's eyes left her cousin to rest lovingly on Buck's craggy face. "Is there a danger of that?" she asked softly.

"Sweetheart, if the sun comes up in the west tomorrow morning . . . I may change my mind," Buck said with a deep chuckle.

"Bernie, have you seen Tandy?" Bonnie asked with a worried frown. "The ride into town didn't do that gunshot wound any good."

"The last I saw of him, he and Gilly were goin' down Center Street toward—"

"Heavens!" Bonnie's worried look turned to shock. "Not *that* place!"

"Well—for cryin' out loud! They're old enough." Her brother shuffled his one foot against the floor.

"They went to Flo's," Rose said loudly. "Them girls'll take their money and make 'em think they're as randy as a two-peckered goat."

"Really?" Gustaf smoothed his hair down with his fingers. "Bernie, you got plans for . . . later?"

"Go on down there." Bonnie plunked a plate of food on the table in front of her brother. "If you're so dead set on gettin' the . . . clap!"

Kristin was not the least shocked by the bold talk. Buck held her tightly to his side. They smiled into each other's eyes, reading each other's thoughts.

*After tomorrow they would be together forever.*

They might just as well have been alone on a mountaintop for all the attention they paid to the voices of the others floating around them. Kristin's caressing fingers stroked the inside of his thigh, his hand on her hip pressed her closer to him.

Kristin's senses reeled with happiness as they always did when he looked at her so lovingly with his beautiful green eyes. She was sure in her heart that the magic would never fade. This was real. This was forever. It was all there in his eyes, and the wonder of it filled her with joy.

# *Epilogue*

Court convened at the appointed time. The judge heard the testimony of Kristin regarding her meeting with Colonel Forsythe and Mark Lee. She swore that she had left town because she feared she would be forced to sell and that she had never signed a document giving Lee the authority to act on her behalf.

Cleve testified that Forsythe had told him the land was sold and handed over a written statement from the Ryersons that they had been forced off their land.

The judge allowed time for the accused to defend himself. In a surprising move the young lawyer threw himself on the mercy of the court. By midmorning it was over and the judge passed sentence. Mark Lee was sentenced to five years in the territorial prison for his part in the land-grabbing scheme. His assets were to be confiscated to pay restitution to his victims, and he would no longer be allowed to practice law in Montana Territory.

The evidence against the banker was not sufficient for a jail sentence. His bank accounts, however, would be tied up for a time to allow auditors to determine to what extent he had been involved in the scheme.

Ruth DeVary was not charged in the death of Colonel Forsythe. The judge ruled that she had acted in self-defense.

Forsythe's assets, which were vast, would also be used to pay restitution to his victims.

There was some discussion between Pablo and Cleve about revealing Forsythe's relationship to Dillon so that he could inherit the mansion in Big Timber. On hearing this, the storm that Dillon raised was nothing short of a cyclone, and he threatened to burn the place to the ground rather than accept anything that had belonged to that dirty, lowlife bastard Kirby Hyde or Franklin Kyle Forsythe or whatever he chose to call himself.

Since Colonel Forsythe had no known heirs, the judge ruled that Ruth DeVary would be considered the Colonel's common-law wife and would therefore inherit the mansion. It would be suggested to her that she use the house as a home or a school for girls. The woman was in bed suffering from the severe beating she had taken before her mind had snapped and she killed her tormenter. The judge volunteered to help her with the legalities when she was well again.

Kristin and Buck were married as soon as the court was recessed, and all walked over to the church to witness the ceremony. Kristin wore a blue muslin with lace at the neck and cuffs that she had brought along for the occasion. Buck had purchased a new shirt, a string tie, and pants for the event. He was handsome, in an untamed sort of way, with his shiny, dark unmanageable hair, dark face, and rugged features. He smiled from the beginning to the end of the ceremony and squeezed Kristin's hand so tightly that it was numb when he slid the gold band he had purchased that morning onto her finger.

When the ceremony was over, the bride and groom emerged from the church to find a buggy decorated with ribbons and Buck's big gray tied on behind.

"A gift from Mr. Lee," the judge said smiling, and then added when he saw Buck's frown, "This fancy buggy would be sold to pay restitution to your wife for his mishandling her affairs. Take the buggy and enjoy the trip home."

"Come see us sometime, Judge Williams," Kristin called, after Buck helped her up onto the seat. "Thank you, for fixing up the papers so my husband's name will be on all the Larkspur land. Thank you, Lieutenant, for seeing that no harm came to him yesterday. Thank you, Rose. 'Bye, Mr. Stark. You and Dillon come see us."

"But not right away," Buck called.

" 'Bye Bonnie. If Gilly gets to be too much trouble, send him home and don't take any sass from Gustaf. And, Gustaf, don't you dare go back to Wisconsin without coming out to the Larkspur."

"I'm not so sure I'll ever go back, cousin. Girls out here are prettier than the ones back home." His merry eyes flicked to Bonnie.

Kristin's eyes filled with tears when she looked at her cousin's familiar face. Until now he had been all that was dear to her.

"Thank you, Gustaf, for insisting I come to Montana and then coming out to see about me. I'll always love you . . . next to my husband, of course."

"Of course." Gustaf tilted his cap at a jaunty angle. "I'll just have to get used to playin' second fiddle. Ya better get goin', Buck, or she'll be rattling on 'bout something"—his voice became thick and he had to clear his throat—"or the other this time tomorrow."

"You're welcome at the Larkspur anytime, Gus. That goes for the rest of you, too." Buck slapped the reins against the mare's back. "Giddy-up, horse. I'm taking my bride home."

The buggy moved away from the church, down the side road and bypassed the town. Neither Buck nor Kristin spoke until they came out of the woods and saw the grassland spread before them.

"I'm Mrs. Buck Lenning," Kristin exclaimed proudly, her eyes shining with happiness. "Mrs. Buck Lenning." The name came shiveringly sweet from her lips.

Buck pulled the horse to a halt, loosed the reins so the mare could eat the grass growing beside the road, then turned and opened his arms. Kristin went into them eagerly. He held her to him gently, carefully, as if she were the most fragile thing in the world. Her hand caressed his face and he became one silent groan of pleasure.

"I'm so proud! I'm the luckiest woman in the world to have you for my husband."

Buck closed his eyes and whispered, "Kristin." His lips touched hers as he whispered again, "I'll always love you."

Whatever had begun within him when he first had seen her asleep in his chair weeks ago had been growing steadily. Now it consumed him. She was so open, so honest, so kind and giving—and so brave. He had been proud of her when she spoke to the judge.

*Dear God, help me never to disappoint her.*

The kiss he gave her was an innocent kiss—soft, generous, uninhibited and incredibly sweet. She responded with parted lips, yielding and vulnerable to the wanderings of his.

His heart was drumming so hard that he could hardly breathe, his love for her was overpowering. He burrowed his face deep into the fragrance of her hair and felt his whole self harden and tremble.

Kristin abandoned herself to the heavenly feeling of being in his arms, knowing that she was his, that he was hers and that they would be together . . . forever. Her fingers touched the wild soft hair she loved and then traveled to his nape and felt along the line of his jawbone. A low moan escaped from her lips when at last they were freed, and she clung to Buck as if to merge with his body.

"I think we'd better go on home before we have more kisses like that or I may carry you off into the woods."

"I'd not mind—"

He locked his arms around her more tightly, traced along the side of her face with his lips and gently kissed her trembling mouth again.

"I may never get tired of doing this, Mrs. Lenning."

"I hope not, Mr. Lenning." She cradled his face with her hands. Her wanton little smile grew into low, throaty laughter.

"Let's go home." She touched his lips gently with her fingertips.

"I don't want anyone to come visit for months and months!"

"You might get pretty tired of just me for company."

"Mrs. Lenning . . . that's impossible. There are things we can do without talking!"

Heartened by her smile and the love for him that glowed in her eyes, Buck felt he could take on the whole world. A surge of love for her flowed through him like a river. How was it possible that this woman, and only this woman, with her soft smile and calm words could make him feel so joyous?

He kissed her again with lusty delight and then picked up the reins and urged the mare on down the road.

Sitting close to him, her shoulder behind his, her hand resting on his thigh, Kristin looked up at the wide expanse of cloudless sky.

*Thank you, dear Moss, Uncle Yarby . . . Papa, for making it possible for me to be here with this man. I hope you are as happy with your Anna as I am with my love.*

# Author's Note

Dillon Tallman, Cleve Stark and Colonel Kyle Franklin Forsythe alias Kirby Hyde were first introduced to my readers in *Yesteryear*, Warner Books—January 1995.

Oil was never found in large quantities in Montana. It ranks seventeenth among the oil-producing states.

Larkspur is an annual plant that grows from one to three feet tall. The flowers are one and one-half inches wide and appear in long terminal clusters. The color varies from clear blue to purple to pink and occasionally to white. Larkspur is distinguished by a spur, formed by the upper sepal of the flower, which bears a likeness to a bird's claw.

Larkspur is listed in *Magic and Medicine of Plants* (Readers Digest Association—1986) as a dangerously poisonous plant. It is second only to locoweed in causing death to livestock that accidentally eat it while grazing.

For centuries Larkspur has served mankind as an agent that destroys human parasites such as lice and itch mites. At the Battle of Waterloo in 1815 the British issued it to Wellington's troops for that purpose. And the Union troops are said to have used it also during the Civil War.

Dorothy Garlock
Clear Lake, Iowa